WITCHING AFTER FORTY

VOLUME TWO

LIA DAVIS

L.A. BORUFF

Witching After Forty, Volume Two

Published by Davis Raynes Publishing

PO Box 224

Middleburg, FL 32050

DavisRaynesPublishing.com

Cover by Glowing Moon Designs

Formatting by Glowing Moon Designs

DavisRaynesPublishing.com

Witching After Forty follows the misadventures of Ava Harper – a forty-something necromancer with a light witchy side that you wouldn't expect from someone who can raise the dead. Join Ava as she learns how to start over after losing the love of her life, in this new paranormal women's fiction series with a touch of cozy mystery, magic, and a whole lot of mayhem.

A Ghoulish Midlife
Cookies for Satan (Christmas novella)
I'm With Cupid (Valentine novella)
A Cursed Midlife
Birthday Blunder (Olivia Novella)
A Girlfriend For Mr. Snoozerton (Novella)
A Haunting Midlife
An Animated Midlife
Faery Odd-Mother (Novella)
A Killer Midlife
A Grave Midlife
A Powerful Midlife (coming soon)
A Wedded Midlife (coming soon)
More to come

BIRTHDAY BLUNDER

A WITCHING AFTER FORTY PARANORMAL WOMEN'S FICTION SHORT

BIRTHDAY BLUNDER

Olivia has to throw Drew a birthday party with the help of the magical menagerie.
And it all goes wrong.
Despite her best intentions, Olivia can't make things happen today. Winston, Ava's semi-aware house, doesn't like the fact that Olivia is there baking while Ava isn't home.
Hey, at least Ava can be sure she doesn't need a security system.

CHAPTER ONE

"Oh, no, darn it." I lurched as the grocery sack ripped, catching the corner so it ripped even further. The big eight-thousand-pound bag of flour hit my foot, making the top of my foot explode with f-bomb worthy pain. But at least my foot, now throbbing, kept the flour from hitting the ground, busting open, and going everywhere. "Darn it, darn it."

Limping, I left the flour, which wasn't *really* eight thousand pounds, even though it had felt like it at the time, sitting on the walkway and headed for the door. I had Ava's spare key in my pocket, which didn't do me much good, considering my hands were still too full. I should've grabbed a tote or something to carry all this crap in, but it was a little too late for that now.

Usually, I was a little more organized than at this moment. But being alone in Ava's house with a skeleton, a ghoul, and well...the house itself left me feeling a little out of sorts. I wasn't used to dealing with all the magical things that went on in there, though I did enjoy them. Most of the time.

Of course, I stumbled up the stairs, but at least I caught

myself. No major injuries; I didn't even skin my knee or shin or anything. *That's good, right?*

Dumping the other bags on the porch in front of the door, I pulled the key from my pocket and slid it in the lock with a sigh.

But then it wouldn't turn. "Seriously?" I bent and squinted at the lock. Was this the wrong key?

I pulled it out to check. No. Ava had painted the side of it with purple nail polish, so I'd always know which key was hers. Not that I would forget, but she insisted because I had a million keys on my ring. Her words.

Not the wrong key. I gripped the handle tighter and jiggled it as I inserted the key. Still not working. "What is wrong with this lock?" I said through gritted teeth. I'd used it before and it had worked fine.

Maybe the door was just stuck. Holding the knob with one hand, I bumped my butt against it as hard as I could, but it didn't budge. Instead, I cried out when a sharp pain shot through the side of my hip.

"Damn it. Open up, you psychotic house!" I stepped back and glared at the house before picking my jaw up off the ground when the door opened all on its own. Okay, that wasn't creepy at all.

Alfred stuck his face around the door and grunted. His clouded eyes searched me for a few moments before he opened the door wider. He nodded, or at least I think he did. His pale, gray skin didn't move much. When he grunted, I understood it as a welcome. He couldn't speak due to a string that sewed his lips together.

At least the door hadn't opened on its own. Although I believed it could if it really wanted to. My adorably insane husband, Sam, who was also Ava's childhood BFF, claimed the house talked to him, and his name is Winston. Ava and I were skeptical about that.

"Hey, Alfie!" The cheeriness in my voice was fake, but I'd get back to excited soon. Now that Winston's door was open, nothing was stopping me. "I've got a bunch more stuff to unload. Can you grab these bags?"

I'd ask the ghoul to help unload, but despite Ava living on the edge of town, her street was pretty busy, especially now that spring was coming. Tourists would flock to the area soon enough. There was too much risk that someone would see a stiff, zombie-like man carrying groceries in. Too bad it wasn't near Halloween, then he could help me.

He grunted again, which was Alfred-speak for a long, drawn-out sentence of welcome.

"Thanks, Alfie," I chirped as I bounced down the stairs, nearly tripping again. Damn, did I wear the wrong shoes? Was the sole loose or something? I stopped for a second and balanced on one foot while I checked my shoes.

Nope. Run of the mill sneakers. No holes or flappy pieces. With a sigh, I hurried back to my car and grabbed another load of bags.

"Decorations, check." Peering into the bags, I tried to think of whatever it was I'd forgotten. It'd been bugging me since I left the party store. I poked through and triple-checked my inventory. Streamers, a happy birthday banner, cheap paper tablecloths. What was I missing?

It would come to me. Eventually.

Gathering another couple of armloads, I grunted as I heaved them up. Good grief. How were streamers this heavy?

I made it to the stairs in one piece, then tripped again, on the same stair I was pretty sure. "Damn it!" I yelled as my bags went flying.

Larry stuck his head... skull... out the door. "Need a hand?" He couldn't come out either, unfortunately.

I sighed and rolled over on the porch before sitting up. "Please. Could you and Alfred possibly start the decorations?

We were going to do the living room only since it's going to be a small affair."

The late morning sunshine illuminated the front porch far too well. I could nearly see through the back of Larry's eye sockets and into the back of the *inside* of his skull. If that was even possible. I shuddered at the thought, though I wouldn't trade a moment of how crazy things had been since Ava came back to Shipton. It kept life interesting. Lord knew we all needed interesting at our age.

Climbing to my feet, I looked away from Larry's shiny skull and started gathering up the far-flung streamers and packs of plates and napkins.

"Thanks, Larry," I called as he went in with a few of the bags.

Hurrying back to the car, I stepped carefully down the stairs, watching exactly where I was going for each footfall.

Somehow, *somehow*, my clumsy ass still stumbled on the last one. And I would've sworn I saw the board move. *Winston.*

"Okay, I'm climbing up the side of the porch next time," I muttered as I glanced back toward the house, suspicion growing in my gut.

Last trip. I got all of the rest of the bags and balanced three rolls of wrapping paper under my chin as I bumped the door closed with my butt. That was when my car alarm went off, blaring the god-awful noise that echoed off the cliff Winston sat on.

I left it blaring and continued toward the house. One crisis at a time. It would go off in a minute.

"Okay, stairs. Leave me alone this time." Glaring at them, I stepped one at a time, slowly, one foot, then the other foot, until I made it up to the porch. The front door stood wide open, thanks to Larry, so I strode forward with my armload.

And promptly dropped it all when I tripped over the door

jamb. The latest and last round of bags slid into the house and halfway down the foyer toward the kitchen.

"Son of a b—"

"Hey, Olivia!"

I snapped my jaw shut so fast I bit my tongue. "Hey, Zoey," I called to Ava's latest house guest, an orphan she raised from the dead when we stopped a shifter fighting ring a week ago. She was a tiger shifter and surprisingly looked nothing like Alfred even though she was also technically a ghoul. Or was she?

Then again, Snooze wasn't a ghoul. I rubbed my forehead and decided to stop thinking about the whys and hows. It always gave me a headache when I tried to understand Ava's power. They went against all laws of logic and nature.

Ava had a habit of collecting the undead. It was like they were drawn to her, which made sense because of her necromancer powers. Alfred, the ghoul, originally animated by a now-dead necromancer. When the old necro died, Alfred had to have a new handler, and by virtue of being nearby, Ava was it. Then, Larry, a fully defleshed skeleton turned up, but *then* he didn't want to go back to being dead.

Trying to ignore the throbbing in my shin, I picked myself up off the ground, again, and smiled at Zoey. "Hey, sweetheart. Are you busy today?"

She shrugged and shook her head. "No, not really. Ava got me signed up for some online classes, but I'm all caught up."

Her long black hair was in one long braid, and the tail draped over her shoulder. On the top of her head were two tiger ears that twitched and moved as if taking in all the sounds around us.

I almost commented about them but decided against it. Zoey could shift into her tiger form just as easily as she had when she was alive. Or so I was told. But for some reason, shifting back to human had its challenges. For example, the ears. Most often, her tiger's tail stayed when she shifted back to human. Her eyes, however, never changed. They were forever stuck as yellow cat eyes.

I breathed a sigh of relief. "Excellent. Here." Snagging the rolls of wrapping paper, I stuffed them into Zoey's arms. "There's tape..." Looking at all the party stuff on the floor, I sighed. "Somewhere. And scissors in Ava's office top left drawer."

Zoey didn't even question that I knew that. I was here more than home, not that I minded. And Ava didn't seem to mind. At least I hoped not. I kept her pretty well-supplied in donuts and cupcakes just in case she minded.

I gathered up the foodstuffs off the floor, leaving the décor items for the undead peeps. Time to make a cake. At least I couldn't trip over anything while stirring the batter.

CHAPTER TWO

"Okay. Now. Cake." I blew out a breath and surveyed the bags on the counter.

Zoey looked over my shoulder. "What kind of cake?"

"Carrot," I said proudly. "It's my specialty, and Drew loves it."

She sniffed as I pulled ingredients from the bags. "I've never had it."

I put the eggs in the fridge, shocked that they'd survived my insane journey, then shot Zoey a look. "Hey, can you even eat the cake? Or anything?"

Was it a rude question?

She nodded with a wide smile. "Yes, I can. Ava says it's odd that I can, considering I'm technically dead. Hey, who am I to complain, right?"

"Oh cool. Dead or not, I think I would eat too. I love food too much to pass it up." I squeezed her hand as she giggled. Her body temp was a little warmer than Alfred's but not as much as a living being. Ava and Owen mentioned it could have something to do with Zoey being a shifter. The magic that made them shifters must've still been there since Zoey had died a few years before. So she was considered a newbie dead.

I snickered at the thought. The undead and magic. I loved my new crazy life. It was much better than my mess of a first marriage.

Pointing to the wrapping paper, still in Zoey's arms, I said, "Go on and start wrapping, okay? The gifts are in one of the bags in the foyer and Ava's gift is on the right side of the couch, out of sight of the door, under the end table."

She saluted me and walked out of the kitchen toward the living room. That was when I noticed her tiger tail swinging with her hips.

"Okay," I muttered. "Bowls, a mixer, what else?" I grabbed a cabinet knob to get Ava's mixing bowl set out, but it wouldn't open. "Weird." I groaned and tugged again.

But the cabinet wasn't having it. "Hey, Zoey?" I called. "Aren't you like, super strong?"

"Sure." She wandered back toward the cabinet. "Let me try."

Centering her base of gravity, Zoey bent at the waist and leaned back with her hand on the cabinet pull. The darn thing didn't budge.

"It's really stuck," I said. "Give it a good tug."

She nodded once and glared at the cabinet, then yanked. From my perspective, she yanked *hard*.

But the cabinet opened easily, so Zoey went flying across the kitchen, sliding on her butt until she thumped into the refrigerator.

"Oh, my gosh, Zoey, I'm so sorry!" I scurried over and held out my hand to help her up. "I must've loosened it for you."

I helped her to her feet and brushed off her back. "Sorry. Go over and work on the wrapping. Thank you."

She nodded once and shot the cabinet a confused glare as she headed across the kitchen.

With a sigh, I glared at it myself. At least the cabinet was still open. I snatched the mixing bowls out quickly before the door slammed shut on my wrist or something. I leaned against the counter and brushed my hair out of my face. Deep breaths. I had plenty of time, and it was all going to be *fine.*

Without warning, something smacked me in the back of the head. I yelped and ducked as I spun around. There was nothing behind me but the cabinets. And one was wide open, one that hadn't been open before. All the cabinets had been solidly closed when I turned around to catch my breath.

Rubbing the sore spot on the back of my head, I stared at the cabinets. "Winston?" I whispered.

Nobody replied, of course. Winston, AKA the house, had somehow absorbed the magic that had been performed in this house for hundreds of years. He could be ornery. And I hadn't thought about Winston twice when I'd agreed to come here and get the party set up. That had been a mistake.

Ava had taken Drew to a movie, then they were supposed to spend the day together. It was Ava's way of making sure the sheriff didn't just pop over to her house unannounced as he and the rest of us often did. After all, this party was to celebrate Drew turning the big five-zero.

I was *supposed* to make the cake last night but as I pulled out my mixing bowls at home, Drew had called and said he'd harangued Ava into a last-minute bowling trip and that we should join. How were we supposed to say no? Drew, being my husband's boss and best friend, knew that our son, Sammie, was at his grandparents'. He also knew that when Sam and I weren't busy with Sammie, we'd always be down for bowling. And any other day, I would've been. Except that I was supposed to have been making a decadent carrot cake. So, the cake making was bumped to today, and it would just have to be iced a little warm. Ugh. That never worked right.

Next. Mixer. I needed a mixer. And for once, it was something I didn't immediately know where to find.

"Okay, Winston. Help me out. I'm doing this as a favor for Ava. Can you please just let me get the mixer?"

Movement out of the corner of my eye had me swinging my head. A cabinet sat with it's door open, just a crack, but I could see the mixer sitting on the shelf. "Yes!" I cried.

Hurrying over to the slightly open cabinet, I reached into it, but as my fingers barely brushed the side, it slammed shut. "Winston!" I yelled. "Come *on*!"

Carefully, wary of the house's antics and totally confused about why he was targeting me, I grabbed the cabinet knob and pulled. Relief flooded me as it opened. I held it open with one hand and snatched the mixer out as fast as I could with the other.

At this rate, I'd only get the decorations up before the guests arrived, and that was only because I wasn't the one putting them up!

CHAPTER THREE

"Who is this from?"

I whirled around and raised my eyebrows at the mug Zoey held up. "Um. I have no idea."

"Larry?" I called. I would've asked for Alfred, but he didn't talk. If I was Ava, I would've long since cut the strings tying his mouth together and forced him to tell me why he didn't want to talk, but she was far more patient than me. Go figure, since I was the one forty-something with a five-year-old. But I loved kids and that kid of mine was my heart. Not that my two adult-ish kids were loved any less.

"Yes, Olivia?" Larry stuck his head in the door. I wasn't sure but I swore he kept looking at Zoey. Then again it could've been my imagination. Or that I was so used to the craziness that I was going insane myself. It was probably all the above. He didn't have eyes, so I really had no idea where he was looking.

I watched him for a few seconds as he turned his head to Zoey then back to me fast enough to make me cringe. Oh, no. *Please don't fall off.*

Larry's head had an unfortunate habit of… well, falling off. Hitting the ground. Rolling, bouncing, the whole nine yards.

"Hey, uh…" I waved him into the room, kind of frantically. "C'mere, yeah."

His bones clacked against the kitchen tile as he came closer. "What can I do for you?"

I motioned toward the mug in Zoey's hand. "Do you know anything about this?"

Larry leaned in, and though he was nothing more than a bag of bones, he somehow managed to squint at the mug. "I do believe that's the one Alfred ordered from both of us."

Pushing the deeply unsettling feeling of the skeleton squinting out of my mind, I looked closer at the mug. "The Devil Made Me Do It."

Of course. Perfect.

"Well… That's great." I smiled eagerly at Larry. "Good job." I paused then held up one finger. "Question. *How* did you guys order that?" I certainly hoped they hadn't gone into town.

Visions filled my head of the two of them in big hats and trench coats, trying to sneak into the curio shop downtown.

Not a comforting image. Funny, sure, but not comforting.

"We used Alfred's tablet," he said. "Wallie logged us into someone's online account." He shrugged one bony shoulder. If Larry was going to be with us much longer, I was going to have to learn the real names of the bones.

I liked knowing things.

"Well, that's nice, Larry. Nice of you to think of him. Ah," I sucked in a deep breath and tried to be tactful. "Do the touch screens respond to your hand?"

He shook his head, his permanent smile somehow looking a little rueful. "No, but we also ordered some gloves that have this bit on the tip that will make it so I can use the tablet as well. I can't wait."

A grunt from the next room caught Larry's attention. "Coming, Al!"

He chuckled. "Probably wants me to take a pic." He wandered off as I wondered why they were taking pictures. Not my circus...But I was a part of it.

I snorted.

No matter, at least not right now. "Well, wrap that for Drew." I smiled encouragingly at Zoey, ignoring the fact that her eyes were permanently shifted. Right then the pupils were long slits in the center of yellow irises.

What wasn't normal, or at least normal for her, was the cute little ears that were still sticking out of the top of her hair. At least her tail had vanished.

We were going to have to do some serious work on that girl this summer before she started her college classes in the fall. She'd been a shifter before her death—meaning sheltered—and now that she was an actual ghoul—or whatever—we needed to lay down some ground rules to keep her seeming normal.

But not today. Today, I had to get this dang cake in the oven.

"Okay, flour, sugar, no. Brown sugar." It was on the counter. "Oh, there you are. Okay."

I stuck my head in the refrigerator and grabbed the eggs. When I turned to put them beside the brown sugar on the counter, it was gone. "Uh, what?"

I turned in a slow circle. That brown sugar didn't grow legs and walk away. It just didn't.

"Larry!" I yelled.

No, wait. Zoey. "Hey!" Whirling around, I glared at Zoey. "Hey, Zo, girlfriend." I gave her a big, cheeky grin. "Did you hide my brown sugar?"

Zoey stared at me, and as she opened her mouth to reply, to say no by the looks of her face, Larry walked in.

But he was a bit distracted. Zoey and I watched, open-mouthed, as Larry tried to get a piece of tape off of the tip of his right pointer finger. Except it kept sticking to his left pointer finger.

Then his right thumb.

Then he grabbed it between his teeth, but then it got stuck to his teeth.

"Drat," he whispered.

How did a skeleton whisper?

Zoey stood and held out her hand like she'd done this before.

This poor girl.

Larry leaned over, jutting out his jawbone so Zoey could grab the tape. She balled it up in her hand and tossed it on the table with a few other scraps.

When I returned to the counter, that French-flapping bag of sugar was right back in its spot on the counter.

What a bunch of bull-hockey.

I really had to talk to Ava about her preference for us not to cuss around Zoey and Larry. She said it was a bad influence, but in order to get in the habit of not flinging around the F-bomb, I had to start saying the non-offensive swear words even in my own head.

Bunch of malarkey.

CHAPTER FOUR

I would get through this cake. I would do it.

Centering my nerves, I practiced the breathing I'd learned at that one yoga class I'd convinced Ava to take with me that one time.

Neither of us had ever suggested going again after I had to watch the class pretend they couldn't smell the little bit of gas that slipped out during my downward dog. I'd been so thankful it was silent, I hadn't stopped to think about the fact that it could be stinky.

Until it hit my olfactory senses.

But no matter now. I was calm. The ingredients were here. Oil. Carrots and a little flat, shredder thingy. I never could remember the name of that thing, but I always shredded my carrots myself. Pre-shredded grocery store carrots were hard and dry by the time they went in the cake.

Something else I knew. I liked knowing things.

I preheated the oven and put in some pecans to toast while I worked on the cake mix. Flour, two and a half cups. Measuring carefully, I put the first two cups in the bowl, but as

I measured out the half cup, another movement out of the corner of my eye caused me to jerk my head. And it was a chain reaction after that. My arm flinched, which made my wrist flex, and my hand shook, flinging flour up and all over my shirt.

Seriously? Son of a biscuit.

I tried to brush the flour off, but it was sticking hard to my sweater. Whatever. Brown sugar, granulated sugar, baking pow —Holy crap!

"Hello, Olivia." Luci's voice behind me made my arm jerk big time, and baking powder went on top of the flour all over my chest.

Turning in a slow circle on my heel, I glared at Luci, Ava's devilish new neighbor, and his girlfriend, Carrie, who was my son's Kindergarten teacher.

"What are you doing here?" I asked in a low voice. It wasn't that I wanted to be rude, but he was a potentially dangerous man, and I didn't feel too comfortable being the only responsible adult around him. He usually only came around to stir up trouble.

There was Carrie, but she was dating him, so she didn't count.

"You know." Luci squinted at my shirt. "Feeding them won't make them grow."

"What?" I narrowed my gaze. "What are you talking about?"

He gestured vaguely to my chest, causing me to look down and belatedly realize he meant feeding my boobs. Great. Okay. "Well, what are you doing here?"

Whirling again, I opened the eggs to add a few to the batter and frustration rose in me so quickly I nearly threw them across the room. "You've got to be kidding me. Winston!" I threw my head back and screamed at the house even though he couldn't or wouldn't reply.

"No need to shout," Luci said. "I believe I can help."

"Oh, thank you, but no, I—"

He cut me off by waving his hand. Eggs lifted out of the carton and plopped right on top of the flour and sugar.

Along with about half of the broken shells from the carton.

"No," I moaned.

Carrie looked over my shoulder. "Hey, Luc, how about you go in the living room and see if you can help those guys in there with the decorating." She smiled at me encouragingly. "And I'll help Olivia pick the shells out of this batter."

Luci shrugged. "Whatever you say, dear."

He wandered from the room.

"Sometimes, he's more trouble than he's worth, but I really think he means well." Carrie gave me a half-grin. "And he's amazing in bed."

Now that was some gossip I wanted to hear, but I noticed Zoey's kitty-cat ears twitching. "Maybe we'll talk about that later."

I nodded my head slightly toward Zoey and Carried widened her eyes, then tapped her nose to tell me she understood.

"Okay, let's get to picking."

The house seemed to calm down a bit with Luci and Carrie there, and we actually got the batter mixed and in the oven before a rattling sound caused us both to turn.

Zoey snickered as Mr. Snoozerton, Ava's fat, immortal Maine Coon cat, came limping into the kitchen. "Snooze!" I cried. "What happened to you?"

Laughter and snickers from the other room caused me to look a little closer as the big cat limped toward me, shaking out one of his front paws with every other step.

"Oh, no." I finally saw why he'd been limping as he yowled loudly at me. Alfred came running from the living room, grunting, and the big, cranky cat veered off course, heading for Alfred, his favorite of the house's inhabitants, rather than me.

Alfred picked him up, then carefully peeled the piece of tape off of Snoozer's paws, then set the fat cat down so he could take off up the stairs, complaining loudly.

"Who did that?" I asked.

Alfred glared, then shifted his angry look to Carrie.

"Ah," I translated. "Luci?"

Alfred grunted, then returned to the living room. "Maybe we should follow," I whispered.

Carrie nodded vehemently, so we hurried out of the kitchen and toward the living room.

"Oh, geez," I whispered as I took in the view in the living room. "I shouldn't have left them alone to decorate."

Carrie snickered under her breath. "I agree."

The decorations actually weren't that bad. Streamers... uh, streamed from the light fixture in the middle of the room out to the corners. A big Happy Birthday banner hung over the fireplace, and they'd found balloons somewhere to let drift across the floors and hang from corners. Balloons! That was what I'd forgotten.

That wasn't the part that made me shake my head in derision.

"Hello?" Ava called. "We're a little early!" She stopped short in the living room doorway. "Why does Larry have googly eyes?"

Ignoring Larry and my question about where in the world Larry had found giant googly eyes to stick to his eye sockets, I turned in a panic as Ava and Drew, the Birthday Boy himself, walked in a solid hour early. The other guests hadn't even arrived yet.

After nudging Zoey, I threw up my arms. "Surprise!" I cried. "Happy birthday!"

Zoey echoed me, clapping her hands. Her ears twitched in time with her hands.

Drew stared at Larry with a half-smile on his face. "Thank you!"

Motioning toward a big stain over her boob, Ava grimaced. "Sorry we're early, I spilled coffee all over my shirt."

Luci leaned forward from the sofa. "Hey, you know, letting them drink won't make them grow."

Okay, maybe that was a little funny.

A HAUNTING MIDLIFE

WITCHING AFTER FORTY, BOOK 3

CHAPTER ONE

Done!

Finally.

After months of hard work, starting and stopping, a paragraph here and a chapter there.

Now it was done. After struggling for the last several weeks with the ending of the novel, I typed 'The End' with glee and a feeling of accomplishment. The next step was to let that book baby sit on my computer and marinate until I returned from Philly. A few weeks of perspective would help me see errors more easily before shipping it off to my editor.

I leaned back in my comfy office chair and stretched. My muscles nearly creaked as they loosened. Ah, how I missed my younger days of writing for hours on end only to jump up and bounce from one activity to the next without a crick in my neck or stabbing pain in my back.

Picking up my coffee cup, I frowned to find it empty. Again. Ugh. It seemed like I'd make a cup and it would set until it got cold, or I'd turn around, and somehow it was empty.

I set the mug back on my desk and ran my hand through my

hair. It got stuck halfway down to my shoulder. What the hell did I have in my hair? Something sticky. Ew. Must have been that late-night... or was it an early morning snack? Leftover donuts from this morning. Or yesterday morning. Olivia had dropped them by at some point.

Wait, what day was it? I'd been holed up in my office for too long.

I needed sleep.

But hey, it was all worth it. Another manuscript in the books. Heh. Pun intended.

Standing, I picked up my cup and my trashcan full of snack wrappers and takeout boxes. Damn, how long *had* I been in the office? Aka the writing cave. By the look of the overflowing trash can, I'd guessed a week. That couldn't have been right. Surely it wasn't that long. I tended to lose track of things when I got in the zone. Clay had always taken good care of me when this happened.

Owen, Alfred, and Larry had been trying to keep my head above water, so to speak, but every time they tried it made me think of Clay doing it. And then I'd get sad again, making it harder to focus on the words.

I opened my office door and stepped out into the downstairs hallway. I had closed the door around midnight—I think—to keep Snooze and his new girlfriend out of the room so I could focus. Lucy, the pretty white cat I brought back to life over the weekend, could talk. Like full sentences. And holy crow. That little kitty was chattier than a teenage boy. Well, boy of any age. Man, could they talk. Lucy would fit right in. Most people thought it was the girls that always had diarrhea of the mouth. I'd never raised a teenage girl, but I had raised a teenage boy, and Wallie hadn't shut up for like four years.

Emerging from the hallway, I caught the scent of bacon and coffee. I gravitated to the yummy scents like they were calling me. When I reached the dining room, just off the kitchen, though it was technically the same room because of the open space, I froze.

Alfred, the house ghoul, stood near the stove, flipping bacon with his Kiss the Cook apron on. Sammie was a few feet behind him, holding out a plate. I soon realized why when Alfie reached over to another skillet and launched a pancake at him.

With a surprising show of skill for a kid his age, Sammie caught the pancake with his plate. "Hey!" I cheered. "Go, Sammie!"

Seven heads turned toward me, staring like I had grown an extra set of arms. Owen, my friend, roommate, and mentor raised his black eyebrows and pushed his dark hair out of his face. Sam and Olivia, my childhood best friend and his wife, who was my current best friend and had taken the central role as my Person with a capital P, grinned as Olivia eyed my hair. Just to be sure, I checked. Nope, no extra arms. But my hair was a mess—half up in a sloppy bun and half down around my face. The latter had the sticky donut yuck in it.

Zoey, my sort-of adopted daughter, snorted and turned back to her pancakes while Wallie, my biological son, barely spared me a glance as he ate. He was long used to my crazy appearance after emerging from my cave.

"Is Sammie out of school?" I asked as I tugged down my oversized tee and pulled up my leggings. Comfy clothes were staples for a writing binge. Again, I wondered how long I'd been in the writing cave.

Olivia burst out laughing while Sam asked, "Did you sleep last night?"

Last night... "Oh! It's morning already."

"Yeah," Olivia said with a giggle. "It's teacher's planning day. No school today."

Oh. I had lost a few days.

Alfred came over and took my cup and the trash can from me. He glared at me and grunted. Then he pointed to the stairs.

I didn't need a translator to know what he meant. I needed a shower. Probably pretty badly.

Owen frowned at me. "You need to hurry, or you'll be late for your flight."

"What? What time is it?" I glanced at the clock on the stove and cursed low enough I hoped little Sammie didn't hear me. That kid was like a parrot. He repeated everything he heard.

"Seven o'clock," Olivia said with a snicker. She loved being right, and I hated that she often was.

I ignored her amusement. No doubt I'd hear about this moment later on. But reality was starting to come back to me. I had two hours to shower, dress, and pack. It was a good thing I'd created Zoey's fake ID the night before. Luci—the devil, not the cat—helped me with a little magic that made her legit in the human databases.

Zoey had been an orphaned shifter who I'd taken in when my friends and I had saved her and a bunch of other kids from a shifter fighting ring. Sort of like dog fighting, but with poor shifter kids. Many of them had been very, very young and we'd found a *lot* of dead kids. Too many.

"Ava," Olivia exclaimed. "Go!"

I jumped and scurried toward the stairs. "Right, yes. Go."

Zoey, Wallie, and I were flying to Philly. The plan was to rent a truck there after we packed up the house and drive it back to Shipton. It wasn't going to be an easy week, getting all of the stuff from my life with Clay packed up or donated. But it was time. It was past time. I had to move on.

After I showered and dressed, I stared down at my half-packed suitcase and tried to remember that I had a house full of my own belongings. I had a bigger wardrobe there than here. I didn't need to take much. A knock sounded on my bedroom door. "Come in."

Owen opened the door but didn't enter. He was a little old-fashioned like that. Polite. "Are you taking Larry with you?"

"I asked and he said he wanted to stay here to help you." I placed my toiletries into the small carry-on. I wasn't checking any luggage, and I'd told the kids to do the same. Zoey would fit into some of my older, skinny clothes I'd hung onto in the hopes of losing weight. As if. If she didn't like them, I'd donate them.

Out with the old. It was time to move on from more than just grieving my Clay. I picked up the mini suitcase and turned toward Owen. "Listen, if the house starts his crap, have Alfred grunt at him." I wasn't sure that would work, but it was worth a try. "Winston usually listens to him." Since my old house had taken on a personality, we'd had to name him. Winston was as good a name as any. He seemed to like it, anyway.

Owen laughed. "Winston doesn't bother with me because I'm a necromancer. I think he gave Olivia crap because she's human. No magic."

Hmm. I hadn't thought about that. "Sam is human."

Owen hummed. "True, but Sam also grew up with you and has spent a lot of time in this house."

That made sense. He'd been in and out so much he'd learned long ago about my family and me being witches. "Are you going to be okay here for a week? You'll have to go get groceries or at least be here for delivery. Alfred knows not to answer the door."

"Ava, I've been a necromancer longer than you and know how to take care of a ghoul, a magical house, and an animated, fleshed-out skeleton who has been dead for thirty-some-odd years." Larry had been a big surprise. When my fat, old, immortal Maine Coon cat, Mr. Snoozerton, led me to a little white dead kitty and asked me to animate her. I figured out I had the power to do more than animate. I could heal the dead. Something as yet unheard of, or only heard in rumor. I'd given it a shot on Larry, a skeleton I'd accidentally animated over the winter.

And he'd grown his flesh back. All of it. To the point that

now he looked perfectly human. Alive. And according to Zoey, 'freaking hot.' "And don't forget two immortal cats. One of which can talk quite well." I frowned. "Maybe I'll call Wade and just have him pack up the house." Leaving this chaotic menagerie to Owen suddenly seemed insane.

Owen broke his unspoken rule of not entering my room and crossed over to me. "Ava. Stop." He took my hands, forcing me to look at him. "You are going. Everything here will be fine. Not to mention, Sam will be here if I need anything, and the coven said they'll help if anything weird happens."

I snorted. The coven—*my* coven because I was the High Witch in charge—loved all the weird stuff that happened in my life. They'd probably be all over it with glee. Not that I blamed them. The insanity that was my life was, most of the time, pretty damn cool.

Owen let go of my hands and moved to the door. "You've put this off long enough. It's time to let go." His words reflected my earlier thoughts almost exactly. That had to mean something. And he was right. I could do this, but boy did I need a nap. And I didn't think I'd be getting one any time soon.

After saying goodbye to everyone in my house—two humans, one small human, one ghoul, one animated dead person, who may or may not be a ghoul now, I wasn't sure, two immortal cats, one devil, who had appeared... I wasn't sure when, but there he was, and one self-aware house—Owen drove Wallie, Zoey, and me to the airport. When he pulled through the drop-off lanes, I spotted Drew and my heart did a little dance while my eyes drank in the sight of how sexy he was in his sheriff's uniform. I'd been planning on sending him a sweet text right before I put my phone on airplane mode, but this was so very much *way* better.

Heart soaring, I got out of the car, and Drew quickly pulled me into his arms. His mouth claimed mine, and I melted into him like I was meant to be there. Like I'd always been meant to be there. Pulling back, I smiled up at him. “I thought you weren’t able to come.”

He shook his head and traced my jaw with his fingertips. “I still can’t. I've got to run, but I wanted to see you off.”

Laughing, I tucked my arms around his waist and hugged him tightly, relishing how much taller Drew was. And bigger. I liked feeling small as I hugged him.

Drew had been with me when I'd gotten the call from Clay's Uncle Wade that the house had sold. Drew had insisted that he would come with me and wouldn’t hear any arguing from me. However, plans changed. He had to help out with a case in Acadia National Park and couldn't leave town. There'd been a murder, so he was assisting the Rangers.

Pulling back, I smiled up at him. “I’ll only be gone a week.” But that felt like forever, knowing Drew wouldn’t be there. Or maybe I just dreaded the coming job. How strange to feel so lost without Drew. I hadn't felt that way in a long time. I'd learned to be pretty self-sufficient.

He eyed me closely and frowned. “Have you been up all night?”

I gasped dramatically. “Who, me?” I looked around at the people milling about the drop-off area. "Surely not."

A crooked grin formed on his handsome face. “You finished the book.”

I flashed him a brilliant smile, beaming with excitement. “I did. And I’ll sleep on the flight, then again when I get to Philly.” The flight would be way too short to sleep long. It wasn’t even two hours.

I wasn’t meeting the new owner, Hailey, for a couple of days so I'd have time to nap, pack, and get my emotions in check before letting a stranger into the house. Into her house, now.

“Make sure you get some sleep. After you've rested, call me.” He kissed my forehead.

I wrapped my arms around him again and held him for a moment. “I will. I promise."

Wallie stuck his head out of the automatic door. "Hey, Drew." He raised his eyebrows at me. "There's not a big line at security. Let's go."

After waving him back inside I popped one more kiss to Drew's lips, then grabbed my small suitcase. "Bye," I called.

I walked back through the double doors, not turning until I had to. Zoey grabbed my hand and tugged me toward the gate. "I read all about flying online. We check in, get our tickets, then go through security."

"Zo, I checked us in at home," Wallie said. "We have all our tickets. Straight to security."

She gulped audibly. "Oh. Time for that?"

Throwing my arm around the young girl, I turned her toward the small line at security. "Stop fidgeting," I said softly.

"I can't help it." Her barely audible whisper was more of a squeak. "What if something goes wrong? I don't exist, at least not as far as the humans are concerned."

"Stop talking about that now." We were too close to the front already. "And chill."

She'd put a ball cap on to hide her ears just in case they made an appearance. We had a glamour on her, but I didn't want to trust that it would definitely, one hundred percent work.

"Okay, take off your shoes and put them in these buckets." I set an off-white tray in front of her. "And put your backpack in there, too."

I'd already coached her not to wear jewelry or a belt, so once the shoes came off, we were good.

"Miss?" A tired-looking woman leaned over. "Hat off, please."

Zoey smiled at her with wide, nervous eyes. We hadn't been able to do anything but glamour for her tiger eyes, which hadn't shifted back to human since I animated her. If that slipped, well, we were just screwed.

I breathed a sigh of relief when the hat came off and there were no ears. "It's okay," I murmured. "Step into that machine and it just scans your body to make sure you don't have a weapon."

This was the big test. Would the machine be fooled by a glamour? I had no idea. If her ears popped up or tail popped out, we were screwed with a capital F.

But it seemed to go well. Then, as Zoey stepped through to the other side and I walked into the scanner for my turn, Wallie hissed at me. "Mom! Her tail."

Turning my head back to Zoey, I gulped when her tail appeared out of the bottom of her skirt. In her relief to get through the scanner, she'd let it slip.

And the agent was turning toward Zo. The whole thing happened in slow motion, like in a movie.

"No!" I yelled and dropped to the floor, pulling all the attention on me. The agent who had been about to look at Zo rushed to my side, as did Wallie. All eyes swung around to me, including Zoey, peering over the agent's shoulder.

"Sorry," I said, getting to my feet and rubbing my butt. "I just tripped and fell on my *tail*bone."

Zoey's eyes slammed shut and she disappeared from sight. I'd forgotten to glamour her tail. All I could do now was hope she either managed to tuck it up inside her clothes or made it disappear.

"Are you sure you're all right, Mom?" Wallie asked with his nostrils flared.

"I'm fine, stop fussing. You know I'm just clumsy."

The security agent gave me a scathing look but backed away. We finished our scan without incident.

We weren't even out of Maine yet. This was going to be a long trip.

CHAPTER TWO

When the cab dropped us off at the house in Chestnut Hill, a suburb of Philadelphia, my stomach churned, and dread froze me in place. The last time I was in this house, I was a depressed grieving widow. Some things hadn't changed. I was still a grieving widow, just not as depressed. I was proud of how much moving back to Shipton had helped me.

With a sigh, I stared up at the split foyer and tried to make myself walk forward.

"Come on, Mom." Wallie put his hand on my shoulder. "We're ready for this. We've talked about it until we couldn't talk about it anymore. Just go in."

He was right. That didn't mean it would be easy, though.

With an encouraging look from Wallie, I unlocked the door and went inside. I didn't fall apart as soon as I set foot in the foyer, so that was a plus.

Wade had turned on the A/C so the house wouldn't smell closed up. I thought it felt amazing.

"Geez, it's cold in here," Zoey muttered.

I pointed at them, my voice full of threat and sweat on my

brow. "Don't touch the A/C. There are blankets in the hall closet and a slew of warm clothes upstairs. Layers." My emotions had triggered my hot flashes. Then again, at my age simply waking up triggered my hot flashes. And sometimes I woke up in the throes of one without doing anything to cause it.

As I moved deeper into the house, I got a strong sense of being watched. I climbed the stairs to the main floor while Wallie took Zoey downstairs. He'd pretty much taken over the entire downstairs when he was in junior high.

As I stood in the upstairs living room, I turned around, looking for the source of the odd vibe. Then a warm sensation flowed over me, and I swore I smelled Clay's cologne for just a moment. Okay, so that was just crazy. It was the grief that made me sense him. Being here for the first time in several months, all the memories of our life together. It had definitely been a good one.

Yeah. It was the grief causing me to feel like Clay was about to walk through the door any second.

I went to the kitchen not thinking about how I'd seen my mother's ghost a few weeks ago. It isn't possible that Clay would be there. Not possible at all. If he was here, I would've sensed him years before.

Opening the fridge, I nodded at nobody in particular. It was empty. Just like I'd left it in October. "Pizza it is," I mumbled and shut the refrigerator door. I'd meant to send Uncle Wade some money to buy a few staples for the week but had forgotten. I'd also gotten way too used to Alfred handling it all. He usually made a list and either put in an order for delivery or sent Owen to the store.

They were spoiling me. To be fair, I was providing them a place to live and food to eat. And for dead things—undead things?— they sure did eat a lot. Not to mention the entertainment. They'd talked me into upgrading the internet service because Zoey had introduced Alfred and Larry to something called Tik-Tok and they wanted fast upload speeds. Apparently, they were *trending.*

It was already late afternoon, and I'd skipped lunch, not to mention I never got my nap. At the moment, my stomach was letting me know *all* about that mistake. The combo of sleepiness and hunger was threatening to make me grumpy. Maybe even hangry.

"I gave Zoey the tour," Wallie called from the living room.

"Great." I brought up the app for the local pizzeria and placed an order for two larges with the works, then at the last second changed it to three. Leftovers were always a good thing.

I'd never taken the app off my phone. Once we were finished here, it would be time to delete all the local apps. I had no plans to return since I'd had Clay cremated. His urn waited, still, in the living room for me to figure out when and where I wanted to spread them.

As a necromancer, even though at the time I hadn't been a *practicing* necromancer, I wouldn't ever bury a loved one. I'd proven even an old skeleton could be animated by someone powerful enough.

But then, once I had Clay's ashes, I hadn't been able to bring myself to actually do anything with them. Instead, he'd gone over the fireplace to watch over Wallie and me.

I didn't bother with asking Zoey what she liked. The child could eat all of us under the table and didn't seem picky about anything. The fact that Zoey, Snooze, his girlfriend Lucy, and now Larry could eat food mystified me. Technically, they were undead. I'd animated each of them at one point or another.

Ghouls. Kind of. If Alfred would let me cut his strings, no doubt he'd join in on the nosh fest as well.

After I placed the pizza order, I stared into the kitchen and breathed out a long, drawn-out sigh. With a flick of my hand, I opened all the cabinets at once to inspect the contents. Not much. Long shelf-life type stuff, like soups. I didn't have the energy to start this. I flicked my wrist again and shut the doors.

Wade had dropped off bubble wrap and boxes, they were piled in the laundry room off the kitchen. But I was too tired from the flight and being up all night to start packing.

A knock pulled me from my haze. Before I got halfway to the door, Wallie was already there. "It's too soon to be the pizza," I called.

Wallie ignored me and flung the door open. "Uncle Wade!" Wallie hugged the older man and stepped back to let him in.

Wade met my gaze and instantly crossed the room to me, pulling me into a tight hug.

My emotions went haywire. Wade was Clay's uncle and had adopted me as his own early in the marriage. He was the only one to keep in touch and make sure I was surviving Clay's death. It had nearly taken me out as well. Clay's parents didn't care for me, so they'd barely been in touch.

That didn't bother me. We'd told them early on that I was a witch, hoping for acceptance and tolerance.

We'd gotten the opposite.

What pissed me off was that they'd also written Wallie off when it became clear he'd inherited my powers.

I buried my face in Wade's chest. Hugging Wade had always felt like what I imagined a hug from my father would feel like.

"It feels like a lifetime since I saw you last." Wade stepped back and framed my face. "How are you?" He'd cut his salt and pepper black hair short, nearly a buzz. It made him look like a big, burly general. He'd always been a big man, but as he got older, he'd kept up his activity level, so he wasn't getting all saggy yet like so many of us did as we aged.

Hell, I was already saggy. No plans to do anything about it, either, except maybe just try not to gain any weight.

Squeezing his hands, I smiled and tried not to look overly tired. "I'm good." I meant it, too. In fact, I realized that I was *better* than good. "You need to stay for dinner. I ordered more than enough pizza."

Wade yanked me into another quick hug. "I think I will."

"Come sit." I looked around for Zoey, wondering where she'd snuck off to.

Wallie noticed my expression and said, "Zoey's taking a shower. She actually beat me to it. She's fast." The water heater in this house sorely needed replacing. While we had two bathrooms, if they both ran the shower at the same time the water went cold in a hurry.

But the small things like that actually made the house sell faster because I put it up at a very cheap price to offset the needed upgrades. I'd never even gotten around to installing a dishwasher and, in this day and age, that was unheard of.

I laughed at Wallie's frustration that he had to wait to wash off the airplane smell. "Yeah. That's called shifter speed."

Turning to Wade, I said, "I'd offer you something to drink, but I haven't been to the store yet."

He grinned like he had a secret. "I figured as much so I brought some things. Wallie, can you get the bags out of the truck?" Wade sat on the sofa and motioned me to come over.

I sat beside him and pulled one of the throw pillows into my lap. "I'm not sure what to do with all this stuff. Yaya's house —my house in Shipton—came furnished."

He shrugged. "You could ask Hailey if she wants any of it and donate whatever is left." He looked around. "I might take a few things. But I know Hailey is coming from a long way and I don't *think* she has a lot of stuff."

"Oh, I didn't think about that. I'd be happy to give her some of this furniture. Good call." I grinned at him. "I guess I got it in my head I'd have to do some sort of yard sale and I *really* didn't want to." I pulled out my phone to put a reminder in it to call the local thrift store and ask if they'd pick up the big stuff.

Wallie came back in carrying an arm full of bags. "This is more than a few things." He struggled down the hall toward the kitchen. "Don't get up. I got it."

I grinned and Wade shrugged as he glanced at the doorway just when Zoey entered the living room.

The tiger ghoul stopped in her tracks and stared at Wade then me. I'd let her glamour go once we got here, and her ears were back on the top of her head. I giggled at her panicked expression as her ears laid down flat. "It's okay, Zoey. This is Wade. He knows about the supernatural."

I'd told Wade about Zoey, but I hadn't gone into details like how she half-shifted on occasion. He stared at her. "I know but knowing and seeing are two different things."

All I could do was pat him on the hand. He only knew the half of it. "I told you my life is crazy now. But I'm loving it."

Before we could go any deeper into it, Zoey turned to the door and sniffed the air. "Pizza's here."

I stood and motioned her toward the kitchen. "Go help Wallie put away the things Wade brought and get us some plates and napkins." Technically, Zoey was of age, but in many ways, she was like a young teen. She hadn't been around other kids her age enough, nor had she gotten enough of an education. We were doing everything we could to help her catch up, so to speak.

Although, she hadn't been absolutely sure she was eighteen. She'd spent almost a decade with the shifter fighting ring and time had been hard to keep track of.

With a nod, she skipped off to the kitchen. When she was out of sight, I answered the door and thanked the delivery guy.

When I closed the door, Wade said, "She seems so alive. How is she a zombie?"

It was my turn to shrug. "Not a zombie, really. They're

people who are turned into mindless animals. She's a ghoul. It's the part of me that is different." I set the pizza boxes on the coffee table and called, "Come eat!"

I didn't bother waiting for plates, just threw the first box open and grabbed a slice. "Owen thinks I'm special and far more powerful than other necromancers. Alfred, Zoey, Snoozer, Lucy-fur, and Larry are all connected to me. When I die, so do they, unless I transfer them to another necromancer. Even then I worry that another one wouldn't be able to keep five ghouls alive without draining their powers."

He grabbed a slice as the kids came back in. "Doesn't it drain yours?"

I shook my head. "That's just a small part of me being *special*, as far as we can tell."

We ate pizza, talked about random things, and told Zoey silly stories about things Wallie did as a kid. Heck, he was still a kid, just a college kid now.

At my urging, Wade stayed throughout the evening and until nearly dark. Finally, I yawned one too many times and he stood. "I'm going." He bent over and pressed a kiss to my forehead. "See you tomorrow."

After he closed the door behind him, I locked up the house using magic, then headed to bed. The kids had gone up an hour ago.

We'd given Zoey the guest room, while Wallie took his old room. It was a good thing I hadn't collected my menagerie in this house. It wasn't big enough to hold all of them. We were bursting at the seams in Winston as it was.

I entered my room and stopped short. A smile drifted on my face as I could've sworn I felt Clay again. The feeling was stronger than it had been in the living room when I'd first arrived. I was beginning to believe that maybe it *was* his ghost. But why would he be here now? I'd never felt him like this before I went to Shipton. It better not be to haunt me.

Moving to the bed, I pulled out my night clothes from the dresser. The feeling was still there. "Clay? Are you here?"

Nothing happened. Dead silence. Maybe it was all in my imagination, wishful thinking.

Closing my eyes, I sent out a low current of magic to see if I could call him that way. Could I communicate with ghosts? Again, nothing happened. *Okay, Ava, you have lost your mind.* Or I was just being hopeful to see him one last time. Like I'd seen mom's ghost and Yaya in the mirror.

Opening my suitcase, I pulled out my toiletries and set them on the counter in the bathroom. As I brushed my teeth, I moved to my walk-in closet. I'd left the door closed, so there shouldn't be much dust in there. I sniffed and looked around, pleased to see it looked fine.

It had to have been the memories inside this house that made my senses and emotions work overtime. Pushing away the feelings, I took a quick shower and dressed in the pajamas from my dresser, some of the many clothes I'd left here in Philly and would be taking back to Shipton with me.

Even though I was so exhausted, it took a while to wind down. I played a game on my phone and tried to scroll social media. That often worked to make my eyes get sleepy.

Finally, it worked, but then the moment I closed my eyes to go to sleep, a noise outside the window pulled me back into full wakefulness. Frowning, I got out of bed to look at what in the world could've been outside my house.

The neighborhood looked normal. Streetlights made shadows everywhere, but it was quiet and still.

A flash of a shadow ran across the street from my neighbor's house. But it was gone before I could get a good look. One of the streetlights flickered a few times. I sighed and rolled my eyes for seeing shadows that didn't exist.

Scanning the area one more time, I froze and locked gazes with a man standing on the front porch of the house directly across from mine, watching me. He hadn't been there a few seconds ago, nor had I seen movement there to indicate the front door opening.

Narrowing my eyes, I considered sending out a tiny bit of magic to warn whoever it was off. I didn't, of course, because he was more than likely human. I couldn't tell from the distance but the odds of him being supernatural were slim.

He sure as hell was staring hard. "Creeper," I whispered and shut the blinds. I crawled back in bed, deciding that I needed to check around about the disturbing neighbor.

Something was way off about him, and I was going to find out what.

CHAPTER THREE

For the first time, possibly ever, I was awake before the rest of the house. For sure I hadn't been the first one up since Wallie was a little boy. I used to try to get up before him to make sure he didn't get into any trouble around the house.

That had stopped the minute he was old enough to be trusted not to completely burn the house down.

Stretching, I thought about life in Shipton. I'd gotten so used to having Alfred around. He was always up early and had coffee made. I missed my ghoul. Not just because he did all the housekeeping and cooking.

No, really. I enjoyed his quiet company. He made me feel settled and comfortable, even though he never said a word.

Another person I'd grown used to having around was Olivia. At least a few times a week, she'd show up at the house earlier than I liked to get up. I thought she did it on purpose, plotting to one day make me a morning person. Not happening. Ever.

Pulling out my phone, I found the contact for my bestie and pressed it.

Olivia's perky voice answered on the first ring. "Morning Ava! I was going to call but Sam said to let you adjust. Then, I thought of texting you this morning...but wow, it's early for you. Are you okay? Do you need bail money?"

I laughed so hard I had to cross my legs. "Why would I need bail money?"

"I don't know. It's before seven so I figured... Anyhoo. How are you?"

I narrowed my eyes, though it didn't do any good because Olivia couldn't see me. She was flustered about something. I could tell by the way she chatted randomly. And she knew I was too old and boring to do anything that got me arrested. I guessed I could've been picked up for raising the dead in a public place. But I only did that the one time. Good thing it had been around Halloween and the residents of Shipton thought we'd been putting on a play in the cemetery. It had worked out.

"What's wrong?" I asked my BFF.

"Why would anything be wrong?" Her voice shifted from chipper to bitter faster than Snooze when I turned on the can opener. That fat cat was fast when it came to his tuna.

With a sigh, I challenged her. "Your tone tells me there's something bothering you. Do *you* need bail money?"

"Just hold on to it. I might need it." She meant it as a joke, but I heard the serious note in her tone.

Propping my feet up, I settled in for a long talk. "Spill."

There was a pause before Olivia spoke. "I just got off the phone with Jess."

I waited. When it was clear she wasn't going to volunteer any information, I decided to drag it out of her. She couldn't leave me hanging like that. "And? Is she coming to visit? What about Devan?"

I hadn't ever seen either kid. All I knew was Olivia's older children were at college in Chicago. She didn't talk about them often, and if I asked about them, she replied in short, clipped sentences.

"No, they aren't coming for spring break or the summer." Her voice fell flat. My chest tightened. I couldn't imagine being so far from Wallie and not seeing him. I couldn't have said when she might've seen them last.

"Tell me," I urged, sensing that she wanted to talk about it or vent. "I'm here for you. Even if I am eight hours away, or by plane a couple of hours."

"You know I was married before." She laughed softly. "Of course, you do. I had two kids with the asshole."

"Yes, I remember you mentioning it." She had married Carter Phillips, the star quarterback of Shipton High. Had two kids and lived the high life. Nothing Olivia wasn't a stranger to since her family had always had money.

She sniffled. "The marriage was shaky from the start. I've grown enough to know I didn't help matters. I stuck the kids with a nanny while I did everything every other rich wife did. I wasn't a mother to them, not properly. Not like with Sammie. They grew up to hate me." Olivia let out a breath then sniffed. "Carter and I fought all the time about all the petty shit I did. I didn't see it, didn't see who I was until I lost everything. Carter packed up the kids and left one day. The next time we talked was in front of the judge."

Damn. Talk about karma. And I truly felt bad for Olivia. Carter could have tried harder. Then again, I hadn't been there. I didn't know how bad it was. But to take the kids? "I'm so sorry, Liv."

"It's my fault. I just hope that one day Jess and Devan will forgive me." She sniffed again. "I've been trying, reaching out a lot. Anyway, I hear Sammie stomping around in his room. Let me feed him. Thanks for calling." She obviously wanted to be free from this conversation. It had to be hard to talk about.

"No problem. You can call me any time to talk. I'm here for you."

"Thank you. Talk to you later." She ended the call.

I set down my phone and stared at the ceiling. As I contemplated getting out of bed and getting started with the day, the ghostly feeling returned. I jumped out of bed. "Clay?" I whispered. Grabbing my old robe from the back of the closet door, I slipped out into the hallway, but the feeling just got stronger. My skin tingled as I moved down the hallway and crossed to the living room. Before entering the kitchen, something cool brushed up against me, like from head to toe. Startled, I whirled around, but nothing was there.

No. That wasn't true. I was sure Clay was there and was trying to make contact. But why? Why was he there now? And why did he need to talk with me? It just didn't make sense that he'd show up now after all this time.

Not that I wasn't happy to feel him again. Actually, my feelings were strongly mixed. I'd begun to move on. So then, guilt washed over me for realizing I'd been in the process of moving on and that felt disloyal to Clay.

Grief was a, well, it was a bitch.

After one search around the living room, then a quick spin around the den and office, I went into the kitchen and proceeded to make coffee. Thankfully, it had been among the items Wade had brought the night before. The dark, rich go-go juice always made it easier to think. I got the water added to the reserve tank and caught something dark moving to my left. Jerking my head in the direction where I would've sworn something moved, I frowned. Nothing.

Okay, I might've been going crazy.

As I reached for the sugar, the entire canister moved. Like several inches across the counter away from me.

Nope, nope, nope.

Breathing heavily, I sent out my senses, putting magic in

the mix, searching for whatever was haunting my house. I sucked in a breath when I felt Clay so suddenly and so strong it was as if he were standing *right* beside me. My pulse kicked up several beats per second which I was sure wasn't healthy. Especially for someone my age.

Whirling around and around, I stopped, somehow. Why I halted in the exact spot that I did, I had no idea, but I lifted my hand and reached out. A cold sensation wrapped around it and with a squeak I jerked it back. Clay was here. "Oh, my." Tears filled my eyes. "Clay?"

I lost focus when I heard footsteps in the living room. No, not yet! I wasn't ready for this moment to be over.

I jerked around to face the coffee pot just as Wallie stumbled into the kitchen. Hiding my tears from him was a must. He didn't need to know his dad was there until I found out why Clay had made a sudden appearance and if he was sticking around.

My son wasn't a morning person, much like his mama. Good thing, too. Once he outgrew the childhood early mornings, I had usually been able to sleep in.

He mumbled, "Good morning," as he shuffled over and grabbed a coffee cup from the cabinet. "I'm glad Wade brought over coffee last night."

The boy read my mind. "Yeah, or you'd be going to the store without it."

He grunted and took his coffee to the table. "I miss Olivia and her donuts."

I snorted. "You miss the donuts."

He shrugged.

Zoey bounced into the room. Literally. She *was* a morning person. I never understood how people could just leap out of bed fully awake and ready to...people. Ugh. Gross.

Wallie stared at her as she grabbed a bottle of water from the fridge. Meeting my gaze, he grimaced. "Is she always like that in the mornings?" He'd been around her enough in Maine to know the answer to his question.

"Yep." I took a few more sips of my coffee. "I'll need the two of you to go get a few more things from the store. Just enough to get through the week."

"We don't have a car," Wallie complained. He wasn't a lazy kid. It was just too early to be functioning.

I rolled my eyes. "Walk to Wade's and get his truck."

He sighed and took his coffee back upstairs to change out of his Star Wars pajama pants.

"You ready to work?" I asked Zoey.

She nodded enthusiastically and opened a cabinet. "What's to eat?"

"There are those toaster pastries you like."

Her face lit up. "Ohh." She rifled through the cabinets until finding the blue box of sugary goodness.

After handing my debit card to Wallie, he and Zoey headed out with an extra silver packet of tarts in her right hand. Wade lived on the next block over, so it wasn't that far of a walk. Plus, they were young. Exercise was good for them. Yawning, I ignored the voice that told me it would be good for me, too.

Nope. Moving all this stuff would be exercise enough this week.

Once I was alone in the house. I used my magic to lock up. Wallie had a key, but I didn't expect them back for at least an hour. It was time to try to get Clay back.

I dug out some candles from the kitchen junk drawer and headed to my bedroom with my coffee.

I put candles around the room, one each in the North, South, East, and West. Sitting in the middle of the bed I had shared with my husband until he died almost six years ago, I lit the candles and created a circle around me with string. With a calming breath, I closed my eyes and sent out my magic, and called to Clay.

At first, nothing happened. Just me sitting on the bed, my left hip starting to twinge. It had given me trouble when I sat with my legs crossed ever since I had Wallie. Focusing, I put more power into it and called out to him. "Clay. I know you're here. I can smell you. Show yourself!"

My skin tingled as the air in the room charged with magic. Magic that I wasn't conjuring. With hope swelling in my heart, I opened my eyes. Gasping and clutching at my throat, I nearly jumped off the bed.

Clay sat in front of me with a big silly grin on his face, his hair falling into his eyes like it always used to. I stared at him, amazed, shocked, absolutely in awe as I took him in.

I'd been right. He was definitely here, and he was definitely a ghost.

CHAPTER FOUR

His voice floated through the air, a sound I'd been dying to hear since the moment I *stopped* hearing it. How was I actually watching Clay's boyish grin widen? "Finally! I've been trying to get you to notice me since you walked into the house." Clay waved his arms dramatically, then he seemed to remember something. The smile disappeared and he glared at me.

Tears pricked at the back of my eyes, but I was still too stunned to speak. He looked like he did the day he died. Not a day older. Also, he was semi-transparent.

A car accident that had only involved him and one other car. I'd been freaked out about driving for a while after, understandable considering both my father and my husband died in car accidents.

He wore the same clothes he'd worn that day to work. Black slacks and a gray button-down top. He needed a shave. He'd woken up late that morning and had left the house in a rush. But his wreck had been on the way home.

My vision blurred as my eyes filled with tears. "How is this possible?"

Clay cocked his head as he frowned and moved forward, reaching out. He let his hand drop, hesitating before touching me. "You haven't let go."

Let go of what? How was he able to touch me? "I don't understand." Hell, I didn't even know ghosts were real until a few weeks ago. I traced the spot on my leg where he'd just touched with my fingertips.

Clay sat on the bed in front of me, but the mattress didn't compress. He didn't weigh anything. "After my body died, I came to the house. At first, I didn't know why I hadn't crossed over, but I didn't care because I got to stay with you and Wallie."

"Wait, you've been here all along?" Now that I thought about it, the house had always felt heavy since he died. Like his presence lingered, making me sad. I could sense him, but he wasn't there.

When I'd arrived at Winnie's house, at Winston, I'd started to feel better. I hadn't put two and two together until now, fully blind to Clay trying to connect with me. I hadn't been able to move on because he was still here with me.

Clay scooted closer to me. That was when I reached out and took his hand. Surprisingly, I felt him, though he wasn't quite warm enough. Closing my eyes, I sucked in my breath, trying to smell that scent that was uniquely him. I'd smelled it last night. My chest tightened and tears flowed down my cheeks as I pulled his hand to my face.

With a worried frown, he swiped the wetness from my cheeks, pressing his palm to my skin. "Don't be sad. You just have to let go so I can move on." His voice, though he was right in front of me, was somehow far away.

My heart cracked, the grief washing over me nearly as hard as it had the day I'd found out he was gone. "I don't know how."

His features turned sad. I tried to gaze deep into his brown eyes, but it wasn't the same. Right in front of me and he still felt so far away. "I tried to reach out to you for so long but couldn't get your attention."

I saw it now, how he'd been trying to reach me. I'd been so blind before, stuck in the mire of my grief. "Why did it work this time?"

His lips lifted. "Your magic. It's stronger now." He shook his head. "I'm so proud of you. You've finally embraced who you are."

That was a change. "When you were alive, you wanted me to subdue my magic."

Clay shrugged and chuckled. "Death gave me perspective. I see now that I never should've encouraged you to block off such a huge part of yourself. You've blossomed since you've embraced your magic."

Ducking my head, I smiled. He was right about that. I'd never felt more myself than since I allowed myself to open up to my magic. "Yeah. A lot of crazy stuff has happened since I moved to Shipton."

"I know," he said. "I can't be with you there; I'm tied to this house and my ashes. But I've been listening. I heard you update Wade last night, and I'm dying to know why Alfred won't let you cut the strings on his mouth."

I'd updated Uncle Wade the night before on pretty much everything.

"I still can't believe Sam married Olivia even though I was at their wedding. They seem like an odd couple." He'd died a few months after the wedding.

I nodded. "I think that's why it works with them. Besides, Olivia isn't the snobby bitch she used to be. She's a lot of fun to be around. And it doesn't hurt that their kid is adorable."

"How old is he?" His eyes twinkled as he gazed at me. I got the feeling he'd missed me as much as I'd been missing him.

"Almost six," I said. "Olivia was pregnant at the wedding but didn't know it. She found out about the baby a few weeks after, but they kept it kind of quiet. I didn't even know. They were worried about complications with her having a baby at her age."

He sighed and laid sideways on the bed and I realized he was floating just above it. "A ghoul, a skeleton that isn't a skeleton anymore, a tiger shifting ghoul, and two immortal cats. You have a zoo of unusual beings."

"Pretty much." I smiled, though. I was proud of those lunatics.

A laugh burst from him and then he said, "You could start your own circus!"

I giggled and pushed him off the bed, but there was no sound when he hit, so I scrambled across the large bed to look over the edge and didn't see him. "Clay?" I whispered. A moment later he shot up out of the floor, scaring the daylights out of me. I squawked and fell back, grabbing a pillow and throwing it in his general direction. Of course, it went straight through him.

After we stopped laughing long enough to breathe, he floated back over to the bed and sat beside me again. "Do you think Wallie can see me?"

My heart ached for Clay. He'd missed so much of Wallie's high school years. "Yeah, I think he probably can. He did inherit my necromancer genes and has been training with me, Owen, and his girlfriend."

"Tell me about his girlfriend." He propped his chin in his palm and gazed up at me.

I crossed my legs, ignoring that ever-present twinge in my hip, and smiled at the thought of Michelle. "She's beautiful and amazing. She's a witch with a strong connection to water. And she loves that I'm a necromancer." I'd never realized so many people would embrace my necromancer side.

“What about this sheriff you mentioned?” Oh, geez. I'd told Wade a bit about Drew last night. Clay had overheard.

My heart skipped a few beats. “What about him?” Jumping off the bed, I blew out the candles and headed out my bedroom door.

I ducked my head as I walked down the hall toward the living room. Clay zipped around to stand in front of me. “That. The way your face lights up when you think of him. The way you said his name earlier. You're seeing him.”

I opened my mouth to deny it, but I could never lie to Clay. “Maybe.” Shame crept up my cheeks like I'd been cheating on him.

He crossed his arms but didn't look mad. “That's a yes.”

Shaking my head, I walked around him. “It's weird to talk about this with you. You're my husband.” He'd been my life partner for so long.

Startling me again, Clay appeared in front of me in the kitchen doorway. “I *was* your husband. I'm dead, so I'm not your husband anymore.” He crossed his arms and narrowed his eyes at me. "Supernatural divorce."

He was wrong. “You will always be my husband.” I pushed past him and went straight for the kitchen. When I got in there I remembered, the only thing sweet in there was pastries Wade had brought over last night.

Sighing, I opened the cabinet. I wanted ice cream, but I guessed a cakey donut would do.

Clay drifted in, and I tried to ignore him. Then he wrapped his ghostly arms around me. I melted into them, but they just didn't feel right. It wasn't him, not enough of him. “I understand what you're saying. I love you and will always love you. But you're still holding on to me, which makes it hard for me to move on.”

What? That made things different. If my clinging to his memory meant he couldn't go on to the next plane or Heaven, or whatever happened next, I had to find a way to let him go. "I'm keeping you? Are you stuck here?"

He shrugged and let go of me. "I thought when you left for Shipton, I would finally be able to cross over, but I can't even leave the house."

Oh no. What had I done? "I'm sorry, Clay. So sorry. I didn't know. I didn't even believe in ghosts until recently."

He laughed and floated to the ceiling. "How can someone who can raise the dead not know ghosts were real?" He had a point, but I wasn't about to tell him that.

I rolled my eyes and took a bite of the dry donut. I needed milk. I sure hoped that Wallie had picked some up. I couldn't remember if I put it on the list.

Focusing on Clay, who was now sitting on the countertop next to me, I sighed. "I was so busy playing human most of my life. I wanted to be normal."

He nudged me. "Hey. I loved that you were never normal." He knew I had hang-ups about my necro powers. "I wish I'd seen how incredibly special you were many, many years ago. Hell, if we'd moved back to Shipton so you could embrace your powers, maybe I'd still be here now."

Tears filled my eyes. "I've missed you so much."

The sound of a truck door closing made Clay and me lock gazes. My heart sank. Our interlude was over. "What is Wade doing back?"

"That's Wallie and Zoey. They went over there to get his truck and some more groceries." I waved for him to leave. "I don't want Wallie seeing you yet. I need to see how he takes it." He hadn't seen his father since he was a young teenager. This wouldn't be easy on him, to say the least.

"Fine. But don't wait around too long. We have to figure out why I can't move on."

I nodded as he disappeared. Seconds later the front door

opened and Wallie and Zoey came in with their arms full of reusable shopping bags.

Wallie pointed at Zoey. "The junk food is her fault." I saw the tops of chips bags sticking up out of the sacks.

Zoey scrunched up her nose at him and took off her hoodie, revealing her tiger ears on the top of her head. "Not all of it."

Hoping they'd remembered the thing I was craving the most, I searched through the bags until I found the double chocolate brownie ice cream. I grabbed a spoon and took it to the living room. I needed to think after spending that last hour with Clay's ghost.

An overload of chocolate was just what the doctor ordered.

CHAPTER FIVE

The house felt empty without Clay visible, but now that I'd seen him, I felt him every time he came near. He was still here, just behind the veil.

Was it a veil? Heck if I knew. I was barely struggling through this necromancer mess.

"Was Wade home when you got the truck?" I plopped down into the kitchen chair and looked at my son. The hair on the back of my neck prickled. I was pretty sure Clay was touching me there.

Wallie shook his head and he put the frozen meal in the microwave. "No. I called him and left a message that I had his truck. He hasn't replied yet."

That was odd. I thought he'd be here by now. He'd made it seem like he was going to be here all day today to help. "I just called him, and he didn't answer." Something settled deep in my gut, a feeling the situation was slightly off.

"We can walk over after we eat and check on him before it gets dark," Zoey suggested before taking a bite of her sandwich. She grunted. "Alfred makes better sandwiches."

I laughed. "Only because you don't have to make them." But hey, she wasn't wrong. And checking on Wade was a good idea. It'd be good to get a bit of fresh air anyway.

Wallie pulled his meal out of the microwave. "She's right. You should've brought him."

Rolling my eyes, I wadded up my napkin. "That would have gone *really* well, getting him through airport security." I had a hard enough time hiding Zoey's tiger parts that kept popping out. Shaking my head, I went to the living room and put on my tennis shoes. I'd spent the day working on my closet, packing some, and donating a *lot*. I'd lost enough weight in Shipton that I needed to go shopping. Happiness was good for my waistline

About fifteen minutes later, the kids were ready to go check on our Uncle. "You know this'll be our last walk around the neighborhood." My heart clenched with sadness that I'd probably never be back. Bittersweet

Wallie shrugged. "I'm okay with that."

I stared at him as we walked down the street. Was he this detached emotionally about his childhood home? "Aw, come on, don't be all bummed out."

Zoey snickered while Wallie rolled his eyes. I just pretended my left ankle wasn't giving me a sharp stabbing pain with every step. "I'm just starting my life," Wallie said as he walked with zero trouble. Ah, the benefits of youth. "Do you think I planned on staying here for the rest of my life?" He scoffed. "Hell, no. I always knew I'd move away and find my place in the world."

I fake sniffed and pretended to wipe a tear from my eye. "My baby is all grown up." I was putting on for his benefit, but it did make me sad. It wasn't that I wanted more children, especially at my age. But it would've been nice to go back in time and relive just a bit of Wallie's babyhood. He'd been such a cute baby.

Chuckling, he playful pushed me. "Stop. You're changing too."

Catching myself before I fell over, I shot him a mom-look. "I know." Sometimes when I was alone at night, after everyone went to bed, I reflected on how much change had happened in my life in such a short time. We strolled down the street, the weather clear and warm for March. I was getting a little sweaty in my jacket.

I'd set a glamour on Zoey before we left, thankfully. Her tail twitched behind her as we strolled down the street.

But then the bright, cheery feeling in the neighborhood changed. A tingle went up my spine and then the sensation poked at my necromancer powers. I stopped and turned to see who or what was watching me. I locked my gaze on the house across the street from mine and narrowed my eyes. We'd walked around to the backside of the street behind their backyard. Which, I didn't remember that house's yard being so huge.

"Wallie." I stopped and narrowed my eyes at the space. "Didn't there used to be a house here?"

"Yeah," he said slowly. "My old friend Jimmy lived there. They moved away when I was about to go into high school."

"Maybe you're not remembering which house it was," Zoey suggested.

Wallie shook his head then looked around with his eyebrows up. "No, it was there."

Now it was just an enormous backyard for the house directly across from mine. Complete with an extra-tall privacy fence. "I don't think I've ever seen a fence this tall," I murmured.

There was movement in the large back window, but the curtains blocked my view to see who it was. Something told me it was the creep from last night. I tensed, drawing on my magic, ready to defend myself. Though, I didn't know what exactly I'd do in our defense. I needed to practice more fighting magic. Just to be safe.

"What is it?" Wallie moved closer to me, standing slightly in front of me like he was ready to protect his mama. On the other side of me, Zoey extended her tiger claws. She too was ready to throw down to defend me. Those sweet kids. I loved them for trying.

I took each of their hands and started walking again. "I felt something but don't know what. The neighbor across from us gives me the creeps." I couldn't pinpoint why, but it was my magic that reacted. Something supernatural was afoot.

Which figured. I went back home to Shipton and suddenly everything was all magic all the time. Why wouldn't things be paranormal here as well?

"I haven't seen them yet." Wallie glanced back, scanning our surroundings. My boy was really grown. He didn't look for his mommy to take care of him anymore. I stuck out my bottom lip at the thought.

When he looked back and met my stare, he frowned. "What?"

"Nothing." We walked in silence for a few minutes, thoughts of Clay swirling in my head. How proud he would've been of his son for being my defender. "Wallie, have you ever seen a ghost?" His eyebrows shot up. "It has come to my attention recently that, like necromancers, we can see them. And call to them." Although to be fair, I wasn't sure how we could do the latter. I had with Clay because I had something that belonged to him. Plus, I was connected to him when he was alive. But I'd never called my mom to me. Not that I recalled, anyway. Surely in all my years of missing her, if I'd been able, I would've pulled her ghost to me.

"No, but it makes sense that we can." He glanced at me. "Tell me what you need to tell me."

I hesitated long enough to make Wallie stop walking. "Mom. What is it?"

We were on the corner of Wade's street. I could just see his house down the road. "Your father is at the house."

Crap that was too insensitive. I was terrible at this stuff.

"You saw him?" Wallie's tone was calm. He wasn't surprised by the news flash.

I met his gaze with wide eyes. "You're not surprised?"

"No. Not really. I felt him when we got there. I just didn't say anything because I didn't want to upset you." He wrapped an arm around my shoulders and pulled me close. I rested my head on his shoulder as we started walking again.

Of course, he'd sensed his father. Wallie was going to be as strong as I was one day, or nearly so at least.

Zoey reached out and took my hand. She must have sensed our emotions in a bit of turmoil. I pulled her into the family hug.

Time to come clean. "I called him out when you two were at the store. However, we have a problem. He says I'm still holding on to him so he can't move on. I don't know how to let go. I didn't even know I was holding him here."

Zoey pulled back and took my hand again, her claws gone now. "But you *have* moved on. You're dating Drew. Right?"

I nodded and realized that I hadn't talked to Wallie about my relationship with the sexy sheriff. "About that." I looked at him out of the corner of my eyes. "Are you okay with it?"

He chuckled and squeezed me tighter. "Of course. I like Drew. Plus, I think he's good for you. You don't have to hide who you are."

Wallie kissed the top of my head and let go of me. "We'll figure out the issue with Dad."

Just then, a woman came around the corner at the end of the road from the direction we'd just come. She had workout clothes on, which made me think that she was on an early evening walk. As she passed us, she smiled and nodded. We all muttered polite hellos, but my greeting died in my throat as I caught sight of what looked like a bite on her neck.

Wallie and I looked at each other but didn't comment on it. It could've been anything. Every injury or strange happening didn't automatically mean something spooky was going on. We kept walking.

When we got to Wade's the sun had begun to set, but there were no lights on in his house. He lived in a house about the size of ours. I'd completely forgotten to get his spare key out of the kitchen drawer, so we walked around the house and knocked, peeking in the windows until we began to worry the neighbors might call the police.

I should've put up a ward to make us invisible, but I didn't think of it until it was too late. "Well." I stepped back and peered up, trying to see into his upstairs windows but it was no good. "We'll come back tomorrow and break in if we don't hear from him soon."

"Agreed," Wallie said. "But that's unlikely. We do have a key."

Oh, whatever.

Zoey sniffed at the door subtly. "I don't think there's anyone there."

On our way back to the house, we noticed a group of people outside the creepy neighbor's house. The one across the street from mine.

At first, I thought they were having a party or something, but the music wasn't loud. I barely heard it as we walked up our driveway. The weird thing was that they seemed to be sunbathing in the moonlight. In lawn chairs. Talking and laughing with sunglasses on.

They were *so* weird!

We went inside and watched them through the windows.

Zoey sat on the couch and said, "They're not human. I don't know what they *are*, but human, they are *not*."

"They're vampires."

I nearly jumped out of my skin when Clay appeared beside me and announced the origin of our neighbors.

Wallie must've heard his dad's voice. He hurried out of the kitchen and stopped short in the living room doorway. "Dad," he whispered.

Clay walked over to him, but his feet didn't quite touch the floor. "Oh, Wallace. I've missed you so much."

Watching them embrace set my emotions over the edge they'd been teetering on.

I gave them a couple of minutes to whisper to each other.

"That's Clay?" Zoey asked, plopping down on the sofa beside me, both of us gazing at the father and son reunion.

"Yup." I eyed my boys. Clay was solid when he touched Wallie or vice-versa. When they weren't in physical contact with each other, Clay took on a translucence.

I gave them a few minutes to murmur together before interrupting. "Welp, ah, vampires? I thought they were a myth."

Clay slung his arm around Wallie's neck and gripped him hard. "No idea. I only knew witches were real, but I've been watching them since they moved in right after you left for Maine."

"If you can't leave the house, how do you know they're vampires?" Zoey asked with her head cocked to the side.

Clay walk-floated over. As soon as he let go of Wallie, he was see-through again. "They only come out at night," he said simply.

Laughing, I shook my head at him. "That doesn't automatically make them vampires."

But them being vampires—in theory, another form of undead—meant my necromancer senses going a little haywire made sense.

And there was that lady out for a walk with the bite mark on her neck.

What were the chances that my new neighbors, from a life that was mostly magic free, were vampires?

I peeked out the window at them again. My jaw dropped as I watched a woman apply what looked like, from this far away, tanning oil on the back of another of the vampires. Errr, people. Not vampires. I couldn't say for sure that's what they were.

Not yet. I added it to my mental list of things to figure out tomorrow.

CHAPTER SIX

"Oof." Leaning back, I stretched my back and then kept going. I'd forgotten how hard moving was. Just the packing was a pain, literally. Forget moving big stuff. I'd begun putting yellow sticky notes on all the furniture I didn't want to keep. If Wallie wanted it, I'd given him strict instructions to remove the yellow paper and replace it with a blue one.

I was in the middle of taping up another box when the doorbell rang. I almost expected it to be echoed through the house. Of course, it didn't because this wasn't Winston. That was when I realized how much I missed my old Victorian in Shipton Harbor.

Not bothering with checking the peephole in the door, I opened it. My magic had already let me know who it was. Another new ability that had manifested since I became High Witch of the Shipton Coven. It was more of a feeling. A knowing.

I opened the door and smiled. Hailey Whitfield was adorable with her shoulder-length blonde hair and bright blue eyes. She was several inches shorter than me with sexy curves.

Wade had told me she was about my age, but she looked like she was aging well. Either that or she'd started using eye cream a lot younger than I had. "Hello, Hailey. I'm Ava." I offered her my hand and she took it.

I chuckled at the confused look on her face. "Hailey. Oh, you said that, okay well, thanks so much for meeting me and letting me take the tour." She glanced around me, making me look out of habit to make sure there were no ghouls or ghosts in sight. If we'd been in Shipton the chances would've been extremely high that something undead would get spotted.

Of course, Clay sat next to Wallie on the sofa. The two of them were talking softly, but at least Wallie had his cell to his ear so it wouldn't look like he was talking to himself. Zoey was out of sight. I'd put her to packing up the attic. It was full of family memories and things I wouldn't want to part with.

Once I was sure everything in the house looked normal for a human, I stepped aside and invited her in. "Wade tells me you're friends with Kendra next door."

Hailey's smile widened. "Yes. We grew up together and stayed in touch when she moved here. I wish she were here, but she's on vacation." She looked around with interest as she talked.

Suddenly everything I'd been meaning to do to the house was glaringly obvious. The wallpaper in the hall had begun to peel in the top corner near the door. And there were dead moths in the light fixture at the top of the stairs. I couldn't see them from here, but I'd spotted them last night and meant to get them out before Hailey came.

Too late now.

I wondered if Hailey knew Kendra was a witch. It would make sense that she would, if they'd been friends for so long, but I wasn't going to mention it just in case she didn't know. Nice and normal. That's what I was today. Just a regular old human.

That was a weird feeling because I hadn't acted like a human in what...six months? Had I been in Shipton that long? In some ways, it felt like I'd been there for years, and in others like I'd just gotten there.

Once Hailey entered the house, I closed the door and frowned. "Sorry for the mess. I started packing up things and forgot the time." Packing supplies were spread across the living room and the dining room, just visible through the door, had become a catch-all of donated stuff.

She chuckled and kept looking around. "Oh, no worries. I understand."

Wallie swatted at his father, which to Hailey probably looked like he was batting at the air. Thankfully, she was looking up at the peeling spot in the wallpaper. Damn it.

I almost told him to take his conversation somewhere else, but it wouldn't have done any good since I was giving Hailey a tour of the whole house.

Ignoring my son and dead husband—ugh what was I going to do?!—I motioned for Hailey to follow me. I showed her the kitchen, letting her know that the appliances would all be staying. "Clay and I bought all new stuff about six years ago, and I didn't cook much the last five years." I'd been too depressed and heartbroken to cook after Clay was gone.

Dragging my mind away from the sad thoughts, I focused on Hailey. "The same with most of the furniture. I won't be taking it with me, so you are welcome to have it." I pointed to the yellow Post-It on the dining room table. "Yellow means it's to be donated." I pulled a black marker out of the junk drawer. "Put an H on anything you can use."

She took the pen uncertainly. "Thank you."

What if she didn't want it? "Seriously," I repeated. "All yellow sticky notes mean donate." I held up one finger and stuck my head into the living room. "You better have everything you want marked," I hissed at Wallie.

He waved me off. On his head be it if there was something left behind that he'd wanted.

I returned to Hailey. "Yeah, mark as much or as little as you want. Anything you don't mark will be picked up at the end of the week."

She relaxed and her grin spread into something more natural. "That would be great. It'll save me some money on buying new stuff right away."

Great. It made me feel good, thinking that this woman, who was starting over herself, might be helped by these furnishings.

Leaving the kitchen, we walked back through the living room. Wallie had his phone put away and now Clay stood from the couch and began following me around.

Wallie stood as well and held his hand out to Hailey. "Hi, I'm Wallie, Ava's son. Sorry, I was talking to my dad when you came in."

Alarm jolted through me. He did *not* just say that.

Hailey glanced at me. "Oh, your husband couldn't make it?" She smiled politely.

Oh, he was here, all right, but she didn't need to know that. "My husband is dead."

"Wow, that was harsh," Clay said in my ear, chuckling.

Blinking and trying very hard not to show a reaction to his words, I almost elbowed him in the ribs but caught myself. I couldn't let myself look weird in front of the human.

Wallie shuddered for a moment then said, "Stepdad." A little late for a correction.

Hailey smiled uncertainly. "Is that Drew you mentioned the other day?"

I ignored Clay and gave Wallie my meanest mom look. "Uh, no, Wallie was talking to someone else, and yes, Drew and I just started dating. We're not married, and don't plan on it anytime soon. Do you want to see the rest of the house?"

She looked from me to Wallie and nodded. "Absolutely."

Why in Hades had thinking of marrying Drew made me panic? It had to be that fact that Clay was hovering so close by. He knew I was seeing someone but that was a far cry from *marriage.*

As we topped the stairs, I heard movement in the guest bedroom at the end of the hall and figured it was Zoey. We went into the master bedroom first. I'd been through most of it, so it was fairly neat and packed up.

Then we moved down to Wallie's room, and I said a silent prayer it was clean after him being here for two days.

It was. Mostly. Boxes were strewn everywhere, instead of neatly stacked like in my room, but the good news was that most of it was packed, at least. "Each bedroom has its own bathroom," I pointed out, which she probably already realized. "I was always thankful for that."

That left the guest room. We strolled down the hall. The door was cracked open, so I didn't think twice about just walking in. Once I did, I froze for a split second, then grabbed the door and pulled it closed as fast as I could.

"Oh," I squeaked. Zoey had shifted fully into a tiger and laid in the middle of the bed, licking her back thigh with her other leg straight up in the air behind her. Like a dang house cat. Except she was more like three hundred pounds.

I turned to face Hailey and forced a smile. "Sorry. Zoey was dressing." Then, I tapped on the door and spoke through it in a loud, cheery voice. "Zo, we have a guest over."

The sound of a very large animal hopping off the bed echoed from inside the room. Thump, thump.

Hailey stared at the door and arched one eyebrow. "Is she okay? It sounded like she fell."

Laughing nervously, I shook my head and stayed firmly in front of the door. "She's fine. Probably knocked something over."

Then Zoey yanked the door open and grinned. "I'm fine.

My books fell on the floor." Hopefully, Hailey wouldn't question the fact that Zo had heard us through the door.

We walked in, and Hailey looked around.

No books in sight. Had Zoey even brought any books? Forcing another grin at Hailey, I said, "See? Fine. Let's move on."

The rest of the tour went on without any craziness. Thank goodness she couldn't see or hear Clay. That man...er, the ghost was determined to make me look like an insane person with ever-increasingly snarky comments. When I showed Hailey my office, Clay had to remind me of the last time we'd had sex on the desk.

In detail.

Hailey went back through the house, writing a big H on each sticky note for the furniture she wanted, then when she was finished, I congratulated her on her new home and shut the door behind her with a huge sigh of relief.

I didn't know how to be human anymore.

A few hours later, I took a break from packing and decided to call Owen to check on things on the home front.

My mentor and friend answered on the second ring. "Hey, Ava."

It was nice to hear his voice. I'd grown very fond of the tall, awkward-looking man. "How is everything?"

Owen was quiet for a few seconds before answering me. Dread began to build in my gut. I had too much to do here before I could return home. Did they need me? Had something gone wrong?

"Everything is good," Owen said and paused again. "Did...did you know that Alfred has an Instagram account?"

A *what?* "No..." That couldn't be a good thing, could it? Instagram was about pictures, and Alfie was desiccated flesh. "Please tell me he doesn't take selfies."

He hissed. "Okay, I won't tell you." Owen chuckled then began laughing out loud.

I closed my eyes and practiced breathing, counting up as I inhaled and down as I exhaled. Not that I needed the practice, but it was good to remind my body to do so every once in a while. "Should I ask?"

His laughter faded long enough to explain. "Mainly they post pictures of the cats, but he most recently took a selfie of him and Larry together. Oh, and Snooze is in the background photo bombing." Owen laughed some more, and I was glad he could see the humor in it because I was kind of freaking out. The last thing I needed was the FBI or Homeland Security showing up at my door thinking I was about to start the zombie apocalypse.

"They put a filter on it, so it looks kind of cartoonish and like it's staged. You have to check it out," Owen said when he came up for air. "He is @ShiptonGhoul."

Of *course,* that would be his user ID. Reluctantly, I opened my Insta app and searched for the Shipton ghoul. The first thing I noticed was the profile pic. It was a selfie of Alfred, looking far too realistic. Then, I noticed how many followers he had. Over two hundred thousand! What in the Hades?

What had they gotten into now?

CHAPTER SEVEN

I laid on my bed, on top of the blankets, looking up at the ceiling, and listening to the ringing of Drew's phone. I'd been here a couple of days and hadn't heard from him, so I'd gathered my courage and hit his contact on my phone.

When he hadn't picked up by the fourth ring, I almost hung up. He was a busy man, after all. I completely understood that he didn't have time to drop everything just because I called. He was probably on the evening shift at the police department.

"Sheriff Walker," Drew barked into the phone, apparently not bothering to look to see who was calling. That was okay with me. I could play along.

I dropped my voice, attempting a sultry sound. "Should I start calling you that from now on?"

"Ava." His voice softened, and I heard a muffled curse followed by a thump or maybe a door shutting. "Sorry, I was distracted with closing this case."

"Don't be sorry." I would have video chatted with him, but

my hair was a mess from all the packing, and I needed to shower.

Movement at the door caught my attention. I'd shut that door before calling Drew. With a sigh, I glanced up and frowned. Clay stood in the opened door and pointed to the floor. "Salt? Really, Ava?"

I waved a hand and magically shut the bedroom door. I hadn't been sure salt would keep the ghost out, but it was good to know it did. The last thing I needed was my husband listening to my conversation with my boyfriend. It was rude and weird. Just calling Drew, knowing Clay was... well, not alive. But *here*. It felt disloyal to both men.

"Everything okay there?" Drew asked.

Turning away from the door, I looked out my window at the moon. "Yeah. We're making good progress with packing things up. Hailey, the new owner, is keeping a lot of the furniture, so that's less to move." I paused, thinking of how I could word the question I wanted to ask him.

I heard the smile in his voice. "Does that mean you'll be coming home sooner than planned?"

The hope also in his tone made my heart bloom. He missed me. Aw, I hated to burst his bubble of hope. "I don't think so. Something has come up. That's why I called you. Besides, I miss hearing your voice." Among other things. A hug would've been nice, too.

Then I felt disloyal to Clay. Sigh.

Drew's voice went on alert. "What's wrong?"

"We're pretty sure we have vampires living across the street."

"Why would you think that?"

"I saw a lady walking around with a bite mark on her neck. And the other night they were sunbathing... at night." And the ghost of my dead husband thought they were vampires, too. I wasn't adding in that part. "I was hoping you knew a little more about them before I go over there and introduce myself."

"You will not go over there." Drew spoke with an alpha male tone that melted my insides.

While it was true, I found it hot that he was so protective, I didn't like to be told what to do. I'd do what I darn well pleased. "I have a tiger shifter and a witch-necromancer hybrid at my back. We'll be fine."

Drew was silent for a few seconds, then in a lower tone said, "I don't know much about vampires. I assumed they were extinct or something because nobody I knew had ever dealt with them. Back when I hunted, I never ran into them or even a rumor of them. As far as I knew, they'd gone extinct or never existed at all. But it could also be that they're exceptionally good at staying to themselves. However, that doesn't make them any less dangerous."

Did he think I was going to go over there and open a vein for them? "I didn't say they weren't dangerous." I rolled off the bed, making a few groaning sounds as I got to my feet.

Drew laughed. "What are you doing?"

Might as well be truthful. He should know the real me. "Getting off the bed. It's not as easy as it once was."

He chuckled, and then the laugh turned a little dark. "Do I need to ask why you were on the bed?"

I rolled my eyes. "Talking to you, of course." I knew what he was implying, but Clay was one line of salt away from me right now.

"Of course," he replied with a chuckle.

I shuddered and sighed. Gods, I missed him. More guilt. "Anything I need to know before I do the neighborly thing?"

"Ava." His voice said he meant business.

A jolt of pleasure shot through me. "Say that again."

He moaned with a bit of growl in it. "You're killing me."

"Not yet. Besides, I'll bring you back before your soul moves on. So don't think you'll get away from me so easily, buster." If I'd been able to use my necromancer powers when Clay died, maybe I could've animated him the way I had Zoey. And Larry. They looked like normal, regular people now. That could've been Clay.

Another sexy as Hades chuckle rumbled through the phone, pulling me out of my regrets. "I'm harder to kill than most."

That was true, and I was thankful for it. The way people had been dying around me lately, I didn't need my beau to be one of them. "Um, the vamps?"

He grunted. "Stay away from them."

That wasn't an option. "You know better than that."

"Yes, I've been warned." There was a low sound of someone talking in the background. "I have to go. Text me before you go to sleep." He paused. "And don't go over there!"

"Okay, talk to you later." I hung up and walked to the door and opened it. Clay was there with his ear pressed to the wood. He pulled back and glared at me.

Stirring up a little wind, I blew away the salt from the floor and gathered it in a little whirlwind. "I see death hasn't made you any less nosy." It was a good thing I didn't have Drew on speaker.

I walked the salt over to the trash can under my vanity, one of the few pieces of furniture I was taking with me.

"You were talking to Drew?" Clay asked.

Crossing my arms, I sighed. "I'm not comfortable talking about this with you."

He sat on the bed—floated just above it. "It's okay, Ava. I'm glad you've moved on. I want you to be happy."

Staring at the ghost of the dead love of my life, I fought tears and whirled around, heading out of the bedroom and down the stairs.

I went to the living room and found Wallie and Zoey on the sofa watching TV. Had they even packed anything today?

I sat in the chair in front of the large bay window. It had a great view of the vampire house. I moved the blinds just enough to look out at our neighbors. Not mine anymore. Hailey's neighbors.

"They're moving about in the front yard. Wait, is he mowing the grass? At night?" Sure enough, a man walked around the front yard with a push mower.

The kids got up and crowded around me, peering out of the blinds like a bunch of peeping Toms.

"We should go over there and meet them," Wallie suggested.

"I plan on it, but I feel I need an excuse to go over there." Plus, Drew would kill me.

Zoey said, "You can walk your pet tiger."

I laughed, picturing just that. "Um, Zo, people don't have pet tigers. Ever. I think humans have a law about it." If they didn't, they probably should. Otherwise, some fool would probably go overboard and declare himself the Tiger King or something ridiculous like that.

"We could ask to borrow some sugar," Wallie said.

"They're vampires. They don't have sugar." At least I didn't think so. I didn't know a damn thing about them. Could they eat? "Okay, I'm going over." Drew would have to understand that I couldn't wait for his help. I had to satisfy my burning curiosity.

As I stood and moved to the door, Wallie and Zoey followed. When I turned around and gave them a stern look, Wallie shook his head. "You are not going over there alone. No arguing."

I crossed my eyes at him. "You're as bossy as Drew."

Wallie snickered. "He told you not to go over there, didn't he?"

"He did. But he's not the boss of me."

Clay drifted over to stand between me and the door. "I agree with your boyfriend. By the way, will I get to meet him?"

That was the last thing I wanted to happen. "No. Drew is working a case and can't take time off to come here." I was more than a little thankful for that. I'd been thankful for a lot of things lately. "Now let's go borrow some sugar from the vampires. I mean, our lovely new neighbors."

Flinging open the door, I headed through the yard before anyone else could try to talk me out of it. I wasn't going to miss out on meeting a new-to-me supernatural creature just because they may or may not be dangerous.

Wallie and Zoey hurried behind me. I eyed the man pushing the old-fashioned lawn mower. If I had to describe a stereotypical vampire, it would be this guy. Pale, tall. He had brown hair, but I couldn't see his eyes from the sidewalk. The only thing about him that I wouldn't say was typical of a vampire was the dude was freaking *huge*.

As we approached the walkway, the other people sitting around, seeming to be enjoying the moon, jumped to their feet. One woman, a sort of dumpy-looking guy, and a gorgeous man. They approached with the hot one in the front and the other two flanking him.

The lawn mower dude stopped pushing the manual lawn mower and walked over as I waved. "Hello," I called. "I'm Ava. We wanted to come over and introduce ourselves."

The one who seemed like he was in charge stepped forward. "I'm Jax. These are my brothers and sisters, Paige—" Jax inclined his head to the woman slightly behind him on his left.

The woman, who was black, yet somehow also pale, nodded her head once. Maybe they were brothers and sisters in the sense that Owen was my brother.

Jax nodded toward the lawn mower. "Ransom."

The big dude grunted and moved to stand behind Paige. Jax nodded his head to his right. "And this is Leo."

Leo didn't look happy to see us. He snarled his lip slightly as he blinked.

"These are my kids, Zoey and Wallie."

There. Now everybody nodded at everybody else. "We're actually here to move out," I explained. "You'll meet a new neighbor in a week or two, Hailey."

Trickling out my magic, I tried to see if any of them noticed me feeling my way.

They didn't give any outward sign, but Zoey shifted behind me as the breeze picked up. Leo stiffened and his gaze flashed to Zo on my right.

All of the vampires shifted, where they'd been still—unnaturally still—moments before. They might not have realized Wallie and I were witches, but they'd smelled Zoey now. "Well," I said brightly. "Nice meeting you. If you need any sugar... Don't ask because we barely have anything in the house."

We laughed, but it even sounded forced to my ears. Jax grinned, as did the lady whose name I'd forgotten and the big dude, whose name I'd *also* forgotten. Leo, the freaky-looking one, just bared his teeth.

"Oh, I noticed something, and I'm just far too nosy for my own good." I tittered a little giggle. "It seemed like you guys were sunbathing the other night... At *night.*"

Jax nodded. "We have an allergy to sunlight."

"Ahh." I nodded as if that made all the sense in the world. "Right, right. Have a good evening."

"You as well," Jax said.

We turned back with Wallie and Zoey walking in front of me.

"Ava," Jax said in a soft voice.

I turned with my eyebrows up. "Yes?"

He stepped forward, but I didn't feel any sense of danger. He wasn't out to hurt me. "Don't worry about the moonbathing. Or anything else you might notice from this house."

The man was looking me in the eye, like, seriously eyeballing me. "Uh, okay?"

"There's nothing going on here that doesn't go on at every other human household."

He'd used the word human. I furrowed my brow at him. "Uh-huh. Whatever you say. Night, night."

I joined the kids on the sidewalk, and we went back to the house together.

That man, that vampire, had just tried to compel me.

And now all I wanted to do was hide behind the curtains and watch the vampires.

CHAPTER EIGHT

I taped up another box just as the doorbell rang. We'd been making great time with the packing, sorting, and donating. Straightening slowly with one hand on my lower back, I glared at the door. I wasn't expecting anyone, and it was daylight, so I didn't have to worry about the vampy neighbors paying me a visit. At least I hoped not. What did I know about what vampires could or could not do? Maybe sunscreen would help them walk in the sun?

Wallie stuck his head out from the hallway and gave me a raised brow. "Ma?" He and Zoey had been packing up the bedrooms. All except mine. I'd done most of it, but I wanted to go through Clay's stuff alone. I wasn't ready for that yet, so I'd saved it for last and didn't look forward to it.

As I crossed the living room to answer the door, Clay appeared beside me. "We have visitors." His brow was furrowed and lips set in a line.

What was up his...I snorted. "*I* have visitors. No one else can see you besides me, Wallie, and Zoey."

And for that reason, I wasn't worried about opening the

door with Clay hovering beside me. Whoever it was would only be able to see him if they were dead or a necromancer. I'd checked last night. Owen had been contrite and apologized for not telling me before.

Twisting the knob and giving a pull, I gasped then let out a little squeal. "Sam, Olivia! What are you doing here?"

"Sam looks good. He's been taking care of himself," Clay said over my left shoulder. "Olivia is a little curvier than she used to be in school."

I pressed my lips together to keep from laughing and thanking the gods Olivia couldn't hear my deceased husband. She was curvier, but it was a good thing. She'd been a little too skinny before having kids, at least in my opinion.

Olivia beamed at me. "Since it's spring break, we left Sammie with Sam's parents and came to help!" The sound of a car door shutting captured my attention. I looked over Sam's shoulder to the front walk. My heart fluttered at the sight of the man exiting a cab in my driveway, then walking up behind my two besties with a duffel bag.

Clay leaned in close. "Is that the stepdad?"

I closed my eyes briefly. *Do not respond to Clay.* He had teased me about Drew being our son's stepdad since Wallie called him that to Hailey. Because to her, we were all just a normal group of humans. Or at least we'd had to act that way.

"Drew." I stepped aside to let Sam and Olivia enter while I waited for the stepdad. Clay, of course, waited with me as my stomach began to cramp with nervousness.

He stopped in front of me for a split second then pulled me into a hug. I melted into him, just happy to be in his arms after nearly a week apart...until my husband started talking again. "Oh, he's handsome. I don't judge guys, generally, but you got a winner there. *Now* I see why you stayed in Shipton." As soon as Drew let me go, Clay moved around to stand between Drew and me.

With what I hoped was a smooth, unobtrusive move, I pushed Clay out of the way and took Drew's hand to pull him inside, shutting the door behind me and ignoring it when Drew ended up walking right through Clay. "I thought you couldn't make it." Part of me was so happy to see him, but part of me was mortified. A big part of me.

Should I have felt guilty to essentially push Clay away and draw Drew toward me? Did that mean I was choosing Drew over Clay? Oh, this was such a mess.

Drew looked around as I locked the door behind him. "I told you yesterday that I was closing the case. Plus, I couldn't leave you to deal with the vampires by yourself." Drew gave me a crooked smile that made my insides melt. This was too hard.

"Oh, how thoughtful and protective of him. Alpha male. Just your type." Clay drifted back to my side, staring at Drew, then he turned to me. "Was I not alpha enough for you, Ava?"

I laughed, though I wanted to cry, then coughed and turned to face Wallie to cover my reaction to Clay's snarky words. My son and Zoey were on the sofa giggling like a couple of schoolgirls. I glared at them. They were no help. Clay had always been a mischievous prankster, but I couldn't retort. What I wanted to tell him was that he'd been more than enough for me, but he was gone now. And with Drew, Sam, and Olivia here I couldn't say a darn thing.

Olivia looked at them, then me. "What's so funny?"

"Yeah, Ava, share with the class," Sam added as he went toward the kitchen. "I'm hungry."

"Those two are being silly. It's nothing." I waved my hand to push Clay behind me, so I didn't have to look at him. Too bad I couldn't stop him from talking.

Time to change the subject. "Who's in charge of the department while you two are here?"

"Charles," Sam said as he came out of the kitchen with a handful of cookies.

Clay snorted. "Charles, captain of the dance team? That Charles?"

I swear if Clay didn't stop talking, I was going to put him in a bubble. "Charles is good. Nice guy." Olivia plopped down on the sofa. "Flying is exhausting."

When no one spoke for a few seconds, I asked, "Are you guys hungry? It's late for lunch but we can order delivery for an early dinner."

Sam nodded with his mouth full of cookies.

Of *course,* Clay had something to say. "Should I get the candles to make it a little romantic for you and my replacement?"

Wallie barked out a laugh, then ran out of the room when everyone turned to stare him down. Traitor. Zoey laughed and fell off the couch, shifting into her tiger at the same time. Her tiger was much bigger than she was, so the coffee table went flying. Drew reached down and stopped its progression as Zoey barked out a roarey-laugh thing.

Frustrated with his interference and my extremely conflicted emotions, I whirled around to face Clay and threw out my hands. "Stop it!"

He vanished instantly in a burst of grey smoke. Oh, no. Did I banish him? I had no idea what sort of power I had over ghosts.

Behind me, Drew closed the small distance between us. "I hope you didn't just kill your husband's ghost."

"Ghost?" Olivia squeaked and sat up on the sofa. She put her hand on Zoey's head.

At the same time, I asked, "You can see him?" Panic flared in my stomach, the cramp from earlier returning with gusto.

Drew chuckled and nodded. "And heard him."

Ohh, I was gonna hurl.

"Clay is here?" Sam moved closer to me. He and Clay had been good friends in high school.

I let out a sigh. "I didn't know until I got back." I scanned the living room and frowned. I hoped I hadn't just killed a ghost. Was that even possible? "Clay? Please, tell me I didn't kill you. I don't want you to be re-dead."

"You didn't kill me." He popped in beside me, making me jump. "I'm still just regular dead.

I studied his deep brown eyes, muted because of his slightly invisible look. "Drew heard every word."

Clay whirled and studied Drew for a moment, while Drew watched him with twinkling eyes. "How is that possible? He doesn't have a witch mark."

Sam and Olivia look at me in confusion. Clay noticed their faces and held out his hand to me. "You can make me solid so they can see me. When you touch me, I'm visible." Oh, yeah. I'd known that. But it was a lot to take in, having my Shipton people here in Pennsylvania.

When I reached for his hand, he snatched it back. "Don't animate me. I don't want to live forever. I need to move on so you can move on."

I nodded, understanding what he was saying. No turning the ghost into a ghoul or any other undead immortal. "I don't know how. But my powers have been pretty advanced since I opened myself up to them. There's no telling what I might be able to do." The fact that he'd been cremated didn't necessarily mean I couldn't animate him.

That meant I had to focus and make my intent clear. I took calming breaths and focused on making Clay solid for a twenty-four-hour period. No, scratch that. I decided to make him solid for three days so we could all catch up. Hopefully, that wouldn't make Drew feel uncomfortable.

I took Clay's hand and pushed my magic into him with the limit of three days, then he'd return to his ghost self.

Sam's jaw dropped as Clay appeared in front of him. "Clay," he whispered.

Clay stepped forward and yanked Sam into his arms. They slapped each other on the back a few times before pulling apart.

"Olivia," Sam said when they were done with their bro hug. "You remember Clay?"

Clay and Olivia hugged, and then she turned to Drew. "This is Drew, the sheriff of Shipton Harbor. Drew, this is Clay, Ava's..." Olivia shot me a panicked look.

"He's my husband," I said in a level voice. "My dead husband."

Clay looked Drew over. "And you're my replacement."

Drew chuckled and held his hand out. "I hope to be. This, you, presents a new complication."

He hoped to be Clay's replacement. Holy crow, Drew wanted to get married.

I did *not* know how I felt about that.

"Why are you guys here?" I asked, avoiding the elephant in the room.

"The vampires," Drew said flatly. "I called my mom, and she said vampires didn't exist."

I shrugged. "They do. We talked to them last night."

Drew looked up sharply. "What? You did what?"

"I tried to stop her," Wallie called from the kitchen. "Mexican okay with everyone?"

"Ohh," Olivia said. "That sounds great. I'll go help." She scurried into the kitchen to look at the takeout menus with Wallie. Zoey the tiger ambled after them.

Clay sighed. "I wish I could eat Mexican food. One of you, please order a steak quesadilla. Maybe if Ava touches me, I can taste it."

CHAPTER NINE

It turned out Clay could *not* taste my Mexican food, but the act of trying broke the ice with everyone. Our dinner was fun and made the evening fly by.

After dinner, everyone went to the living room to watch TV. The cable was still on for another day. I stayed in the kitchen with Drew, cleaning up, which consisted of throwing the paper plates and plastic utensils away. I told the stubborn sheriff that he didn't have to help, but he did anyway.

Standing in the doorway, facing the living room, I checked my phone for the millionth time in the last hour. Wade still hadn't replied to mine or Wallie's texts, and I was getting worried. If he didn't call soon, I was going to go break his door down.

Drew came up behind me and took my phone. "It's late. He's probably asleep." His fingers teased my hands as he pulled them away.

I nodded, then leaned over and snatched my phone back to check the messages one more time. But there was nothing.

With a sigh, I threw the phone down on the table. "We'll

check on him in the morning. If he isn't home, I'm calling a search party. It's not like him to go this long without replying to my messages." Especially when I was in town. This was nuts.

"I'm sure everything is fine," Olivia said then added, "What are the sleeping arrangements?"

Ugh, I hadn't even thought about that.

I looked around, suddenly panicked about whether Drew expected to sleep in the bed with me, but Wallie said, "Sam and Olivia can have my room. I'll sleep on the pull-out sofa."

"That works." I turned to face Drew and frowned. The butterflies that had taken up residence in my belly woke up and were fluttering their little hearts out.

A sexy smirk formed on his face, which only added heat to the winged creatures. "I guess that leaves me with you."

Holy crap. *Oh, holy crap.* Panic washed over me. *Breathe, Ava.* I wouldn't be getting any sleep with Drew next to me. In my bed. Holy crap. What would Clay say when he found out? Would he be in there, too?

"Breathe, Ava." The sound of Clay's voice next to me made my hysterics worse. Would both of them be in my room? I looked at my husband and then my boyfriend. This whole situation was getting out of control.

Clay took my hand. "I don't sleep. Don't need to. So don't worry about me. I'll be roaming the halls doing the ghostly thing. Maybe leave the TV on for me." He grinned at me before adding, "And have fun. "

He was not helping at all! Not even a little bit.

"I hope you can do it quietly. Some of us need our beauty sleep. Also, gross." Wallie got up from the sofa and then disappeared down the hallway. He was probably getting some sheets and a blanket for the sleeper.

Practicing my even, steady breathing, I completely ignored Drew as I waited on Wallie. My guess was right. He reappeared a few seconds later with the items in his hands.

For a second, I forgot myself and glanced at Drew. Immediately, my cheeks heated. This was going to be a long night. "Come on," I mumbled.

Grinning, Drew followed me down the hall to the master bedroom. My stomach churned with a nervous need to make dinner reappear. Ta-da! Right on the carpet.

But I managed to keep it all in. Thankfully.

It'd been five years since I'd shared a bed with another man. Or another woman, for that matter. Anyone. It wasn't that I made a habit of inviting people to sleep with me.

Good gods, I might as well have told Drew he could have the bed so I could go sleep with Wallie. At least I'd actually be able to sleep that way.

Inside the bedroom, my gut churning like an angry ocean, I watched as Drew went to shut the door but stopped halfway and looked at me. I waved my hand and closed the door with my magic just to rip the darn bandage off and get it over with. Then I took a deep, calming breath. "We are both adults."

There was nothing wrong with us sleeping together. I mean, actually sleeping and not the other thing that had my insides twisting and burning with desire. And guilt for having my boyfriend in my room. In the house I shared with my husband.

Okay, stop this. I wasn't a teenager anymore. And Clay was dead, even if he was in the house with us right now. Undead. Clay was undead.

Drew took his shirt off and a storm of desire whirled inside me. Good gods, he was hot. He had the body of a thirty-something bodybuilder, just not as huge. Broad shoulders, wide chest with more dips and valleys than the mountains. Then I remembered he worked out at the Shipton gym often. A few times a week, I believed. At least according to the rumor mill, aka Olivia.

Older men like Drew were why the label silver fox was created. He personified it from head to toe.

Was I going to lay beside him with no shirt on? How would I keep my hands to myself?

Tearing my gaze from him, I went to the box where I'd packed my clothes and dug out a clean pair of pajamas, then shut myself in the bathroom. Inside, I pressed my back against the door and tried to slow my heart rate.

Why was I so nervous? It wasn't like Drew would do anything that I didn't want him to. He wasn't that sort of man, anyway. He was honorable and decent.

And so freaking hot!

I knew for a fact he only had good motives. I'd have sensed it if his intentions were bad.

That was another heightened ability I gained after taking on the High Witch position in the coven. My empathy was gaining strength. As far as I knew, it was part of the gig. After all, I'd need to be able to tell if someone was set on harming the coven, which was my responsibility now.

Especially after the mess with Bevan cursing the witches to die by odd and crazy accidents. It made sense that the High Witch spell would make the necessary magical adjustments to protect us all. I needed to get all this stuff wrapped up in Philly and get home to my proper place as High Priestess of the coven.

Pushing away from the door, I changed quickly and then stared at my reflection in the mirror. My long brown hair hung around my shoulders, wild and free. My green eyes were a little dull, giving away how tired I was. Or how stressed I was. And worried about Wade. Or all three.

Leaning forward, I brushed my teeth and gave myself a very quiet pep talk. "Okay, Ava Harper, you are a grown woman and there is nothing wrong with finding companionship after the death of your husband. It is the natural state of healing and moving on." But Clay was here. Not in my bathroom or my bedroom, at the moment, but in the house. Sure, he was a ghost, and he was waiting on me to let him go so he could move on into the afterlife. At least I'd made him solid so he couldn't sneak up on me or watch us sleep.

"Ready or not." I rinsed the toothpaste out of my mouth, stuck my tongue out at myself, and exited the bathroom.

When I stepped into the bedroom, Drew was already in bed with the blanket pulled up to his waist. Looking sexy as Hades--the god and the place, both. My heart rate kicked up again and my flesh heated. I sure hoped he had shorts on under that blanket. If he was naked, I was *so* running away to sleep on the pull-out with my son.

"I have shorts on," he said with a grin. How had he known? It was like he'd read my mind. Maybe it was my face. I tended to wear my emotions all over it. Half the time it was some version of resting bitch face.

But his face... Oh, gods, that grin was wicked and full of temptation.

Once his words sank in, I started moving toward the bed. I had to stop standing there like an idiot. This was no big deal.

Shrugging, I tried to play it cool. "I wasn't worried. We're adults. There is no harm in us sleeping together." Oh, no. That sounded wrong. It sounded like sex. "Erm, I mean sleeping in the same bed...beside each other...um, actually sleeping."

I was an idiot. A total idiot. Why did my brain not work? It sent stupid words to come out of my mouth.

He pulled the blanket back, and I caught a glimpse of his black shorts against the creamy white sheets. "Come on Ava. I promise to keep my hands to myself."

That made one of us that would behave at least. I was *so* not going to say that out loud. Pushing myself forward, I made it to the bed and under the covers without hyperventilating. Yay, me. Why the heck was I so nervous? Besides the obvious and the fact that Clay had been my first and only lover.

We laid in silence for a few minutes with Drew's body heat seeping toward me before Drew asked, "Hang on. Charles was the captain of the dance team?"

Drew's question broke through my nervous thoughts and made me laugh. "Yes. I'm surprised Sam hadn't told you."

He shook his head and chuckled. "It never came up."

I rolled to my side to face him. Instantly, he did the same. "Charles used to be a great dancer. He might still be, I don't know. Haven't talked to him since I've been back." He'd been so popular in high school that nobody had even teased him for being such a good dancer.

That didn't mean there weren't a few chuckles, but they were generally good-natured. Not bully-ish.

"Somehow, I can see that he is. Not in a bad way." Drew paused and reached out to brush a stray hair from my face. My pulse jumped and heat pooled in my belly. "What's with the stepdad thing?"

I laughed then snorted, which made both of us laugh. I told him about what Wallie said to Hailey when she stopped by. "Now Clay refers to you as a stepdad or his replacement."

"I've been called worse." Drew reached over and ran his knuckles down my cheek.

I sighed and leaned into his touch. Then I frowned. "Does it bother you that he's here? I mean, it's got to be awkward for you."

"No. But I have wondered why he is here. Is he stuck?"

"Yes, and it's my fault." I averted my gaze to stare at the window.

He furrowed his brow. "How is it your fault?"

I shrugged and met Drew's stare. "He says I'm holding him here, but I can't think of how. He says I just need to let go. But somehow I think there is more to it."

Drew took my hand and tugged as he rolled to his back, making me scoot closer to him. A few seconds later, I was snuggled into his side. It felt great. And I was so turned on. "What is the one thing you haven't done yet?"

"I'm not sure. Other than the promise I made to not grieve him for long and to move on with my life. But I'm *doing* that now." I didn't think the semi-broken promise was holding him there. It had to be something else. "Oh, his ashes. I couldn't bring myself to spread them, especially when I wasn't sure where I'd end up."

The house had been mine and Clay's. I hadn't seen me starting over without him there. Yet, I left the ashes here when I went to Shipton because I hadn't planned at the time to stay in Maine. I wasn't sure where I'd end up.

But now, I was sure. I was starting over in Shipton with Winston and my new extended, partially undead family.

"I think you may be right. Ask him where he wants them to be spread, then do it. Say goodbye, get your closure." Drew traced his fingers down my arm in feather-like touches that calmed me.

He was right. "I already know where he'd want them." I glanced up at Drew, then kissed him lightly on the lips. "Thank you."

I snuggled into him more and wondered how I'd gotten so lucky to find a man that I could possibly spend the second half of my life with.

Wait! Where the heck had that come from?

CHAPTER TEN

For the second time in a week, I woke up before anyone else. My mind wouldn't let me sleep any longer. I'd dreamed that we found Wade dead and after that, I couldn't get back to sleep.

While making coffee and warming up leftover Mexican food for breakfast, I paced the kitchen. Every car that drove by, every person that walked in front of the house, and pretty much every sound from outside had me running to the front window, peeking out to see if it was Wade. Of course, it was never him. I must've messaged him a hundred more times since I got up this morning. Typing on my phone, I made it a hundred and one.

Not long after my breakfast and first cup of coffee were done, Olivia joined me in the kitchen. Drew wasn't far behind her. Sam came stumbling in a few minutes later looking like he hadn't slept a wink.

I tapped my foot and sent off another message, then put the phone to my ear to call again.

"Stay calm," Drew said. "He's a grown man and has run his own life all this time without you."

I rolled my eyes and poured another cup of coffee. The three of them could tell I was ready to bolt out of the house and head straight to Wade's. I'd already toyed with the idea of calling Dana and Rick Johnson to see they knew a shifter who was a tracker to hunt down Wade. Maybe they had connections in the area.

Dana and Rick were ferret shifters and became my liaison for the shifters. Their oldest son died in the same fighting ring Zoey had. I'd saved their youngest son by finding and taking down the whole thing. I'd managed to bring Zoey back, animate her, at least, but the rest of the shifter kids had been too far gone to save long-term.

Drew sat in the chair beside me, pulling me from my plots of searching for and saving Wade. I met his gaze and smiled. He smelled good and was a sexy distraction, but he didn't smile back. He just leaned forward, cupped my cheeks, and claimed my mouth like he was making all kinds of promises of pleasure.

Moaning deep in my throat, I scooted closer in my seat and returned the kiss. Tingles skittered over my skin. He tasted of toothpaste and spice. Mmm, I could've kissed him all day.

When he broke the kiss, he sat back in his chair and held up his cup. "I just need one cup, then we'll go to Wade's."

I nodded, unable to take my eyes off him. We'd kissed before, but not like that. That wasn't just a kiss. It was a claiming. Drew was marking his territory. Or maybe I was going insane and hanging out with shifters too much recently.

Sitting back in my chair, I said, "Was that a distraction or an attempt to get your way?"

"Both," Drew said before taking a sip of coffee.

I laughed softly. That man was dangerous on so many levels. Across the kitchen table from me, Olivia stared at us. Then she said, "Sam, I want a kiss like that."

Sam walked to the table, bent down, and poked out his lips

to make a fish face. Laughing, Olivia put her palm to his face and pushed him away. "Goof-ball."

Clay came drifting into the kitchen, glancing at each of us like we lost our minds. "Have you heard anything?" He knew as well as the rest of them that I was freaking out about Wade.

I shook my head. "Nothing."

He sighed. "I'm worried too. I wish I could leave this damn house and go look myself."

I checked my phone again to make sure I hadn't received a message in the last thirty-five seconds. Then I was up pacing again. Where the heck was he?

And why wasn't he returning my calls or messages?

Another car went by outside, so I rushed to the window. It was just a random car. Not Wade. A random thought crossed my mind. "The vampires have him," I said to no one in particular as I stared at the house across the street. That was the only thing that made any sense.

Wade could've been dead. My heart squeezed, and it became hard to breathe.

Drew came over to me and took my hand. The next thing I knew we were walking out of the house with his arm around me. Sam and Olivia walked right behind us.

"Where does Wade live?" Drew asked, locking his fingers with mine.

I pointed to our right. "Turn left at the stop sign, then left on the next street over."

When we reached the stop sign, we heard footsteps behind us. Turning, I spotted Wallie and Zoey jogging toward us. So, we waited.

Once the kids joined us, we walked as a group to Wade's house in silence. However, we did slow down as we passed the backyard to the vamps' house. Even though it was morning, the sky was overcast and looked like it might rain later. The sun wasn't quite out, and I noticed a few of the fanged ones in the yard. Jaxon wasn't outside and I didn't recognize any of them from the other night. How many vampires lived in this house? Was there an underground labyrinth?

One of the vampires growled out the word hunter as we passed. Drew tensed beside me, then a spark from the magic he kept a very tight lid on tingled in my hand.

I met Drew's gaze and arched a brow, but he shook his head to let me know he was okay. I didn't dare say anything that close to the vamps, but I was eager to know about this magic spark.

When we reached Wade's house, something was off. My dream flashed in my mind. I pushed it away as I was worried, but I didn't have the power of foresight. I had no reason to be worried yet.

"Someone else has been here," Zoey said as she scented the air. Her perky nose wrinkled. "A vampire."

I *knew* it. Letting go of Drew's hand, I rushed toward the front door and dug out the spare key to Wade's house. I had forgotten it the last time, so I'd made sure I grabbed it and put it in my pocket first thing this morning when I got up. I hadn't been about to head over here without a key again.

As I stuck the key into the lock, Drew covered my hand, stopping me. "I'll go in first."

I rolled my eyes. "No one is inside." I knew he was a hunter, but he didn't have to be so macho. I was the big, bad witch, after all.

"How do you know?" He raised his eyebrows at me.

I stared at him with my lips pressed into a thin line and one corner dipped in a half frown. "Necromancer, remember? I can sense dead and living people. If there was someone inside, I'd know. *Especially* if that someone was paranormal."

His lips twitched as if I'd amused him. Then he leaned in close. "I'm still going in first."

To stop me from arguing, he gave me a quick kiss while

unlocking the door and pushing it open. The kiss was nothing like the one in the kitchen minutes ago, but it was enough to stun me. Dating someone was so new to me. I felt like a teenager again.

We walked in and emotions flooded me. Mostly panic because the living room was a total mess. The coffee table had been knocked onto its side, one of the lamps laid shattered on the floor. Pictures knocked off the walls. It looked like the aftermath of a bar fight. Turning to Zoey, I inhaled deeply. "Do you smell blood?"

She nibbled her lower lip and nodded. She didn't want to tell me but couldn't lie to me either. It was the necromancer-ghoul bond we shared. It was possible for them to lie to me, but it was difficult.

Crap. The panic spread to my fingertips. "We need to search the house."

Sam held up a hand, "No one touches anything. You lot stay here. Drew and I will go through the house."

I crossed my arms over my more than a handful of breasts and glared at the men as they went off in different directions. Olivia nudged me and pointed to the sunroom off the back of the house. "Let's go check out there."

I nodded and led the way. While we checked out the sunroom and the backyard, finding nothing, the guys searched the rest of the house while hopefully leaving everything as it was. I knew they were being careful just in case Wade's disappearance wasn't paranormal related. If it was just a home invasion involving a regular old human, then we'd have to call the local police and let them handle it.

Yeah, right. I was betting it was paranormal and a vampire was involved. I'd bet Winston on it.

We met back in the living room. Drew said, "No signs of him. The rest of the house hasn't been touched. That makes me think the fight or struggle happened here."

"Did you find the blood?" I asked.

Sam and Drew both shook their heads.

"It's not like we can call the police," Olivia said, looking at Sam for directions.

Sam shook his head. "No, this isn't a human crime."

Zoey growled low in her throat. "This was vampires."

I hugged my waist and moved toward the front door. "I'll ask Jaxon. When we went over there the other day, he seemed to act like he was in charge. It was like the others looked to him as a leader. I say we march right over there and ask him if he knows anything."

Drew and Sam looked reluctant, but finally, Drew nodded. "I don't think this is going to go well," he grumbled.

Hurrying out of Wade's house, we rushed toward the vamp house and stopped at their backyard. Waving my arms, I got the attention of one of them. It was a huge backyard. When he got closer, I realized it was Leo. The one I could tell didn't like me. Well, it was okay. The feeling was mutual. "Is Jaxon up?"

"No." Leo snarled. "He doesn't want to talk to *you*."

Balling my hands into fists, I was about to zap him with a little power when Drew tugged me away then glared at Leo and the other two who had joined him. "Tell him I want to talk to him at nightfall, or I will be back. Alone." He snarled his lip and even though the threat wasn't aimed at me, I felt the severity of it.

Leo watched us leave and I watched him watch us.

Drew pulled me close. "Don't taunt the vampires."

"He started it." I sighed and cuddled into him as we walked back home.

We got around the block and had turned back toward my place when Sam pulled something out of his pocket. "You know, I found a bowl of these in the kitchen. I grabbed one just in case because each of them had one or two matches missing."

He held the object out, so I took it and studied the cover. It was a small, red matchbook with a white X on it. Flipping it over, I found a phone number. "What in the world could this be?"

"Probably some exclusive club," Drew said. "If he's got a bunch, he's grabbed one every time he was there."

"Well, call the number," I said. We hurried into the house. "Come on, we'll get some privacy and do it in here."

We huddled around the coffee table as Olivia dialed the number.

"Password?" A deep, resonating voice said.

Panicking, I looked around at everyone and spread my hands. "Uh, I don't know it. Wade Harper gave me your number."

"Oh, okay. Sure. First time, eh?" He chuckled.

"Yes, uh, yeah. First time." I shrugged and exchanged a wide-eyed glance with Olivia.

"Okay, well the address for tonight is 550 Suarez Loop. Knock three times. Don't come alone. Six pm." The line went dead.

"What now?" I whispered.

"Let's just go over there now," Drew suggested.

I shook my head. "No, if whatever it is happens at six, we shouldn't go until then. It might be empty before."

Wallie turned his phone around. "550 Suarez loop is just a house. Maybe it's like a book club or something."

I jumped up. "Well, until we can go, we can pack. Everyone pick a room and get busy."

Olivia handled the small stuff, floating around, refilling tape guns, refilling coffee cups. She handled lunch and an early dinner and helped schlep full boxes to the living room.

Clay was surprisingly helpful, and we went through his stuff and decided what to do with it all. Mostly it was to be donated, but he had a few things he specifically wanted Wallie to have, and there were a few family heirlooms I packed for Wallie's future children.

Finally, as my stomach chewed a hole in itself, the hours passed, and it was time to head to the house.

We piled into the truck. Zoey and Wallie rode in the truck bed while Drew drove and Sam, Olivia, and I scrunched in the bench seat.

When we got close, as planned, Zoey and Wallie hopped out of the back. Zoey was using her nose to help them snoop around while we got the lay of the land inside.

Drew pulled the truck up to the curb and we looked around.

"Maybe it's just a party?" I suggested. The whole cul-de-sac was filled with cars. Every available spot to park was taken and we were nearly an hour early. Drew backed up the street and parked a block away.

"Everyone ready?" I asked.

We smoothed our clothes when we got out and started walking, Drew and I arm in arm, and Sam and Olivia did as well. We walked right up to the front door like we were meant to be there and had done it a dozen times and knocked three times.

The door opened and a smiling woman spread her arm. "Please, come in. We're happy to have you."

As we walked by, she looked Drew over and nearly purred. "Very happy to have you."

As soon as we walked through the hall and into a large living room, a few things sank in.

"Please," the woman said in a sultry voice as she ran her fingers up Drew's arm. "Dive right in."

The room was full of couples, and most of the couples were writhing with one another on the floor, on the couches, pressed against the wall. There were two men and a woman all over each other on the coffee table.

And the woman wasn't wearing a *shirt*!

"Oh, my goddess, Olivia," I whispered.

She lurched forward and put her arm around my shoulders. "I know. I think this is a swinger's party."

"Excuse me," I said, gingerly pulling the woman's hand off of Drew's arm as he stared into the living room with a startled expression on his face. "Ma'am?"

The woman who let us in gave me a sharp look. "Yes?"

"We're looking for Wade Harper. Have you seen him?"

Her posture changed and she sighed. "No. Not in about a week. If you talk to him, tell him Kristen misses him. He should come back soon." She winked and turned her attention back to Drew.

I tugged on his arm and backed into the hallway with Olivia pretty much glued to my back.

"Hello," a husky voice said. We turned to find another woman, a fairly gorgeous one, if I were being honest, pretty much drape herself around Sam. "Would you like to come upstairs with me?"

Sam stammered and looked at Olivia with wide, terrified eyes. "Oh, no, I uh, no, see, we, uh."

Olivia stood up straight and pulled away from me. "Bitch, you better get your hands off of my husband!"

She lurched for the woman so fast I barely had time to get my hands around her waist. "Sam!" I yelled. "Get her out of here!"

Sam jerked his arm away from the woman and hefted Olivia up over his shoulder, then made a beeline for the door.

That didn't matter to Olivia. "You even look at my man again and I'll scratch your eyes out. And I'll curse you! Do you hear me? Your titties will shrivel up and you'll never have another moment of horniness!"

Drew crowded me as the entirety of the writhing, sexed-up, frenzied people turned to stare at the still shrieking Olivia as Sam carried her outside.

"Thanks for having us, we had a lovely time!" I squawked as I ran after them.

Holy hellchops in a handbasket. That was a swinger's club, and Wade—*Wade*—was a member.

Once we hit the sidewalk, Sam put Olivia down and we ran for the truck. "Zoey!" I called. I knew she'd be able to hear me. "Come on, now!"

Wallie and Zo came running from around the back of the house. They hopped in the back as Drew put the truck into drive and took off.

"Well. That was..." I sucked in a deep breath.

"Fun," Olivia said.

Sam put his arm around her. "My little spitfire was ready to fight for her man."

She snuggled into him as I turned to Drew and pretended to stick my finger down my throat.

But she was right, really. It was fun.

CHAPTER ELEVEN

Once the sun set, I decided to go out the front door to take the trash out so I could be obvious about wanting to catch Jaxon out and about. And because I was taunting the vampires, as Drew called it. Hey, I needed to take out the trash. I had a legitimate reason for going out there. It wasn't entirely because I was anxious to see the vamp leader. Only mostly.

Glaring at the vamp house, I didn't see Jaxon, but that didn't mean he wasn't home. In fact, I was betting the fanged one, Leo, never even told him I wanted to speak with him.

Well, I'd give him ten more minutes, then I was going over there. And I wasn't going to be nice about it.

I opened the trash can lid and tossed the bag inside, making as much noise as I could. I dropped the metal trash can lid and slammed it against the concrete on the driveway a few times as I picked it up.

When I turned to go back around to the front of the house, a dark figure stepped out in front of me. I stepped back out of reflex, then stopped and glared at the man in front of me. Only he wasn't a man, was he? *It* was a vampire. I could tell by the way my necromancer powers flared as soon as he stepped in front of me. My nature wanted me to control him.

And this was not the blood sucker I wanted to talk with. No, it was the liar. Leo.

"Has Jaxon woken up yet?" I asked, giving him one more chance to lie to me.

He snarled, but it didn't scare me. Somehow, I knew I could handle him. "It doesn't matter, because you won't be talking with him."

I *really* didn't like to be told what to do. Or what I wasn't going to do. I put my finger on my chin and cocked my head. "You see, that's where you're wrong. I'm a grown adult and can talk to whomever I want." I sidestepped to move around him, but he blocked me.

My witchy senses went haywire. I had to think quickly, and I needed backup, though I was still pretty sure I could take this sleazeball. What to do?

If I yelled, it was possible his buddies would come to his aid. Since I was connected to Zoey, from raising her from the dead, I sent out my magic to her with a message. It was kind of like telepathy without actually having the ability. And I hoped it worked, but I had no idea if it would. "*Zo, get Drew and come outside. There's a vamp with a bully complex.*"

I felt a nudge along the magical connection and hope bloomed inside me. Did she get the message? Maybe I wouldn't be handling this psycho on my own after all. I inched left, and he inched left. I went back to the right and so did he. I gathered my power, ready to use it if I had to.

My question was answered just a few seconds later when Drew came into view a few yards behind the vampire.

The vamp turned to glare at Drew, then faced me again. "You called for backup? What kind of necromancer are you?"

Now that I had backup, I felt even better. I smiled wide. "A powerful one." I threw out my hands and sent a blast of energy toward the fanged freak, but it didn't pack as big of a punch as I'd hoped. He stumbled back a few feet, then rushed forward faster than I expected him to. Before I could react, he plowed into me, knocking the wind from my lungs as I hit the ground. Holy crap he'd moved so quickly.

I couldn't breathe. I tried to gasp in some air, but it was like blowing bubbles in jelly. Nothing would make the air go into my lungs. All the while fear flowed inside me. I hoped Drew hurried. I didn't want to be turned into vampire feed tonight.

Leo stood over me with a smirk on his face, but Drew didn't let it go for long. Drew's hands glowed with power as he punched the vamp in the jaw. As the air began to slowly seep into my lungs, Leo stumbled away, surprised at how hard Drew hit. I was a little impressed. Okay. I was a lot impressed.

Leo ran at Drew, but my man was ready for the vampire. He moved seconds before Leo's fist touched him. Then Drew punched the vamp in the chest, sending him flying into the side of the house. I cringed and was glad the house was brick. I'd already sold it, and it would be a lot of paperwork if I handed over a damaged house to Hailey in a few days. But holy *crow* Drew was fast. And strong. And just dreamy.

In a flash, Leo was up on his feet. Then he flew at Drew like a linebacker on speed. Leo's shoulder connected with Drew's stomach, pushing him back almost faster than I could track. They slammed into the large tree in my backyard with Drew taking the full force of the impact. I gasped and then crouched. Panic was setting in, which made it harder to breathe. The vampire was too strong, Drew would lose.

I still struggled to breathe as I sat up. If I could get on my feet, I could try more magic to at least help Drew, but both breathing and standing were hard to do at the moment. Suddenly, Zoey appeared beside me in tiger form. She let out a choked meow sound and rubbed her head against my shoulder. As soon as I sank my fingers into her fur, the pain in my chest lessened and my lungs opened up. I sucked in a large bubble of air and released it.

I didn't have time to process how my tiger ghoul was able to heal me because nothing about my magic was normal. I just had to roll with it. I stood and faced the vamp and the hunter, then held out my hand. "Stop." Oh, my necromancer magic had burst out. Odd.

The vampire instantly stopped, frozen in place. Oh, wow. I'd said stop, so he stopped.

So cool!

Another weird magic moment. I'll ask Owen later. "Don't move," I commanded.

Drew stumbled to me with his arm around his waist. His handsome face was a total mess. When he reached me, I touched the wounds, healing them as quickly as I could. The healing power seemed to be more powerful than the last time I used it. I didn't have time to dwell on that, either. Lots of questions for later.

He shuddered and studied me for a moment. "Are you okay?"

"Yeah." Looking at the vamp, I asked, "Is Jaxon home?" Lacing my necromancer magic into my voice, I lowered it. "Tell me the truth."

"Yes," he replied with his stare blank like he was under compulsion.

That was interesting. "Why did you attack me?" I narrowed my eyes at him.

His nostrils flared. Some part of him was able to resist. "You were being nosy. I couldn't let you go to Jaxon about that human."

My anger rose, and I closed my fist and stepped forward. The vamp made a choking sound. Was I doing that? To test it, I opened my fist and he let out a breath. It *was* me. Nice. "Where is *that human*?"

I squeezed as he replied so his words came out sounding choked. "In an alley about a block from Catch and Release."

I was about to ask where that was but decided I needed to make an example out of him. I walked across the street to Jaxon's house. The vampire followed because he didn't have a choice. It was easy to control him. All I had to do was want him to do something, then filter my magic into him and he did it.

Leo was under my spell. Now that I thought about it, vampires were undead. That meant I could control them. At least I could control Leo here, and it seemed likely he wouldn't be the only one.

Jaxon met us on his front porch. His brows raised as he looked from me to Leo. "Why are you controlling him?"

He'd sensed that I controlled the vamp without me having to tell him. "Leo here did something with Wade, and I wanted you to hear his confession." Then turned to Leo, asking, "What is the Catch and Release and why is the human, who has a name, Wade, in an alley?"

Fear made the vamp's eyes grow large. "I turned him." I was guessing it was against the rules to turn humans. Oops. Sucked for him. Pun intended.

Jaxon growled and snapped his fingers. "Paige." The female vamp from the other day appeared and grabbed Leo by the arm. That was when I released him from my power.

Paige, who I believed was like a vampire cop, took the creep inside. Jaxon motioned to his car. "I'll take you to get your uncle."

"How do you know who Wade is?" I had to power walk to the car to keep up with him. As I reached it, Drew opened the back door for me. He didn't even ask if he could go. Not that I would've turned him away. Heck no. Not after that impressive performance I saw in the backyard.

Once inside the car, Jaxon said, "I know everyone in this neighborhood."

CHAPTER TWELVE

My nerves were like a live wire and my stomach churned. "That vampire said he turned Wade."

I kept my voice low. I was more talking to myself than anyone else, trying to wrap my head around the fact that my uncle was a fanged one. What did that even mean? How did it happen? Would we be able to take care of him?

"*That* vampire has a name, not that it matters now." Jaxon frowned. "Leo will be turned in to the Elders for punishment. We aren't allowed to kill, harm, or turn humans. For the latter we need permission. There is a process both the human and his sire needs to go through."

"Is that how your kind stays undetected?" Drew asked.

"Part of it." Jaxon stared at Drew for a long while. "I've never met a hunter."

Drew shrugged and took my hand. "I've never met a vampire." He snorted. "Honestly, I didn't believe your kind existed."

They could bro it out later. "What do I need to know so I can help Wade adjust to this life?" I was already making a mental list of what Winston needed to do to make room. There was no way I'd let Wade stay here by himself. Not after this. He'd just have to come home with me. Once he adjusted, if he wanted, he could move back here.

Jaxon shifted his gaze to mine in the rearview mirror. "He can't be allowed to live."

Oh, no. He didn't get to go there. "Stop the car." I reached for the door handle but Drew tightened his hold on my hand. "Stop the car. I'll be damned if I let you near Wade."

I didn't curse often but Jaxon was peeving me off. I hadn't yet used my magic on him, which was why he was still driving.

"It is the law—" Jaxon began but stopped as I glared at him, my magic bubbling to the surface.

"I don't live by your rules. Wade will be coming back to Shipton with me. *Alive.*" Well, alive as an undead vampire. Unalive. Alive 2.0. One more undead being in my house. What did one more matter? Winston was going to have to make room somehow. We could add to the house. The coven would help.

Jaxon worked his jaw and focused on the road. "You will be held responsible for him."

"That's a given." I glared back at him. Wade was my only living relative, besides Wallie, and I wasn't about to let anyone take him from me.

We pulled into the alley next to a club in downtown Philly called Catch and Release. Peering out my window, I fogged it up as I spoke. "What is this place? Leo said he dumped Wade in an alley a block away."

Jaxon got out, and I exited the car right after, scanning the area for Wade. "I got a call about an unknown vampire wandering around right before you brought Leo to me." Then Jaxon pointed to the building. "This is an exclusive club for members only. It's a safe place for vampires to feed. The humans inside are aware of what they signed up for and are willing."

"That's an unusual name for a club," I muttered and walked farther into the dark alley.

Jaxon chuckled. "I named it after our catch and release rule."

I turned and lifted my brows at him. "Your what?"

"I told you. We are not to harm or kill humans. That extends to feeding. We catch them, seduce them, then release them with only memories of a good time. Catch and Release." He flashed his fangs at me. Drew stepped in front of me like he wanted to protect me from the vamp. I held my tongue and kept from reminding him that I could control vampires just as well as I could a ghoul.

Jaxon was old, I knew that much. I felt it. However, I was betting that I could take control of him like I had Leo.

"Wade was brought here until I could arrive." Jaxon moved to a door on the side of the building and opened it.

I noticed he didn't add, "to kill him" to his statement. That would happen over my dead body. Which would be unfortunate, as several undead things would end up dying when I did.

After Jaxon entered through the side entrance to the club, Drew and I followed. The music inside wasn't as loud as one would expect from a club. It was still upbeat, electro-dance-type music but not overly loud. I could hear myself think.

My necro powers went haywire inside the place though. There were a lot of vampires. And they all seemed to turn and stare at us as we walked through the place. They gave Jaxon respectful glances and nods while Drew and I got a few snarls and a lot of curious stares.

Drew placed a hand on my lower back and moved closer to me. He didn't have to tell me that his skin was tingling because I felt his power. It was like a hum of energy that flowed around him, fueled by his need to protect me.

I poked at his magic with my own just to see what would happen. He sucked in a breath and placed his hands on my hips, digging his fingers in a little. With his lips near my ear, he said, "I wouldn't do that."

Desire flared deep in my belly. "Why not?"

He pulled me back until our bodies were pressed together. "Oh." His hard length pushed into my hip, heating the desire. Even through the jeans he wore, I got a pretty good idea of the size of that package.

"Have you not used your magic during sex?" Drew's voice dropped lower and there was a roughness in his tone that put images in my head I didn't need at the moment.

I shook my head and noted that Jaxon glanced at us, then chuckled softly as he walked away. Turning, I studied Drew's features. "Have you?"

It was at that moment I realized that I didn't know my boyfriend at all. He frowned and something dark passed through his depths. He opened his mouth as if to say something then stopped.

"I've found Wade," Jaxon said, making me jump because I didn't hear that damn vamp walk up behind me.

I poked Drew in the chest. "We will have this conversation later."

He kissed my forehead. "Later."

I turned and followed Jaxon to a corner in the back of the club. Wade sat on the floor with his knees pulled up to his chest. When I got close his head snapped up. His eyes were so dark it broke my heart to see him like that.

Jaxon held out a hand to stop me from advancing any further. "He could bite you and necromancer blood isn't good for our kind."

Interesting. "Why?"

Jaxon stared at me like he didn't want to answer my question. Well, that was too dang bad, but he was the one who brought it up, so he had to explain it. After a few more seconds, he gave in. "A necromancer can turn us into slaves with their blood."

Oh, wow. That was interesting. I understood why he didn't want to tell me. "I have no interest in having slaves. I don't need them. I have two ghouls and a fleshed-out skeleton—although I shouldn't call Larry a skeleton anymore—and two immortal cats linked to me. I don't need anyone else." I pointed to Wade. "I will not have to link him to me, and I have no reason to."

Wade was family. I squatted down in front of my uncle. "Wade."

At the sound of my voice, his eyes turned normal, with the inky blackness receding, and he frowned. "Go, Ava. Leave me."

"I will not. You are coming home with me. And by home, I mean Shipton." I made my tone firm and put a tiny bit of magic into it. He couldn't argue with me.

I hated the fact that I would have to control him at first. I stood and held out my hand to Wade. He took it and let me pull him up.

Jaxon shook his head. "He'll need to feed and learn how to do it without killing." He turned and waved us to follow. "You'll get a crash course on vampire feeding, and I'll answer any questions you have."

I *particularly* didn't want to learn about vampire feeding. However, Wade needed to and as the one who would ultimately be responsible for him, I needed to know these things as well.

Jaxon led us to the upper level where we sat on a high-backed sofa with arms. It was basically like a fancy booth without the table attached to it. In front of us was a circular table about the height of a coffee table.

Within moments of taking our seat, a waitress appeared. I hadn't even seen her walk over. One moment it was just us, then bam. She was there. Creepy.

"The usual for me and a bottle of red." Jaxon glanced at

Wade and added, "And someone nice and pretty for our new friend."

I frowned, not comfortable with ordering a person for Wade to drink from.

Before the waitress left, Drew held up one finger. "A water for me."

She glared at him for a long moment until Jaxon said, "That's all."

There was power in his voice that seemed to make the woman snap in line and do as she was told. I eyed him. "Are you like the leader of them?"

He nodded once. "I'm the master vampire of this area."

That made sense, especially from the way the other vampires acted around him. And the fear that had rolled off of Leo when I'd forced him to tell the truth. I met Wade's gaze. "How are you?"

He shrugged then scanned the crowd of the club. "I'm dead."

"Undead," I corrected in a flat tone. "What happened? And don't tell me you were turned into a vampire. I already know that much."

I didn't care if my tone was a little too firm. I'd worried about him for days. At least he could've called me. But maybe he just hadn't been able to. Maybe he'd been scared.

"A vampire followed me home the night I left your house. He asked questions about you and why you were there. He didn't make sense. He went on about necromancers coming back to turn them into slaves." Wade made eye contact with me and frowned. "You don't turn people into slaves, do you?"

I stopped myself from rolling my eyes at him. Sure, Wade knew what I was and accepted me for all my weirdness, but we'd never gone into great detail about necromancers or witches. He'd never asked. "No. I don't turn people into slaves. I don't even control my ghouls." That was an understatement.

Jaxon added, "But you can."

He was not helping. "Yes, I *can*, but I don't and won't unless I absolutely have to."

Wade relaxed. "The vampire insisted I knew something. When I told him to get out of my house and to leave you alone, he went crazy. We fought, but he was too powerful. I remember..." He shuddered. "I remember him killing me. Then I woke up craving blood."

Jaxon made a low growl-like sound. "Leo will be dealt with. Like I told Ava on the way here, Leo broke our number one rule —no killing or turning humans."

"Isn't that 2 rules?" I asked with a grin.

"Two of the most important rules that we will classify as one. We haven't lived this long without discovery by making humans aware of us." He nodded to the waitress. "Our drinks are here as well as Wade's human."

The human was a beautiful brunette with short curly hair and large brown eyes. She was about my height with curves that looked amazing on her. She smiled at everyone as she went to Jaxon and sat in his lap. "Hi, Jax. It's been a while since you called on me."

Jax caressed her cheek and smiled. "I'm old, Honey. I don't need to feed as often. But tonight, I have a new vampire that needs to learn to feed properly."

That was when Honey met each of our stares and stopped on Drew. "Oh, he's handsome. Silver Fox."

"No, no," I said in a loud voice. "Wrong silver fox."

Drew grinned at me like he'd just had a big compliment. "You think I'm hot."

She stood and moved to stand in front of Wade, who had sat on the end of the semi-round sofa. Holding out her hand, she said, "Hi. I'm Honey and will be happy to service you."

Frowning, I watched her for a moment before turning to Jaxon. "This is like a brothel for vampires? Are they paid?"

He chuckled. "In a way. But all the trusted humans who work here have the final say in who sinks their fangs into them. I take good care of my employees. And before you ask, no, Honey is not her real name. We use stage names here to protect their privacy. They do have a life outside of working here."

I nodded and stood, then asked Drew, "Switch with me?" I wanted to be close to Wade in case he lost control.

Drew scooted over so I could sit closer to my uncle. "So how does this work?"

Jaxon explained to Honey who I was. "This is Ava. She's a...witch and will be responsible for the newbie."

I expected him to go into more details than that, but Honey seemed to understand what he wasn't saying. I rolled with it. After all, what did I know? Not a whole lot.

Honey sat on Wade's lap like she had Jaxon's and spoke in a soft, caring voice. "You can take from my wrist or my neck. Wherever you feel comfortable."

Wade glanced at me as if seeking some kind of permission or just some support. I took his hand and squeezed. "You have to learn to do this. Don't worry. I won't let you kill her."

He picked up Honey's wrist and brought it to his mouth. Then he bit into her flesh. She sucked in a breath then relaxed into him with her fingers playing with his hair. "That's it. Nice and gentle."

Honey continued to speak words of encouragement, and I was starting to see why Jaxon had called on her to feed Wade. Turning to Jaxon, I asked, "How many new vampires has she broken in?"

"Broken in?" Jaxon lifted a brow. "We don't turn many. There hasn't been a new vampire in this area in decades. Honey has a way with people and vampires. She can soothe their worries."

That was interesting. I focused back on Wade, feeling like I was invading something intimate. After a few minutes, Jaxon said, "He's taking too much. Stop him before he can't be stopped."

I opened up my necro powers and touched Wade's arm. "You've had enough."

He let out a growl and tightened his hold on Honey. Okay, so the gentle approach wasn't gonna work. I put a little firmer mean-mom into my tone and my magic. "Wade, stop."

He froze and pulled his fangs from her wrist. "I'm sorry. It was, I don't know how to describe it."

Honey smiled at him like he hadn't just tried to drain her and held up her wrist. "You have to lick the punctures to seal them."

Wade did, and Honey stood up. "Would you like me to come back before you leave?"

Before Wade could answer, Jaxon said, "No need. You should take a break and eat something."

She nodded and gave us a little wave before leaving.

We spent another few hours there, drinking, talking, laughing, and dancing. Wade had moved. Who knew? Not me, that was for sure. Drew was a good slow dancer. Or maybe I just liked being in his arms.

Jaxon brought a few more people for Wade to drink. He was able to stop himself more easily each time he fed. Jaxon assured me it would get easier within a matter of days.

By the time we were ready to leave, Wade was fairly comfortable with feeding on humans. I only had to intervene once since Honey. Jaxon said he was impressed by how well Wade had adapted in a short time.

I was sure Wade still had a long road ahead of him to adjust to his new life. I would be there with him and for him. He was my family, and I would not let him fail.

CHAPTER THIRTEEN

Mornings were never going to be my strong suit. And I didn't want them to be. I enjoyed my evenings and sleeping late, and I wouldn't let anyone give me a hard time for that. I had just stumbled into the kitchen to start coffee when my phone dinged with an incoming text. Before I could wrap my thoughts around what was going on—because it was way too darn early to get up—a cup of warm coffee was pressed into my hand. Humming, I raised it to my nose and inhaled deeply. "Perfect," I murmured.

Then Drew kissed me on the cheek and directed me to the table. "Morning." I let him shuffle me along.

"Morning," I said as I read the text from Owen.

Luci was just here looking for you. Just FYI

"Crap." I did *not* want to deal with the devil today. Not even a little.

"What?" Drew asked. He was cute when he first woke up. A little piece of his black hair was sticking straight up in the back.

I turned my phone so he could see it. "Owen said Luci was

looking for me."

Just then, the doorbell rang. I sighed. Too early.

Drew and I locked gazes then looked toward the living room. Drew pointed to the table. "Enjoy your coffee. I'll get the door."

I muttered, "Thanks," as I sank into the chair and sipped my coffee. Drew had made it just how I liked it. How did he know?

I heard Drew open the door and then dropped my head to the table when I heard a familiar voice that I thought I wouldn't hear while in Philly. Dang it. Why was Lucifer here? And why had he bothered with the doorbell? Why hadn't I known he'd be at the door? Normally he'd just come right in, or I should've known it was him at least.

I got up and went to the living room. When Luci saw me, he smiled and rushed right over, holding something in his hand. "I come bearing gifts."

That was ominous.

Frowning, I looked at the envelope in his hand. I wasn't sure I wanted gifts from Satan. Not today. "Your gifts come with conditions. No thanks."

Luci rolled his eyes and opened the envelope. "So untrusting." He pulled out what looked like tickets. "You'll enjoy this, I promise."

I stepped closer, cradling my coffee. At the same time, Olivia and Sam entered the room. Luci handed them an envelope too. "I didn't forget my favorite deputy and the little wifey."

Olivia pulled out two pieces of paper and scrunched up her nose. "Train tickets?"

Yes." Luci grinned. "It's a luxury train, fully inclusive. It'll take you to Portland, where I've arranged for a car to pick you up and drive you home. The view is spectacular this time of year."

I shook my head. "We don't need to take the train."

Luci pouted, sticking his bottom lip out. "I tried to think of something good for you. My intentions with this gift are strictly honorable."

I shook my head. "No, we have to drive the truck home." Shrugging, I tried to hand the tickets back to him, but he wouldn't take them.

"How will you all fit in the truck?" Luci asked. "At least a few of you will need to either fly or rent a car. Why not use these tickets I've already purchased?"

Olivia had been busy on her phone while we talked. "They're legit." She stepped close and showed me her screen. "At least, mine are."

I took her phone and typed the ticket numbers from the tickets into the website. They were registered for a luxury suite and all meals and drinks included.

"Look." Luci walked around us and pointed to the screen. "I made them open-ended. You can pick your time and register when you want to go. I wasn't sure what time of day you'd want to leave."

He'd made the offer pretty attractive. It was hard to refuse. And a train ride on a romantic locomotive in a luxury suite sounded *heavenly*—haha a heavenly gift from the devil—after the week we'd had.

"I have one condition," I said.

Luci's eyebrows flew up. "What's that?"

"You magically pack Wade's house and load it into the trailer we're going to send Wallie to rent. That will take a huge weight off my mind."

Lucifer sighed and cocked his head at me. "Really? I have to bribe you to accept a gift from me?"

I just stood there with one eyebrow cocked.

The devil burst out laughing. "I guess that's fair."

"One more thing. Anything we don't move into our house

of Wade's, that he doesn't want to get rid of, you'll store in one of your amazing rooms," I said. "You've got plenty of space."

Luci glared at me but inclined his head once. "Done. Get the trailer, and I'll help."

I handed our tickets to Olivia for safekeeping. "Then we're taking the train."

Why did I have a bad feeling I'd come to regret this decision?

I expected Luci to leave after giving us the train tickets, but he didn't. Just my luck.

It was our last day here anyway. We needed to get Wade's truck and the rental trailer loaded ASAP so the kids could head out right after dark. We had most of the house packed, though. And Hailey had agreed to handle the pickup of the donated stuff, so we just had to take our stuff and put out the trash and leave.

We'd covered Wade's furniture with blankets and sheets until he decided, later on down the road, whether to stay in Shipton or come back here to Philly. His house was paid off, so it could sit until he knew his plan.

My son had yet to make an appearance, and I'd already had a cup of coffee and dealt with the devil. "Wallie!" I couldn't believe that kid had slept through the doorbell and our conversation. Then again, he *was* my child. "Wallace Harper!" I yelled toward the pull-out sofa sleeper where he laid with his mouth open and a trickle of drool escaping his lips.

"Huh?" He sat up, looking around. When his gaze landed on Luci, he frowned. "What is Satan doing here?"

"He gifted us with train tickets so you, Wade, and Zoey will be driving back. Tonight. That means you have to go get a trailer so we can start packing everything inside." I turned toward the hallway to go check on Wade, who was asleep in my walk-in closet. Jaxon said he'd sleep all day.

When I reached my room, I noticed I was being followed

by my husband's ghost and Luci. He'd lost the spell I'd done to make him corporeal and was back to being a regular ghost.

Seeing Clay reminded me that today was also the day I would say goodbye. Forever.

Clay floated around to stand in front of me. "You're leaving today."

I didn't have much choice. It was time to go. "Yeah."

"But you haven't let go." I didn't want to look at his face; his voice was slightly pitiful.

I glanced at Luci, who now sat on the bed as he watched us with interest. I was so glad my struggle was so entertaining for him.

I reached for the closet door, and Clay stopped me. "Hang on. What's your plan?"

Letting out a sigh, I took his hands. "I do have a plan. But I'm not saying anything until Wallie gets back from picking up the trailer."

"Okay." He didn't look convinced as he moved away from the closet door.

"I know what to do. If I tell you right now there is a strong chance you will move on, and I want Wallie here when you do." I gave his hands a squeeze and let go of them. "We'll wait."

I eased the closet door open and peeked inside. Wade was on our twin-size air mattress, sound asleep. My heart ached for him. I hoped I was able to help him adjust. I'd find a way. He was family.

Closing the door, I looked at Clay and my heart broke all over again. "Can you hang out a little longer?"

He nodded but looked so sad. "Putting it off will only make it hurt more."

I turned away from him, not wanting to have this conversation just yet. He flashed to stand in front of me, his brows bunched together. "You promised me you wouldn't grieve me for too long. It's been five and a half years."

"I know that!" I pushed him and started walking toward the door again.

He rushed up behind me and threw his arms around me. I turned without a second thought and buried my face into his chest the way I had for so many years while we were married. Every time I needed comfort, he'd hold me like this.

My spell had worn off and he was back to his ghostly form. As long as I was touching him, he was solid—like he had never died. I could potentially keep him with me forever. "I made that promise when I believed we would both live to be over a hundred and would die within days of each other." I looped my arms under his to hug him tighter.

Glancing at the door, I saw Drew standing just inside the room. He watched us, but I didn't feel any jealousy coming from him.

Clay turned so both of us looked at Drew and Luci, who had gotten up from the bed and stood beside my boyfriend as my dead husband held me. "Ava is a fascinating creature," Luci said quietly.

Drew chuckled. I rolled my eyes and pointed at Luci. "Clay, this is my new neighbor, Satan. I summoned him during Christmas while attempting to summon Santa Claus."

Clay studied Lucifer for a moment then focused back on me, shaking his head. "My time on earth is done. I need to go and prepare for my next journey. You have a purpose, and it begins with letting go of the past."

I released Clay and stepped away. "I know. But not until Wallie gets back. I'm not doing it without him."

Then I left the bedroom to go finish packing the last-minute items, leaving my old flame and my new flame hanging in a bedroom with my undead uncle. And Satan.

Just a normal day, really.

CHAPTER FOURTEEN

I'd been avoiding Clay all day. In my defense, I'd been busy loading the back of the truck and the trailer once Wallie got home. The house was empty now except for the furniture that Hailey said she wanted to keep and the donation stuff, which was marked clearly or neatly boxed.

Luci had even helped with the loading, a miracle. He'd used magic so he could sit on his rear end and surf social media. I guessed I could have used magic too, but I'd needed the physical labor to distract me from what had to be done.

I'd put it off as long as I could. Walking over to the mantel, I picked up the urn with Clay's ashes and hugged it to me. "Wallie, can you come here?" I called.

He was outside doing a final check and tying down the tarp over the bed of the truck. He walked into the house and stared at the urn in my hands. Sadness filled his eyes as he closed the distance between us and took my hand. "It's time," I said.

He nodded then glanced at the hallway. Wade stood in the archway. The sun had just set, so he was safe to move about the house. I waved him over to join us. He was Clay's uncle after all. Since Wade was now undead, it was possible he could see Clay.

Once Wade joined us, Drew directed Sam, Olivia, Zoey, and Luci into the kitchen to give us a little privacy. That man deserved a kiss.

Clay appeared in front of us, and Wade jumped. "Holy effing hell!" He looked at me then back to Clay. "How?"

Clay pointed at me. "She hasn't let go, so I can't move on."

Frowning, I looked down at the urn. "You were right when you said I'm meant to stay and find my purpose. I'm grateful for the time we had together, and I hate that it had to end." My heart thumped so hard I had to take a deep breath and release it slowly. Wallie and Wade rubbed my back as I gathered my strength. "Drew helped me figure out the one thing that I haven't done. I wasn't ready to say goodbye and that was unfair to you. I broke my promise." I'd kept Clay at arm's length the whole time I was here because I'd known that this would be the end game. In reality, I wanted to push everyone away and cling to Clay. We could live here together in the house until I was old and shriveled up.

But that wouldn't be fair to him. Or me. Or my new life and family in Shipton.

My vision blurred as tears filled my eyes. Before Clay could say anything, I held up his ashes in the center of our little circle. "I'm taking your ashes back to Shipton where the three of us will spread them into the ocean. You'll be near me that way, always."

As soon as the words left my mouth, I knew it was the right thing. My grief didn't feel so heavy. It was still there, but not as crippling. I had to let him go, and I was ready. The Universe had plans for me that didn't include my past.

Clay smiled and became solid. He also glowed with an inner light as he stepped closer to me. Then he pressed his lips to mine softly. After he pulled back, he hugged Wade, then

Wallie. They'd spent some good time together, bonding and saying goodbye while we were here.

Clay turned to me and cupped my face. "I love you and always will, no matter where I end up."

I believed him. Somehow, someway, and someday, we would meet again. I bit back a sob. "You will always be in my heart and a part of my soul. Go enjoy your next life and journey." I gripped his arms. "Until we meet again."

Wallie nodded. "Everything Mom said. Thank you for being my dad. It was too short, but you were the best father."

Clay hugged his son again and turned to Wade. "A vamp. I never saw that coming. You *have* to tell my mom."

We laughed at Clay's joke. His mother hated anything that wasn't human.

Clay turned back to me and kissed me lightly on the lips. "I love you, Ava. The best part about moving on now is that I can do so knowing you are happy and found someone to share the rest of your life with." He nodded toward the kitchen. "If you treat him half as well as you did me, he's a lucky man."

I wasn't sure about the rest of my life, but I was starting to learn I needed to live in the moment. For now, I had Drew. But this wasn't about him. It was about Clay. "I'll love you until the end of time."

And then, I let him go. Something deep inside me unclenched, and I breathed out and with my breath, Clay blew me a kiss, and quietly, lovingly, he faded away, moving on to his next big adventure.

I collapsed against Wallie and Wade, sobbing my heart out. Someone took the urn from me, and Drew came out of the kitchen and wrapped me in his arms. I sank into him, burying my face into his chest. "He's gone," I wailed against his shirt.

"I'm here to listen when you're ready to talk." He kissed the top of my head.

When my tears were spent, I sucked in a deep breath and

glanced up at him. "I feel like a weight's been lifted. I got to say goodbye. I got closure." I knew he was at peace, gone to whatever happened to us next.

Stepping out of Drew's embrace, I turned to Wallie. He had the urn. "Keep this safe during the drive. I don't need your father haunting me the rest of my life."

Wallie chuckled. "We'll do a ceremony or something at home."

Just then, a knock sounded on the door, interrupting us. I opened it to Hailey's smiling face. I returned the smile a little shakily. "Hi! Come in."

"Thank you." She entered the house and looked at everyone standing around. "Are we having a sendoff party?"

I laughed and introduced her to everyone, including Luci, and tried to silently encourage her to not make eye contact with the devil. Wade excused himself and headed to the kitchen. I guessed that he was packing his cooler of bagged blood that Paige had dropped off. And probably drinking one in the process.

I handed Hailey the keys. "It's all yours." Sucking in a deep breath, I took one last look around and let go of the house. I'd brought my baby home to this house. But it was just a chapter closing as another began. It felt right.

Hailey took the keys. "Thanks. I'm so excited about this move and so ready to start over." She paused and studied me for a moment, then her gaze drifted to my inner wrist. "So, uh, are you a witch?"

I choked and coughed, then laughed. Her bold question shocked me. "I am. I figured you might know about us since your BFF is Kendra."

"Yeah." She paused again and scanned the living room like she was looking for something. "Kendra says that houses can absorb magic."

Ha! If only she knew. "You don't need to worry about this

one. My in-laws didn't like that I was a witch, so I suppressed my magic while living here. At the time I wanted to live a normal human life." No more normal for me. I was happy about that. "Now I know who and what I'm meant to be."

I felt Hailey's relief as if it were my own. I understood. She didn't need to move into a house that might mess with her.

While Hailey watched, wide-eyed, I conjured a pen and a notepad, then wrote down my phone number and handed it to her. "If you need anything or have questions or even just need to talk, call me." I considered telling her about the fanged ones across the street, but I thought it was better not to. It was possible the sale was still so new she could back out.

Besides, Jaxon had said they don't mix with humans outside his club or the small group of trusted humans who knew about them. It was how they had gone unnoticed by the hunters for so long.

Once Hailey left, I saw my son and uncle off. They had an eight-hour drive to Shipton, which was why we were leaving just after dark rather than early in the morning. Wade would be awake and able to drive. Once the sun came up, the poor man would be out, and he'd have to go in the back of the trailer if they didn't make it to my house first. Newbie vamps were weak in the sunlight and slept most of the day. Jax said after a hundred or so years, Wade would be able to stay up more during the day.

About ten minutes after they drove off, Luci turned to us. "I bid you farewell and safe travels." Then he dematerialized just as our cab pulled up.

Drew, Sam, Olivia, and I were taking the train home. While it sounded fun, I was still suspicious of the gift Luci gave us.

Why had I agreed to take the darn train?

CHAPTER FIFTEEN

Holy crap on a cracker. This train was glorious. We boarded a car with a green carpet. "If I take my shoes off and sink my feet into this carpet, I'm telling you, you won't be able to see my toes," Olivia whispered.

"I know," I squeaked. "This is luxury like I didn't know even existed!" I'd thought trains were all worn-out velvet and smelled stale. But then again, I'd never been on a train, so what did I know?

As we walked down the narrow pathway, the porter showed us two rooms. "These are our two luxury suites. Please, press the button on the phone if you need anything at all." He bowed his head and Drew held out his hand. As they shook, I caught the slightest flash of green exchange hands.

"Was that a twenty?" I asked as we all crowded into the first room.

"Yeah. We're in their best suites and they obviously think we're some richy-riches." Drew chuckled. "Might as well tip extravagantly."

We oohed and aahed over the room. It was small, but every bit of material in the room was either incredibly soft or overwhelmingly silky. The sofa and armchair were made of the highest quality and on the other side of the room, a double bed was piled high with pillows.

"Oh, skylights," Olivia crooned. "Come on, let's go see if the other room has skylights." She jumped up and down a couple of times.

"If not, I call dibs on this one!" I threw my bags on the couch. I'd move them if I had to.

Both rooms were identical, so Sam and Olivia stayed in the second to get settled in while Drew and I went back to the first one.

I walked through the suite with big eyes, then hopped on the bed and tested it out. "It's super squishy," I called.

Drew watched me with a twinkle in his eyes. "I'm glad you like it. I still think this train has a big fat string attached to it that we haven't seen yet."

I grunted. "I totally agree."

A bell dinged in the car. "What was that?" I asked.

Drew shrugged and looked around. A pamphlet sat on the little table beside the only armchair. He picked it up and rifled through it. "Oh, that's the last bell for dinner. It says the kitchen is open until ten, so one more hour."

"Let's go grab a bite to eat," I said. "I'm not starving, but I don't want to miss out on having dinner on this fancy train."

Drew chuckled and held open the door. "Let's grab the lovebirds before they start doing the horizontal tango."

I stuck my nose in the air and sashayed past Drew out the door as if I were a snobby lady who would find it perfectly normal to ride on a train like this. Once out in the hall, I walked on tiptoe toward the room next door and then when I got there, banged on it as hard as I could, hoping to startle them.

Seconds later, Olivia answered with her blonde hair disheveled. I snickered. That hadn't taken long. "What?" she croaked. "Give a girl a break!"

"Last call for the dining car," I said. "You coming?"

She looked back into the room, at Sam presumably, then her grin widened. "Nope. We'll eat later."

"Okay," I tried to warn her, but she slammed the door shut. "But you can't eat later," I whispered.

Olivia jerked the door open and stuck her head out. "Don't do anything I wouldn't do," she said in a sing-song voice. Then she slammed the door again as I giggled.

"There's not much she wouldn't do, but she's gonna do it hungry."

"Maybe they're planning to live on love," Drew said. "But *I'm* starving." He held out his elbow. "Shall we?"

Smiling, I put my hand in the crook of his arm and let him walk me out of the hall and through a door. We entered a car with a few people sitting here and there on luxurious blue couches. "I guess this is where the people who didn't get suites ride?" I whispered.

Drew consulted the pamphlet. "Yep. Dining car through the next door."

Nodding politely at the people sitting around, we walked straight through and into the next car. Row after row of four-top tables lined the walls, one at each window. We moved to the middle of the car and Drew pulled out a chair for me. "My lady."

This train ride was the perfect distraction and pick-me-up after the emotionally tumultuous evening I'd had.

With a giggle, I picked up the menu and browsed the options. It all sounded delicious. When a server walked over, Drew ordered a bottle of wine, and I pointed to a chicken dish that sounded good. "This pasta, please, no mushrooms."

When the waiter left, I stared at Drew for a long moment, thinking that I had gotten lucky a second time in my life. "Thank you."

"For what?" He bunched his brows together.

"For being understanding with Clay. I didn't know he was still there. It had to be awkward for you."

Drew covered my hand with his. "I understand the loss you feel, and I want to be there for you."

I turned my hand over so we linked our fingers together. "You lost someone?"

He nodded. "It feels like a lifetime ago. I was a different person then—a hunter. She was a witch."

My heart sank while my intuition told me that another hunter took her from Drew. "I'm so sorry."

"I was sent to kill her. When I got there, ready to take the shot, I saw something I never expected. She had a child. A girl around Sammie's age." Drew frowned and pulled his hand out of mine and sat back while scanning the dining car. "Before that night I didn't associate witches with being mothers or daughters or people, really. I'd been taught they were monsters and should be put down. It's the blind prejudices that all hunters have."

"Is that why you stopped hunting?"

He nodded. "I was already on the way out by then. I just hadn't fully made up my mind. Seeing Dawn with her daughter made me want to look into why she was marked for death. Once I found out she was innocent, I told her that she'd been marked. We ran with the little girl and hid out for a few years before my father and a few others caught up to us."

I gasped, my heart aching because I knew this story didn't have a happy ending. "They killed her?"

He nodded but said nothing.

"And the little girl?"

He gave a jerky nod and looked out the window. The backs of my eyes stung with unshed tears. The hunters had killed the child. A baby!

Drew sighed. "That was a dark time for me. After my grief of losing them subsided somewhat, I hunted down everyone who was there when she was killed and repaid the favor. All but my dad. I left him alive to remember what I am capable of. What he created."

"Good." We fell silent when the server brought the wine and poured it.

The rest of the meal was spent between a comfortable silence and light conversation of all the things we needed to do when we got home.

When we finished eating, Drew stood and offered his elbow again. "Shall we retire to our bedroom?"

"I—" My intent was to say something like I'd love to, or I can't wait. Instead, I just squeaked.

"What was that?" Drew asked with a wide smile.

Clearing my throat, I tried again. "I'd love to."

My stomach swirled in knots at the idea of going to bed with him. And not for sleeping. The memory of the kiss he gave me that morning at breakfast came rushing back. My insides heated and my private regions tingled with anticipation.

My mind was a different story. It scared the crap out of me to think about having sex with another man.

Apparently, the wine with dinner had done nothing to calm my nerves.

I was an adult. I could have casual sex and not so casual. But what if I screwed up somehow? Drew would never want me again.

I didn't speak a word as we walked through the dining car, through the car full of plush seats, and into the hallway of our car. Ours and Olivia and Sam's suites were the only two rooms on it. I tried to close off my ears as we passed Olivia and Sam's door. I didn't need to hear that mess. I definitely didn't need any visuals those sounds would create.

As soon as Drew closed the door behind us, I scrambled forward and grabbed my suitcase. "Be right back," I squawked in a way-too-high voice.

I opened the door to the bathroom to find it was a closet. Whoops. Whirling around, I opened the only other door, near the bed, and found a teeny-tiny bathroom with a toilet and sink and the world's smallest shower. I wasn't even sure my bag and I would both fit inside.

Cramming inside, I opened the bag with my back pressed against the wall and rifled through it until I found the only sexy thing I'd packed.

Ugh. Now that I looked at it in the harsh fluorescent lighting of the bathroom, I wasn't impressed. Ugh, ugh, ugh! The beige gown was wrinkled.

And it was all I had. Damn it. Stripping quickly, I avoided looking at myself in the mirror under this lighting and turned on the faucet. Pulling out my razor, I gave my legs and armpits a quick once over.

I looked at my hair down... there. I liked to keep it pretty short, but since Clay died, I hadn't been keeping up with it. Had no reason to. Until tonight.

There was nothing I could do about it now. I hadn't brought my trimmer with me. Drew was just going to have to care about me with grass on the field.

What if he liked a woman to be clean-shaven? Was that in style again? Clay had always said it made him feel like a perv for me to be completely bald down there.

Well, I was as good as I was getting on a train, at least. I'd had the same makeup on all day. I could at least freshen that up a smidge.

After swiping on another layer of mascara, I pinched my lips to make them pink but didn't do any gloss. He'd just kiss it off.

I'd put this off as long as I could. It was time. Sleeping beside him at the house had been pure bliss and at the same time, torture. Since then, I'd resolved my lingering grief with Clay. I set him free and in return, it felt good to know I had his blessing to find love again. Or just to be in a relationship again.

Nothing held me back except my sheer terror.

With one last deep breath in and out, I forced myself to open the door.

Drew sat on the edge of the bed, unbuttoning his shirt. He'd taken his shoes and socks off already. He jumped up when he saw me.

"Hey." Drew sucked in a deep breath as if he were just as nervous as I was. At least that was reassuring. "You ready for bed?"

I nodded mutely as he finished unbuttoning his shirt, revealing a wide, strong chest.

Oh, okay. The nerves were fading. I fiddled with the hem of my wrinkled, silky gown that only came to mid-thigh. "Um."

The uncertainty I'd seen a few seconds ago in Drew had disappeared. Or maybe he was just better at hiding it or banishing it. He stepped forward and put his hands on my bare arms, rubbing them up and down. "You're freezing," he whispered.

The word echoed in the room. "Freezing."

Stiffening, I looked around. "What?"

"What?" Drew raised his eyebrows. "You know, if you're not ready for this, we can just cuddle," he suggested and pulled me closer. His voice was a mix of seduction and calm. "I could hold you in my arms, close to my heart." His deep voice lowered into a rumbling tone, almost a growl. "Press your body against mine, your ass into my crotch, and my arms around your waist." He pulled me even closer and the evidence of how much he wanted me pressed into my lower stomach.

"Maybe we could, just, uh, cudd..." I lost my train of thought as Drew's lips lowered against mine. Moaning, I opened my mouth to him, relishing the feel of his tongue slipping into my mouth. "Drew," I whispered into his mouth. It sounded more like a moan. Oh, geez, did that sound sexy or just weird? The last thing I wanted to sound like was an asthmatic gorilla. Biting off the sound, I pulled back and looked up at Drew with sultry eyes. He'd succeeded in getting my motor revved. I hadn't put panties on under the gown. If I sat on the bed, I'd probably get a big damp spot on the back of it.

And I was overthinking everything. *Stop thinking, Ava!*

In an attempt to *not* embarrass myself and look sexy, I lowered myself gracefully onto the bed, sort of sideways. But then I needed to scoot over so that Drew could join me. My gown got trapped halfway underneath me as I slid over. It tugged on the top of the gown, and the momentum had already started.

As the gown yanked down and I scooted over and kinda up, the material gave way and my boob popped out. Just... plop. There was my titty.

Drew's gaze flew straight to it, and the last thing any girl would ever want to happen...did. He laughed.

I scrambled up and tugged the gown straight, then stuffed myself back down into it. "Thanks," I muttered.

"No, no." He lowered himself onto the bed beside me. "I wasn't laughing at you. Actually, I should say, you have a glorious breast. I'd very much like to see the other one. It was just the manner in which it was exposed. I'm sorry, Ava, but it was funny."

I ducked my head as a blush spread up my chest and neck toward my cheeks. "I suppose it was."

He scooted closer. "May I?" Trailing a finger along my decolletage, he dipped it under the elastic neckband and tickled the top of my breasts as his lips met mine again.

Shuddering, I arched my back, pressing my breasts against his hand until he dipped his finger lower and stretched the top until both breasts came out.

The material sort of lifted them and tucked them together. I was *not* complaining about that.

With a low growl, Drew pulled his lips off of mine and lowered his head to one of my rosy, pink buds. And then it disappeared into his mouth, and I lost all sense of reason.

I could've sounded like a gorilla birthing her first baby for all I knew as Drew's hands roamed my body. If he cared one whit about how long the hair between my legs was, he gave zero indication as he found my core and teased it until an orgasm shook through my body.

And it didn't stop there. After slipping a condom on, he looked deeply into my eyes. "Are you sure?" he whispered.

"Yes," I exclaimed. "And hurry!" The orgasm hadn't stopped. It just waned and ebbed, but if he hurried up and— "Oh, yes, just like that!" I yelled in a garbled, strangled voice.

As Drew moved above me, proving his abilities lived up to his looks, another big O came over me as I matched him thrust for thrust. It washed away the guilt about Clay, the nerves about sleeping with the second man I'd ever dated, my trepidation of taking tickets from Luci because that meant trouble in some way or another.

I let go, fully, completely, overwhelmingly, for the first time since I'd opened myself up to my powers. My magic danced through me, enhancing the La Petite Mort until the lights in the room popped and sizzled, and Drew growled at me. Actually growled! "Ava," he whispered. "Your magic."

"I know!" I yelled throatily.

As I came down from the extreme climax, all the other stuff

tried to crowd back in, the first thought being that though I'd always been supremely satisfied with Clay, it had *never* been like that. Not even a little bit.

If I didn't know better, I would've thought the world had shifted. But that was silly romance novel kind of stuff.

CHAPTER SIXTEEN

With a sigh, I leaned back against Drew after he collapsed beside me. As his chest's heaving slowed and his breathing regulated, I patted him on the pec. "Wow," I whispered, trying to calm my rushing heartbeat while also trying to enjoy the happy bliss feeling. "That was... Wow."

Drew chuckled. "I don't know about you, but I can honestly say I've never had better. Is it like that every time with a witch-necromancer hybrid?"

A soft giggle escaped me. His tone was a mix of let's do that again and concern for what that level of power could do. I was feeling the same way. "I've never had sex with my full powers unlocked. So, I have no idea." I arched an eyebrow with him. "I'm game to try it a few more times and see, though."

Drew squeezed me, burying his nose into my hair. "I think your magic broke the lights."

It was pretty dark in here. "Urgh, I think so. Let me go see if it's in the hall, too." I still had my gown on. I just popped my boobs back inside. He'd worn a condom, so no mess to clean up. Nice.

Still, I was barely dressed, so I just stuck my head out into the hallway. Something wasn't right. "Hey, Drew? Can you come here?"

His voice floated from the other side of the room. "I already know what you're talking about. Something isn't right."

Scrambling down the hall, I knocked hard on Olivia and Sam's door. Olivia answered in one of Sam's t-shirts. "What the hell, Ava?"

I pushed inside her room, much to her distress. "Cover your junk, Sam, but it's nothing I haven't seen before."

He was covered from the waist down in the bed and just rolled his eyes at me. "Nice dress," he replied.

I looked down and realized my headlights were on. Crossing my arms, I looked around their room. "Yep, it's weird in here, too."

"What are you..." Olivia's eyes widened as she looked around. "Oh."

It wasn't that my magic had messed up the lights. Everything was dimmed—like the colors were dulled. It was *odd.*

Drew walked in wearing only his jeans just a few seconds later. "It's like the whole world has faded," he said. "What's going on?"

"Everyone get dressed," I said. "Let's go see if we can find anyone on the train who might explain this, ah, lighting situation."

Drew shrugged and followed me to our room, where we dressed quickly, then met Olivia and Sam in the hallway. "Let's go toward the dining car," I suggested.

Drew grabbed my shoulders. "Let me go first."

"Uh, hon?" I gave him a grateful smile. "I appreciate it, but I'm kinda powerful. Maybe let me go first."

He cocked his head at me as he mocked me. "Uh, *hon*? No."

With that, he turned and led the way into the other car

we'd seen earlier. Stubborn man. Well, at least I got to watch his backside as we made our way to the next car. It was a fine backside, after all.

When we stepped onto the plush carpet of the seat-car, my jaw dropped. "Nobody's here," I whispered.

"Maybe everyone's asleep," Sam suggested.

"No," Drew said. "Earlier, there were at least twenty people spread out in this area. This is where people who can't afford the suites ride all night."

We looked around, but something wasn't right. I narrowed my eyes. "Weren't the couches blue earlier? And they weren't velvet." The seats were dark red now.

As we looked closer, we noticed other things that were off. "These light fixtures are gas, not electric," Olivia said.

"And the windows are very old fashioned," Drew pointed out.

"But where is everyone?" I exclaimed. "Let's go look in the dining car."

Rushing forward, I didn't wait for Drew to jump in front of me. But when I opened the door to the dining car, I wished I had. "Whoa," I whispered.

This car was also empty, but where earlier the walls had been paneled in rich, dark wood, now it was all metal. Metal seats with leather, or maybe pleather, cushions. Vinyl? I didn't know. The tables were shiny silver. And previously the whole thing had been filled with tables, but now on one side was what looked like a soda counter straight out of the fifties.

And it was also metal.

"Holy crap," Drew said. "This isn't right at all."

"Again, where is everyone?" I threw up my arms and turned in a circle. "What is happening?"

"Okay, Ms. All Powerful," Sam said. "Use your magic and get us an answer."

Oh, good idea! I sucked in a deep breath and focused on my

powers. Casting out my magic, I blanketed the train and let my senses seek out any sign of life. There was none. So, I started looking for signs of *un*life.

And found one right away.

A ghost popped into sight right in front of us. "Hey," I exclaimed. "Finally!"

The ghost, a boy with neat, short hair, froze. His eyes widened as he looked from me to Drew. Olivia and Sam couldn't see him, so their gazes floated around in the general direction of the ghost, but really, they were only looking there because Drew and I had.

"Can you see me?" the ghost asked. "Truly?"

Drew and I nodded. "Yes, we can. Is there any chance you could explain why we're on this strange train?" I smiled consolingly.

"How can you see me?" he asked in a voice that broke as if he'd died while going through puberty.

"I'm a necromancer," I said. "And Drew here is a witch hunter. And if you touch me, I can make it so the other two can see you, too."

Olivia waved with a hesitant smile, but she was looking away to the left of the kid.

That didn't sit right with the little man. He backed up a few steps, shaking his head. "If you're a necromancer, doesn't that mean you can control me?"

I shook my head. "No, no. I can only control actual bodies." Hesitating, I bit back the words I'd been about to say, that I suspected I could make a ghost permanently corporeal. He didn't need to know that. It would just freak him out.

He nodded, relieved. Hesitantly, the boy stepped forward and held out his hand. I touched it and did the same thing I had done to Clay, making him appear to Sam and Olivia. At the same time, I made my intent to be temporary. It would only last a few minutes.

They rushed forward, which kind of freaked the kid out. He backed away with his hands clasped together.

"No, it's okay," Olivia said. "What's your name?"

He looked around and sniffed before shuffling forward again. Now that he was solid and a little more vibrant, I was able to get a good look at his clothes. They were pretty old. His pants went to just below his knees and he wore a pair of white socks that came up to meet.

"Peter," he said.

Peter's jacket was more like a tunic with a wide starched collar and a black silk scarf. "Peter," I said carefully. "Do you know you're dead?"

The ghost blinked at me. "Of course," he said with a note of derision in his voice. "I've been dead for over a hundred years. How else would I still be around?"

I held up my hands. "Sorry, I'm new to talking to ghosts. In the human world, it's widely believed that sometimes ghosts don't realize they're ghosts."

He nodded. "Yeah, I've seen movies."

Drew and I exchanged a glance. "How?" he asked.

"Also," Sam interjected. "How is a boy who died in the, what, early twentieth century?"

Peter nodded.

"Okay, so how are you on a train that looks to be from the early 1950s?" Sam walked over and touched one of the sterling booths. It was solid to his touch, so he sat down.

"Maybe older because of the gas lamps." So far nothing on this new version of the train made sense.

"It's a ghost train," Peter said simply. "We don't have electricity in this reality. And the train goes wherever we steer it. If it happens to go through a home with a ghost, the ghost comes along with us."

A ghost train. Of all the... "So, do you have any idea how we're on here with you?"

Peter shook his head. "All we know is that we were hit with a massive wave of magic a little while ago and the train we'd been paralleling suddenly went to the right and when we went straight, you came with us."

"How long ago, exactly?" Drew asked.

Ah...I had a feeling where Drew was going with that question.

Peter furrowed his brow. "It's hard to keep time now." He closed his eyes but then looked to the right suddenly, sucking in a surprised breath. He nodded then turned back to us. "About a half-hour. Maybe not that long."

"Were you just speaking to someone?" Olivia asked, looking around.

"Of course." Peter looked at us like we were utterly daft. "I'm not alone here."

Drew leaned over and whispered in my ear, "It was about the time you orgasmed."

Oh, geez. Now I had to worry about my magic doing insane things if I had an orgasm? Nothing crazy had ever happened when I gave myself one.

Then again, the ones I gave myself were nothing like the one Drew gave me. And I opened up my powers... Crap.

"Okay, Peter, so, we were on a train. I accidentally let some big magic out, and it shoved us onto your train. Does that mean this train is now visible? Can other humans see us?" I walked closer to him. "Are we in danger here?"

Peter cocked his head at someone beside him. "No, he says he doesn't think so. We're staying on the tracks just in case, and if we approach another train, we'll steer off long enough for it to pass." He nodded a couple of times. "Captain is going to go drive the train himself." Peter turned his attention back to us.

"Trains have captains?" Olivia asked.

Peter shook his head. "No, he was a captain in the Army."

"Oh." Olivia gave me a wide-eyed look. "Okay, then."

"Peter, dear." I put my hand on his shoulder. "Would you like us to try to help you move on?"

He blinked several times. "You can do that?"

We all nodded vigorously. "We think so. You've got unresolved problems that prevent you from going on to the next great adventure," Drew said. "If we can help you resolve them, you can move on."

Peter furrowed his brows again, his little button nose wrinkling. "I'm afraid of what comes next. I think I'll stay here for a while."

"Okay, sweetie. We need to figure out how to get off this train, though," I said. "Any ideas on that one?"

Peter shrugged. "Your train is long gone. And while Captain can steer this train, he can't make it stop or go backward or anything."

"Does your crew even know where it is going?" Sam asked.

A woman appeared beside Peter, suddenly. All of us jumped a little. "Hello," she said. "I'm Sue. Can you please help me?"

CHAPTER SEVENTEEN

Somehow, this was Luci's doing. He knew this was going to happen. I didn't know *how* he knew. But he did. He'd planned this.

Dang it. I was going to make him pay. Preferably by sending him back to his home in Hell.

"Okay, Sue. Tell me what I can do for you." I smiled encouragingly at her and sat down in one of the booths. "How can I help you move on?"

She wore contemporary clothes. Her jeans said nineties, as did her poofy, teased hair. "I need to tell my daughter I'm proud of her," Sue said.

I raised my eyebrows. "Is that it?"

She nodded. "But she lives in Australia. The ghost train won't go over water. So, we can't travel to her so I can try to talk to her." She sighed and blew a breath up. Her bangs didn't even move. Hairspray? Or a ghost thing.

"Hey," Olivia said. "Touch her so we can see and hear her, too."

"Oh, sure. Do you mind, Sue?" I held out my hand.

The woman nodded and grabbed my fingers. Once she was visible, she repeated to Olivia and Sam what she'd told me and Drew.

"Would it work for you if we called her?" Olivia asked.

Sue shrugged. "I don't see what else we could do."

Sam pulled out his phone. "I've still got service. Video chat?"

To check, not that I didn't believe my childhood BFF, but I was curious about how we had cell service, so I took his phone and studied it. Then I called Drew. His phone rang. With a raised brow, he answered it. "Hi."

I giggled. "Just seeing if it actually works here."

Peter laughed. "I think it works because of you. Your magic is strong. I can see it."

See it? I glanced down, not seeing anything. Maybe only dead and undead things could see it? I'd have to remember to ask the ladies in the coven if they saw it.

Drew leaned in and whispered, "Your power is a hum of energy around you. I don't see it; I can feel it. So maybe ghosts can see magic like an aura or something."

"That makes sense." But I was still asking my coven about it.

Focusing on Sue, I noticed her staring at Sam's cell in my hand. She frowned and pointed. "What's that?"

"Uh, phones nowadays can show one person to another," I explained.

Sue's mouth parted in awe.

"Okay, so what's her name?" Olivia asked. She took Sam's phone and had it poised, ready to search for Sue's daughter. "If we can find her, maybe we can find a way to contact her."

"Yolanda. Yolanda Perez. Unless she's married. Then, I don't know." Sue sniffed as Olivia typed.

"Do you know where in Australia?" Olivia asked. "There are a couple of different Yolanda Perez."

"Perth, before I died." Sue dabbed at her eyes. "If she's still there."

"Yep. One Yolanda Perez in Perth, Australia." She pressed a button. "She has a social media account so I'm trying to call her through their messenger pro—" Olivia cut off when someone answered.

"Hello? Who are you?"

"Oh, um, uhhhh..."

I snatched the phone from Olivia's hand.

"Hi, Yolanda?" I smiled encouragingly.

A beautiful young woman blinked at me. "Yes. What's going on?"

"Just making sure I have the right Yolanda. Can you tell me your mother's name?"

Yolanda's black eyebrows furrowed and her face hardened. "It *was* Sue."

"Okay, great." I sucked in a deep breath. "I have something rather unbelievable to tell you, and it's even harder to explain and will be hard for you to believe over the phone. But it can't be done in person. So, just promise me you'll listen until I'm through explaining, okay?"

Yolanda looked like she was already ready to hang up the phone.

"Seriously, Yolanda. This is no trick. And it's important."

She rolled her eyes. "Fine."

"Okay, so the first unbelievable thing. I'm a witch." I waited for that to sink in.

She just arched her eyebrow. "My best friend is a Wiccan. What of it?"

Okay, that didn't go over as I thought. There was nothing wrong with Wiccans. I had a few join the coven recently. They were great help with rituals and potions. Some could even create low-power spells. "No, I'm a born witch with magic powers. I could prove it if we were together, but over the phone, anything will look like special effects, so I'll just jump right in. I can see ghosts. And the ghost of your mother came to me and asked me to help her move on."

Yolanda mouthed silently at me. Before she had a chance to get pissed, I continued. "I've made it so you can see and talk to her, but you must know. She is *not* alive. You will not see her again other than this phone call, okay?"

Yolanda still looked stunned, but she nodded mutely. I stood and turned the phone so that Yolanda and Sue could see one another.

"Mom," Yolanda said with a sob. "It's really you?"

Sue nodded. "Honey, it's really me. There's something I have to tell you."

Yolanda nodded with tears rolling down her face. "I'm sorry, Mom. I'm so sorry."

"No, honey, I'm the one who is sorry. I haven't been able to move on because I never told you."

"Told me what, Mom?" Yolanda moved the phone closer to her face.

"I'm so proud of you. I'm so happy you followed your dreams and didn't listen to me. I hope you can forgive me, and always know how incredibly proud of you I am." Sue had tears going down her cheeks as well.

"Oh, Mom. I forgive you. And I love you so much."

Sue smiled and sighed, and the sigh went on until she began to fade. I caught the phone as she faded out of sight. The air was filled with a sense of peace and contentment and as she disappeared.

"Mom?" Yolanda's voice cracked. "Mom?"

I turned the camera toward me. "I know this is upsetting, but try to come away with the knowledge that you helped your mother move on, okay?"

Yolanda nodded. "She's gone?"

"Yeah, but she was so peaceful and happy as she went. I'm

sorry for your loss."

"No, she's been gone for years, but... I never knew she was proud of me." With another nod, she cut off the call. I hadn't done anything magical, but the end of the call left me feeling oddly drained. Maybe it was just emotionally.

"Peter?" Drew asked. "Are you still here?"

He appeared beside me. "Of course."

"You said this train doesn't stop?" Drew was going somewhere with this, but I had no idea where.

"No," Peter said. "We can make it slow down, but it will not completely stop."

"Could you get us to Shipton Harbor?" he asked. "We could jump off."

That was a disaster waiting to happen. But hey, it was a risk I was willing to take to get home.

We rushed up to the front of the train to talk to Captain. It was the first time I'd seen him, and I realized that the ghosts could control which supernatural person could see them. That was interesting.

Captain was still in his army uniform and by the looks of it, if I remembered my history lesson correctly, he'd died during the Civil War. He looked at all of us and gave a short nod. "What can I help you with?"

"We were wondering if you could take us to Shipton Harbor, Maine," I asked and Olivia nodded.

Then Olivia said, "Wait. Shipton doesn't have a train station."

Captain smirked and winked at her, not that she could see him. "I don't need a station. But you are aware you'll have to jump."

"Yeah, we're aware." I wasn't happy about it, but what other option did we have?

"All right, then. Next stop...well, next slowdown will be Shipton Harbor."

CHAPTER EIGHTEEN

We pulled up to a train station. Or at least I thought it was a station. Captain said he didn't need a station, but maybe he'd meant not a real one. He made his own? Squinting, I tried to make out the sign, but we passed it too fast.

"Okay," Captain said. "We'll work together to slow this thing down, but we can't stop it. You need to get ready to jump."

"Question." Drew held up one finger. "Will jumping off the train take us off this ghostly plane?"

Captain arched an eyebrow. "No idea. Come now, we're getting close."

"This way." Peter ushered us toward the back of the car, where a door waited. I was sure that door had not been there moments ago. He opened it. "Now, I'm going to help them slow the train down. You guys get ready to jump when Captain yells."

He disappeared. "Bye," I called. "It was nice to meet you, Peter."

Peter reappeared for a split second. "Nice to meet you, too, Ava. I hope we meet again someday."

"How do they slow down the train?" Olivia whispered.

We didn't have time to ask, though, because suddenly the car shook and slowed enough that it nearly took us off our feet.

"Steady, men!" Captain yelled, steering the train closer to the station. I began to recognize Main Street in Shipton, but there'd never been a train station in town for as long as I'd lived there.

"We have a train station?" Drew asked, looking bewildered.

"This whole trip is nuts," Olivia muttered, then broke out into a huge grin. "I love it!"

I laughed. She would. I swore the only reason she liked me so much was *because* my life was crazy.

Drew chuckled. "At least Luci didn't zap us anywhere." He shuddered. "That was the worst."

"Get ready," Captain called. "Almost time."

The train slowed even more. We grabbed our bags. "Throw your luggage," Captain said.

Drew threw them one at a time onto the wooden walkway lining the train station.

"Now!" Captain yelled. "We can't hold it much longer!"

Holding out his hand, Drew turned toward me. But it turned out the ghosts had done a great job of slowing the train down. I was able to just hop off and skip forward a little bit before stopping. I turned to find Olivia and Sam already off and Drew stepped foot on the walkway just in time for the train to take off like a shot.

It blurred as it went by, but I spotted Peter waving from a window as it rocketed off into the darkness.

"Well," Olivia said. "We're still on a ghostly plane."

As soon as the train was out of sight, the train station disappeared. We landed on the concrete sidewalk of Shipton with a thump, right in front of Imaginary Homes Bookstore, where Owen and I worked part-time.

"We gotta find out if that train station was ever actually there," Olivia said as she looked around.

"The sun's almost up." Drew looked down Main Street. "But you're right. We didn't come out of the ghostly plane."

He was right. Everything was still dull and almost greyed out. I extended my magic to see what I could figure out, but it didn't feel a hundred percent right. "Yeah, we're still ghostly."

We turned in a circle, looking around at each other and the town. "Can anyone see us?" I asked.

Whistling along the sidewalk, the owner of Peachy Sweets, our local—and delicious—bakery where Olivia got her sweets every morning, walked around the building, jingling her keys.

"Hey," Olivia said. "Kelly!"

But Kelly didn't hear her. On light feet, Olivia crossed the road and stood directly in Kelly's path.

And Kelly walked through her.

"Ahh!" Olivia screeched. "That tickled!" She hurried back over and tucked herself in Sam's arms. "Not in a good way. I don't want to be dead anymore."

"You're not dead." I giggled. "None of us are. We're just in an alternate reality, I think."

"Now what?" Drew asked. "How do we get out of this reality and back to our own?"

"Let's get back to the house." I started down Main Street in the direction of Winston. "Owen will be able to see us. He can call the coven and we'll figure out how to come through."

With a sigh, Olivia followed. "I can't see what else we can do." She sniffled. "This was fun at first, but now I'm kind of freaked out. What if I never see Sammie again?"

I looped my arm through hers. "You will. Don't worry."

We started walking with the guys following, and then I

spotted Clint exiting his car. "Oh, I forgot. He's doing inventory this week and coming in several hours early."

An evil thought crossed my mind. We could have a little fun while no one could see us. "Want to lift your spirits?" I asked, nudging Olivia.

Olivia looked at me with narrowed eyes, suspicious. "What are you thinking?"

Stepping forward, first I tested to make sure Clint couldn't see me. When none of my silly faces I made got a response from him, I giggled. Then, I followed him into the store.

Olivia was stuck outside, though, because he shut the door before she could slip through. As he walked toward the back of the stacks, I focused on trying to unlock the door, but couldn't because my hand slipped right through it. "Oh." I laughed. "Just walk through."

Olivia, Sam, and Drew walked through the bookstore's glass front door. I laughed some more. This was going to be fun.

"If we're going to mess with Clint," Drew said. "The thing is, how? We can't touch anything, and he can't hear us."

That was a valid point. "Let's see if that old movie from the early nineties holds up. The more we focus, maybe we can move stuff in this world."

He rolled his eyes but then chuckled. "What else do we have to do?"

"Yeah," Sam added. "Plus, if we succeed it'll be hilarious."

Clint walked back to the front with a pile of books in his hand. He set them on the counter.

Focusing on the top book, I tried to touch it. I pushed my index finger into the book, and it really went into it. The book didn't move. Dang it. Olivia sidled up next to me and tried. And failed.

"Focus," Sam encouraged. "Envision yourself touching the book."

We both kept trying, but our hands passed through the book. Crud. That wasn't working.

"Why aren't we falling through the floor?" Drew asked. "There's a basement here, isn't there?"

I shook my head. "Not that I know of."

He stomped around, clomping his big boots on the floorboards. "Odd," he said. "Can I go upstairs?"

Drew gave a particularly strong stomp, and Clint heard it. My boss's head jerked up and he looked around in surprise. "Hello? Is anyone there?"

We all burst out laughing. "Drew, you've got the gift," I exclaimed. "Come try to move this book."

He stomped toward us. Clint didn't seem to hear each footfall, but he did some of them. And the ones he did hear were effective enough. He backed away from the counter until he had his back pressed against the far shelf.

"Hello?" Clint whispered as he leaned so far back, he nearly knocked over the coffee maker.

"Hello!" I yelled.

Nothing.

Olivia joined in as Drew worked on trying to move the book. Sam moved forward and tried as well, while Olivia and I jumped and waved our arms, yelling and screaming.

He heard one of us because Clint stiffened again with wild eyes. "Hello?" he said weakly. "Is someone playing a prank on me?"

Just then, Sam succeeded in moving the book. It didn't go far, just over a few inches. It wasn't even enough to knock it off the stack.

But it was enough for Clint to see. Throwing his hands in the air, he yelled throatily and ran through me—yuck. Olivia was right. It was a disgusting feeling—and toward the back.

Snickering, we watched him go. "Was that mean?" I asked.

Olivia and Sam held each other up while Drew wiped tears

of laughter from his eyes. "If it was," he said through his chuckles, "then we're all mean."

Olivia waved her hand at me as she calmed down. "He'll be fine. He'll convince himself he imagined the whole thing."

She turned toward the door. "Come on. Let's head on to the house."

We walked down Main Street for a little while before seeing another person. It was just too early for many people to be out and about.

"You guys give *me* a hard time about causing trouble." Luci's voice made us all freeze and turn around. He stood in front of the grocery store's roadside sign, leaning against it with his arms crossed. "But you just put me to shame." He shook his head. "You try to send me to Hell for having a little fun, but you guys take *one* trip to the in-between, and look at the lot of you." He tsked his tongue. "Shameful."

"Oh, lighten up." I waved my hand at him and kept walking. "You're no fun."

"Excuse me." Luci hurried forward. "I am *nothing* but fun." He wiggled in between me and Drew. "Want me to pop you home?"

"No," Drew said quickly. "I puked for days last time."

Luci shrugged. "Suit yourselves."

"This is all your fault, anyway," I said, supremely irritated with the devil. "You caused this. Do you care to explain why?"

Sticking his nose in the air, Luci shook his head. "No, I do not care to, thank you very much."

He looked like he was about to disappear, but Olivia shouted his name. "Hey, Luci!"

Blinking slowly, he turned. "Olive, isn't it?"

She scowled. "You know my name."

With a laugh, Luci winked roguishly at her. "Of course. What can I do for you?"

"Can you get us out of the in-between?" she asked. "We're

still not sure exactly how we got in, but we're going to need to get back to normal."

He hummed low in his throat and eyed Drew and me. "I think some of you do know how you got here. But, no, I won't help you."

He stopped and spread his arms, then bowed. "Not yet anyway."

And with that, the devil disappeared.

I sighed. My feet were starting to hurt. And we'd forgotten to find our bags. Would they be moved to the real world since they came from it? Or were they lost here forever?

I had no idea.

CHAPTER NINETEEN

By the time we got to my driveway, I'd had enough. It was full daylight, finally. We trudged up the driveway—well, I trudged. Olivia seemed a bit tired, too, but Drew and Sam were bright-eyed and bushy-tailed. Of course.

But then, they stayed in pretty good shape for their job. Me staying in shape for my job meant keeping my fingers limber. And my magic.

As we crossed the lawn, Snooze walked around the house. He stopped and stared then heaved a big, irritated kitty breath before continuing on his way. A few seconds later, before we even got to the front porch, Lucy-Fur, his new girlfriend, trotted around. "There you are," she called. I'd healed her and animated her and now she could talk.

Snooze turned around and glared at her.

Uh-oh. Was my Mr. Snoozerton having regrets about keeping his girlfriend around?

Snoozer yowled at her, lifted his tail and twitched it, and kept walking.

"You haven't gotten out of talking to me like that, you know," Lucy-Fur yelled as we watched on.

She turned and noticed us, then gave the tiniest hiss. "What are you fools looking at?"

We all shook our heads and watched the little, long-haired white cat stalk back around to the back of the house.

"So, I guess we're not sneaking up on Snoozer, then?" Sam said, snickering.

"Yeah, we're sort of ghosts to them. And they can see ghosts." I watched the little kitty turn the corner as an idea popped into my head. "Lucy! Wait, please."

The slender, white feline sighed as she stopped.

"Lucy?" I asked.

She didn't look my way. As she stared off into the distance, I waited for her to acknowledge me.

"Uhmmm." I glanced back at Olivia, Drew, and Sam in time to see Wade's truck turn up the driveway, hauling the rental trailer. I wasn't sure what had taken them so long to get here. And where was Wade now that the sun was out? But I had a question to ask Lucy. "Hey," I called. "Snobby cat?"

She sat on her haunches and licked her front paw. "Yes?"

"You can see ghosts, right?" I scrambled forward and dropped to my knees in front of her. "You can see me?"

She sighed, which came out a bit hiss-like, and finally looked at me. "Yeah? So?"

"Have you seen a blonde woman? She'd look younger than me. It's my mother. She died when I was a kid."

Instead of answering me, she bowed her head and then proceeded to hack up a hairball. It was gross and disturbing.

She sniffed the brown ball disdainfully, then got to her feet. "No. I haven't seen a blonde ghost. Are we done?" Without waiting for me to reply, she sauntered away.

"Argh," I muttered. I couldn't follow her, not when Wallie was parking the truck right by the front door.

Owen and Alfred came out the front door, smiling at Wallie and Zoey, but then the four of us turned and walked closer. When the rest of our family noticed us, their collective jaws dropped.

Larry came hurrying out of the house, his gaze glued to the little tiger ghoul. "Zoey! I'm so happy you're ba—" At that point, he also noticed us. "Ah, my holy shit. Are you guys dead?"

We all rushed forward, denying his question. "No," I called. "We're just stuck here!"

Wallie ran full tilt around the truck. "Mom, what happened?" He looked panicked.

"Don't worry," I said as I rushed toward my son. "I'm not dead, I swear!"

"Then what's going on?" Zoey asked. Larry had descended the stairs and they held hands as they walked toward us with Owen to get the whole story.

"Where is Wade?" I asked. "And what took you guys so long to get here?"

Wallie shook his head. "No, no. You guys first."

"Ah, yeah, we somehow got on this ghost train," Drew said. "And we're still stuck on the ghostly plane."

I very carefully didn't look at Drew, but Olivia noticed me as I purposefully didn't notice Drew. Her eyes narrowed. I rushed forward and grabbed Wallie's arm. "Where is Wade?" I asked, pushing the subject of how we got into the ghost world to the side.

"We got a flat," Wallie said. He pointed to the truck. "That's the spare. Full-size spare, luckily. But it put us behind. When the sky started to lighten, we were still a good hour away, so we put Wade in the trailer. He's under a blanket and out cold. We'll have to leave him there until it gets dark."

That was unfortunate. Poor Wade. He was going to wake with a stiff neck.

Chortling, I got my own inner joke. Stiff. Cause he was dead. As a vampire. I was a hoot.

"Come on in the house," Owen said. "Alfred made breakfast."

Olivia and I exchanged a glance. "Can we even eat?" I asked.

She shrugged. "We can try. But I doubt it."

We traipsed into the house. It was nice to be home, but everything was still so subdued. Like looking at it all through a smokescreen. I wanted to *actually* be home. To go to bed for like a week in my Shipton bed. In Winston, as weird as that sounded.

"Okay, so what's the plan for Wade?" I asked. "Where can we put him?" We'd pretty much run out of rooms.

"I guess I'll give up my office," I said. I hated to do that. The only way I got anything written was to lock myself in there and put on music and completely ignore the rest of the insanity I called home.

"No, Mom, you can't do that," Wallie said. "I'll just give him my room. I'm not here all the time, anyway."

We sat for a minute as Olivia, and I tried to pick up cups of tea Alfred had set in front of each of us.

Didn't work.

With a sigh of exasperation and a grumble from my stomach, I gave up and sat back. "I want to echo Drew's earlier question. How can I sit in this chair but not fall through it, yet can't grab the teacup?"

Nobody answered.

"We could convert the living room into a bedroom," Olivia said. She didn't live here, but she was here often enough to think she had a vote.

Heck, I didn't mind her voting. "That could work. We can entertain in the kitchen."

Owen shook his head. "No, we need somewhere to hold coven meetings."

Drew held up a finger. "Won't he need somewhere light tight?"

Oh, darn. We lapsed into silence, trying to figure it out. "Maybe we can rent a house nearby?" I asked.

Wallie snapped his finger. "The basement! We'll renovate it. I mean, we have magic. We can even dig out and give him his own entrance so it's like a little apartment down there."

Nodding, I grinned at my son. "I love that idea."

Everyone seemed in agreement, so I slapped my hand down on the table. It went right through the wood. "It's agreed. We'll renovate the basement."

The house began to rumble under our feet. Everyone jumped up and looked around in a bit of a panic. "Is that an earthquake?" I asked.

But then the wall behind the table began to... There was no other way to explain it. It grew.

"What is happening?" Drew asked, his voice shaking from the vibrations in the house. The shaking intensified, nearly taking me off my feet. Drew threw his arms around me and helped steady me. "Thanks," I whispered as the rumbling quieted.

We all took stock of the room. "This room is bigger." I studied the wall. "And looks kind of great. Where else?"

"I'll look downstairs," Sam said.

Wallie pointed upstairs. "I'll check up."

I peeked out and studied the deck. It was definitely a lot longer. When I turned around, Sam was emerging from the basement stairs. "Uh, it's exactly like we described it." He scratched his head. "With the walkout and everything. Winston even dug out a little dirt path leading up to the basement door."

Wallie bounded down the stairs. "There's an extra bedroom upstairs on either side of the hall!"

Larry grinned broadly. "Yes! Finally, I can stop sharing with Alfred."

As we exchanged amazed glances, Lucy ambled in the open back door. "Hey, you were asking about a blonde ghost?"

I nodded. "Yeah?"

She stopped and licked her paw four times before licking her lips, *then* speaking. "She's out back."

CHAPTER TWENTY

We bolted out the back door. Everyone let me go first, but I got the sense that they were all fighting behind me, each of them trying to get out first. It occurred to me that Sam, Olivia, and Drew could just go through the walls, but I didn't wait to see what they did. I just kept going.

As soon as I hit the deck, I saw her. She stood out by the cliffs, staring at the ocean with her blonde hair billowing on the breeze. "Mom," I whispered.

She was too far away to have heard me, yet she turned to face me when I said her name. I ran as fast as I could toward her.

The ghost world, the in-between, whatever it was called, didn't save me from being a little too heavy and a little too old to be running full tilt. I was going to regret these shin splints later. As I hurried across the grass, I lamented the fact that I couldn't heal myself. Stupid obscure magical rule I didn't understand. Zoey had healed me while in tiger form. Maybe that would work again.

"Oh, Ava," Mom said as I reached her.

This time, we were on the same plane and this time, I knew if I touched her, I could make her solid. I flew into her arms with a cry of relief to finally be in my mother's embrace after all these years.

"How are you here?" I asked with my face buried in her hair. "Why are you in this place?"

"I'm trapped here, but I'm not sure why." Mom looked around as if looking for something or someone.

Trapped? In the in-between? "I don't understand." Then I knew. Or I had a guess. It had something to do with the curse that killed her. Bevan Magnus had hated my mother enough to add a little something extra in her curse. Like a restless afterlife.

"Darling, I'm being stalked here. I can't stay in one place for too long." She looked around worriedly. "You've got to get out of here. You're lucky it hasn't found you yet."

Pulling back, I grabbed her shoulders and looked into her green eyes. "What is it? What's stalking you? I might be able to stop it. I'm actually here, physically. I can do magic, I think." I'd been practicing defensive and offensive magic with Owen and the coven. Not as much as I would've liked, but hopefully I was strong enough to make up for what I didn't know.

But Mom shook her head. "No, it's too strong. You can't defeat it, Ava. Not yet anyway." She stiffened. "No. Run, Ava! It's here!"

Mom looked out toward the ocean, and gliding over the water was a huge, sickly black blob. Squinting, I tried to make it out as it came closer, but I couldn't figure it out. Every time my mind focused on it, it shifted, like an unnatural liquid that flew over the water.

"What the hell?" Drew whispered from behind me. I jumped, startled. I hadn't realized he was there.

"What is it?" Wallie said. He was a few feet behind, looking around wildly. "I can see Grandma, but what are you guys looking at?"

I pointed to the ocean, where the enormous black... thing... was coming closer. "You can't see that?"

Wallie shook his head. "No. And hi, Grandma. It's nice to meet you."

My mother smiled softly at Wallie. "And you, my boy. I'm so proud of you, Wallie. So glad to have you as a grandson."

Turning her attention back to the approaching threat, Mom blanched. "Honey, get out of here. It can't hurt you in your world. But it can hurt you here. You must go."

"What is it?" I cried. "I don't know how to get out, so I've got to fight it."

We backed up as it neared, and still, my eyes didn't want to focus on it. Mom moved in front of me, but I yanked her backward and prepared my magic. "Wallie?" I called. "Can you still not see it?"

It had arrived. It loomed over us, enormous, liquidy, and ever-changing, ever-moving.

"No, Mom, I got nothing."

A black tendril reached out toward me, like the tentacle of an octopus, searching for something to snatch toward its mouth.

"Owen, Wallie, blast right above us!" I backed up from the tentacle and raised my arm. "Everyone else, touch me so I can draw on your power!"

I felt hands on my back, so I raised my arms and gathered my magic, both my earth power and that rich darkness that gave me power over the dead. I waited until the big black thing was very close, gathering power and drawing from Drew and even Sam and Olivia. They were human, but they still had power, they just couldn't tap into it.

When the ball of energy was as big as I could get it, and the black tendril was nearly at me, I released the magic, hurling it at the center of the mass as hard as I could, screaming my frustration with it.

The magic hit the blob but instead of going into it, hurting it, it smacked against it and barreled back toward us. I had just enough time to gasp out two words before it hit us. "Mom! Run!"

Everything went dark. I knew I was unconscious, oddly. But I couldn't bring myself back to the awareness, return to consciousness.

What felt like hours later, I managed to swim to the surface of my mind. Forcing my eyes open, I squinted against the bright sunshine.

"Mom, wake up!" Wallie yelled. "Please wake up."

"Oof," I grunted. He was leaning on my chest. "Get off."

"Oh, thank goodness." The weight on my boobs lifted as I cracked my eyes open.

"What happened," I whispered.

"You came flying out of that ghost world like you'd been hit with your magic," Owen said as I squinted at him.

"I'm in the real world?"

"Yes, and I have questions." This was Luci. When had he gotten here? I jerked my head around to find him peering down at me with an interested look on his face. "Now that you're home. How did you get to the in-between, really? And how did you get out?"

I shot him a glare and turned to find my friends. Were they okay? I felt like I'd been run over by a semi-truck.

All three of them laid behind me. Olivia was pretty much on top of Sam, both of them face-up. Drew was face-down a few feet away. I hurried over and put one hand on each of Sam and Olivia, pushing magic into them until they began to blink and moan. If they were injured, I could help more, but for now, I crawled over to Drew and pushed my healing magic into him, as well.

Once he began to wake, I sat back and rested a minute, giving the three of them time to get their bearings. "Anybody need healing?" I asked once they looked at me owlishly, looking as confused as I felt.

"Ava," Luci said insistently. "How did you do it?"

"Do what?" I asked, irritated at his questioning. I looked up at Owen, ignoring the devil. "Did you see where my mom went?" I asked. "Did it get her?"

Owen shook his head. "You yelled for her to run and she disappeared, but I never saw what you were fighting. What did it look like?"

I mouthed at him silently. "I don't even know how to explain it."

"It was enormous," Olivia said.

"Like a gigantic blob of liquid ink," Drew added.

Sam shuddered. "Unnatural. Evil."

Luci's eyes flashed. "I've never heard of such a thing. Tell me how you got there and how you got back, and I'll help you."

I thought about what had happened at the precise moment we crossed over from the real train to the ghost train. Then I glared at Luci. "It was some sort of big magical surge," I said. "It had to be. That's how we got back out. I gathered all that magic, surely you saw that part?"

He nodded. "Yes, but how did you get *in*?"

Straightening my spine, I sniffed and climbed to my feet. "That's none of your business," I said stiffly. "Now, leave us. I want to try to find my mother."

Everyone else stood with me and we stretched and tried to get our bearings. My magic had literally bounced off of the inky blob, so it was still in the ghost world with my mom, tracking her. Why? I wasn't sure. Deep down, I knew it had something to do with how she died, but I had no idea how to stop it. But I would. And I would help my mom find peace.

"Let's go call a coven meeting," I said. "Owen, maybe you can reach out to any necromancers you know?"

He nodded. "Of course. There aren't many of us, but maybe they've had experience with ghosts before. We can ask."

"Luci," I said sharply.

He arched an eyebrow at me. "Yes?"

"Tell me about that place. What's the big deal about it?" I stared at him until he sighed.

"It's called the in-between. It's where souls go when they die but refuse to pass on." He rolled his eyes. "And I've never been able to get in there."

"Why did you set it up for us to be on that train?" I asked.

Luci grinned wickedly. "That was a particularly genius plan of mine. I'd been told by other, shall we say, informants, that the ghost train would be passing near that train line. The ghosts have a bit of a network thing going on, and I happened to know there was a ghost near Philly that was supposed to be picked up."

"A ghost that, what?" Olivia asked. "They didn't say anything about picking up ghosts."

Luci gave her a dry look. "How do you think there are so many ghosts on the train?"

Olivia shrugged and we exchanged a glance. I hadn't thought about it either. "We haven't exactly had time to go over all this stuff in detail."

Luci waved his hand. "Anyway, I want you to do whatever you did and help get me on the ghostly plane. It sounds like a kick. And maybe I can help you with your big blobby thing." He wiggled his eyebrows at me. "What do you say?"

I couldn't stop my gaze from drifting to Drew.

He looked like he'd swallowed a frog.

"I say no!" I said quickly. "Me getting there was a case of being at the right place at the right time. I can't just..." Oh, it was so hard not to look at Drew. "Do that again."

Luci's shoulders slumped. "You're going to have to try, aren't you? Gotta save mommy dearest. When you figure it out, let me know? I'll help in exchange for a ride in and out of that realm."

I narrowed my eyes at him. "What is so—" but he snapped his fingers and disappeared.

With a sigh, I turned toward the ocean in the distance, in the direction of where I'd seen my mom both times. "Mom, if you can hear me, I'll come for you. Just keep safe from that thing. I'll get you out of there."

Sniffling, I sank into Drew's arms and let him guide me back toward the house. As we reached the deck stairs, a big thump drew my attention. Snoozer was in front of Alfred, trying his darndest to jump up and grab Alfred's string, the one threading his mouth together.

Alfred kept pushing him away, but it was like Snooze was a kitty obsessed. He kept trying, thumping back down on the deck when Alfred pushed him. This happened several times.

"Wallie, get that fat cat," I said. "Tell him to leave Alfie alone."

But as Wallie reached for the big idiot feline, it happened.

Snoozer's claw caught the edge of the string and stuck. And as the oversized kitty fell back to the deck, the string came with him, yanking Alfred forward as his mouth unthreaded. He grunted low in his throat. Oh, geez, I hoped it didn't hurt.

Apparently, it did. As the string's end tugged through the stitch marks, his grunt turned into a high-pitched squeal.

And then it was out. Snooze sat back on his haunches and licked his paw, looking particularly proud of himself.

My jaw dropped as Alfred opened his mouth for the first time and spoke. "Snoozer, you're a complete asshole and you always have been!"

Everyone gasped.

It was a female voice!

"Aunt..." I clutched my chest, shocked to my core. "Aunt Winnie?"

WE ARE SO sorry about the cliffy! There's just so much you guys are going to LOVE and most of it is coming in an Animated Midlife. We'll be hard at work to get it out for you ASAP!

IF YOU'D LIKE to read more about Hailey and the vamps across the street, check out Fanged After Forty: Bitten in the Midlife. Hailey's going to think her new neighborhood really *sucks*.

IF YOU HAVEN'T ALREADY CHECKED, BE sure to head on over to www.instagram.com/shiptonghoul. **insert cheezy grin here**

AN ANIMATED MIDLIFE

WITCHING AFTER FORTY

PROLOGUE

"Mom, wake up!" Wallie yelled. "Please wake up."

"Oof," I grunted. He was leaning on my chest. "Get off."

"Oh, thank goodness." The weight on my boobs lifted as I cracked my eyes open.

"What happened," I whispered.

"You came flying out of that ghost world like you'd been hit with your magic," Owen said as I squinted at him.

"I'm in the real world?"

"Yes, and I have questions." This was Luci. When had he gotten here? I jerked my head around to find him peering down at me with an interested look on his face. "Now that you're home. How did you get to the Inbetween, really? And how did you get out?"

I shot him a glare and turned to find my friends. Were they okay? I felt like I'd been run over by a semi-truck.

All three of them laid behind me. Olivia was pretty much on top of Sam, both of them face-up. Drew was face-down a few feet away. I hurried over and put one hand on each of Sam and Olivia, pushing magic into them until they began to blink and moan. If they were injured, I could help more, but for now, I crawled over to Drew and pushed my healing magic into him, as well.

Once he began to wake, I sat back and rested a minute, giving the three of them time to get their bearings. "Anybody need healing?" I asked once they looked at me owlishly, looking as confused as I felt.

"Ava," Luci said insistently. "How did you do it?"

"Do what?" I asked, irritated at his questioning. I looked up at Owen, ignoring the devil. "Did you see where my mom went?" I asked. "Did it get her?"

Owen shook his head. "You yelled for her to run and she disappeared, but I never saw what you were fighting. What did it look like?"

I mouthed at him silently. "I don't even really know how to explain it."

"It was enormous," Olivia said.

"Like a gigantic blob of liquid ink," Drew added.

Sam shuddered. "Unnatural. Evil."

Luci's eyes flashed. "I've never heard of such a thing. Tell me how you got there and how you got back, and I'll help you."

I thought about what had happened at the precise moment we crossed over from the real train to the ghost train. Then I glared at Luci. "It was some sort of big magical surge," I said. "It had to be. That's how we got back out. I gathered all that magic, surely you saw that part?"

He nodded. "Yes, but how did you get *in*?"

Straightening my spine, I sniffed and climbed to my feet. "That's none of your business," I said stiffly. "Now, leave us. I want to try to find my mother."

Everyone else stood up with me and we stretched and tried to gather our senses. My magic had literally bounced off of the inky blob, so it was still in the ghost world with my mom, tracking her. Why? I wasn't sure. Deep down, I knew it had something to do with how she died, but I had no idea how to stop it. But I would. And I would help my mom find peace.

"Let's go call a coven meeting," I said. "Owen, maybe you can reach out to any necromancers you know?"

He nodded. "Of course. There aren't many of us, but maybe they've had experience with ghosts before. We can ask."

"Luci," I said sharply.

He arched an eyebrow at me. "Yes?"

"Tell me about that place. What's the big deal about it?" I stared at him until he sighed.

"It's called the Inbetween. It's where souls go when they die but refuse to pass on." He rolled his eyes. "And I've never been able to get in there."

"Why did you set it up for us to be on that train?" I asked.

Luci grinned wickedly. "That was a particularly genius plan of mine. I'd been told by other, shall we say, informants, that the ghost train would be passing near that train line. The ghosts have a bit of a network thing going on, and I happened to know there was a ghost near Philly that was supposed to be picked up."

"A ghost that, what?" Olivia asked. "They didn't say anything about picking up ghosts."

Luci gave her a dry look. "How do you think there are so many ghosts on the train?"

Olivia shrugged and we exchanged a glance. I hadn't thought about it either. "We haven't exactly had time to go over all this stuff in detail."

Luci waved his hand. "Anyway, I want you to do whatever you did and help get me on the ghostly plane. It sounds like a kick. And maybe I can help you with your big blobby thing." He wiggled his eyebrows at me. "What do you say?"

I couldn't stop my gaze from drifting to Drew.

He looked like he'd swallowed a frog.

"I say no!" I said quickly. "Me getting there was a case of being at the right place at the right time. I can't just..." Oh, it was so hard not to look at Drew. "Do that again."

Luci's shoulders slumped. "Well, you're going to have to try, aren't you? Gotta save mommy dearest. When you figure it out, let me know? I'll help in exchange for a ride in and out of that realm."

I narrowed my eyes at him. "What is so—" but he snapped his fingers and disappeared.

With a sigh, I turned toward the ocean in the distance, in the direction of where I'd seen my mom both times. "Mom, if you can hear me, I'll come for you. Just keep safe from that thing. I'll get you out of there."

Sniffling, I sank into Drew's arms and let him guide me back toward the house. As we reached the deck stairs, a big thump drew my attention. Snoozer was in front of Alfred, trying his darndest to jump up and grab Alfred's string, the one threading his mouth together.

Alfred kept pushing him away, but it was like Snooze was a kitty obsessed. He kept trying, thumping back down on the deck when Alfred pushed him. This happened several times.

"Wallie, get that fat cat," I said. "Tell him to leave Alfie alone."

But as Wallie reached for the big idiot feline, it happened.

Snoozer's claw caught the edge of the string and stuck. And as the oversized kitty fell back to the deck, the string came with him, yanking Alfred forward as his mouth unthreaded. He grunted low in his throat. Oh, geez, I hoped it didn't hurt.

Apparently, it did. As the string's end tugged through the stitch marks, his grunt turned into a high-pitched squeal.

And then it was out. Snooze sat back on his haunches and licked his paw, looking particularly proud of himself.

My jaw dropped as Alfred opened his mouth for the first

time and spoke. "Snoozer, you're a complete asshole, and you always have been!"

Everyone gasped.

It was a female voice!

"Aunt..." I clutched my chest, shocked to my core. "Aunt Winnie?"

CHAPTER ONE

"Winnie?" I staggered forward, staring at Alfred's dry, cracked lips and completely bamboozled that my Aunt Winifred's voice had come out of it. "How?" I gasped.

That crazy fat cat had finally done it. He'd removed the string from Alfred's lips and my aunt's voice had come out.

Alfred looked down at Snoozer again and hissed. Snooze stood, twitched his tail, and walked slowly through the door into the kitchen.

This was impossible. My aunt was dead. I'd gone to her funeral, mourned for her, and carried her ashes home in an antique silver urn that had been blessed by the coven. How in the H-E-double hockey sticks was she inside a ghoul's body?

At my side, Drew rubbed circles on my back but wisely didn't comment. He was probably rethinking the whole dating a crazy necromancer. I was definitely rethinking being one. I hadn't signed up for any of this. It wasn't in the plan.

Alfred shuffled forward. Winnie did... no, the ghoul named Alfred with Winnie's voice shuffled forward. I tensed, watching him...her intensely as she spoke again. "Oh, honey. I wanted to tell you. There's so much you need to know."

Oh, this was freaky. Alfred reached out a hand, and somehow I knew if the skin on his, uh, her face could move, Winnie would've looked remorseful.

Sam inched his way toward the door. "I'm going to go get Sammie from Grandma and Papa."

Before I could demand that he stay, he disappeared into the house. Great. Coward!

I stared at Olivia with my brows raised, wondering if she too was about to desert me.

She grinned. "I'm staying. This is better than the town gossip at the hair salon."

I rolled my eyes and almost told her to make popcorn and pull up a chair so she could enjoy it in comfort. But I refrained from being snarky with my BFF. I was tired. And grumpy. And in shock.

Focusing back on Winnie-Alfred, I asked, "So, who is Alfred? Was it ever him or was it always you?"

They dropped their hand. That was easier. Alfred-Winnie would be they...for now, at least.

"He's in here, too," they said in the female voice. Winnie said it like it was common knowledge. Which it was not. I didn't know a thing about my dead aunt being raised in the body of a ghoul.

I held up my hand. "I need so many explanations."

I was so glad Drew still had a hold of me because my behind would be on the floor.

They turned toward the house. "Well, sit. I'll make breakfast while I explain. I need something to do with my hands." Of course. Why wouldn't they need to keep busy?

We all gathered in the kitchen, every eye trained on the ghoul. My entire family pressed against my back. My blood and not my blood, but still, all family.

If my eyes had been closed, I could've imagined it was really Winnie moving around, making pancakes and sausages. It had been all along. That broke my heart because I wanted nothing more than to run to her and wrap my arms around her. But I wasn't doing it with her in Alfred's body. Assuming that was Alfred's body and not some other random guy. Oh, this was too much. I needed a drink. A good stiff one. Was it late enough for whiskey?

"That's why Alfred's pancakes taste like Winnie's," I whispered, dropping down into a chair at the table. "I just figured you'd found her recipe."

They shook their head. "If you'd asked, I had a recipe all prepared to show you. I was a bit nervous that it would give me away, though."

Yeah, it might have. Then again I'd been so busy with all the craziness going around. Training to raise the dead. Searching for dead children so I could shut down an illegal shifter fighting ring. Not to mention dealing with my new neighbor, Satan, aka Luci.

"I have unfinished business," Winnie said as I closed my eyes again so I didn't have to see her voice coming out of Alfred's lips. And how was her voice so clear when his dried-out mouth wouldn't possibly bend enough to allow them to really enunciate?

Another entry for the weird as heck file, alongside *all* my questions about Larry.

"But how'd you get in this body?" Olivia asked, taking the seat next to me at the table. Wallie sat silently beside her, still staring at Alfred in shock.

Drew sat on my other side and remained quiet as he watched and listened to the family drama unfolding.

A few seconds later Zoey and Larry took a seat beside Owen. Neither one said a word, just watched Alfred-Winnie make breakfast with wide eyes.

"Well, when I died, I haunted Bill until he agreed to raise me. But he wasn't the most powerful necromancer. Because I had been cremated, instead of my own body being raised, I was shoved into Alfred and we both came up." They shrugged and continued to cook.

Yeah, no big deal. They both came up.

Geez. Maybe I was a little shocky.

Bill, William Combs, had been a family friend and a necromancer. He'd died back in October, not long after I got into town. No, before you think that, I didn't kill him. A rogue hunter by the name of Carmen who hated necromancers had. She'd also tried to kill Owen. That was how we met and how he became my mentor, friend, and roommate.

"But, he could've fixed you. And why didn't you tell me?" I asked.

"Bill? No, he couldn't have. He wasn't nearly strong enough." They waved one hand at me dismissively. "Unfinished business. I was afraid you'd get in the way."

Me? Get in the way? The way of what? She was being very dismissive of this. This was a huge freaking deal! "What's your unfinished business?" I watched them put the first pancake in the hot pan, casual as you please.

"That's for me to deal with," they said. They turned and pointed the spatula at me. "But I tell you what, if you could figure out how to get me into my body, that'd be great. I saw what you did with Larry. He looks normal now! I want that."

Blinking rapidly, my mind whirled with possibilities. Could I do that? Could I make a body out of her ashes? Winnie's cremains were on the mantel in the living room, beside my mother and Yaya. What could I do with them? Was I *that* good? "I wouldn't begin to know how to do it, though. With Larry, there'd already been a skeleton, like a guide." Like painting in a color-by-number kit.

They slid a pancake off the skillet and handed it to Wallie, who was closer to them. "Might as well start eating while they're hot." Then they glanced at me. "Bill has all kinds of spells like that in his office," they said.

"What about Alfred?" Zoey asked, ears just twitching away. "Can he talk?"

"Don't burn my pancakes," Winnie said in a stern voice. Then, they shook their head and looked around at us.

"It's very nice to meet all of you properly," Alfred said in a mouse-like, smoky voice. It was like a cartoon mouse trying to be sexy.

Weird.

It was all I could do not to burst out laughing, and I knew, beyond a shadow of a doubt, if I looked over at Olivia or Drew, or even the younger adults at the table, I'd lose it. I was too tired to keep it together. I was really surprised at my progress so far.

Don't look at them.

"Are you happy about this situation?" I asked him in a strangled voice. Hey, I managed not to giggle.

The ghoul flipped the pancake. "I'm not *un*happy. But I have to admit it would be nice to have my body back to myself. Perhaps if Winifred isn't inside me, you could restore me the way you have the others."

This was beginning to feel like I was going to have an army of ghouls that looked totally normal. Just another day in paradise. "I'm certainly willing to try," I told Alfred. "And I'm sorry that you're in this situation."

He handed Zoey a plate with a pancake on it and then poured more batter into the pan. "It's okay. I'll let you talk to your aunt again. Nice to meet you."

A few seconds later, they turned and looked at us. "So, are we going to get me my body?" Winnie asked.

"I guess," I said slowly. "But if I can make a body out of

cremains, what's stopping me from raising any and everyone I want to?" I asked no one in particular. "And further, if I can figure out how to pull your spirit out of Alfred's body and into your own, then I could move anyone around. I could make Olivia and Sam walk a day *literally* in one another's shoes."

Everyone snickered at that thought, even me.

"It doesn't work that way," Owen said. "Your power isn't limitless."

"Spirits at peace are untouchable," Winnie said as she flipped the pancake. "Only spirits in the Inbetween are accessible to necromancers."

"What about Larry?" I asked. "Where did he come from?"

"I was in the Inbetween," he said. "Not at peace. I had unfinished business."

Yes, Larry showed up at my door on Valentine's Day wanting me to find his killer. I was getting ready for my first date with Drew when someone knocked on the door. Imagine my surprise when I opened it to a skeleton who could talk.

Now he was fleshed out and looked like a normal young man in his early twenties. After I raised Snooze's girlfriend, Lucy-Fur and Larry saw that I healed her in the process, he asked me to try it on him. Make him a living being instead of an animated skeleton. And it had worked.

"Why am I so special?" I asked Winnie. "Do you know? Why am I able to have this many people raised without it draining my magic? Why do people keep telling me that I'm the most powerful necromancer in the world?"

I wasn't sure they used those exact words, but it sounded good.

WinFred-Alfred stopped and turned to look at me. "You're the last female witch of your bloodline on both sides. You have all the powers of your ancestors."

She said it like it was so simple, but I wasn't so sure it was.

There was always a price that came with power. I didn't want to owe any debts for something I hadn't asked for.

"Um, okay," Wallie said. "I get nothing?"

Winnie chuckled and shook her stiff head. "You get the same powers you would've had. But when the last female, me, died, the bulk of the Howe family power hit Ava. She already had her father's power, though suppressed by her own choosing. Now the Howe family power just intensifies it."

Wow. So that was why. It was nice to have an answer, finally.

"Men always get the short end of the stick," Wallie muttered.

With my eyebrows raised and my best *mom* expression on my face, I turned to give my son some pertinent information about being a woman, but Olivia took care of it.

She slapped him upside the back of the head. "Don't be an idiot, Wallie."

I went back to the problem at hand. "If I can raise you, put your ashes back together and give you a body... And I was able to pull Larry out of the Inbetween... Why couldn't I raise mom's ashes and pull her out?" I asked.

Winnie's eyes went sad. "We figured that out years ago. Bill and I tried. She's in the Inbetween, but something is holding her there. I was there with her briefly until Bill got me out. Beth has unfinished business, but something in the curse Bevin put on her holds her there."

We ran out of questions to ask, so we had breakfast, just thankful to be here with Winnie and to have a game plan and more information. My mind buzzed with new information while at the same time I found it hard to think with so little sleep. The trip home from Philly had taken longer than it needed to with being jerked onto a ghost train in the Inbetween. Jumping in and then out of the Inbetween had drained me.

"I'm exhausted," I said after I finished my pancakes. "I'm napping."

Oliva rose from her chair and patted my shoulder. "I'm going to snuggle my little Sammie. Call me when you wake up."

I nodded and rose to my feet, yawning as I followed her to the door. Drew was close on my heels. When I turned, I slammed into him. His arms circled my waist, and I leaned forward, resting my head against his chest. He smelled so good and was warm. I wanted to burrow myself into his arms and sleep.

Before I realized what was happening, he scooped me up in his arms and carried me to my room. Then he removed my shoes and tucked me under the covers before kissing my forehead. "I'm going to check in at the station and then go home for a nap of my own. Call me if you need anything?"

I rested my palm on his cheek and smiled sleepily at him. "Thank you for being so amazing." He really was the best.

He winked at me. "Any time."

Then he left, closing my bedroom door on his way out. I laid there, listening to his footsteps fade down the stairs. When the front door opened and shut, I closed my eyes.

Just as I was about to drift off to sleep, my phone rang. By the ringtone, was Melody, my second in command with the coven. What did she want? Did she have a tracker on me to tell her the exact moment I fell asleep?

I answered with a graveled, "Hello." At least I thought that was what I said.

"Hey, Ava, something strange is going on," she said. "We found something on the beach that you need to see."

"Okay," I said, too exhausted to do it now. "Can it wait like three hours?" I asked. That would be enough time for me to get a bit of energy back, at least.

She hesitated. "Yeah, I *think* so. Come down to where we like to do our rituals on the beach as soon as you can."

I hung up, sorry to make them wait, but I literally couldn't convince my eyes to stay open. I had to grab a little sleep. After cracking my lids enough to set an alarm, I was out.

CHAPTER TWO

Yawning, I made my way downstairs. A three-hour nap and long shower had been just the ticket. Well, almost. Fatigue still clung to me like a bad hangover, but I was upright and refreshed. At least for a little while anyway. Enough time to see what Melody wanted and then go back to bed.

Alfred... err, Winnie—one of them, anyway—held out a small cup. The dark rich aroma filled me with pleasure. I actually sighed.

"I thought you'd need a quick shot, so I made espresso instead of coffee." Winnie's voice. We were going to have to figure out how to tell when they were Winnie and when it was Alfred. This was going to get confusing real fast. Or maybe it was my tired mind not processing everything at the moment.

"Thanks." I started for the door and stopped and turned. "Can you have Owen or Wallie check on Wade? He's in the moving van still."

"Why is Wade in the van?" Both of them said at the same time. The mix of Winnie's soft, motherly voice and Alfred's mouse-like tone threw me. It was like a creepy stereo sound. I snorted and covered my mouth. The lack of sleep was making me loopy.

Under my feet, the floor timbered slightly, making me laugh more. Winston also thought the sound of them speaking at the same time was funny. After I stopped laughing, I blew out a breath and explained about Wade. "You know Clay's Uncle Wade?" Alfred-Winnie nodded. "Well, he was turned into a vampire when I was in Philly selling the house. I don't have time to go into the story right now. New vampires sleep while the sun is up. If he does wake, cover him with a blanket or something. I don't need to lose another family member."

If Wade did wake before the sun was down, he would probably be confused and step out of the van not realizing the sun was up. The thought gave me pause, and I almost turned around. Wallie was there, and I had to trust he'd take care of Wade. Plus, I didn't plan on being gone long.

I shook my head at Winnie, not wanting to explain any more than I had to at the moment. Winnie could be long-winded, and I didn't have time to catch up on how her afterlife was going. "I have to go. We'll talk more later."

I rushed out the door and down the steps, trying to hurry. Melody and whoever else from the coven were waiting on me. But I'd made them wait just another minute longer because I had to have two of Winnie's espressos. They were darn good.

It took me a few minutes to get down there. I wasn't walking as quickly as I would have hoped, given how tired I still was. All the activity and magic use lately had helped me tone up quite a bit but my poor body was just exhausted.

Several yards from the house, down a slope of large rocks, I stopped short. I was halfway down the path that led down the cliff to the beach.

Lucy-Fur sat on the path, staring at me. "Um, hello," I said.

"Why is there an undead creature in the back of your vehicle?" she asked. Lifting one paw, she licked the beans on the bottom of it once. "Why are there so many undead things around you?"

I kept walking, stepping carefully around the unpredictable white cat. "That is an explanation that would take far too long for right now. Ask me again another time."

"Okay," she said from behind me as I continued on down the beach. "But it's about to get worse."

How in the world did she know that? I shook my head and considered what a cat could possibly know about it as I hurried as fast as I could along the beach to a hidden alcove with a cave, where the coven liked to do rituals and spells. Some of the coven members often hung out there just for a fun beach day as well, since it was on my property and rarely did anyone else ever trespass. Plus, we had the place warded against nosy people. Humans would ignore the area. Paranormal beings would sense the magic and know it was a warning to stay away.

As I got close to the spot, I started to realize something was way off. There was a dark energy floating in the air that made the hairs on the back of my neck stand on end. Fish, crabs, birds, and all sorts of different plant life had washed up on the shore.

It was an eerie sight. Closer to the woods, one of the trees was all of a sudden drooping. The last time I was down here, it was *not* like that. Even though I spied Melody, Cade, and Leena near the cave, I moved closer to peer at the tree. There was a black tar-like substance on it. Oh, no.

They joined me at the tree. "What is that?" Melody asked.

"I have no idea," I answered. "But it reminds me of something I saw last night." It looked like the black blob from inside the Inbetween. My gut twisted and my intuition screamed that this wasn't a good thing.

"What do you think it is?" Cade asked.

I didn't have any answers I was willing to share right now. I especially wasn't going to tell them that I might have been the one to let this evil out. Damn it.

But I had to trust someone. Who could I trust in the coven with information about my mother? Should I involve them at all? I had no idea. And I wasn't making any major decisions on so little sleep.

Without warning, the tar substance on the tree began to move; it shifted and wiggled and then lifted itself off of the tree.

The three of us jumped back as one. Not good. I shivered all over as if zapped by something.

"Take my hand," I commanded.

Melody, Leena, and Cade formed a circle behind me.

I held on to Melody's hand and tried to control the blob as I would a ghoul or like I had the vampires back in Philadelphia.

It didn't work. So whatever that thing was, it wasn't dead or undead.

Then again, I was still feeling pretty depleted.

"Here," Melody said, and a surge of magic rushed into me. Her's, then Leena's and Cade's. I channeled their power and tried to control the goop again. This time it worked.

Melody pulled a bottle out of her bag, just a plain water bottle. "Try this," she said, dumping the water out into the sand then thrusting it toward me.

Good thinking. My brain was still tired, and I was a little freaked out that a piece of the blob was on this plane. Focusing on the dark entity, I was able to *will* it into the bottle.

Once Melody put the lid on, I released the magic, and the blob went kind of wild inside the clear plastic, but it couldn't get out. And that was the important part. To be sure, I added a magic bubble around the bottle to hold it there.

I sat down on the sand and scrubbed my face, trying to figure out what to do next. My magic was powerful, but I was exhausted. And I didn't have the skills needed without a lot of research or help from my coven and my friends to be able to deal with this effectively.

Leena sat beside me and put her hand on my arm. "Are you okay? You look tired."

I waved my hand and smiled at her. "I've only had about three hours of sleep in the last two days. I'll be okay."

"What do we do with this thing?" Cade asked. "What is it?"

I stared at the bottle and knew I couldn't take it into the house. This thing was dangerous. And I definitely didn't want to leave it alone.

"Do any of you know how to do a barrier spell?" I asked. "I'd do it, but my magic is depleted until I get more sleep."

One way to see if you could trust someone was to admit to a weakness. Right then I was as weak as they came.

Melody nodded. "I do, and if we combine power, it should be fairly strong. And give you a little pick-me-up in the process."

I looked over my shoulder toward the cave. A pick-me-up sounded nice but I doubted it would work. "Let's put it in the back of the cave. I have my suspicions about what it is but I need to research and consult with Owen and Drew."

And pin down Luci to spill what he knows about that dark entity. But I didn't say that out loud. I felt deep down that I could trust the three witches with me today. The problem was I didn't *know* them. Loyalty was a fickle thing.

I wasn't the type to give mine to just anyone so I didn't expect others to either. Besides, a betrayal within the coven was why the former High Witch was dead and I'd taken her place. Bevin Magnus had been a member since he was a teen. He grew up with my mom and almost every single member. And he'd betrayed them all by creating a curse that killed witches in bizarre accidents. He hated everyone with more power than himself.

To make things worse he was involved in a shifter fight ring. He and his sister—a dear sweet, deceitful woman—had been running it. They'd kidnapped shifter children and forced them to fight each other to the death. About half of the coven had either known about it and did nothing, or they'd been involved in one way or another. I'd banished those members after stripping them of their powers.

As for Bevin and Penny, Luci sent them to Hell to live out their punishment. It hadn't been my first choice but it had worked. At least this way they suffered as much as those children had.

Fury uncurled inside me, and I glanced down at the bottle still in my hand. The black blob had stopped trying to break out of it. Now it just moved in a slow rippling motion. And it felt like the creepy thing was watching me. Feeding me it's anger. Ew.

And on that note..."If you can get the barrier spell to work, I can figure out exactly what this is, and hopefully, deal with it. As soon as I know something solid—no pun intended—I will update the Coven. This thing needs to be contained and I don't want anyone coming down here without me."

"No problem," Cade said and held out his hand to me. "That thing gives me the creeps and it's dark."

He shivered and made a face. I was right there with him, and I was the one holding it.

Cade and Leena hauled me to my feet, and we put the plastic bottle in the far corner of the cave. Once it was out of my hands, I felt lighter and less angry. Letting the three witches step forward, I touched Melody on the back and pushed what magic I could muster into her to help make and strengthen the barrier.

Melody, Cade, and Leena started chanting and magic rose up, making their skin glow. It wasn't bright. It was more like different color shimmers of tiny lights dancing over their flesh.

The air around us electrified as they weaved the spell, commanding it to form an iridescent box around the bottle. Once the box was fully formed a snap of power puffed out from it and the box went invisible.

It was done. I reached out and tapped my finger to the barrier and smiled. "That's pretty strong."

Melody nodded, eyeing the bottled-up blob. "It'll hold for now. We'll keep an eye on it."

"Yeah, definitely. I'm going back to bed. But call me if anything else weird—er, weirder than normal happens." I waved at them and trudged back up to the house, thinking about all the magic I'd used in such a short time. Getting in and out of the Inbetween, on the train, dealing with the blob and now this baby blob.

I needed rest.

It was near dark by the time I made it home. I walked into the kitchen to find Owen with Winnie-Alfred.

"I need sleep," I said. As I accepted a plate of sandwiches from Winnie, a bump from the basement caught my attention.

"That's just Wade," Owen said. "He'll be up here as soon as the sun is all the way down." He rolled his head from shoulder to shoulder. "Until we can get a supply of blood, I think I could draw it myself. I was a phlebotomist in my younger years, among many other things. I can give him some of my blood without him having to bite."

We didn't think we had any supplies for drawing blood and nobody wanted to volunteer to be bitten. I certainly couldn't do it. I could already control him because of my necromancer powers. If he took my blood, it might turn him into some sort of Renfield.

I wasn't about to rob a blood bank. With my luck, I'd get caught or something else strange would happen. I was too tired for all that nonsense. Uncle or not, I was not doing it.

Just as I was about to go upstairs, Olivia and Sam walked in with Drew. That gave me an idea.

"Hey," I said, looking at Owen. "It might not be good to give Wade your blood. You don't want him to be your stooge."

"He can have mine," Olivia volunteered. Sam and Drew nodded their heads as well.

Owen rustled up—or maybe conjured up—some supplies, and I stayed downstairs long enough to watch Owen draw blood from Olivia, Sam, and Drew and put it into three small glass jars so as not to mix the blood. It was one of the oddest things I've seen. I was thankful he thought of it. I should have, but I was *so* tired.

Wade came out of the basement door once the sun had fully gone down and just as Owen finished. He immediately rushed to the counter and grabbed one of the jars, slurping the blood down quickly and disgustingly. He drank the second jar slower and put the third in the refrigerator.

"I'm satisfied for now," he said. "I don't feel like I'm in any danger of hurting anyone with bloodlust."

"Okay," I said once I knew he was okay. To test him, I hugged him.

He hugged me back, and I swore he sniffed my neck. He whispered, "Thank you for saving me."

I squeezed him a little tighter. "Don't thank me yet. We still have a lot to learn. We'll do it together."

Just as soon as I slept and dealt with the baby blob and created Winnie a new body. I need a to-do list. Or a clone.

Maybe not.

Yawning again, I waved and headed toward the stairs. "Night."

CHAPTER THREE

"Your phone won't stop beeping."

I cracked an eye to stare at Lucy-Fur. She'd become part of the family very quickly after Snoozerton had me raise her from the dead to be his girlfriend. She was a beautiful snow-white cat. And she could also talk. I wasn't sure if she could before I'd turned her into an immortal ghoul-cat like Snooze was, or if my magic had given her the ability to speak.

She twisted one white ear around. "Please make it stop. I'm trying to nap."

I blinked at her, not fully awake to process everything. At least she said please.

To prove her point, my phone beeped rather obnoxiously. It was a miracle I hadn't heard it.

"See? It doesn't stop." She stared down at it as if she wanted to knock it off the end table. Then she looked back up at me. "I think there is something wrong with Snooze. He's making a God-awful noise."

Jumping down from the end table, she walked to the door

then stopped like she was expecting me to get up. With a sigh, I said, "I'm sure he's okay."

"No, I don't think so. I'm really worried. You need to come to check on him." She stared at me until I got up. For a cat, she sure did have the mom-stare down pat.

Throwing the covers off, I stood and followed Lucy down the hall to Alfred's room. When Winston expanded himself to make room for Wade, the house had added more bedrooms upstairs. I still wasn't sure how he did it other than by magic. I learned in the last six months not to question the things that happened around me. Just roll with them.

The extra rooms threw me off a little. I didn't know where anyone's bedrooms were anymore, which was crazy since I grew up in this house.

I heard Snooze before I walked in. As soon as the noise hit my ears I started laughing. It sounded like a grown human man was in there snoring like a foghorn. It was louder than I ever heard that crazy cat snore before.

"See," Lucy said, head-butting the back of my leg as if to push me closer to the snorting cat. "That's not normal."

"He's fine. Just snoring." Just as the words left my mouth Snoozerton let out a loud snort and a growl.

Lucy moved closer to Snooze and watched him. "Should he go see the vet? He could have something wrong with his nose or throat."

"The only thing wrong with that cat is he loves food too much. Besides, he's immortal like you. He can't die unless I do." That was something I planned on not doing. Not anytime soon.

Leaving the cats to do whatever they did, I went back to my room and laid across my bed as I checked my messages.

Drew: I'm starting to get worried.

Olivia: Call me when you get up.

Melody: We reinforced that barrier spell. No worries. Let us know what that stuff is.

Wallie: Headed back to school. Call me if you need me. Love you, Mom!

Drew: Seriously, how long are you going to sleep?

Olivia: Please answer Drew so he'll stop bugging me.

Sam: Olivia and Drew are driving me crazy.

Owen: Where do we keep the electric screwdriver? I think Winston hid it from me.

Owen: Nm. Found it.

I replied to Drew first. **Why didn't you just come over? I'm up now.**

Then, I told Wallie I loved him, and Sam and Olivia I was awake and fine. After sending a thanks message to Melody, I snuggled in to read Drew's reply.

Drew: I considered it. But if you really were sleeping all this time, I wanted you to get your rest.

He really was so sweet. Typing quickly, I explained about my powers being depleted. Although, I hadn't meant to sleep since yesterday at sundown until today late afternoon. Wow, that was almost twenty-four hours. Apparently, I needed the sleep. It was almost dinnertime. Speaking of, I invited Drew to come eat with us and hoped, as usual, Alfred...Winnie had made enough to feed a small army.

I also invited Olivia and Sam and heard Owen talking in the hallway, likely to Zoey. Since we got back home she'd shifted and went hunting in the woods and most likely swimming in the ocean. Tigers loved the water.

When Olivia replied to let me know they were on their way and bringing little Sammie, I rolled off the bed, then shuffled into the shower.

After I got up the energy to actually bathe and not just

stand under the steaming spray, I dried off, threw my hair in a ponytail, and dressed in my most comfortable clothes. When I got downstairs, everyone had already turned up.

They were waiting on me while I took my long hot shower. It'd be okay. I felt ten times better.

Once everyone was seated around the table, I started to explain the blob. "Okay, so a piece of the black blob from the Inbetween is currently being held in the cave by the ocean."

They stopped chatting and handing food around and stared at me in complete shock. "What?" I wasn't sure who asked. It didn't matter, really, because everyone was waiting for me to answer.

"Maybe I should've told you before," I said in an apologetic tone. "But I couldn't stay awake. I felt like I was about to pass out."

They continued passing around the potatoes but did it with their eyes mostly on me. So I continued. "When I went down to the beach, I saw a lot of marine life on the sand, dying. Fish washed up, even stuff like coral and jellyfish. And on one of the trees was a piece of the black blob."

"What did you do?" Olivia cried as she cut up Sammie's chicken.

He ate happily, surrounded by people who were all completely normal to him. He'd never batted an eye at Larry no longer being a skeleton, and when Lucy-Fur deigned to talk to him, he just chattered back like she was his best friend.

And it was totally, completely normal for a cat to talk.

He was either a great kid or so utterly screwed up he'd never be able to have a functional relationship. Only time would tell.

"Anyway, Melody, Cade, Leena, and I got it contained, but we need to figure out more about it. It's going to be the key to helping us get back to the Inbetween and get Mom. Maybe we can kill two birds with one stone." I took a bite of potatoes.

"What about my body?" Winnie asked.

"I haven't forgotten that. But dealing with the blob is more pressing. We'll get to Bill's and find the spells. I promise." One thing at a time. Winnie was okay where she was for the time being. If we didn't take care of the blob then she wouldn't have long to enjoy her new body anyway.

I didn't say that out loud because of Sammie. That kid was a master at looking like he wasn't listening while picking up every word that was said.

"Let's divide up some tasks," Owen said. "I'll start researching the ghostly plane. Surely there's information somewhere on the internet about it."

That would help speed things along. I nodded, agreeing. "I'll look in the occult books at the bookstore. I'd agreed to work a shift for Clint tomorrow before I knew all this mess was going to happen."

"Hello, everyone," Luci said as he swept uninvited into the room. "Oh!" He breathed deep. "I love chicken masala."

"Not today, Satan," I said with one hand up. It was my favorite way to greet him. Besides, I really didn't have time to deal with him, especially with how strange he was being about the Inbetween. He was way too interested in it and how to get there.

He believed I held all the answers. He was wrong.

He bowed his head. "I promise to be on my best behavior."

I sighed and relented. "Fine. Sit."

"I wondered if you'd had time to give any thought to going back to—"

"No," I said severely, cutting him off. "We have other things to deal with first. I'll deal with them, then I'll think about how to get back in there."

I wasn't sure if I had to go back into the Inbetween to get Mom out. At least I hoped not. But I needed to worry about the blob first. Luci could wait right along with Winnie.

He deflated a little, like a small child being told they couldn't go to the park or have their favorite toy. Men—no matter what species—were big freaking babies.

"Okay," he said sullenly. "I heard you talking about the blob, though."

I hadn't realized that. Darn it. Although I shouldn't have been surprised. He probably had my house magically bugged. "Oh?"

"Yeah. I might be able to help but I need to see it."

I shook my head. That didn't feel right, not at all. "I don't think so."

He squinted at me. "That thing is evil. I'm the *King* of all evil things. It makes sense if anyone could make heads or tails of it, it'd be me."

He had a point, but as entertaining as it had been to have Luci around for the last few months, I still didn't trust him.

"You keep saying blob." Olivia drank a big swig of lemonade, washing her food down. "Didn't you guys see the person in there when we were in the Inbetween?"

It was my turn to look at her, shocked. "Person?"

"Yeah. It was a woman with blonde hair and what looked like navy blue eyes. A slightly oval, somewhat square jaw. She was beautiful and scary." Olivia took another bite of chicken.

Luci stiffened. "Are you sure you saw this?"

Olivia nodded with one eyebrow arched. "Absolutely."

"You probably hit your head extra hard," Sam said. "There was nobody in that blob. Just a mass of evil."

"Right," Luci whispered. But then he stood. "I've just remembered something I need to do. I'll talk to you all soon." And instead of walking out, he just dematerialized. As he did, though, he was looking at Olivia with the strangest expression on his face.

How odd.

CHAPTER FOUR

"Welcome to Imaginary Homes Bookstore," I called automatically when the bell over the door rang. "Let me know if I can help you find anything."

I glanced up from the book I was reading in time to see the woman smile at me and move through the stacks. Apparently, she didn't need any help, so I went back to reading the book on the occult, the latest of several I'd been combing through.

None of them said anything about an evil black blob or the Inbetween. That got me thinking if it was even called the Inbetween. It might be one of those realms that had several names depending on the mythology and culture.

A few minutes later, the bell jangled again. This time, Olivia and Carrie walked in with Zoey.

A spike of excitement fluttered through me at the sight of my girls.

"Hey. Good to see you, Carrie." It felt like forever since I'd seen her, which was funny considering she was sort of dating my neighbor, Luci.

Before she could respond, the customer who'd come in

moments before they did walked to the front and set a book on the counter. It was one that I'd read before. "I enjoyed this series," I said in a way of greeting and in my best happy-happy customer service voice.

She smiled at me. "I hope I do too. I like to read, but I've been in a slump lately."

Olivia chuckled. "I hate that."

"Me too," said Carrie.

I nodded, agreeing with them as I rang up the lady's purchases. "That will be $7.43 with tax."

She reached into her shirt and wiggled around in her breasticle area, and then pulled a ten out.

Olivia and Carrie recoiled with looks of horror while Zoey snickered. Wide-eyed, I locked gazes with Olivia, who was getting ready to voice her opinion on the situation.

Oh, no she wouldn't.

I didn't need the drama this morning. With little effort, I waved my hand like I was swatting a fly away and spelled my bestie so no sound came out of her mouth while the woman was in the store.

The sight made me giggle, which I covered with a single cough then cleared my throat. Olivia was a few feet behind the woman waving her arms and talking. Or trying to. When Olivia realized what I had done to her, she glared at me and folded her arms over her breasts.

I gave her a toothy grin as I took the money gingerly between two fingers and set it to the side. Oh, it was moist.

Yuck. Maybe I should have let Olivia speak her mind after all. Then again, I didn't need Liv and the customer to start arguing in the store.

After hitting ten and total on the register, I counted out the woman's change, put the book in a bag, and kept a big smile plastered to my face. Until she left, at least. As soon as the door closed behind her, Carrie and Zoey burst out laughing.

Olivia glared at me. "You spelled me!"

I shrugged. "I will not have you picking fights with the customers."

"I wasn't going to pick a fight. I was going to let her know how gross and unsanitary that was." She shuddered and wrinkled up her nose.

"I couldn't agree more with you, but that would have started a feud and I'm not in the mood to deal with it." I set the ten on the counter behind me to dry before putting it in with the rest of the money. Gross. I grabbed a can of disinfectant spray and gave the boob money a coating for good measure.

"So what brings you ladies in today?" I asked.

Olivia had taken Zoey under her wing and helped me make sure the eighteen-year-old was staying on the straight and narrow as she took her GED classes online through the local community college. I appreciated Olivia's help with her.

"We were headed to lunch. We thought we'd stop in and see if you could sneak away." Olivia leaned against the counter and studied the book I had opened.

I shook my head as the bell went off again. This time it was Clint, the bookstore owner. He looked frazzled. I frowned and waved. "Afternoon. How are you?"

He looked from Carrie to Olivia, to me, then quickly glanced back at Zoey. "Do you ladies believe in ghosts?"

"No," we all said, nearly in unison. Except for Zoey. She just looked bewildered. Of course, she didn't know what he was referring to because she hadn't been in the Inbetween with Drew, Olivia, Sam, and me.

Aw, now I kind of felt bad that we'd freaked him out when we were in the Inbetween. While there, we could interact with the natural world. The realm of lost souls, as I'd started calling it, ran parallel to this one.

I made sure not to look at Olivia. She seemed to make me burst out laughing in cases like these. And that wouldn't have been a good thing. Clint was already stressed. Laughing at him would've been rubbing salt in the wound.

Poor guy. I'd find a way of explaining his experience. But later, after I dealt with the evil baby blob and its parent in the Inbetween.

"Why, have you seen a ghost?" I asked Clint, acting a little bit like he was crazy. I know that didn't help, but what was I to do?

He shook his head. "No, of course not." He glanced at the stack of books on the counter. "You just seem to like those occult books, so I thought I'd ask." Muttering to himself, and looking a bit twitchy, he headed for the back.

We all watched him disappear into his office.

"So, Olivia says you need to know about other dimensions," Carrie said softly once Clint was out of earshot.

I nodded. "I do."

"Well, I know a thing or two. But if you can't get away for lunch, do you want to plan a girls' night? I'm free tomorrow night."

That sounded heavenly. "Yes," I said with a little too much glee. "Tomorrow works for me."

Zoey nodded eagerly. "Can I come?"

Olivia winked at her. "I don't see why not, but you're drinking sparkling grape juice."

Zoey deflated a little. "Okay, fine. But I still want to come."

"Great. Then it's settled. You guys can come over to the house. I'll have Alfred make snacks." I wasn't sure what Olivia had told Carrie about the whole Winnie-Alfred ordeal.

They looked around for a minute, and Carrie got an early reader book for her Kindergarten class, then they left for lunch. I didn't mind not going with them. I'd see them soon, and I owed Clint this shift to give him time to chill out after the prank we pulled on him.

Not long before I was about to close up, Sam and Drew

walked in wearing plain clothes. "Hey, officers," I greeted as I drank in the sight of Drew in a dark grey t-shirt and faded blue jeans. "I'm getting all the VIP guests today."

"We figured out we both wanted to come to see you, so we came together," Drew explained, reaching out to take my hand.

"To what do I owe this pleasure?" I asked my boyfriend and my life-long best friend. Though, Sam had to share the best friend title with his wife now. I didn't think he minded, though.

"I wanted to ask you to dinner tomorrow night." Drew gave my hand a little squeeze before letting go.

"And I came to say goodbye. I'm taking Sammie and my dad on a weekend fishing trip tomorrow." Sam grimaced as I widened my eyes at him.

"This isn't a good time for you to be going out of town," I said. I couldn't protect him if he was out of town. Then again he and Sammie would probably be safer out of town, especially if I couldn't find a way to destroy the blob.

Sam held up his hands. "I know. But there's not a lot I can do to help, and we paid for this cabin ages ago. Plus, Olivia pointed out that it wouldn't be the worst idea to get our son out of town while things are getting a little dangerous."

After sucking in a deep breath, I nodded. This was why we were best friends. We thought alike. "I guess that's true. I just always expect you to be around."

Sam clapped Drew on the back. "Well, you'll have to settle for this guy."

Drew puffed out his chest and winked at me. "I'm good for a thing or two." He leaned onto the counter and gave me a wink. "How about dinner tomorrow night?"

"I'd love to, but we're having girls' night. Carrie is going to tell us what she knows about uh... *traveling*." Drew and Sam nodded. They knew what I meant. "Can I postpone you to Saturday?"

"Sure. I'm off tomorrow and Saturday. That'll work."

"Take care of Olivia," Sam said. "I tried to get her to leave the danger, too, but she wouldn't. And I'll have very spotty service on the lake, so you might not be able to get a hold of me. Olivia has the phone number for the closest ranger station if anything does happen."

I grabbed his hand. "We'll be okay. We have Luci and the Coven." I said that last sentence very quietly. "Enjoy the time with your dad and Sammie."

He finally nodded. "Okay. I'll go and try not to worry. I know you'll protect her."

I snorted. "More like she'll protect me. She's pretty fierce."

"Yeah, she is." The smile on his face warmed my heart. I was so glad they'd found each other.

Drew went to kiss me on the cheek and I turned my head so our lips met. He let the kiss linger for a few and my insides twisted. I was so close to just leaving with him and escaping into bliss and all kinds of pleasures that he could ignite in me.

But I couldn't let myself be distracted. We had to solve the mystery of the baby blob. And create Winnie a body. *And* stay alive in the process.

Drew broke the kiss and moved toward the door with Sam.

As soon as I got off work, I headed for the beach without going into the house first. I wanted to make sure the blob was still contained.

Inside the cave, I stared at it behind the invisible barrier, which was much stronger and sectioned off the back corner of the cave where the entity was.

I tilted my head and studied it. It was kind of hard to tell with it being in the bottle, but... was it a little bigger?

No. It was probably spread out against the inside surface of the plastic, making it look bigger. It was fine.

Really. Everything was fine.

CHAPTER FIVE

Even with the internet, the Coven, and the books on the occult from the bookstore and the library, we knew basically nothing about the Inbetween by the time Carrie came over for girls' night.

Olivia had brought her stuff over earlier that day, intending to spend the weekend with me since her house would be empty. Sam, his dad, and little Sammie had hightailed it out of town for a guy's weekend. Olivia didn't want to stay in her house alone and she would be over at mine all the time anyway. Staying would save on drive time. That was fine with me. What was one more house guest?

"Okay," I said once we settled down with popcorn and wine. What a combination. Zoey sipped her sparkling grape juice from a wine glass. I hoped we didn't make her want to drink younger than she would've. Then again, she was eighteen and most kids her age were going to college or would be soon, where they would partake in all kinds of alcohol-induced activities. She was safer with us.

Turning my full attention to Carrie, I asked, "What do you know about other dimensions?"

Carrie Treehill was a teacher at Sammie's school. Well, the only elementary school in Shipton Harbor. She'd gone to school with Olivia and me. After she'd had an orgasmic run-in—literally—with Luci, Liv and I had discovered that sweet Carrie was Fae. As in Faery from another realm. Although I believed she'd been born in the human realm. But don't quote me on that because I could be wrong. A lot has happened since we found out.

Olivia and I included her in our world of the weird. She fit right in.

"Why don't you start by telling me the whole story." Carrie sat back and waited.

So I gave her the short version, leaving out the part about sex and having an orgasm that sent a blast of power out and pushed us all into the Inbetween. At least that was the running theory of how we'd got there.

"Luci sort of arranged it all," Olivia explained. "We think he knew the ghost train and the real train were going to line up on that night."

"Still, it would've demanded a considerable amount of magic to make it happen." Carrie paused and studied both Liv and myself. "Moving from one dimension to another is a big power suck."

I blushed and shifted in my seat. "Tell me about it. I slept over twenty-four hours the other day."

"What?" Olivia asked, looking directly at me. "What do you know?"

Clearing my throat, I avoided looking at them, especially Zoey. "Drew and I were um... *together* in the moments that we switched over to the Inbetween."

Olivia burst out laughing. "You mean your orgasm is what pushed us over?"

My face had to have been bright purple by now. But I nodded, still not making eye contact with them.

Alfred walked in with a fresh bottle of wine and a cheese tray. "That would be hard to duplicate."

Ah, Winnie's voice. Nice. Now my aunt knew I'd had sex with the Sheriff.

"I have a confession," Olivia said. "Sam and I were doing it right at that moment, too. I can't say for sure I had an orgasm right then, but it was close." She didn't look embarrassed in the least.

"Yeah," Carrie said. "But you're not magical."

Winnie-Alfred—*WinFred*?—started to walk out of the room.

"You can join us, you know," I called out before she made it to the kitchen.

She turned and smiled, that stiff, creepy Alfred-smile. "Thank you. I didn't want to push in on your girls' night."

"You're not a push-in at all," Carrie said. "I was so happy for you guys when Olivia and Zoey told me it was you in there all this time."

WinFred came back in and sat beside me on the sofa. Carrie leaned forward. "But why didn't you tell them sooner? What stopped you?"

Waving a hand, WinFred topped off everyone's wine glasses. "Unfinished business. I'll figure it all out once I'm in my real body. In the meantime, I'd appreciate it if we didn't spread it far and wide that I'm in Alfred's body."

Carrie held up a hand. "You got it, Winnie. Your secret is safe with me."

"We made our way back here," I said, finishing the story of the lost souls and the black blob. "But when we got to the house, this big black blob of evil came for us. Mom appeared and told us to run."

"But they didn't see the face," Olivia added. "They think I

hit my head too hard, but I'm telling you, there was a woman in that blob."

"Tell me again, what did she look like," Winnie said. "I didn't really absorb what you said the other day, I was too shocked that everyone now knows who I am."

Olivia described the woman again. "Her blonde hair had a little more gold in it than mine and her eyes were the darkest blue I've ever seen. They seemed to sparkle. But there was so much rage and pain in those depths."

Winnie nodded her head. "That sounds so familiar. I wonder..." But she sighed. "I wish we could talk to your mother."

Carrie sat up straighter, her eyes wide and a grin pulled at her lips. "Why don't we try a seance? It's the Witching Hour, the time of day when the veil between the worlds is supposed to be the thinnest."

I raised my eyebrows. Oh, that would totally work. "I never even thought of doing that. Let's!"

We traipsed up to the attic because that was where the ritual room was and there was a permanent pentagram carved into the hardwood floors. After placing candles in a circle in the center of the pentagram, we sat cross-legged around them, joined hands, and put one of Mom's shirts that I'd kept in the center.

"Ava, you lead," WinFred said. "You'll be the strongest, both because you're a necromancer and because you're her daughter."

"You're her sister," I said.

WinFred cocked their head at me. "Yeah, but I don't actually have any magic anymore, being dead and all. I'm completely pointless in this circle."

"You're not," I said. "I want you here. And I'm glad you're here."

If she could've cried, she might've. Her eyes, though filmy, looked touched. "I'm glad I'm here, too, Avie." She hadn't called me Avie since I was a pre-teen.

I pushed aside my emotions and focused on the shirt and the memory of my mother. It didn't take long before we connected, which was both surprising and a relief. She appeared in the circle, a very faint outline of herself. I wanted to jump up and hug her.

"What is it?" she asked in a panic. "I can't stay in one spot for long." She stared down at me and smiled. "Oh, it is always so good to see you, Ava."

"I love you, too, Mom." I didn't want to make her stay here any longer than necessary and risk the blob getting to her. So I got straight to the point. "Do you know anything about the blob? Can you tell us anything that will help destroy it?"

Mom's head swiveled until she stared at Alfred. "Winifred," she said severely. "It's Phira. We were wrong about her. It stripped everything good and light from her. They weren't meant to be here. They were never meant to be here."

Fee-rah? "Who is Fee-rah? Is it a person?"

Mom wasn't making any sense to me.

Before she could answer me, Luci appeared inside the circle beside my mother. She disappeared without another word. I didn't cut off the connection. She must've severed it from the other side. I hadn't known ghosts could even do that.

"What did you do?" Luci yelled at Winnie in a deep, demanding voice. "What happened?"

I scowled at him. It was becoming obvious that he was spying on us and listening in on our conversations. That pissed me off.

Before I could call the devil out for spying, WinFred sighed. "This is why I didn't want Snoozer to take my string off." She met my gaze. "This is my unfinished business."

"What is it?" I put my hand on her knee. "Whatever it is, we'll figure it out."

Luci still looked like an imposing thundercloud. "Sit down," I barked. "You're not scaring any of us." I'd had about enough of him.

He glared at me, but sat beside Carrie, then turned his attention back to WinFred. "Spit it out. What did you do?"

She sighed and spilled it. "Beth, Mom, and I were approached when Beth was pregnant with you, Ava. The Fae King asked us to do a spell to send a Faery into the Inbetween because that was the only realm Lucifer couldn't get into."

Winnie's reference to 'Mom' was Yaya—her mom. The three of them were pretty powerful and combining their magic would have been just enough to open a portal to the Inbetween. I wasn't sure how I knew that. It was like the information revealed itself to me because I needed to understand it in the current moment.

Magic sometimes worked like that.

Luci's face darkened as he stared at my ghoulish aunt. "Tell me you didn't do it."

Do what? I glanced between the two, wishing they would share their little inside secret with the rest of the class.

WinFred kept their gaze on me, ignoring Satan. "The Faery wasn't supposed to have a romance outside of her own kind, and she especially wasn't supposed to get pregnant."

Luci stiffened. Carrie took his hand and squeezed. "Hey," she whispered. "Are you okay?"

"Then what happened?" he asked through his teeth. Even though anger flowed around him, he held Carrie's hand gently and ran his thumb over her knuckles.

"We did the spell. If that's Phira, then she's gone very dark while in the Inbetween. I saw it briefly while I was there before Bill brought me back. But I didn't recognize it as anything other than evil and blob-like. If what Beth said was right, the Fae were never meant to go to that realm. It's meant for witches and humans. Even other paranormals don't go there."

I hadn't heard that. "Why?"

"It's sort of a purgatory for humans. The running theory is that witches have enough human DNA that they also can gain access. Other creatures simply don't go there." She shook her head. "We got it so wrong."

"Okay, so assuming this blob is Phira," I said. "Is she after revenge? Does she know Mom is one of the witches who put her there?"

WinFred shrugged one stiff shoulder. "I suppose so. I was only in there for a short time, but you said it came after her."

I nodded. "For sure. But why didn't you ever tell me about this?"

"The Fae King made us promise not to tell anyone. We swore an oath and the only reason I can speak of it now is because the Fae King is dead. He said Lucifer was pure evil and would kill Phira and her child."

"What about the child?" Luci asked in a deadly whisper. A dark sadness rolled from him and hit me in the chest. No one, not even the devil, should suffer the loss of a child.

WinFred looked stricken. "The child went in with her."

I turned to Luci. "Is this the true reason you came when I summoned Santa?"

He blinked at me. "I tracked Fee to Shipton Harbor, but the trail went cold here. I've been keeping a close eye on the town ever since. Your summoning gave me a way in. Gave me a way to investigate in person instead of hidden and secret."

"Well, that King went mad. The Fae killed him. He was totally evil." Carrie's tone was serious and sad. "I know this for sure because I'm in contact with my Fae family."

Luci gripped her hand. "He and I fought for years. I tried to help free your people from his grips. I was thrilled to hear he was gone, but it also meant I'd lost one possible lead to my Fee's location."

"Why would he want to hurt your lover, though?" Carrie asked.

Luci shook his head. "It's not completely true that the Fae aren't supposed to mate outside of Faery. Fee was royal and was forbidden to seek a mate outside her kind. She was his daughter. But that never meant a punishment like this. He did it because he hated me. His own daughter! All because he wanted to punish me. And he did." He met my gaze. "I was her lover. The baby was mine."

Holy crap.

"We trapped an innocent there?" WinFred asked in a small voice. She shook their head. "Luci, I am so sorry. We had no reason not to believe him. We thought she was evil and that she had to be contained."

"Don't apologize," he replied, clearly not forgiving her. "Just get her out."

CHAPTER SIX

"I'm not sure what to do." I'd spent the day poring over more books and the internet.

Bupkiss.

Drew sat across from me at a table at a new barbeque restaurant called Blowin' Smoke. I had to say it was the best food I'd tasted in a while. He watched me with a mix of helplessness and affection. Holding his stare, I admired the swirl of teal and blue of his irises.

"I could try to feel out some of my relatives," Drew suggested. "But they're still active hunters. If they catch wind of why I'm asking, it might bring them down on us."

I shook my head. That was another problem I didn't want in my town. While Drew's family might respect his wish to claim Shipton as his territory—for lack of a better term—and may sometimes show up out of curiosity, other hunters would come to rid my town of all paranormal activity. Yes, it was *my* town. I'd claimed it. And would do anything to protect it. "No. Don't do that. We'll find a way to get to the bottom of this."

I raised a bite of brisket to my lips and savored the melt in my mouth yumminess. As I sighed and enjoyed a moment of calm, Luci stole that moment and appeared out of nowhere. I nearly choked on my food. It was a miracle the whole restaurant didn't see him and flip out.

Why in the heck couldn't I have a normal dinner with my boyfriend without Satan showing up? This was how the whole trip to Paris happened on Valentine's Day. While that had been a nice surprise, I didn't have time for spontaneous trips overseas or whatever shenanigans the devil had planned.

I was on a date. Dang it.

"What are you doing here?" I hissed.

He sat in the empty chair beside me and grabbed a fork. I hoped he didn't think he was going to join us.

But he pointed the fork at me. "Why aren't you trying to get Fee out of the Inbetween?"

"Excuse me? It took three witches to get her in there," I spoke through my teeth to keep from yelling. The humans around us didn't need to know that I'd set loose an evil entity. Or even a small part of that entity. He glared at me. I snatched the fork from him and added, "It's not as easy as just *willing* her out of there."

He was this all-powerful archangel turned King of Hell. Surely he had contacts that could help him. Why did it always have to be me?

Luci's glare sharpened, and for the first time since he first appeared in my attic, a little trickle of fear danced down my spine. "You have a Coven. You have resources. Get it done."

He disappeared and Drew and I looked around the restaurant, but nobody seemed to have noticed Luci was ever there.

"I guess I should call an emergency Coven meeting." I sighed and pushed my plate away, no longer hungry. But I wasn't wasting good brisket. That baby was coming home with me. "He's right. I'm not using all my resources. I haven't even told the Coven what the blob is."

"Do you not trust them?" Drew motioned to the waitress for the check and to-go boxes.

I met his gaze and lifted one shoulder. "I think I do. I don't know." Being in charge of a coven was still new to me.

Grabbing my hand, he leaned forward and lowered his voice. "They swore an oath to you. They know how powerful you already were and how much more you have become since becoming the High Witch. Any of them who betray you at this point has a death wish. Besides, you have your own personal hunter."

"You're not a hunter anymore." I didn't want to put him in a position where he felt he had to reinstate his active duty status.

He brushed his thumb over my knuckles and a spark of his hunter magic flashed in his eyes. "I will do whatever I need to do to protect you and this town. I'm older and wiser and no longer blind to the prejudices drilled into hunters from the time they are born. Because of that, I'm much stronger than they would ever be."

I smiled. "Because you have powerful allies."

Cupping the back of my head, he pulled me in for a lingering, toe-curling kiss. "So do you."

He was right, but guilt still washed over me. I'd left my mother in the Inbetween longer than necessary because I didn't want to use all of my available help. The fewer people I exposed to the danger the better. Or so I thought. It was stupid and selfish. I couldn't do everything myself, and I shouldn't have tried.

I pulled out my phone and texted Melody. **Emergency Coven meeting. My house in an hour. Attendance is mandatory.**

She'd get the ball rolling.

"I'm sorry to cut the date short. But he's right." I met Drew's gaze. "I need to go."

"It's okay," he said. "I shouldn't have tried to get a date out of you. It was bad timing."

On the heels of his statement, the waitress showed up with the check and to-go boxes. Five minutes later we were headed toward the house. I texted Owen on the way to let him know about the coven meeting. Olivia would already be there, and Carrie didn't need to show for this. She couldn't have helped anyway. Not that Olivia could, but she would've killed me if I didn't include her.

All in all, ten of us were there who could loan power to the operation. Owen and me, of course, plus Melody, Cade, and Leena. The twins came, Brandon and Ben. They were still creepy, the way they spoke together or mirrored one another. A few members I didn't know so well who came were Joely, Mai, and Alissa. They seemed really nice, though. Hopefully, they'd be willing to help.

"Why isn't Luci here?" Olivia whispered. "Surely he can give some power."

I shrugged. "I have no idea what goes on in his mind. He pitched a fit that I hadn't done this yet, and he was right. I should've. But then he disappeared."

Once WinFred had served everyone a beverage, something she'd insisted on, I gave them a minute to settle into the various chairs spread around the room. I needed to purchase some folding chairs or something for moments like this. Instead, the living room was crammed full of kitchen chairs, yard chairs, and desk chairs pulled from all over the house.

I held up one hand. "Thank you all for coming on such short notice. So, the thing is, my mother, grandmother, and aunt did a spell a very long time ago, just before I was born. They helped the then-Fae King trap a rogue Fae in the Inbetween. Everyone familiar with the Inbetween?"

I waited while they all nodded. "Okay, that saves me a big speech. So, we're just now learning that the trapped Fae wasn't rogue. The King was evil. We need to set right what they did wrong." Meeting their gazes, I lowered my voice to sound more serious and compelling. "I can't compel you to help. You have to volunteer. It could be dangerous, and we might end up releasing a massive evil into the world."

That caused more than one raised eyebrow. Ben stood. "Give us more information about this evil."

Olivia and I described the blob. She told them about seeing the face, and that we suspected that she was, for whatever reason, able to see the Fae inside the evil.

"This poor woman has been trapped there, in pain and miserable," Olivia said. "Please help us help her."

In the end, everyone agreed. We decided to do the spell in the cave so that if and when the blob came out, we could contain it within the barrier spell. Now that I was rested and recovered, I hoped to be able to significantly strengthen the magical enclosure.

We traipsed as a group down to the beach. The dead things weren't quite as bad and focused closer to the cave. "So, the blob being here is still affecting things, even behind the barrier," I mused when we stood at the cave entrance. "I have a bad feeling about this."

But, I went forward with it anyway. We joined hands, and I spoke the spell that Winnie had told me while focusing my intent. The members of the Coven followed in line, adding their powers to mine. The cave filled with illuminating power that only other magical beings could see. After the third time repeating the chant, nothing happened. We had all this power rushing around, and no dice.

I turned and looked back at Olivia, who stood with WinFred. WinFred shuffled forward. "Maybe you need more family magic. It was our bloodline that put her in there, after all. You could try it with Wallie in the mix."

With a sigh, I smiled at my Coven. "Thank you for trying.

I'll see if Wallie can come up here and we can try again. Could you all come back tomorrow for the Witching Hour?"

Everyone agreed, and we slowly disbursed. When it was just me and my normal crew left in the cave, we inspected the blob.

"Is it bigger?" Owen asked. "It seems bigger."

"So does the magical box around it," I muttered. "We need to figure this out, and soon." I just prayed once we brought Phira through, she'd come back to herself and not be a blobby rage monster.

CHAPTER SEVEN

"Good morning, my sweet girl."

I cracked an eye to see Alfred sitting on the corner of my bed, but that had definitely been Winnie's voice. I really wanted to get her in her own body.

"So," Winnie said cheerfully. "When do I get my own body?"

"Stop reading my mind." I moaned and stretched, closing my eyes to pretend that she was sitting there with smooth skin; her curvy self instead of all dry and withered ghoul-man. "Come on, Auntie, you know that we have to save Mom first. Plus, that poor Faery you guys had imprisoned, *and* we don't know what's happened to her kid." I peeked over at them, then looked away. "Is it so bad here with us, even in Alfred's body? You could still be stuck in the Inbetween."

"No," she said, brushing my hair out of my face. "You're right. This is better than that horrible place. And I do want to get my sister out of there as soon as possible. It would just be nice to do that in my own body, and who knows? Maybe once I'm out of this dried-up shell—no offense Alfred—"

Alfred's voice came through. "Offense taken." The mouse-like voice squeaked on the second syllable of offense. I giggled and then couldn't stop.

"Well anyway," Winnie said, ignoring her body-mate and my giggling fit. "Once I'm in my skin, maybe I'll be able to do magic."

Taking a deep breath and holding until the urge to laugh passed, I shook my head as I stared up at the ceiling, still intentionally not looking at my aunt. After letting out my breath, I said, "It doesn't work that way. Magic won't cooperate with a dead body. So unless I can find a way to make you alive again, which isn't possible, you won't have your magic."

She sighed, and their body creaked as they stood. "Still. It would be nice to not creak when I walked down the stairs."

I chuckled and got up behind them. Hopefully, Wallie had gotten up early and was already on his way back. I hated to bring him in for one day because he would have to go right back for classes tomorrow, but if we were lucky the spell would work. And that would be the end of my needing him.

Moseying around the house, I tried to familiarize myself with the new bedrooms as I drank my coffee. I couldn't think of anything I could work on to prepare for tonight, and we'd decided to do the spell in the Witching Hour to maximize the natural magic in the air.

In the absence of any current magical purpose, I headed to my office to check my email. I hadn't checked in with my editor since I submitted my latest manuscript.

Ugh, she'd already sent the first half back to me. I figured I'd just open it quickly and take a peek at what she had to say.

"What the...?" I peered at the many notes on the document and couldn't help answering one or two.

"Ava?"

A few minutes later, Olivia interrupted me. "Yeah?" I

turned in my desk chair and stretched. My neck had gotten stiff while I worked.

"Are you going to get ready? Dinner is ready and everyone should be here soon." She stared at me like I was crazy.

"Dinner?" I looked out the window. What time was it? "I haven't had breakfast yet."

Olivia chuckled. "Go shower. Your hair is greasy. You've been in here working on that book all day."

"I did it again, didn't I?" It was far too common when I started working on my books for me to totally lose track of all things.

Olivia just smiled and closed my laptop. "Let's go."

By the time I finished my shower and put my face on, Winnie had finished a big meal. And then after dinner, the Coven began to trickle in. WinFred had made enough to feed all of them, and they gratefully dug in. They'd figured out that there was always food being prepared in this house. Now there would be no getting rid of them.

Wallie strolled in just in time to finish off the pancakes and bacon. Winnie'd made breakfast for dinner, a favorite meal of hers. I smiled at my handsome son. "Are you ready for this?"

He shrugged and swallowed the coffee his great-aunt-ghoul had handed to him. "I guess so. What choice do I have?"

"None if you want to get your grandmother out of that place," I said with a little zing in my voice.

Wallie rolled his eyes. "Of course I do, I'm just not so sure about pulling out a giant blob of evil."

The kid wasn't wrong about that part.

Once everyone had eaten, we headed down to the beach and into the cave. The light had begun to dwindle. Turning on my phone's flashlight, I aimed it at the bottle and squinted. "Does it look bigger to anyone else?"

Melody did something complicated with her hands and a

ball of light attached itself to the ceiling, illuminating everything clearly so that everyone could have a look.

"I think so," Ben said, and Brandon echoed the same.

With a sigh, I tore my gaze away from the black inky darkness. "Well, let's get this show on the road," I said. "Whether this is the right thing to do or not, we might as well get it over with."

Once again, we all held hands. Wallie was at my side. I waited until each member connected and opened their powers to me and Wallie. Then I started the chant and everyone followed suit. Our voices grew louder as I pushed more magic into the direction of the blob.

Again, nothing happened.

When we finally gave it up and walked back to the house, Owen sidled up to me. "You know, we need to go look around Bill's office anyway. Maybe he's got some notes about the Inbetween. He didn't seem to be particularly powerful in his life, but he did seem to be well studied."

I shrugged. "It's worth a try. And I know Winnie is dying for us to go get his books and stuff."

Melody, who was walking right behind us, tapped me on the shoulder. "I don't think anyone has been to Bill's house. They lived across the street from me. And ever since his wife disappeared, it's been quiet. I'd say most of his stuff is probably still there. I don't think his daughter has even been there at all."

I exchanged a glance with Owen. I'd met Bill and Penny's daughter the day I found Bill's body behind the bookstore. I'd driven Penny home, and it was there that she'd told me to take Alfred. "Well, I guess I know what we're doing the rest of tonight."

Olivia skipped forward and grinned at me. "I'm in. I just have to run home and get my stealthy ninja clothes."

Of course Olivia had stealthy ninja clothes.

Good gods, I hoped she didn't show up in a leather catsuit.

CHAPTER EIGHT

"Crap, I dropped my flashlight." Olivia bent down and grabbed the little light and almost fell over in the process. "Will you hurry up with that door?"

I rolled my eyes and kept trying the spell Owen had taught me earlier in the day. How he knew a spell for unlocking doors off the top of his head, I hadn't a clue. It made me wonder if he'd been a thief in an earlier life.

The spell used magic to blast the lock from the inside so it would seem that it simply stopped working. It was clever, and again I wondered about my mentor's extracurricular activities.

This little unlocking, well, lock breaking spell wasn't like the more complicated ones where I had to learn words in Latin. Then again, witches originally used Latin and other dead languages to keep humans and other beings from learning their spells. Some still thought it was cool. All the spells could be spoken in English, or Spanish or any other language. Intent was the important thing.

For me, magic seemed to flow and do what I wanted it to do

no matter what language I used. Well, most of the time it obeyed.

Right now was not one of those times.

As soon as the Coven had gone home, Olivia and I set out to go on our little breaking and entering adventure. Now we were at Bill and Penny Combs' back door. I had tried the easy way of getting in first, using an old credit card to try to slip the lock out of place, but it was a deadbolt, of course. The last thing I wanted to do was break the glass on the door, but if I couldn't get this spell to work, I would have to.

"Seriously, Ava. What is taking so long?" Olivia tapped her foot on the wood deck. While she was whispering, it was a loud whisper. It reminded me of Sammie when he wanted to share a secret but everyone could still hear what he was saying.

"I'm trying," I hissed. She sighed but piped down.

I put a little more magical elbow grease to the spell. A few seconds later, a click from the handle told me I had succeeded. Wicked glee fluttered inside me, and I almost jumped up and down with excitement.

I would make a bad thief.

We crept into the house, and almost immediately I tripped over a large potted plant. "Why can't we just turn on the lights?" I rubbed my shins and tried to let my eyes adjust. Creepy demon eyes, that freaking hurt. Who put a plant in the middle of the walkway?

Olivia flicked on her flashlight. "We have to make sure nobody is here first."

Once again, I rolled my eyes. We'd been loud enough to wake the dead as we broke in. If someone was here, they already knew we were too. "We know that no one is here. Their daughter lives out of town and Melody said she hasn't seen anybody since we put Penny in Hell."

"Still," Olivia said. "Best that we're careful and don't draw any attention to being here."

Using our flashlights, we crept around until we found Bill's study. I'd been to the house once or twice before, so I sort of knew my way around, but it was difficult in the dark. Once we got into the little office, we got busy using our flashlights to go through volumes and volumes of books, notes, and paperwork. The man's whole magical life was in this office.

"We're looking for anything that mentions the Inbetween or necromancy," I said in a quiet voice.

I considered taking everything, but there was just too much to carry out of the house. Someone would for sure call the cops on us. Not that we'd get in trouble. Even though the sheriff and his deputy didn't know what we were up to exactly, they wouldn't throw us behind bars for it. They'd understand why. Besides, Sam was out of town. But I didn't need to draw the attention of the neighbors by carrying boxes of crap out to my car, parked down the street.

"I know what we're after," Olivia said. "I'm not new here."

We got quiet and kept looking until something behind me crashed. I jumped and whirled around, shining my flashlight toward Olivia, who had knocked a big stack of papers off of the rolltop desk in the corner.

I didn't know what I expected to find when I turned. This was a necromancer's house once so the possibilities of creepy things jumping out at us were endless. Hence why I was so jumpy.

"Shh. You'll wake the dead. What happened to the stealthy ninja?" Speaking of, her outfit wasn't a skin-tight catsuit like I feared. It was, however, all black and form-fitting. At least it wasn't leather.

"I'm being stealthy-ish," she said and pointed to the papers she'd knocked over and the desk. "I think this is what we're looking for."

"What in the world are you two doing?" The light flipped

on and Olivia and I both screamed and spun on our heels to find Drew glaring at us with his arms crossed.

"What are you doing here?" I asked, clutching my chest, checking to see if my heart was still there and hadn't jumped out and run away.

Drew smacked his hand over his forehead dramatically. A little *too* dramatically in my opinion. "We got a call about someone breaking into the house. Did you two seriously go through here with your flashlights?"

Olivia and I exchanged a glance before she focused back on Drew. "We were trying not to draw attention."

Drew shook his head and eased forward. "You'd have been much better off parking out front and walking in the front door like you own the place. Anyone who saw you would assume you had permission because no thief would do that."

Ha! I knew it.

I glared at my friend, and she smiled sheepishly back. Then I focused on Drew. "Exactly what I told her we should do." I bent down to rub my shin where I had kicked the potted plant earlier. It was tender, and I bet I'd have a bruise by morning. "Maybe then we wouldn't have had to pull Drew off duty, and I wouldn't have a sore leg."

Olivia waved us off. "It doesn't matter. I think I found what we needed."

We divided the papers between us and started skimming through them. My stack was all about moving souls from one body to another. With the papers, there were a couple of journals and a laptop. I scooped up every sheet of paper, the journals, and the laptop and shoved them inside the tote bag I'd brought with me.

Once I gathered up all that I could stuff in my bag, Drew ushered us toward the door. "Okay, ladies. You got what you needed. Let's get out of here before someone else calls the police because I've been in here so long."

We exited with Drew and held our heads up high so that the nosy neighbors might think we weren't *actually* causing trouble. Still, I wouldn't be surprised if rumors were floating around town by morning.

The hazards of living in a small town.

Drew offered to give us a ride back to our car down the block, but I waved him off. "We're fine." I rose on my toes and pressed a kiss to his cheek. "As you said, we want it to look like we were meant to be here."

Once we got home, we dumped our loot in my office and began to pour over the papers and journals. I gazed at Winifred with hope. "According to these notes, I should pull a soul from the Ever After and put it into a ghoul, and then they become alive, which we know it's not actually alive, *but* it ties that soul to the necromancer and can drain the necromancer's powers."

Winnie smiled that stiff, creepy Alfred smile. "It's not draining you that much. You're special."

"Hey, I've got a lot of interesting notes about the Inbetween," Olivia said. "It's called the Ever After in here, but it's got to be the same place."

"Here is a spell to put a soul into a living body," Owen said in a hushed voice. "But it only works if the body's original soul is gone."

We all stared at each other in shock. I said, "That could be supremely helpful."

CHAPTER NINE

"It definitely looks bigger." Owen nearly had his nose pressed to the barrier, squinting at the blob. "I mean, it's nearly filled up this bottle."

Yeah, I noticed. "And the bottle looks bigger too."

This couldn't be good. What did it mean? I tapped the barrier spell and, yep, it was still as strong as ever.

"What happens when and if it busts out?" Olivia asked. When did she become a mind reader?

I shrugged and pressed my hand against the barrier. "This thing is pretty strong. I don't think it can escape, especially in this form."

Like it had another form to turn into. Umm, what if it did? That was a scary thought. But hey, I was the one trying to pull the bigger one out of the Inbetween, aka Ever After.

Olivia inched forward. She'd been hanging back at the entrance to the cave, which was not like her. "Maybe if we leave it long enough the lady in the blob will just bring herself through and you guys won't have to figure out how to do it."

We chuckled at the thought. Then I studied my friend. "Can you see anything in this? Come on in here."

Olivia sighed and eased forward. The whole time she stared at the blob in a bottle, she complained. "I don't like this. It makes me feel sad."

I looked at her in surprise. What was going on with her? "You didn't mention anything before. I mean you were here the other day with the Coven and me."

She shrugged. "I haven't come this close, and I just figured you all felt the same thing."

"Noooo," I said, letting the word drag out a little bit. "I don't feel sad."

Scared maybe. Determined, absolutely. I wanted it gone. The blob and the threat on my town. And I wanted my mom safe.

Olivia peered at the bottle in the light from our flashlights. Neither Owen nor I were good at making balls of light like Melody was. I probably had enough power, just not enough skill. Yet.

"No, I can't see anything but black, inky... gross. But the closer I am, the more I want to cry. I want to sob and pitch a huge fit." Olivia cocked her head. "It feels like grief. Deep, bone-weary grief."

Owen and I exchanged a look.

"How can she feel it but nobody else can?" Owen asked.

I shrugged. "Maybe she's a bit empathic."

He raised his eyebrows and opened his mouth to say something, but Olivia beat him to it. She whirled and smiled at me with wide eyes. "I've always thought I was a bit of an empath. I can totally tell when someone is upset. Or lying."

Clicking off my light, I turned toward the cave entrance and laughed at my friend. "Sure, Olivia. Whatever you say."

She hadn't been very empathic during high school. But that had changed, hadn't it? I knew it was the sucky wakeup call she'd gotten when her first husband left her and took the kids. Her two oldest children were in college and didn't have much to do with her. Olivia said it was because she'd been a terrible mother and her ex had further turned them against her.

Whenever I thought about what she'd told me over the phone while I was in Philly, I wanted to hug her and tell her it'll be all right. But I didn't know that for sure.

Her first marriage hadn't been great and Olivia raised her kids just like she had been raised—with nannies and little comfort from her parents. It was how most wealthy families were, though. Both of her parents had high-paying professional jobs that demanded their attention. Children were left with nannies. I understood why Olivia hadn't been close to her now college-age kids from that marriage. Liv hadn't had a loving parental role model.

It didn't help that her ex was a dirtbag who made it his second career to make Olivia feel like a bad mother. He made the kids believe she didn't care for them and hadn't even wanted them.

That was not the case at all.

The fallout of the marriage and losing her children had opened her eyes. Sam's influence on her when they'd started dating had helped Olivia learn to love and be the best mom she could be.

"No, really," she exclaimed, following me out of the cave. "Ever since I was a little girl."

"You've never once mentioned this to me."

"Well, I don't mean like a witchy-empath, but like a human type of empath. Not as a superpower."

I studied her for a little while. She had changed so much since I knew her in school. It was possible that she could've found a natural ability to sense others' feelings or care for what they think and feel.

Empathy wasn't a power. Everyone had it. Witches had an

intuition that enhanced our natural empathy. Some even could use it to heal emotional wounds, but those witches would have to have another power that was connected with healing. Like me.

Although I wasn't sure what exactly gave me the ability to heal others. I'd thought it was my necromancer magic. Apparently not.

Owen chuckled behind us as we continued to bicker about it on the walk back to the house.

The break from reading the mounds and mounds of papers had been nice, but it was time to get back to work.

WinFred handed out fresh cups of coffee as we walked in. "Here you go. I'd help you read, but it's hard for these eyes to see that well. That's why when we get on the iPad, we have to turn the brightness all the way up."

I nodded and sipped the rich brew. "It's okay. The coffee is more than enough."

But when we walked into the living room, we found Larry and Zoey on the couch, sitting way too close together with piles of papers in their laps. I started to say something but thought against it. They were both adults *and* they were undead. That didn't mean they couldn't fall in love. Maybe I should have a talk with both of them at some point.

Now wasn't the time. If they wanted to date, who was I to interfere?

"Winnie recruited us to help read," Larry said. "What are we looking for?"

I smiled gratefully and resumed my spot in the upright chair by the coffee table. "Anything about the Inbetween or the Ever After. Anything about resurrecting a body from ash or moving a soul from one body to another. And definitely anything about a black blob thingy."

I wasn't holding my breath about the latter, but it was on

my wish list. Right next to that easy button that hadn't ever arrived.

"Oh, I found that already." Zoey sorted through the pile in her lap for a minute while we waited with bated breath.

WinFred shuffled into the room. "Please be something useful," she whispered.

"Uhh," Zoey skimmed the handwritten pages. "It would help if his writing was legible," she muttered. "Oh, here it is. Making a body from ashes. It says to assemble the ashes on a flat surface. It needs a surge of power, so it recommends using something to focus power or a group. As long as the person leading the spell is a necromancer, there's no need for words, the necro will instinctively know what to do." She skimmed a bit more. "Something about candles and the winds, too."

That made sense to me, though it probably wouldn't have to her. "Great," I said, reaching out for that piece of paper. "That's one of the spells we needed."

I read over the rest of the spell. "It also says this is just to reassemble the body. It won't put the soul back in." Oh, gross. "It also says the body will begin to putrefy immediately. This puts the body in the same state it was in at death."

"So, Beth's body will look like it was struck by lightning," Winnie said. "That's not going to be great."

"If I can get her soul in it, I should be able to heal that." I smiled at my aunt-slash-ghoul. "We can do this."

Renewed purpose and a sense of accomplishment swirled inside me. This was *so* doable. I'd have my mom back and out of the Inbetween.

"Once her body is whole, you should be able to just pop her back in it, right?" Olivia asked. "Since she's in the Inbetween."

I nodded. "Yep. Shouldn't be difficult."

Snooze walked in from the kitchen carrying something in his mouth. His huge fluffy tail was straight up in the air and the tip of it flipped from side to side. Lucy-Fur was fast on his heels. "Give that back you oversized fluff ball."

Snooze let out a growl that sounded a lot like, "No."

Olivia leaned into me. "What is in his mouth?"

Hoping it wasn't something alive or gross, I looked closer as the two cats raced up the stairs. "It's one of the toys that comes in that subscription box." I raised my voice. "Hey, Lucy, there's one just like it in the toy box."

The white cat poked her between the railing at the top of the stairs. "The jerk stole that one too."

Then she was gone, yelling at Snooze to give up the toy or she'd drown him in the toilet. I thought about reminding Lucy-Fur that Snooze was immortal. If he could survive Drew accidentally shooting him, then drowning wouldn't kill him either. But I left the two crazy cats to deal with their drama.

I had enough of my own.

"This is relevant," Olivia said a few minutes later. "Every time a soul is moved, it weakens."

I looked at WinFred. "You've already been moved once."

She sighed. "Great. What sort of shape is it going to leave me in?"

I didn't know. It would be another mystery for me to solve.

CHAPTER TEN

After I read over the spell about a dozen times, we got our candles, Mom's urn, and headed to the attic. Excitement filled me while anxiety clawed at me. Seeing Mom in the flesh, being about to hug her was almost too much. But I refused to be overwhelmed. I wasn't doing this for me. I was doing it to save her from the evil in the Inbetween.

"I'm not sure we can do this with just us," Owen said, concern leaking from every word he spoke.

Wallie was back at school. He'd left Sunday as soon as the spell to get Phira out of the Inbetween had failed. We couldn't borrow him again until Saturday unless we interrupted his classes. I didn't want to do that. He had a chance at a normal life. Well, as normal as he wanted.

I really didn't have anyone else to call. "This feels so personal. It may be silly of me, but I really don't want to involve the Coven. Not yet."

After we spread out a tarp, Olivia took the candles and began making a circle. "It won't hurt for you to try it on your own. It'll either work or not. If it doesn't, maybe you can ask just one or two of the Coven to come help. That might not make it feel like you're putting on a big show."

I nodded. "That sounds like a good plan."

Once we had the candles lit, I dumped Mom's ashes out on the middle of the tarp. Then I used my handy wind spell to keep Mom's cremains from going everywhere. Sometimes, with witches, their magic stayed with their bones or ashes. This was one of those cases. Mom's ashes tried floating away.

"Whoa. I don't know why I didn't expect someone's ashes to not float around in the air." Olivia stared wide eyed as she watched the light winds from my spell form the ashes into the rough shape of a body and keep them from floating.

"Yeah, without this spell, as soon as we opened this bag in the urn, the whole attic would be filled with...well, with my mother," I said with a lame laugh. "This spell keeps that from happening."

My heart was both heavy and hopeful, seeing my mother's remains spread out on the attic floor. Owen took my hands and we stood on either side of the remains.

"It says you'll know what to do," Zoey said. "So, go for it."

Centering myself, I reached deep and pulled my magic to the surface. Stretching forward with my mystical powers, I let them drift all over the tarp. As with all of my necro powers, I didn't fully understand how it worked. I just knew they were doing what they needed to do. Focusing, I went into a sort of trance and let my magic do exactly what it wanted to.

And before my eyes, the ashes moved. They formed together, then transformed into bones. From there, they kept going, the way Larry's had. Muscles formed, and tendons, veins, organs. It was all there, and only my magic would keep it from turning into dust again.

Sweat beaded on my forehead as the spell took more and more power from me.

And several minutes later, it was done. My mother's body

laid on the floor of our attic, eyes closed. She looked like she was sleeping. Peaceful.

"Why is she bruised all over?" Olivia asked in a hushed tone as I released the magic and stared at my mother in person for the first time in over thirty years.

"It's from the lightning," Winnie explained. "It caused her blood to burst from her capillaries and to pool under the skin like a bruise."

I called to my healing magic and added a bit of extra power to her body. The evidence of the lightning strike disappeared.

"Now," I said, stepping backward and taking a deep breath. "Let me pull her from the Inbetween."

This part was easy. I focused my magic the way I had so many times before. Then I called to her. "Mom, grab onto my power and let it guide you."

But nothing happened. Furrowing my brow, I focused again, trying to draw her spirit toward me and out of that place.

"It's not working," I muttered.

I kept trying, focusing on my mother and ignoring everyone else. I vaguely sensed them going in and out of the attic. Eventually, I had to sit down as I tried, over and over, to pull mom into her body. At some point, Snoozer came in and curled up in my lap, purring, comforting me.

I hadn't realized until then that I was crying.

"Ava."

I jumped and turned my head to see Wade in the attic doorway. "Hey," I said. "What are you doing up?"

"It's almost midnight." He shrugged and crossed the room toward me. "I've been up for hours."

He handed me a mug. "Hot cocoa."

Settling beside me, Wade looked at my mother's face. "She was a beautiful woman."

I smiled. "Yes, she was. But I can't get her back. It's not working."

"It's time to stop trying." Wade lifted his mug to his mouth and took a sip. "Oh," he said, pulling the mug away and looking inside it as if he didn't trust the contents. "This blood tastes different."

I raised my eyebrows at him. "Where did you get it?"

He shrugged. "It's part of what Owen got for me. I think it was from Sam, Drew, and Olivia."

"Maybe it's Drew's," I said. "He's a hunter. They have a bit of supernatural in their blood."

He shrugged and drank more. "It might be better I don't know. This tastes amazing. I'd be tempted to get more."

We chuckled, and I kept trying to raise my mother. Once my hot cocoa and Wade's blood were gone, he stood and held out a hand. "Come on, girl. Time to rest."

"Mom's body will start to deteriorate," I said. "She can't stay here."

"She can go into the basement with me." He put his arm around me. "I'll carry her down. You've got an extra fridge down there. I'll clean it out and lean it back so she can stand up in it. She'll be safe there until you figure this out."

That sounded perfectly horrible, but it was a good idea. The fridge was usually full of extra drinks, and was the kind that didn't have a freezer on it, so it was tall. If he took out the shelves it would work. "Thanks, Wade."

"I'm here for you. I might only be here at night now, but it's you and me, babe."

I hugged him tight and when he returned it, I sank into his arms and rested my head against his shoulder. He was the closest thing I had to a dad. He'd always been there. Even in high school, before he moved back to Philly. "I'm glad you're here."

He pulled back and framed my face. "Me too." He kissed my forehead then stepped back. "Let's get your mom down to the basement. Then figure out why you can't reach her with your powers."

As he bent and carefully scooped Mom up in his arms, his words sank in. My powers couldn't reach her. She was killed by a lightning strike, which was part of the curse Bevin placed on her. The crazy freak accident curse.

I pressed my lips in a firm line as I followed Wade down the stairs. What if the curse kept her from being animated after death? That would explain why I couldn't pull her out.

There was one person who could tell me.

CHAPTER ELEVEN

"Luci! Will you please come here?" I knew he could hear me. He showed up all the time when we were talking about different things that interested him.

I stood in my bedroom the next morning. Wade had put my disappointed butt to bed as soon as we went downstairs last night, with Olivia and WinFred backing him up.

But that was then. It was late morning, I'd slept in, had breakfast and a shower, and I was ready to hit it. My powers felt strong. "Lucifer Morningstar or whatever your last name is, don't make me summon you!"

My bedroom door creaked open. Not that it is actually creaky. Those were new hinges—part of the renovations I did when I moved in. The old creepy door sounds came from Winston, the house.

From behind the creaky door, Lucy-Fur poked her head in, then pranced inside like she'd been summoned to do so. She sat in front of me and glared. "What do you want? I'm trying to get in my mid-morning nap."

All that cat did was nap. And curse at Snoozer. Although I

had seen the two of them curled up in my office chair the other night. Oh, gods, I hoped they didn't *do it* in there. I had to make a note to have Alfred clean extra well in my office to be safe.

Snapping back to the issue at hand, I said, "I wasn't calling you. I was calling Lucifer."

"Doesn't he have a phone? It's quieter if you use a phone." With that, she strutted out of my room with her head held high and her tail dancing in the air.

Well then. I guess I've been told. Rolling my eyes I decided to try again, this time in a softer tone. "Satan, I summon you."

But he didn't show.

"Damn it," I muttered.

Stomping out of my room, I headed across the hall to Wallie's room, where Olivia'd been crashing. "You awake?" I called as I knocked.

"I'm down here," Olivia yelled from downstairs. "Listening to you shout the roof off of the house."

As if agreeing with her, Winston shook the floor under my feet.

I hurried downstairs. She hadn't been down when I'd come to eat earlier. "I can't get Luci. Walk with me to his place?"

"Sure."

We headed out with Snoozer and Lucy on our tails.

"Would you hurry?" Lucy-Fur said in a bored voice. "It's cold out here."

I glanced back at the haughty feline and chuckled. It was far from cold. It was late March and felt like spring. Well, spring for Maine anyway. "Are you a good representation of how all cats think? Because I feel like you are."

She sighed as if I were boring her. "I just want to get out of this field full of grasshoppers and other vermin."

I was about to remind her that I hadn't asked her to come along. Snooze usually followed me everywhere unless he was napping or eating. But before I spoke, Lucy-Fur stopped and stared at a spot in the grass. Olivia and I turned to see what it was.

Without warning, Lucy launched forward, trapping something between her paws. "Got you, you nasty little Junebug."

Olivia and I burst out laughing, but it died when Lucy exposed the huge brown beetle. I recognized it. Not a Junebug. A water bug. Before it could escape, she grabbed it between her teeth and chomped.

"Oh, ew." Olivia grimaced. "I heard that thing crunch."

Shuddering, we turned and hurried toward Lucifer's place, leaving the cats in the field to catch more of the so-called vermin.

I rang the doorbell and waited, tapping my foot. Olivia was less patient. She tried the handle. To our surprise, it opened easily.

"Hello?" I called into the massive house, then looked at Olivia. "He gave us permission to go in before. I suppose we can enter to look for him."

We didn't even make it out of the entryway before Luci appeared. He strolled out of a door to our left in a red velvet robe, holding a mug of something steaming. "Ava!" He grinned. "And Olivia. Two of my favorite ladies. Have you come to tell me you've freed my Fee from the Inbetween?"

I shook my head. "No, but we need your help to keep working on it."

He pursed his lips, then took a sip of his drink. "I'm listening."

"We need to get my mother out of there. She can help us open a portal to get Fee out," I explained. "Even with the whole Coven, we couldn't make it work. If it doesn't work with Mom on this side, we have a spell to put her and Winnie in human bodies. We *think* that will allow them to reach their powers again." I'd read more about this spell when looking for one to reform Mom's body. It'd been an idea in the back of my mind, but if it helped convince Luci to get us to Bevin...

"What do you need from me?" he asked.

"We can't get mom out of the Inbetween, and we really should be able to." I clasped my hands in front of me. "I need to question Bevin."

Luci shrugged, then snapped his fingers.

Now crumpled in the middle of Luci's entryway, Bevin looked up at me, squinting his eyes. "Ava?" he breathed.

His brown hair looked dark. Upon a closer inspection, I realized it wasn't darker, it was caked with dirt and something slimy. His clothes were worn with tears in random places and nasty. I tried to not make a face at his appearance, but I failed.

But there was no way I could feel sorry for him.

"Yeah," I said in a flat voice, trying to hold in my anger. "It's me."

He shuffled forward on his knees. "I knew you'd be merciful. Please, if you free me—"

"Shut up," Olivia snarled. She lifted one foot and put it on his shoulder, shoving him backward. He landed on his butt hard. "Why can't Ava get her mom out of the Inbetween?"

Bevin scrambled to his knees again. "I don't know. Please, be merciful, I beg—"

With one wave of my hand, I cut off his vocal cords. He couldn't speak now. "You will tell me the truth," I snarled. "What did you do to make it so my mother is stuck in the Inbetween?"

He mouthed at me. Tapping my foot, I waited for him to talk.

Luci leaned over. "Ava, dear. The man can't tell you the truth if you don't unfreeze his voice."

"Oh, yeah." I waved my hand again and Bevin gasped.

"Her ashes." He whimpered. "I put some of her ashes in

that realm. If any part of her is there bodily, her soul can't leave."

"Where are they?" I snarled again, curling my hands into fists. Definitely not feeling sorry for the dirt worm.

"In a small box." He sighed and slumped down. "Under your front porch in that realm."

I shook my head. I'd been right there. If I'd known, I could've grabbed them. I sucked in a deep, steadying breath. "How do we get into the Inbetween?"

He looked at us like we were nuts. "I thought it was common knowledge. All you need is a lot of power. But going there and back is dangerous. That's why witches don't do it much. You can lose part of your soul."

He said 'much'. That made me wonder how many witches crossed between the realms. And why.

One thing at a time.

"That's it?" Luci asked. "Just a lot of power?"

Bevin nodded. With a snap of his fingers, Luci made him disappear again.

"We gather power, get my mom's ashes, and get her here," I said. "Then she can help us get Phira out."

"No." Luci straightened his spine and glowered at us. "Fee comes out with us."

Okay, then. Fee was coming out with us.

CHAPTER TWELVE

"Come with me," Luci said.

Olivia and I exchanged a glance of worry. "Should we?" I asked.

Luci stopped in the doorway and turned back toward us. "Seriously? After all this time and all the help I've given you, you still don't trust me?"

He wasn't wrong, not exactly. He'd been a constant thorn in my side, but he'd never done anything strictly harmful to us. "Okay," I said reluctantly. "You have to understand... you're *Lucifer*. It's ingrained in us not to trust you."

He waved me off and walked through the large, swinging wooden door.

Olivia grinned wickedly. "He's fun, if nothing else."

She hurried after him.

When I stepped through the door, I gasped and staggered back. The room, which I'd assumed was the same kitchen we'd explored once before when we'd been on the hunt for Snoozer, who had gone temporarily missing, was nothing like it had been. Or else, we weren't in the same house.

"Where are we?" I asked, gaping at the lush foliage. There was color everywhere. Grass so green it didn't look real. And all the trees either had blooming flowers or colorful leaves. Some had both.

The air was *so* clean and free of pollution. There was a mix of floral and herbal scents. It was amazing.

"Welcome to Faery," Luci said, sweeping his arm out. I kept looking around, marveling at the picturesque landscape, noting a waterfall not too far from us.

"How are we in Faery?" Olivia asked, wearing an expression of shock on her face that surely matched my own. She kept turning in circles, admiring everything. "It's so colorful and amazing."

Carrie walked out from between a couple of impossibly huge trees. She looked like a tiny sprite compared to these behemoths. "Oh, how nice to see you," she cried. "Come, meet my grandfather."

She wore a long pale pink gown that barely covered her bare feet. The silky fabric flowed perfectly with her modest curves. The three-quarter sleeves looked like a shimmery web woven around her arms.

She took one of my hands in her left and one of Olivia's in her right, then pulled us toward the trees she'd come through. Luci strolled behind us. I looked over my shoulder, still wide-eyed and impressed that we were in an entirely different realm. "So you turned your kitchen into a portal?"

He laughed and clasped his hands behind his back in a smug sort of way. "Oh, gosh, no. Just the doorway."

"I've been in discussions with my grandfather," Carrie said. "And he's agreed to help you and Luci get Fee back."

Olivia and I exchanged a glance behind our friend's back. "Carrie," I said gently, pulling her closer to me. "You're helping Luci reunite with his long-lost love."

Carrie chuckled. "I'm not in love with him, Ava. He's fun,

and I care about him. But I'd rather see him happy with his true love than continue using him for the best sex I've ever had." She paused as she let go of our hands and pulled aside a curtain of vines. "Though I will really, *really* miss the sex."

Olivia and I giggled as we walked under the vines, but as soon as we stepped through we both stopped and fell silent.

"Whoa," I whispered. "Who in the world is your grandfather?"

In front of us was a royal throne room, in the middle of a forest. Large trees with leaves of purples and pinks served as a natural canopy over the outdoor room. The ground looked like cobblestones with grass growing in the cracks. The throne, deade center, had hand-carved vines and flowers on it.

The man sitting on the throne looked a little like Carrie except he had a short gray bread that matched his shoulder-length hair and lavender eyes. He watched us as we approached.

Carrie stepped in front of us and bowed deeply. Her dress spread over the soft grass. "Grandfather, I bring you the Earth's Queen of the necromancers, Ava, and her loyal human servant, Olivia." He cocked his head at Liv when he spoke to her. The guy must've seriously disliked humans.

"Hang on a second," Olivia said hotly, but Luci stepped forward and pulled her into a side hug, clapping his hand over her mouth.

"Go with it," he hissed.

Olivia did not look too happy with this development, but she kept her lips shut after he removed his hand.

Carrie's grandfather rose from the throne, all flowing gold robes. Just like out of a storybook. "Whoa," I whispered.

The man walked down stairs which formed beneath his feet a split second before each step he took. When he reached the soft grass, flowers bloomed so that he didn't have to step one leaf-clad foot on the ground.

"Daaaamn," Olivia whispered.

Yeah. This really was a damn sort of moment. "Ava and Olivia, I present my many-times great grandfather, King Laneo of the Sprite Courts."

Laneo stepped close to me and peered down into my face. "You have character."

Before I could respond, he stepped over to Olivia and stood equally close as he peered down at her. "You have mischief."

That was a pretty accurate description of Olivia. He stared at her for another couple of seconds while she stood there looking pretty dumbfounded.

Then, lips pursed, he stepped back. "I will send a contingent of Fae Mages to help you open the portal to the Inbetween. They will only be able to provide power. We do not have the necessary magic to actually perform the spell that opens it."

"That will be enough," I said gratefully. "Thank you."

He turned without another word and walked back up his stairs, which had disappeared and now reformed.

"We're dismissed," Luci whispered. "Time to go." He snapped his fingers and we appeared in his entryway again.

It appeared we'd be having help from the Fae.

CHAPTER THIRTEEN

"Are you ready for this?" Drew asked.

Nope.

I sucked in a deep breath, then had to release it to speak. "You mean am I ready to channel magic from some of the most powerful beings on the planet to release my mother from a world I never knew existed a few weeks ago, using powers I'd barely ever used a few months ago?"

Amusement lit up Drew's face as he nodded slowly. "Yep. That about sums it up."

I grinned at him, totally contemplating asking him to run away with me. We could take the next flight out to...anywhere. "Sure! Let's do this."

With a chuckle, he put his hand on my back and followed me out of my bedroom. The warmth of his touch seeped through the fabric of my t-shirt. It was comforting and soothed my nerves.

The doorbell rang as we descended the stairs.

"They're here," Olivia squealed. She ran by as we hit the bottom step, stopped at the doorway, and turned in a circle before sucking in a deep breath and opening the door. "Hello." Her voice came out deep and calm as if she hadn't just been flipping out like a little girl about to walk in DisneyWorld for the first time. "Please come in."

I'd never seen her so excited to meet people before. Of course, our guests weren't just people. They were Fae. I shook my head at her as she led five tall, impressive people into the house.

Moving over so Drew could come off the stairs, I inclined my head at the Fae. "Welcome."

They gathered in the foyer and looked around. One, with inky black hair and terra-cotta skin, stepped forward. The leader. I could tell by the way he held himself above the rest of us. It wasn't rude, it was the way he was raised. He inclined his head back at me, but only barely. "We are honored to be working with the Queen of Necromancers. I am Eodh. I will be the voice of the Fae while we are here."

The sound of being called the queen of anything made me want to laugh. It was a miracle I hadn't burst out a giggle when he said it.

Carrie peeked around the backs of the large people and gave me a big smile. Three women and a man stared at me as I waved my fingers at her. "Hey, Ava!"

I winked at Carrie, then gave my attention back to Eodh. "Thank you for coming."

Eodh blinked once. "Phira is my sister. I have waited for this opportunity for many years."

He stepped aside and motioned toward the other Fae. "These are Phira's sisters and younger brother."

I nodded to each of them in greeting. These Fae looked absolutely nothing alike. Clearly, I had no idea how the Fae worked. The three women ranged in skin tone from the fairest to the darkest, like a color wheel. They were all beautiful beyond belief, of course. They did share that trait. The male was somewhat similar to Eodh, but a bit fairer.

"Hello." I greeted them. "And your names?"

"Will not help you open the portal," Eodh said. "Are we ready?"

I stopped short at his tone and Drew pinched my side. I gave him a sharp look and almost cracked up. But still, I didn't much care for Eodh's sass.

Before I could politely answer him, Olivia stepped around Carrie and waved at the fairies. "Hello, I'm Olivia."

The group turned to look at Liv as one. Then, all five cocked their heads at her at once, like a group of kittens following a toy. It was odd how they studied her, trying to figure her out. Well, I could tell them that it was a waste of time. I gave up figuring Olivia out a long time ago.

She grinned at them a little crazily, even for Liv. "I am so very happy to meet you all, but I can't stay. I'm only here because I wanted to say hi." Olivia stuck out her hand and grabbed Eodh's.

The expression on his face only changed minimally, yet I got the sense that he was deeply amused by her cheek. "We are happy to please you."

Nice veiled insult.

Jerk. Again, Drew pinched my side, making me twitch. Could he read my mind? We were going to have to talk about that later.

One of the women stepped forward and took Olivia's hand. The regal Fae leaned over and peered into Olivia's eyes.

Liv leaned back. "Uh, hey," she said quietly. "Nice to meet you."

"You will be a big surprise, I think," the woman said. "A big surprise, indeed." She sighed. "Mischief."

Olivia backed away and glanced over her shoulder at me. "I'm a delight." She clapped her hands together. "But I really do have to go." Turning, she grabbed me into a quick hug. "Be careful. I'll be back later."

As she opened the door to leave, she nearly ran face-first into Melody and pretty much the entire Coven. "Oh," she gasped. "Hello, hi."

Nodding and waving as she passed all the people we'd begun to know from the Coven.

"It's getting a bit crowded in here," Drew whispered against my temple.

"Yeah. You good? With all this power?" I kept my voice as low as his.

The Fae had magic that seemed to float around them. It tingled my skin but not in a threatening way. For Drew, since he was a born hunter with powers that I didn't fully understand, all this magic under one roof wouldn't feel so great.

He kissed the side of my head. "I'm not leaving you."

My heart expanded. He was *so* the alpha male when it came to protecting those he cared about.

Louder, so those in the back could hear me, I said, "Okay, everyone, if you will, please follow Owen." I pointed to the left at Owen, who stood in the doorway to the kitchen. "He will lead you out the back door and to the site of the spell."

Eodh led the way with his Fae siblings flowing behind him. Melody and the Coven shuffled in and gaped at the tall fairies as they headed out of the kitchen and onto the back deck toward the path down the cliff and to the beach.

"Well," I said with a sigh. "Here we go!"

Drew and I brought up the rear. As I closed the backdoor, leaving an irritated Snoozer and indifferent Lucy staring out the window at me, Luci popped in.

"Oh, good," he said. "I'm not late."

Proud of myself for managing not to jump out of my skin, I turned on my heel, took Drew's hand, and ignored Luci as I hurried to catch up with the group. I hadn't even seen him in the house. Even WinFred had gotten well ahead of me. Not that they could do any good, but they'd insisted on coming. I didn't see the problem with it.

The group waited for me at the entrance to the cave. Something occurred to me and I groaned. "Okay. I'm going to have to go into the Inbetween. I can't lead the spell myself."

Eodh cocked his head. "Nor can we."

I was, by far, the most powerful. Melody furrowed her brow. "Are you sure?" she asked. "You might be able to go in and still hold it open." She looked around. "Why are we opening the portal here and not right by the front porch where the ashes are supposed to be?"

"Because if Phira comes through, we need her to come through into this barrier." I motioned toward the cave. Last night the Coven had gathered and helped me increase the size of the barrier. Now the entire cave was spelled to hold in anyone magical who went inside it. "If the portal is open here and I'm not there to stop her, she'll come through and be trapped."

Melody grinned. She'd known that, of course, but now everyone else did, including the Fae and Luci. I appreciated her playing dumb so that nobody could question me.

"Are we ready?" I asked.

Nobody protested, so I held out my hands. "Here we go."

CHAPTER FOURTEEN

"Okay, Ava," Winnie whispered. "We were able to open the portal with just your mother, Yaya, and me before, but we only had to hold it open for a second."

No pressure. "Yeah, I'll have to keep it open. More power." Geesh I hoped the Fae power was enough.

Hands touched my back and their magics danced over my skin and inside me seeking mine to aid in opening a portal to another world. I knew the chant by heart now after trying on my own so many times.

Ready or not.

I lifted my hands with my palms out and recited the chant, allowing the magic to flow through me and out my palms. The Coven joined in, speaking the words in a soft rhythmic way. The Fae chanted with us. The power built, and I directed it to my purpose.

In front of my eyes, what looked like a hole opened up. As if the veil of time and space was being pulled apart to reveal the Inbetween.

I gasped when it was done, and staggered forward. This

was far more draining than I'd expected. The energy to hold the portal open had to stay at a consistent cycle. And I was in the center of it. My Coven and the Fae were pushing power into me while the portal pulled it out. It took everything I had to breathe. I stepped through the portal and turned to walk through this shadowy cold version of the real world.

Gasping, I tried to move up the beach, toward the path to get to the house. I'd never felt a power drain like this. It was unbelievable.

"Ava," Drew said from the other side. "Let me go get it."

I stopped and turned back, realizing I'd only moved a few feet. "Yeah," I called back. "I can't make it. Not while holding this portal."

Drew took off running. "Just keep it open," he yelled as he went by. "I'll be back."

I moved back to the real world and watched him grow smaller and smaller as he climbed the rocks. Once he was out of sight, I turned to see the people funneling their magic into me.

They didn't look any better than me. Even the Fae had strained expressions on their faces.

Luci, grimacing, darted through the portal. "I have to find her."

He took off running. "Fee!" he screamed. "Where are you?"

"Luci!" I staggered toward him. He was crazy. "We can't hold it open and wait for you to bring her back!"

He stopped short, then turned slowly. "Open the portal again in twenty-four hours. I'll have her here, waiting."

"What? No—"

He took off, not listening to me. I didn't have a clue how he'd do it, but I nodded. The whole point of this was to get my mom *and* Phira out. However we had to do it.

Luci disappeared in the same direction Drew had gone. I didn't have time to question how long this was going to take before Drew appeared over the sand dunes, holding a black box in his hands.

My heart lurched at seeing him. And damn. That man was fit.

And *so* hot.

I stepped through and into the real world again, clinging desperately to the portal. He was so close, but it felt like it was slipping through my fingers like water draining out of cupped hands. "Hurry," I yelled desperately.

The portal began to shrink. Oh, no. "Faster," I urged under my breath. "Come on."

Drew must've reserved a burst of energy. He moved as fast as he could, pumping his arms with the black box held in one like a football.

As the portal slipped away from me, Drew lunged through, speeding out into the real world with a ferocious yell.

Staggering back, I plopped down in the sand and panted. "You did it. We did it."

Eodh sighed and looked down at me. "That was impressive, necromancer. It was a pleasure working with you today." He turned to leave.

"Hang on." I scrambled to my feet, barely mustering the energy to do so. "What about tomorrow?"

"We will return," he said. "We will help you bring Phira home."

"Meet us here in twenty-four hours?" I asked. "Or you're welcome at my home, of course. Any time."

Carrie stepped up beside me to watch them walk away. "Is it me, or is Eodh really freaking hot?"

I glanced at her in surprise. I personally believed that Eodh had something stuck up his rear end and he needed a personality. But hey, to each his own. "You're really giving Luci up that easily?"

She stared at me with a flat expression. "Ava, stop being so sentimental. Luci is in what amounts to purgatory, searching for his long-lost love. I'm not the heroine in his romance novel. I'm the one he leaves for his lady love."

I looped my arm through hers, mostly for the physical support, and pulled her closer. "You're a strong woman."

"Here," Drew said. "Lean on me."

I gladly let go of Carrie and moved toward Drew. He still held the box in his other hand. "I sure hope these are the ashes," he said. "I didn't take the time to double-check."

"Surely there wouldn't have been *two* random containers under my front porch in the Ever After," I said with a chuckle.

"Um, Ava," Larry said, coming up beside me and holding up his arm. "This doesn't look good."

I glanced at his arm and frowned. The skin was peeling off. "How did this happen?"

WinFred looked over and shook their head. "Your powers are depleted. You must be drawing on your ghouls to even be awake right now because I don't feel so well."

"Neither do I," Zoey said. She groaned.

Snoozer and Lucy-Fur met us on the front porch and both of them looked rough. Their fur was patched and grimy-looking.

For the second time since we made the dating thing official, Drew lifted me up with one arm under my knees and the other one supporting my back. Then he carried me up the stairs and tucked me into my bed and told me to rest. He gave me a lingering kiss before leaving.

Seconds later, I was sound asleep.

CHAPTER FIFTEEN

"Have you slept long enough?"

Ugh. I threw the pillow over my head. Why couldn't anyone just let me sleep?

Once again, Aunt Winnie woke me up with her sweet voice. I would never grow tired of listening to her talk. She used to tell me bedtime stories when I was young. I hadn't wanted Mom to do it. Always had to be Aunt Winnie.

I peeked out from under my pillow at her. "I don't know. Maybe."

"It doesn't take that much of your power to do the spell, right?" she asked, hope laced in her tone.

She was ready for her body. And I was too. Right after a few more minutes of sleep.

"Is it dark yet?" I asked with my face still under the pillow.

"Yes." She wiggled on the bed beside me.

I almost asked how long I'd been asleep but didn't have the brainpower to hold onto a conversation at the moment. Instead, I said, "Have Wade bring Mom's body up to the attic. Then come wake me up."

That should buy me a few extra minutes.

"It's already done. Everyone is waiting, even Olivia."

Or not.

I rolled over and looked up at the ceiling, taking stock of how I felt.

Not that bad. I'd slept most of the day, but now my power felt back to normal. I studied WinFred for a moment. "How do you feel?"

"Better."

"And Larry? Zoey? The cats?"

"All fine. How do you think I knew it was safe to wake you?" They tried to grin but failed.

I snorted and sat up. "Did Drew leave?"

"Yeah." WinFred held out a mug of coffee, judging by the smell. "He had a shift. Said he'd be back later tonight."

"Later tonight?" Was he planning on staying? Like the whole night? A sleepover with my boyfriend. Hey, that sounded like fun. I knew a spell for soundproofing my room.

And on that note...

"Okay." I jumped out of bed, ready to do this. "I'm ready to get Mom back. And to see you again. I can't wait to hug you."

My energy spiked, and excitement filled me. There was a really good chance this was going to work this time. How could I lay around in bed? I'd be seeing my mother for the first time since I was ten years old. "Let's do this!"

Moving fast, I changed clothes, then headed up to the attic with WinFred on my heels. Someone had pushed back all the junk up there, piling it against the walls to give us a bigger place to work. Two circles had been set up, and as I walked in, Olivia put down the last candle beside my mother's body. "I'm sorry I missed all the excitement this morning." She held up the black box. "I hear Drew was quite the hero."

Beaming, I nodded, unable to help myself. Drew was pretty great. "I know, right?"

I started my spell to keep the cremains contained in the spell area, then picked up Winnie's urn and dumped her ashes in the middle of the second circle of candles. I let my power surface as I spoke the chant, turning ashes to bone, muscle, and flesh.

"Whoa," WinFred muttered. "That's so cool."

At first, I was surprised that she'd be so amazed, but then I remembered she wasn't used to seeing the necromancy side of things. My father had been the necromancer. Winnie was a green witch. I'd done necromancy in front of her and Alfred before, of course, but it had to be a whopper for her to see her own body lying there.

When it was done, WinFred gasped as they stared at the ashes in the shape of her body. "It's so strange to think that's me."

"Soon you'll be your vivacious self."

"Without magic."

I nodded sadly. "Yes. But I have an idea about that. We'll talk about it when all of this is settled."

There was a spell for putting a soul in a living, yet soulless body. I wanted to explore the implications of that.

But not right now.

Owen, Zoey, Olivia, WinFred, and Larry crowded around the two bodies. Wade was watching from the attic door. He wasn't used to all this magic. Well, he certainly would be in no time hanging out with me and mine.

I sat between the two circles, turned first toward Winnie. Mom was no doubt just as eager to get out of the Inbetween, but Winnie was actually in front of me, staring and waiting.

"Okay," I said, looking up at her. "You ready for this?"

WinFred nodded and if a ghoul could beam, they would've been. They held out a piece of paper. "The spell for moving me out of this body and into that one."

I nodded and looked at it again, though I'd seen it a few

times already. And put it to memory. Besides, it wasn't too different from the one to pull mom out of the Inbetween. "Everyone ready?"

Owen sat beside me. "I don't think you need it, but I'll lend you a bit of power."

I shook my head. "No, but thank you. I want to do this myself."

He scooted back a little. "I'm here if you need me."

Sucking in a deep breath, I reached out with my magic, probing into Alfred. I found him quickly. His soul took up most of the body, filling it with happiness. Alfred was a cheerful guy. I looked forward to getting to know him.

And there was Winnie. Her warm, bubbly personality was tucked into the head of the ghoul. No wonder she was the one to speak most of the time. Plus she seemed to be the one controlling things now that I thought back to everything up until this point.

I hadn't realized the location of the soul determined which of them steered the ship, so to speak.

How freaking weird.

"Come on," I muttered. "Time to go home."

Wrapping tendrils around the essence of Winnie, I pulled her out of Alfred.

Her soul was a light green, almost sheer orb of light floating out of Alfred's mouth and over to Winnie's body.

"Can anyone else see it?" I whispered. "Her soul?"

"I can," Owen said. "It's beautiful. What a rare sight."

Olivia sighed. "No." She pouted a little. "I wish I could."

The floor creaked to my left, and I glanced over to see Snoozer making his way to me. When he saw the orb, he lowered his body and started to do that wiggle-butt thing he did before pouncing. "Snooze. No!"

Just before he leaped into the air, Owen grabbed him and almost dropped him. Snooze was a lot of cat. But Owen managed to wrap an arm around Snooze's lower body and hold him while I finished. I pointed at the fat cat.

"You can stay if you are going to be good. One wrong move and I'll lock you out of here."

Snooze meowed and it sounded like the grumbling backtalk I used to get from Wallie when he was a teen. Boy those were some challenging times.

Crazy cat.

As I sank Winnie's aura into her body, Alfred sat up straight. "Oh, this feels nice," he said in his mousy voice. It really didn't match his look at all. "Not that I minded having Winnie piggybacking on me, but this is great!"

Winnie sat up and sighed. "Oh, my." She looked down at herself. She was a curvy woman when alive and now it looked like she'd lost fifty pounds. And she looked a little younger. Her short salt and pepper hair was shiny and full of life and her green eyes were clear and sparked with my magic. "I look amazing!"

"Yes, you do." More than amazing.

Olivia pulled a compact out of her back pocket. "Here."

After studying herself in the mirror, my aunt lunged forward and wrapped her arms around my neck. "Thank you," she whispered. "Thank you so much."

CHAPTER SIXTEEN

I looked over at Mom's body. "I hope you're ready," I whispered.

With a sigh, I searched deep inside for that part of myself and my magic that kept her body animated, then released it.

Her body returned to ash within a minute. With a creak, Owen opened the black box. Inside, loose ashes drifted around. "Add them, please."

There wasn't much. Maybe a teaspoonful. But apparently, it was enough to keep me from pulling her out of the Inbetween.

"We probably didn't have to add it," he said. "Just get it out of there."

Oh, he had a good point. It wasn't possible to get every speck of someone's remains after they'd been cremated. But as long as they weren't in the Inbetween, I probably could've just pulled her soul into her body. But I wasn't taking any chances. "Add it all."

Once all her ashes were there, I focused and spoke the spell to make her body whole again. Staring down at my mother, who I'd missed so badly all my life, I grinned as I did my thing and animated her. I'd done it enough times now that it was like second nature.

And to my intense, overwhelming joy, she gasped and blinked her eyes. I kept pumping magic into her to heal the bruises from the lightning strike and stopped only when she looked completely normal and like a healthy thirty-five-year-old. Because that was her age when she'd died.

Shoot, she looked younger than me! How would I explain that to people in town? I didn't care. I had her back.

"Mom?" I asked in a quiet voice. My eyes stung as tears filled them.

She sat up and looked around the room, and her eyes landed directly on me. "Oh, Ava. You did it."

I choked back a sob as Winnie and I crawled toward her, the three of us collapsing in a pile of hugs. But before long, my tears broke through, and I cried against Winnie's shoulder with Mom's arms around both of us.

"If a ghoul was able to cry, I'd be sobbing, too," Winnie said, rubbing my back. "Let it all out."

"Come on guys," Olivia whispered from behind me. "Let's go let them have some time together."

I barely registered the rest of my crew leaving the attic but managed to croak at them before they shut the attic door. "Someone text Wallie."

"Don't worry," Olivia said. "I already did."

When my tears had been spent, I scooted back. "I can't stay sitting on this floor for much longer," I joked. "I'm more fit than I used to be, but wooden floors are no place for a forty-something to hang out on. Or to sit on."

"Come on," Winnie said, climbing to her feet. "Let's take a walk and let your mother get the hang of commanding a body again."

We moved slowly through the house and out the back door.

Winnie was right. Mom was a little bit wobbly, but then, she'd been a ghost for over thirty years. I couldn't blame her.

As we walked, I filled her in on my life. "I can't wait for you to meet Wallie. It was torture while he grew up, not having you there to dote on him. Or for me to call and ask questions."

"I tried to play that role," Winnie said. "But with mom and you both gone, it was a bittersweet thing, for sure."

Mom clasped both of our hands and held them to her chest. "I was there. I was watching, as much as I could, with the evil constantly hunting for me. It used to hang out near Philadelphia as if it knew I'd want to go there to see Wallie."

"I'm so sorry," I whispered. "Maybe if I'd embraced this part of myself years ago, I could've gotten you out sooner. I could've saved you."

Mom shook her head and moved closer to me as we walked over the sandy beach. "You did the best you could. I'm just happy to be here now."

"Me, too," Winnie said. "This is amazing compared to sharing that old crusty body."

We laughed and kept walking until we got to the cave. "You can't really see the part of the blob that's here," I said at the cave entrance, inches from the barrier. "It's in the corner, in a bottle."

All three of us screamed and jumped back when the blob in question slammed against the barrier. That corrected me on them not seeing it. And holy freaking cow, that scared the bejesus out of me. I clutched my chest. "How did it get out of the bottle?"

And it was a lot bigger now. Crapola this wasn't good.

It kept slamming itself against the barrier, alternately in front of Winnie and Mom. I motioned for them to move further away from it. "That thing really hates you guys."

"Yeah. If I got locked up away from the love of life, I'd be pissed too." Winnie wrapped her arms around her waist.

Mom's features turned sad and remorseful. "I regret doing it. We never dreamed the Fae King would lie to us."

"I know, Mom. We'll figure it all out in time." I waved my hands at them to back up some, then moved closer to the barrier. "I'm just going to add a little extra power to this thing to strengthen it. You know...peace of mind."

"Good thinking," Mom and Winnie said together.

I pooled some of my magic and directed it to my palm as I held it inches from the barrier. With a little push, the magic flowed out of my hand and coated the barrier. Green and blue streaks rippled over it, then settled into the existing magic, making it stronger.

Blob hit the invisible wall again, but I didn't move or even flinch. It hovered in front of me, watching. Pain of loss and fury drifted in the air between us. "I'm sorry for what you went through. We'll find a way to heal you."

Turning to Mom and Winnie, I said, "Come on. While we wait for Wallie I can give you a slideshow of his life."

Ten minutes later, we were in the living room with Zoey and Larry with two dozen picture albums. They were all of Wallie.

"Oh my gods, he was so adorable." Mom smiled wide as she relieved Wallie's childhood with pictures.

"He really was. He looks so much like Clay."

Mom hugged me close. "I'm sorry you lost him."

"It's okay." I sniffed. "I saw him in Philly. He had unfinished business and got stuck inside the house. It was nice to say goodbye."

Mom squeezed a little harder. "Why didn't you bring him back?"

"He didn't want to. He made me promise not to. Besides, he thinks Drew is good for me and Clay wants us both to be happy." I turned my head just as the front door opened and Wallie entered.

He stopped in the doorway and looked in horror at the stacks of albums. "No. Mom, you didn't."

"What happened?" A sweet female voice sounded behind him as Michelle, his girlfriend, pushed him out of the way. She smiled wide at me and noticed the albums. "Looks like I came at the right time."

I stood and walked around the sofa to give Michelle a hug. "I'm glad you came. Meet my mom and Wallie's grandma, Beth." I motioned from Mom, then to Winnie. "This is my Aunt Winnie. Mom, Winnie, this is Wallie's girlfriend Michelle."

Michelle nodded to both of them. "It's nice to meet you."

Wallie moved past me and pulled Winnie into a hug before turning to meet his grandma for the first time. "Hi."

Mom's bottom lip trembled as she lunged forward and hugged her grandson. "Your mom gushed over you and gave me the highlights of your childhood. I feel like I know you already."

A little while later, Drew showed. I answered the door since Wallie and Michelle were still reliving his baby years with Mom and Winnie. "Hi."

Drew smiled and stepped into my space while circling my waist with his arms. "Hi." He glanced up and frowned. "This isn't a good time."

I felt his arms loosen, and I gripped his forearms. "It's never a good time. That is why we have to make our own good times. Besides, Mom wants to meet you."

I pulled him inside and closed the door before he decided to make a run for it. I had news for him. He was stuck with me for a while.

Drew introduced himself to Mom. Alfred came in with wine for the adults over twenty-one and we all fell into a normal, fun family conversation with laughs and stories of the past.

With a sigh, I leaned back into Drew, sipping my wine and

feeling tipsy. Michelle and Wallie were playing a game with Zoey and Larry.

Everything was so normal. I would enjoy it for however long, or short it lasted. Because tomorrow was another day full of mayhem for me and my crew.

CHAPTER SEVENTEEN

Eodh and his siblings were waiting for us the next evening near the cave. Everyone was able to return, and even though in theory I wouldn't have to hold the portal open for long, it was nice to have all of them here to help. I still felt a little drained from yesterday.

So, yeah, I really hoped things went smoothly.

Once the Coven filed into a half-circle behind me and the Fae, I took a deep, cleansing breath and released it slowly. It helped me center my magic and open my senses to every bit of power around me. The Fae. The Coven. And the natural energies from the earth.

"Everyone ready?" I asked, holding my hands up like I had the day before. "Let's hope this works."

Drew smiled encouragingly. Because he didn't need to run into the Inbetween to get anything, he placed a hand on my shoulder, opening his own powers. It wasn't as powerful as a witch's but it was enough to help boost what was there.

Olivia had come with Sam. She'd said to cheer me on. Sammie was back in school now that his spring break was fully over and was spending the evening with his grandparents. They hung back with Larry, Zoey, and the rest of the non-magical gang. Everyone had wanted to watch Luci and the blob come out of the portal.

"Okay, everyone," I called. "Here we go!"

Even though I was tired, it wasn't any worse today, because Wallie was still here. He took my hand and power began to flow into me. I focused it on the Inbetween and opened the portal and immediately leaned on my son when the drain began. "Luci?" I called through the opening as it widened.

Luci ran out. "Move it, she's coming and she's pissed!"

Focusing, I pushed the portal through the barrier and into the cave. When the inky black blob began to pour out of the opening, she slammed into the barrier. I waited until I was sure she was finished coming through, then released the magic holding the portal open. It rebounded, knocking me on my ass.

I stood and staggered backward. Drew had come up on my other side to help Wallie support me. Leaning on them, I tried to get my bearings without passing out.

"Where is the baby?" Luci screamed, as close to the barrier as he could get without going through it. If he entered the cave he would be stuck in there until I figured out how to turn Fee from a raging evil blob to her normal Fae self. There was no way I'd drop that barrier before then.

I sighed and watched the blob undulate beyond the ward. "I'd hoped she would turn back into a Fae when she got back here."

"Fee," Luci cried. "Where is the baby? What happened to the baby? Do we need to go in there and get it?"

The blob seemed to grow more agitated and pushed itself against the barrier.

"Will it hold?" I asked. Fear crept up my spine even though I added a little more power to the ward the night before.

Melody held her hand up to it, not quite touching, for a few moments. "Yes," she said, backing away. "She's not even straining it."

"Well, thank goodness for that." I sagged against Drew.

I looked back at Olivia, Sam, Larry, and Zoey. Zoey's tiger ears were out and half her face was covered in fur. It was like she was struggling to hold one form or the other. I looked at Larry and noted his flesh was flaking off again.

Crap. I couldn't keep doing this to them. I had to find a way to keep them animated without depending on my magic.

"Phira." Eodh stepped close, drawing me from my thoughts and worry.

"Don't touch it," I warned. "You'll get sucked in there."

He nodded to me, then got as close as he could. "Phira, please try to come back to us. We've missed you terribly. King Novus is dead. King Mitah is in charge now, and he wants you to come home."

The blob calmed.

"Can she hear him?" Wallie whispered.

"I think maybe."

The other Fae walked close, keeping their distance from Luci, who was so close to the edge as if he wanted to jump in there. Each of them murmured something to the ever-shifting blob, words I couldn't hear. I wasn't sure they were speaking in English anyway.

Eodh walked over and bowed a little. "With your permission, Highness, we will come visit this place with our mages. See if we can get her back to herself."

"As long as you don't touch the barrier, that's fine with me. And don't enter the cave. I will not lower the barrier for anyone. I can't risk her getting out. She is far too pissed right now." I watched Luci, knowing he heard me. My words were for him just as much as the others.

He inclined his head once. "You have my word."

The Fae walked away while Luci continued to ask. "Fee,

please." His voice grew quiet and desperate. "Please tell me what happened to the baby."

There was so much hurt in his voice it made my chest tighten. I wanted to pull Wallie and Zoey to me and hold them tight. Zoey wasn't my child, but I claimed her so that was close enough in my book.

Winnie walked up with Olivia and sat near me, Wallie, and Drew. "What's up with the baby?" I asked.

Mom joined us. "Tell them, Win."

Winnie sighed and shot Luci a guilty look. "I kept my mouth tied and tried to keep anyone from knowing who I was because of the baby."

Luci froze and turned to look at her. "What?" he asked quietly. "What do you know?"

"You have to understand, we thought you were pure evil," she said. "We truly believed at the time what we were doing was for the best for everyone."

Mom nodded. "We had no reason not to believe the Fae King."

"I know!" Luci yelled. "Where is my baby?"

Mom tensed and dropped her shoulders as she gave me a sad look. "We were approached by the Fae King and asked to send Phira into the Inbetween, but what we didn't tell him was that Phira had the baby."

The blob grew ever more agitated. It had started moving faster and hitting the barrier again once Mom and Winnie sat down.

"The Inbetween was the only realm Luci couldn't reach. But we couldn't send a baby in there. We just couldn't do it."

"Where is my child?" Luci asked through gritted teeth moving closer.

Mom and Winnie exchanged a glance. "She was put up for adoption," Mom said. "The adoption agency did it closed. We have no idea where she ended up."

Luci leaned down and got in Mom's face. "What agency, Beth," he growled.

Mom sighed. "Dear Hearts."

He straightened and smiled. "Closed or not, there will be a paper trail." With that, he disappeared.

Mom and Winnie exchanged another glance. "This isn't going to go well," Winnie muttered.

"I know." Mom sighed. "We made a big mistake all those years ago."

"Yup."

We watched the blob still slam itself against the barrier. "Come on," I said. "Let's get home. Maybe she'll calm down if we're not here."

Wallie and Drew helped me to my feet, and we walked slowly home. Drew linked our fingers and tugged me close to lean on him as we walked. I leaned my head on his shoulder and wrapped an arm around him.

Suddenly, Snooze ran past with Lucy-Fur on his heels. The fat cat was really moving and he had something in his mouth. "Snooze!" I yelled. "What do you have?"

Lucy-Fur didn't break her stride as she called back, "Larry's finger."

"What the..."

Larry ran by us then. "Give that back you crazy fat cat!"

I started laughing so hard I had to stop and cross my legs. This was my life. It was totally normal for a cat to carry a ghoul's finger in his mouth.

Nothing at all weird about that.

CHAPTER EIGHTEEN

It'd been a few weeks since Luci returned with Fee and we'd locked her behind the magical barrier. The coven and I had tried and failed to find out how to change Phira back to the caring Fae she once was.

Today, we were having our weekly coven meeting slash thank you party. We all need something positive and time to just relax.

Winston had kindly added on a glassed-in sunroom about the size of the living room. There was a folding wall between the two rooms. For meetings and parties, I opened the wall and it became one modest-size ballroom with furniture. We'd cleared out the attic as well as Olivia's and Drew's garages to make sure there was enough in there. Even Luci had brought over a few pieces.

It was pretty handy. It also made me wonder where Winston got his power from. How was he able to create things like wood, nails, metals, and glass to build onto his structure? And why did Winnie act like it was the most normal thing in Shipton?

I could drive myself crazy with all the questions about my family, my magic, Winston, the hunters, vampires, and the list goes on because new things were added almost daily.

Taking a breath, I pushed away the overwhelming thoughts from my mind and focused on the now. Next objective was to help Phira. That's why we were here today with the folding wall opened and the appetizers out.

I exited the kitchen, heading for the center of the large room. Sammie ran by, chased by Snoozer, with Lucy-Fur hot on their tail and one of the witch's daughters behind her. I thought the cute little brunette belonged to Melody. She was around Sammie's age and they got along great.

"Take it out back," I yelled. "Sammie, keep everyone in the yard."

"I'll go keep an eye out," Larry said and scrambled after them, followed closely by Zoey.

"Okay, Aunt Ava!" The back door slammed, then I smiled at the group. "Thanks for coming, everyone." I looked around at the gathered Coven. "This is a combo meeting and thank you party for all your help." I nodded toward Melody so she could do her part.

Melody stood up. "Okay, so first on the agenda. Has anyone come up with any ideas for how to help the Fae return to her natural form?"

Nobody stepped forward, but then Ben raised his hand. "I've got some old family spells that induce calm. I'd be happy to try them."

I smiled encouragingly at him. "We can definitely try. You never know what will work." We went around the room, discussing any other options. "Everyone please look through your family spellbooks and grimoires, see what you can find." I sucked in a deep breath. "She's unbelievably angry, which is understandable. My mother and aunt were fooled once. Thank you all so much for helping me put it right."

Mom and Winnie waved from their seats. "Thank you," Mom said weakly.

"Next on the agenda, also about my mother and aunt. They can't be members of the Coven, as they can't perform magic, but they have shown that they can sense it. The coven voted to let them join our meetings as we prepare to do a spell to put them in human bodies again. We'll tell you more about that when the time comes." I smiled and sat back down, but then jumped back up. "Oh, and as far as any human who might ask, Mom is my cousin from out of town, and Winnie had a twin sister who moved away as a child and is now back."

It was a ridiculous story, but how else would we explain her coming back from the dead?

We went through the rest of the lingering Coven business, then I stood again. "Everyone, there's a ton of food in the kitchen and I know many of you are eager to catch up with Mom and Winnie. Enjoy the party!"

I headed out of the living room and stepped to the side while the Coven came in to eat. Wallie stopped and put his arm around me. "Dad would be proud of what you're building here, you know?"

I smiled up at my son. "I think so, too." I missed him every day, but he was at peace so I'd finally been able to fully move on.

"Where's Drew?" Wallie asked.

I chuckled. "He doesn't sit comfortably around quite this many witches," I said. "He would come if I needed him, but I let him off the hook today."

Wallie was flagged down by his girlfriend, Michelle, who I'd invited for the party. "Excuse me," he said.

Mom and Winnie replaced Wallie. "He's right," Mom said. "About Clay. But I think your father would be beyond proud."

I looked at her in shock. "My father?" She'd always hated talking about him before.

But now, she winked at me. "Ghosts talk," she whispered. "And I have some unfinished business."

Unfinished business. With my father.

Here we go again.

EPILOGUE

OLIVIA

I skipped up the stairs, glaring at them as I went. I was excited to be here, but Winston liked to mess with me. Especially when Ava wasn't around. It was a good thing she was here. Still, I wasn't having any of Winston's nonsense today.

It was check-on-the-blob day, and that was always interesting.

Sad, too, but since I was the only one who could see the face within the inky stuff, Ava had started letting me come while she tried numerous things to get the mass to revert into the beautiful Fae she used to be.

"Ava," I called when I walked inside. Winston was behaving today, which meant Ava had to be inside.

For whatever reason, Winston didn't care for me. Either that or he just liked to mess with me. I hadn't figured out which it was.

Larry walked by with a bag of chips in one hand and the TV remote in the other. "She just got out of the shower, by the sound of Winston's pipes," he said. "She'll be down in a minute."

I nodded and joined him and Zoey in the living room to wait. For a ghoul, he sure did eat a lot. So did Zoey. As I eyed them, I couldn't help but wonder. Did they have to poop? Pee?

Ew. Some questions didn't really need answers. No way was I asking. Magic was freaking weird.

A few minutes later, Ava bounded downstairs and stopped short. "What the heck?"

I looked at her, no idea what she was on about. "What?"

She held out her hands, standing at the bottom of the stairs, then looked toward the kitchen, where she could just see the kitchen table. "Where are the donuts or pastries?"

I moaned and rolled my eyes. "I've spoiled you. That's why I need to stop. You're worse than Sammie."

Normally, when I came over early like this, I brought breakfast. Some sort of pastry or yummy thing. I'd dropped Sammie off at school this morning late, so I'd come straight over here. "You're cut off."

Alfred came shuffling around the cabinets in the kitchen, holding a stack of pancakes. "Are you hungry?" he asked in his high-pitched voice. "I made breakfast."

I arched one eyebrow at Ava. "See? You're covered."

Since I hadn't taken the time to eat, I sat down across from Ava and dug into Alfred's delicious cooking. "I don't even miss Winnie being in you," I told the ghoul. "You're the real MVP of the kitchen, aren't you? Don't be modest."

He inclined his head and chuckled. "I suppose so."

After Ava and I gobbled up the pancakes, we headed down for the beach. "So, where are Beth and Winnie today?" I asked.

"Volunteering at the hospital," she said. "They're on a covert mission to find women of the right age who are in comas or whose souls have moved on but their bodies are in pretty decent shape. We're hoping I can move them into actual living bodies."

I whistled through my teeth, impressed. "That sounds complicated, though. Will they take on the persona of the person whose body they're taking over?"

She shook her head. "We'll have to do glamours, at least for a while. They're even thinking about renting a house a few states over, looking for a hospital far away to do this so that the family of the body won't be nearby."

I grunted. "Maybe they could go to Philly. Stay with those vampires."

She stopped and stared at me. "You know, Wade could probably use some more training. That might not be the worst idea."

We reached the cave, and the inky blob appeared at the front of the cave, against the barrier. As usual, the woman's face turned from sad and dejected to desperate, almost frantic. She slammed against the barrier, shouting something, but no sound came out. Not in that form.

"She's doing the same thing," I said, describing the face to Ava in hopes of giving her some clue that would help her figure this out.

"Okay, I brought some herbs to try to let her absorb. Calming things like ashwagandha, camomile, valerian, lavender."

I shrugged. For all I knew, that would work like a charm. "Want me to do anything?"

Ava held out a satchel. "Yeah, hold this open for me, right near the barrier, okay?"

Keeping my eyes on Phira as she freaked out, I shuffled closer and held the bag open for Ava to combine the herbs in a bowl.

But then, I tripped. "Whoa," I yelled as I went sideways. "Help!"

I managed to catch myself, but the bag went flying, and as I got upright, I gasped in horror.

I was inside the barrier.

Lunging, I tried to get out but bounced off of it. Recoiling, I looked up in horror at Phira. She loomed over me, and the face inside looked as shocked as I felt. Once again, I tried to push out. "Ava!"

I could barely hear her on the other side of the barrier, but she was screaming too by the look on her face. "I thought this thing only worked on supernaturals!" I yelled as loud as I could.

Phira came closer so I backed away, but then stumbled again, hitting the back wall hard. "Ah," I yelled and gripped my arm. Blood poured out of a long cut and dripped past my fingers. "Ava!" I screamed as the ink reached out.

It touched my blood, and then... it changed. Light glowed from behind Phira's face. Warmth, happiness, and love poured toward me, wrapping me in a cocoon of safety and caring.

"What is going on?" I whispered. "How is this happening?"

The darkness receded, replaced by a nearly blinding light. I had to look away, out toward Ava, who stood with her hands up and jaw unhinged.

As I watched, the barrier dropped and Ava rushed in. She grabbed my arm and pulled me out of the cave.

When the light faded, we looked back to find Phira, a beautiful, graceful Fae, strolling toward us with the happiest smile on her face.

When the sunshine hit her face, she stopped and looked around, then her gaze landed on me. "Oh, Olivia, my daughter."

Her what now?

She kept searching outside the cave as if trying to find someone. "But where is your father? Where is Loki?"

"Loki?" Ava and I exclaimed at the same time. We stared at each other in shock. "Don't you mean Luci?" Ava asked.

Phira furrowed her brow. "No. I mean Loki. The man who has been trying to help you get me back to myself. My true love. Olivia's father. Loki of Asguard."

~

HOLY COW. How about that ending, huh?

READY TO READ MORE about Ava and Olivia? Preorder Ava's next book, A Killer Midlife here!

AND YOU CAN ALSO GET Olivia's first book in her own series, **Faery Odd Mother**, in the Girdles and Ghouls Paranormal Women's Fiction Anthology here.

IF YOU DIDN'T GET the Eat Your Heart Out Anthology, Olivia's short book, Bumbling Birthday (formerly titled Feeding Them Won't Make Them Grow), will be available soon. Don't miss out on any of the crazy adventures in Shipton Harbor!

FAERY ODD-MOTHER

A WITCHING AFTER FORTY NOVELLA

PROLOGUE

OLIVIA

I skipped up the steps to Ava's house, glaring at them as I went, not trusting that the boards would stay in place. I was excited to be here, but Winston—Ava's magical house—liked to mess with me. Especially when Ava wasn't around. It was a good thing she was here. Still, I wasn't having any of Winston's nonsense today.

It was check-on-the-blob day, and that was always interesting. The blob, in case you haven't heard, is what my witch best friend Ava pulled out of the Inbetween, which is a sort of spirit world.

Sad, but since I was the only one who could see the face within the inky stuff, Ava had started asking me to come while she tried numerous things to get the mass to revert into the beautiful Fae she used to be.

"Ava," I called when I walked inside. Winston was behaving today, which meant Ava had to be home. But I already knew she was. It was too early for her to be up most days.

For whatever reason, Winston didn't care for me. Either

that or he just liked to mess with me. I hadn't figured out which it was. It made me cautious. I didn't fear him, exactly, because somehow I sensed that he would never intentionally harm me. He just liked to be annoying.

Larry, an animated dead person, brought back to life by Ava, walked by with a bag of chips in one hand and the TV remote in the other. His brown eyes twinkled with renewed life. He nodded his head to the side to move a swoop of his brown hair from his eyes. "She just got out of the shower, by the sound of Winston's pipes. She'll be down in a minute."

I nodded and joined him and Zoey, an undead tiger shifter also animated by Ava, in the living room to wait. For a ghoul, he sure did eat a lot. So did Zoey. As I eyed them, I couldn't help but wonder. Did they have to poop? Pee?

Ew. Some questions didn't really need answers. No way was I asking. Magic was freaking weird. But I loved it.

A few minutes later, Ava bounded downstairs and stopped short. "What the heck?"

I looked at her, no idea what she was on about. "What?"

She held out her hands, standing at the bottom of the stairs, then looked toward the kitchen, where she could just see the kitchen table. "Where are the donuts or pastries?"

I moaned and rolled my eyes. "I've spoiled you. That's why I need to stop. You're worse than Sammie."

Normally, when I came over early like this, I brought breakfast. Some sort of pastry or yummy thing. I'd dropped Sammie off at summer camp this morning kind of late, so I'd come straight over here. Didn't pass go and all that jazz. I cast her a playful scowl and said, "You're cut off."

Alfred, yet another ghoul animated someone else, but then the control of the ghoul had been transferred to Ava—she was pretty powerful—came shuffling around the cabinets in the kitchen, holding a stack of pancakes. "Are you hungry?" he asked in his high-pitched voice. "I made breakfast."

I arched one eyebrow at Ava. "See? You're covered."

Since I hadn't taken the time to eat, I sat down across from Ava and dug into Alfred's delicious cooking. "I don't even miss Winnie being inside you," I told the ghoul. "You're the real MVP of the kitchen, aren't you? Don't be modest." Alfred had previously housed Ava's dead Aunt Winnie within his undead body. She was currently in her *own* undead body, thanks to Ava. And yes, there are more. Ava gets around. Heh.

He inclined his head and chuckled. "I suppose so."

After Ava and I gobbled up the pancakes, we headed down for the beach. "So, where are Beth and Winnie today?" I asked. Beth, Ava's mom, was also—you guessed it—undead. Another ghoul. Ava had enough power to make all these creatures look normal, though. A passerby would never know they were essentially zombies.

"Volunteering at the hospital," she said. "They're on a covert mission to find women of the right age who are in comas or whose souls have moved on but their bodies are in pretty decent shape. We're hoping I can move them into actual living bodies."

I whistled through my teeth, impressed. "That sounds complicated, though. Will they take on the persona and life of the person whose body they're taking over?"

She shook her head. "We'll have to do glamours, at least for a while. They're even thinking about renting a house a few states over, looking for a hospital far away to do this so that the family of the body won't be nearby."

I grunted. "Maybe they could go to Philly. Stay with those vampires."

She stopped and stared at me. "You know, Wade could probably use some more training. That might not be the worst idea."

Of course it was a good idea. I'm a delight.

We reached the cave, and the inky blob appeared at the

entrance, against the barrier. As usual, the woman's face turned from sad and dejected to desperate, almost frantic. She slammed against the barrier, shouting something, but no sound came out. Not in that form.

"She's doing the same thing," I said, describing the face to Ava in hopes of giving her some clue that would help her figure this out.

"Okay, I brought some herbs to try to let her absorb. Calming things like ashwagandha, camomile, valerian, lavender."

I shrugged. For all I knew, that would work like a charm. "Want me to do anything?"

Ava held out a satchel. "Yeah, hold this open for me, right near the barrier, okay?"

Keeping my eyes on Phira as she freaked out, I shuffled closer and held the bag open for Ava to combine the herbs in a bowl.

But then, I tripped. "Whoa," I yelled as I went sideways. "Help!"

I managed to catch myself, but the bag went flying, and as I got upright, I gasped in horror.

I was inside the barrier.

Lunging toward the shimmering wall and away from the evil blob, I tried to get out but bounced off of it. Recoiling, I looked up in horror at Phira. She loomed over me, and the face inside looked as shocked as I felt. Once again, I tried to push out. "Ava!"

I could barely hear her on the other side of the barrier, but she was screaming too, by the look on her face. "I thought this thing only worked on supernaturals!" I yelled as loud as I could. Supposedly humans would've been able to pass through or back just fine. And I was human!

Phira came closer so I backed away, but then I stumbled again, hitting the back wall hard. "Ah," I yelled and gripped my arm. Blood poured out of a long cut and dripped past my fingers. "Ava!" I screamed as the ink reached out.

It touched my blood, and then... it changed. Light glowed from behind Phira's face. Warmth, happiness, and love poured toward me, wrapping me in a cocoon of safety and caring.

"What is going on?" I whispered. "How is this happening?"

The darkness receded, replaced by a nearly blinding white light. I had to look away, out toward Ava, who stood with her hands up and jaw unhinged.

As I watched, the barrier dropped and Ava rushed in. She grabbed my arm and pulled me out of the cave.

When the light faded, we looked back to find Phira, a beautiful, graceful Fae, strolling toward us with the happiest smile on her face.

When the sunshine hit her face, she stopped and looked around, then her gaze landed on me. "Oh, Olivia, my daughter."

Her what now?

She kept searching outside the cave as if trying to find someone. "But where is your father? Where is Loki?"

"Loki?" Ava and I exclaimed at the same time. We stared at each other in shock. "Don't you mean Luci?" Ava asked.

Phira furrowed her brow. "No. I mean Loki. The man who has been trying to help you get me back to myself. My true love. Olivia's father. Loki of Asguard."

CHAPTER ONE

My mother was a Faery.

As soon as Phira had announced I was her daughter, I'd turned tail and ran back to the house with Ava and Phira hot on my trail.

We sat in the living room while I processed the bombshell and planned what to do next.

"I don't understand what's going on." I stared up at Ava, ignoring the freaking *Faery* sitting next to me. The Faery who claimed to be my mother. The one that also claimed that Luci, aka Lucifer, and apparently aka Loki, was also aka my father. "I mean, of course we all know I'm adopted, but I'm not magical. I'm over forty for frick's sake!"

My brain buzzed with confusion and questions. I was half Fae and half demon? Or was Luci a god? Archangel? I wasn't even sure what mythology he fell under.

"I know. It's a lot to accept," Ava said. "But your blood healed her, Liv. We can't look past that."

She was right. My blood *had* brought this freaking willow tree beside me out of that blob. Not that I was calling the woman an actual tree. She was graceful, whimsical, and beautiful like a willow. And there was no way she was my mother. "How do we know it wasn't just blood in general?"

Ava froze, obviously trying to think of a reason. "Um. No, I think it was yours. She was changed by magic from the Inbetween. Only magic could change her back."

I was afraid she'd say something like that. Even though I found magic fascinating, I wasn't sure I wanted to be magical.

"Why won't you look at me?" Phira asked softly.

I didn't know the answer to that. I just really didn't want to turn my head in her direction. My confusion was screwing with my need to have full control over everything in my life. I couldn't control this and that scared me. "Because this is ludicrous," I said.

As much as I'd been jealous of Ava for coming into major powers, and as much as I would've loved it for myself, this felt too easy. Wham-bam, now I have a magical mom?

And we hadn't even talked about Loki. Luci. Whoever he was supposed to be.

Alfred shuffled into the living room with a tray of tea. As if tea was the answer to everything. "Thought you might want a drink," he squeaked.

"Thank you," Phira gasped. "I haven't had a cup of tea in forty years." She leaned forward and picked up a cup, spooning a bit of honey in before raising it to her lips, then making a small moaning sound. "That's delicious."

"Thank you. Carrie got me hooked on that one. It is quite good. I believe it is from the Fae realm," Alfred said. "Enjoy."

He shuffled backward out of the room. While the Fae was busy with her tea, I let myself peek to my left. Her long blonde hair shined in the light from the windows.

As soon as she noticed me noticing her, I jerked my gaze away. "How can we prove this?" I asked. "How can I know?"

Ava gaped at the both of us. "You look alike," she whispered. "Her hair is a lighter blonde than yours, but it's on the same color wheel."

Leaning forward, Ava squinted at me and Phira. I couldn't see the Fae beside me, but I assumed she was looking at Ava as I was.

"Your eyes," she whispered. "Phira's are a different blue. But the shape is exactly the same, as is your brow line."

I shook my head and held up a hand. This just wasn't possible. "It makes no sense. If I was her daughter, I'd have magic."

Okay, so I might be looking for excuses or things to disprove Phira's claims on me.

"They bound your magic," Phira said. "So that the king wouldn't find you."

My curiosity at her words overcame my nerves, and I looked at her. Another layer of the WTF lifted. "What?"

"The witches, the ones who live here." She indicated to the house. "The ones who put me in the Inbetween. I couldn't convince them I was innocent, but I did manage to extract their promise that they'd make sure my baby was safe." She shrugged and took another sip of her tea. "I'm immortal. Forty years in a prison realm is nothing. I've had to go to one before, when I was young, for a minor infraction. I was there for a decade, then."

"In the Inbetween?" Ava asked incredulously.

Phira shook her head. "No, that was the bad part. The Inbetween wasn't created for Fae. It changed me. We have other dimensions usually reserved for punishments."

"And the baby?" Ava prodded.

"I convinced the witches to let me stay here, in a room they'd spelled, until I gave birth. It didn't take long. They gave me one day with you, then took you away." She smiled sadly at me. "I regret not being there for your childhood, but I'm so happy to see you now."

"I'm going to call Carrie," Ava said quietly. "I'll be right back."

She left. And cue the awkward silence.

Before I opened my mouth to ask Phira a question, Luci appeared in front of us. I jumped back, but he hadn't even noticed me. Did he not know I was his daughter? That was right. He'd been away. Ava had said something about Philly and helping Hailey with something or another. Hailey Whitfield was the woman who bought Ava's old house in Philadelphia. Not long after moving in she was turned into a vampire and became a bounty hunter. Talk about life altering.

And I had joined the paranormal club. Maybe. I still wasn't convinced.

Luci staggered forward and dropped to his knees, and when he spoke, his voice was higher than I'd ever heard it and held a strong dose of vulnerability. I swore I spotted a shine in his eyes that might've been tears. My chest tightened at the love and joy rolling off of him.

"I can't believe it's you." His voice was barely a whisper, but I was close enough to hear it.

Ava walked into the room and crowded onto the couch on my other side. She took my hand and mouthed, "Wow."

I nodded. The connection between whatever Luci was and the Fae was was real, electric, and beautiful.

Phira reached up and brushed a lock of hair out of Luci's forehead. Belatedly, he seemed to realize we were in the room. "Where are Beth and Winnie?" he growled.

Ava blinked rapidly. "They're at the hospital, volunteering."

He didn't need to know more than that, but they'd been looking for appropriate bodies, in hopes that Ava could transfer their souls from their ghoul bodies into human bodies who no longer had souls.

"Hold on," I said. "Who *are* you?"

He furrowed his brow, finally looking away from Phira's face, though he didn't release her hand. "What?"

"Phira called you Loki," Ava said. "Have you been lying to us?"

He shook his head, then looked back at my supposed mother. "No. I'm Loki. And Luci." With a chuckle, he dipped his head. "I'm not the devil. But I play one on TV."

When we didn't laugh, he rolled his eyes. "I'm all of the above. And half of the other mythological figures you've heard about over time. I've been many people over the ages, but Luci is my favorite persona and the one I most often affect."

Phira looked over at us. "When I first met him, he was Loki. I've called him that ever since." Her blue eyes were full of tears.

"Loki," Phira said. "It's her." She looked at me. Luci did too, but he looked confused.

"She's who?"

"That is our daughter, Loki. That is our Breena."

Luci rocked back on his heels, blinking rapidly. He nearly hit the floor. Catching himself in time, he stood and slid toward me, then sat on the coffee table in front of me. I had to force myself not to run out the door. Ava tried to let go of my hand, but I gripped it tight. She wasn't going anywhere. I wouldn't let her leave me alone with these people.

"Breena," Luci whispered. "I can't believe it's been you all this time."

He reached out for me, but I jerked back and used Ava's favorite line, whispering fiercely. "Not today, Satan."

CHAPTER TWO

"Olivia?"

Sam's voice drifting into the living room as he opened the front door settled me down. It was amazing, that man and what he'd done for me. He was my romance hero, my happily ever after.

"In here," I called. Luci stood and backed away, crossing the living room and staring at me.

My husband came into view, and I drank him in, like I always did. Because I loved that man and everything about him. It was one of his night shift weeks. He and Drew and the other officers rotated their schedules. The town wasn't huge and neither was the department. So Sam wore a pair of snug jeans and a black t-shirt that formed to his fit torso. He didn't have rock hard abs, but he kept his body in shape. And I was thankful for it. Yum.

Sam hurried into the living room, stopping short when he saw Phira. "Whoa." But he only paused for a moment before making a beeline for me. I stood as he got close, finally letting go of Ava, and enjoyed his strong, capable arms wrapped around me.

"Are you okay?" he whispered.

"I don't know," I said truthfully. "She says she's my mother."

His big hands ran up and down my back before settling at the base of my neck, and for a moment, it was like we were the only two in the room. "Ava told me when she called. And Luci is your dad? How do they expect us to believe that?"

"That's precisely what we were discussing," Phira said, watching the two of us.

"Actually," Luci interrupted. I looked around Sam's shoulder at him and glared. Really? "We were discussing how happy I am to finally know you."

"You have known me," I said with more than a little venom in my voice. "For what, close to a year now?"

"I didn't know it was *you*. That you were my daughter." Luci's gaze hadn't left me except to keep glancing at Phira. His tone was just as soft as the one he used with her earlier. "My girls," he whispered.

I sat beside Ava again and scooted closer so Sam could sandwich me between them. That was a lot better. Having them around me made me feel safe. Secure. Like the freaking *Faery* and dadgum *devil* who wanted me to be their kid couldn't touch me.

"I'm not your girl," I retorted. "And I'm still not convinced you're my parents at all. Like, I'm going to need some real proof."

I took a deep breath and held it for a little while before releasing it slowly. I'd hoped that would help, but it didn't. It definitely didn't make the power couple vanish.

Watching them for a few more minutes, events over the last few months reminded me of the Fae who helped Ava get Phira out of the Inbetween. Her brothers and sisters. I only knew the older brother's name. Eodh. They were some kind of High Fae, which I thought was like royalty.

"Like magic?" Ava asked. "I can see how she might not get one of your powers or the other, but I can't imagine the daughter of the devil-slash-a minor god and a High Fae wouldn't have some sort of powers."

"Oh," Phira said, sitting straighter. "I can help with that."

She stood and glided across the hardwood floor toward me. I pressed against the back of the couch, completely uncomfortable with her getting closer. As cool as it would've been to have been the daughter of two such powerful beings, I wasn't. I couldn't be.

"What are you doing?" I asked.

Phira smiled patiently. "I'm just going to touch your forehead. If you're not my daughter, it won't do anything to you. If you are, I believe I'll be able to unlock your powers."

Sam and I exchanged a long glance. I knew he could see my panic and probably sense it. We could always connect with each other on a level I'd never reached with anyone else. "It's up to you," he murmured, covering my hand with his.

"She wouldn't hurt you," Ava said. "I don't think..."

"Of course I wouldn't." Phira looked at Ava like she'd mortally offended her. "She's my daughter."

My heart thumped faster as I sat up. "Fine," I said with far more confidence in my voice than I actually felt. "Do it."

She touched my forehead, and nothing happened for a moment. I opened my eyes and looked around, confused and a little disappointed. I'd thought it was a long shot, but part of me had always wanted to be special. Wanted to belong to something. But I did. I was Ava's right hand in the craziness of magic.

So, maybe I was never meant to learn who my real parents

were. That was fine, because I'd come to terms with that a long time ago.

As Phira backed away, with every gaze in the room on me, I felt like running away and hiding. What a major disappointment. Talk about anticlimactic.

Winston even hated the situation. He moaned and rumbled, the ground under us shaking as we all sat, holding our breaths in anticipation.

"Oh," Ava breathed. "What is that?"

I followed her gaze to the floor, where a small leaf was pushing up between the floorboards. "Aren't those sealed?" I asked.

"Yes." She leaned over and plucked the leaf. "When we remodeled."

Winston groaned again, and that's when it hit me. Somehow, at the same moment, I became unbearably exhausted, while simultaneously feeling like I'd just taken the biggest hit of speed imaginable. I wanted to run a marathon while sleeping through it.

"Guys?" I whispered. My body began to hum and tingle while my heart raced.

All gazes swung to me again. "I feel really weird."

More rumbling from Winston, and Ava jerked her feet up onto the couch and in my lap when a vine erupted from the fireplace. "What is going on?" she cried.

"Her powers," Phira said in a regal tone, smiling like she won the lottery. In every state. "She's my daughter."

Winston rumbled again.

"What is happening?" I screeched.

Without warning, the front door burst open. I could just see it in the entryway. "Who is here?"

Luci jumped up and ran to the entry, then backpedaled quickly as a gigantic vine snaked in through the front door and into the living room. It kept growing, twisting, leaves sprouting all over the place as Winston protested by making the house vibrate.

It felt like a battle was about to begin between Winston and the vines. Was I doing that? How? I didn't know how to stop it.

"Outside," Luci thundered, waving at me to go. "Now!"

I jumped to my feet and launched myself over the vine, sprinting for the front door. As I leaped off of the porch, Winston must've needed the last word, because something caught my foot. Something that felt deceptively like the edge of a plank of wood from the front porch.

And I went flying. Straight into the yard, ass over end, but to my absolute shock, I didn't hit the ground.

Instead, I landed in the softest patch of greenery I'd ever felt, and I'd always been the outdoorsy type. As a child I'd spent sunup to sundown outside.

Slowly, I looked around. I was a good three feet off the ground in a pile of... clover? I'd never seen clover grow this high, never in all my dang life. I climbed off and looked over at the porch, at Sam and Ava, Phira and Luci, Larry, Alfred, and Zoe had joined them. Every single one of them held the same expression on their faces. Slack jawed.

Belatedly, I realized I felt a lot better. I bent and buried my hands in the clover, and the anxiety and overpowering need to expend energy subdued a lot.

"Take off your shoes." Phira pointed at her feet as if she needed to show me what she meant. "Bury your feet in the dirt."

Standing, I did as she suggested, digging my toes into the sandy dirt as quickly as possible, then sighing in relief. "Oh, that is nice."

I could actually feel the energy from the earth. Since Ava and I started hanging out with Carrie, I'd asked questions and did research on the Fae, learning most of their magics came from nature. And if the earth calmed me that meant I was Fae, right?

"You'll itch if you get too far away from nature," Phira said, walking toward me like she was on some sort of conveyor belt. Were her feet moving? I couldn't tell, and I was too interested in lying down on the ground and letting it take away the overwhelming feeling of the magic.

CHAPTER THREE

"It's true."

The male voice spiked my interest, and I sat up to find the High Fae, the one who had been helping us try to break Phira out of the cave, standing in the middle of the yard.

Phira's brothers and sisters stared between Phira and I, not at all surprised by my new powers. Assuming they could sense them. But they would have been able to, right?

And where had they come from? How had they just appeared? If all this was true, and I had *powers*, this was some information I'd need.

Luci seemed to be just as surprised to see them as me. He moved closer to Phira, stepping up to stand in front of her. Again, his actions intrigued me. He was so protective of Phira.

My attention shifted when Ava joined me on the ground, sitting shoulder-to-shoulder. It was like she wanted to join in some fun she was missing out on. Or she was being just as protective with me as Luci was with Phira. I didn't mind. Having her close made me feel even more grounded, connected. Part of nature and the world and blah, blah, blah.

"This is freaking wild," Ava whispered as she linked our hands and extended them out in front of us. That was when I saw the magic. Hers and mine. It was a mix of light green—mine—and dark blue—Ava's—energy that swirled around our connected hands.

The movement distracted me from the Fae, and I was thankful for it.

"You're telling me." I glanced over at her, replying to her statement. "It feels better when you touch me."

She shrugged. "I'm half earth-witch. Maybe that's why."

It really was wild. I had magic. The tattoo on the inside of Ava's forearm I'd never noticed before caught my attention. A small dark green pentagram. I reached over and touched it lightly with my free hand.

Ava smiled and pressed her shoulder into mine. "You can see it. That's proof enough for me that you're magical."

She let go of my hand and put her arm fully around me to squeeze me close, then whispered in my ear, "You won't go through this alone."

Sam put his hand on my back to let me know he was close, too. His touch comforted my psyche, but I wanted to roll all over Ava, scratching an itch I couldn't reach.

Oh, not like that. A dirty mind is a terrible thing to waste.

I looked up at the Fae as Phira approached Eodh, supposedly the oldest of these regal-looking Faeries. He was also Phira's brother, which made him my uncle. And so was the other man with them. I sensed that he was younger, but it was hard to tell. The three women would be my aunts.

A frown pulled at my lips as I watched them. The siblings were overflowing with joy at the sight of Phira. As was my mother. Wow, that would take some getting used to.

"Brother," she whispered. They touched their foreheads together, then Phira moved on to touch her forehead to each of her sisters'. The three women ranged in skin tone from the fairest to the darkest. Their hair was the same. The one with the fairest skin had blonde hair like mine and Phira. The light brown haired Fae had a slightly dark complexion like she tanned regularly.

The third woman had dark golden skin and dark brown hair.

They were all beyond beautiful.

Once done with their greeting, Phira backed away and smiled serenely.

"That's it?" Ava asked, looking at Eodh, Phira's oldest brother, as far as we'd been able to tell. Though I wasn't sure if he was older than Phira. "You lot have been helping us try to free her for months, and now that she's free, you're just going to touch foreheads?"

Yeah. The same thought had crossed my mind but somehow I knew it was more than just simply touching heads.

The corners of Eodh's lips tipped up, but only slightly. He inclined his head once. "We have been separated for much longer than this in our lives. It *is* nice to see my younger sister again, however."

Ah. So Phira wasn't the oldest. I guess that got me out of ruling Faery. But I had to be sure how it all worked. "So, do you have any other, older brothers or sisters?"

Phira shook her head and chuckled. "No. I think six of us is enough."

Ha! Fair enough. I was an only child. In some ways I loved it, because I didn't have to share my things with siblings. On the other hand it had been lonely growing up in a huge house with no one to play with.

Absently, I ran my fingers through the grass. I wanted to lay back down and press my whole body against the dirt to quell the itching just underneath my skin, but I was far too interested in what was happening with these behemoths.

"If you're my mother, why am I not six feet tall like you guys?" I asked.

Phira blinked. "I do not know."

Okay. Fair enough. "How does this work?" I asked. "Are you guys like royalty?"

They'd been sent by the King, so they could have been like messengers or something. But I didn't think so.

Eodh nodded again. "Indeed."

Phira sat on the ground across from me, her knees to mine, spreading her skirts around her and holding her spine straight and graceful. "We are the High Fae. The original Faeries, and as such, the most powerful."

Excitement tingled in the back of my neck. If all this was true, that would mean I'd be powerful. Even more so since Luci—I would *not* call him dad or father or daddy or anything besides Luci—was a lower god.

If I could ever get this feeling of bugs crawling under my skin to go away, I could really get into this whole powerful child of a Fae and a god thing. "That's kinda cool," I whispered to my best friend. "Assuming all of this is true."

Okay, so I realize that I was in denial. Things like this just didn't happen to me. Ava, maybe, but not me.

"I think it is, too," she whispered back.

Eodh, who had sat down as well, and Phira watched us with amused expressions. I had to assume they could hear us just fine.

Ava kept whispering. "I can't sense any deception."

Whoa. I slumped against her, finally acknowledging to myself that this could actually be happening. I wasn't dreaming. This wasn't an elaborate prank. And there was nothing else for my denial to grab hold of.

I was the daughter of a god and a powerful Fae. "Out of curiosity, how powerful?"

Phira leaned close. "Well, Eodh tells me that our uncle is the King now."

No. Way. My jaw dropped. Ava put her fingers under and pushed it back up. "Your uncle?" My voice squeaked as I asked the question.

"Yes." Eodh smiled, one of the biggest I'd seen from him yet. "Meaning you're now in the line of succession for the throne, albeit pretty far down."

Say what now?

I shook my head and arched an eyebrow at him. "No. Nope. Not happening. I mean, I could get behind having some powers. That's pretty cool. But I'm not on board with being a Queen."

Phira touched my hand, and even more of the itchy magic calmed. "If it helps, the lines of succession for Fae aren't very different from how humans do it. King Novus was our father, our uncle's older brother. He didn't want to dilute the High Fae line. Most Fae are allowed to mate as they please, but High Fae are only allowed to mate other Fae."

I nodded slowly. "Okay, so he didn't want a mixed species baby in the family."

Ava snorted, but Eodh and Phira nodded slowly. "Yes, precisely," Eodh said.

"Our uncle, Mitah, doesn't care about such things. He would prefer we keep the blood strong, but I can't imagine combining our bloodline with the gods would weaken it." Phira cocked her head. "There really is no telling what you'll be able to do."

"What about Carrie? She's a sprite." Ava asked.

Eodh smiled. "Sprites are of a much less powerful bloodline and have been allowed to mate with humans for centuries. She is descended from the Sprite king, so that makes you both princesses."

I snorted and glanced at Ava. "And you thought you were the powerful one."

Ava rolled her eyes and ignored me. "You never said what has to happen for Olivia to take the throne."

I turned back to my mother and uncle. "Yeah." I was hoping it would be a very, very long time before that would happen. Or never.

"Our uncle is the youngest and only remaining of his brothers and sisters and their children. The next heir is myself. Technically, I should be on the throne now, but there is an archaic law that the ruler must be at least five hundred years old. I am four hundred thirty three." Eodh turned and indicated the women and the man standing behind him, my aunts and uncles. "After my five hundredth birthday, if I have no children and something happens to me, Scorpia would take the throne when she reaches five hundred."

I glanced up at the woman he indicated to. Scorpia was the blonde haired, fairest skin Fae. She smiled at me in greeting. I returned the smile and focused back on Eodh as he continued.

"She has children, so her offspring would be the next heirs. In the event something happened to *all* of them, Phira would take the throne with you as heir. If something happened to both of you and your children, it would go to Evie, then Octavia, and then Aeden." Each of the women, my aunts, nodded as their names were mentioned.

I paid attention to who Eodh pointed at as he said their names. Evie was the one with tanned-looking skin and dark brown hair. Octavia had the darker skin tone with the light brown hair. Aeden was easy to point out because he was the only other male Fae there. He resembled Eodh in hair and skin tone.

"You'll have to be trained," Phira announced a little too happily. "In the eventuality that our entire line was killed, you'd need to know what to do to lead the courts."

I gulped. Leading the courts sounded... intimidating. And in that case, I'd have to make sure my aunts, uncles, and cousins didn't die.

"It's okay," Sam whispered. "You've got this. We've got you."

I loved the man and his support. He was taking this a whole lot better than me. Then again he grew up knowing about magic thanks to Ava. I'd only known about magic for a couple of years.

"Of course," Phira said, smiling at my husband over my shoulder. "The likelihood of that happening is miniscule."

That could be true. I hoped so because the last thing in this world I wanted was to be a queen.

CHAPTER FOUR

My phone rang as I sat on the grass, pretty much having a come-to-reality moment. The sound of the popular Frozen song ringtone—Sammie's favorite at the moment—made me jump. I yanked the phone out of my back pocket. "It's Carrie."

I knew who it was before I looked at the screen because Sammie had picked that ringtone for his favorite teacher. Odd that she'd call me now. She was running a day camp for kids in the town, and I'd signed Sammie up. "Hey, Carrie, what's up?"

My gut churned with the certainty that something had gone wrong. My magic crawled over my skin like it wasn't sure what to do.

"Olivia, can you come to camp? Sammie passed out."

I gasped and sprang to my feet. "What? When?"

"About ten minutes ago," she said. There was something in her tone that told me she wanted to say more but couldn't with all the human kids around. "We've got him awake and you know there's a medic here on site. He seems fine now but he probably should be seen."

"On our way." I hung up and looked at my friends and new family. "Sammie passed out about the same time my powers manifested."

Luci strode forward. "Come on, I can take you to get him."

"Oh, no," I muttered, but Ava put her hand on my back.

"It'd be a lot faster. We could get him here and have a look at him."

I looked up at her, and we stared at each other for a few blinks. I really hated the idea of having Luci teleport me. "Okay, but not me. You're taking Sam with you. Do it."

Luci grinned at my husband, and poor Sam gulped audibly. He eyed me briefly like I would be in trouble later. I almost giggled because I liked when I was in trouble with Sam. It made bed time so much more fun and naughty.

"How does this work?" Sam asked.

With one hand out, Luci bowed his head slightly. "Just hold my hand."

Sam carefully laid his hand on top of Luci's and they disappeared.

The minute they were gone, I turned toward my...mother, but my phone rang again. "It's Jessica," I whispered as I looked at the screen. My heart seized in my chest for a split second before it started pounding like a jackhammer. "Holy crap, I didn't even think about it affecting Sammie, Jess and Dev."

I tapped the screen and looked at Ava with my body tense with worry. "Hey, sweetie, are you okay?"

"No!" she yelled with panic. "I'm not! I passed out and now my bedroom is filled with vines!"

She kept shrieking but it was so shrill and panicked I couldn't make it out. "Honey!" I yelled to get her to stop. "Get outside. Touch the grass as soon as you can. That'll help the vines stop growing. I'm going to send a man to pick you up. It's going to be really freaky but he's going to bring you to me, okay?

You can trust him." Gods, I hoped so. "I promise, I'll explain it all. Just get outside!"

"Okay, mom."

My phone beeped. I checked the screen, and it was Devan. "Your brother is calling," I said. "Go outside, now. Luci will be there soon to pick you up."

"Mom," she yelped. Her voice echoed, hopefully because she was in the stairwell. "I thought you said it was a man."

I sighed. "He has a weird name, but it is Luci, and I have to answer your brother. Wait outside." I didn't give her time to reply, just switched over to Dev. "Hey, hon, you okay?"

"Mom, I'm really freaked out," he whispered. "Dad's not answering, he's on some business trip in Majorca or something. I started feeling really strange. I was on a date, Mom, so I went to the bathroom. Now I'm in the movie theater bathroom and it's full of vines."

"Okay, honey, this is happening to me and your brother and sister, too," I said. "I know it's scary but do not call 911. Get outside as fast as you can and touch dirt. Don't ask why, don't take time, just do it."

"Okay," he said breathlessly. "I am."

"Run past people, ignore the vines, and get out of there."

"Okay."

As banging sounds came over the phone, Luci, Sam, and Sammie appeared in front of me.

"Oh, good," I said. "Text me your address, honey. A man named Luci is going to get your sister, then he'll get you. He'll be there in just a few minutes. Trust him, he'll bring you to me right away."

"Mom, what—" But I didn't have time to placate them any more. People could see him. Sam held Sammie. They were safe. I ran to Luci and grabbed his arm. "Please. Please go get my son and daughter."

His face softened as he looked down at me. "Of course I will. What are the addresses?"

I rattled off the address of my ex-husband's house. The one I'd raised Jess and Devan in before the divorce. "Jess is out in the yard. She's expecting you."

The text from Devan came through with the address to the theater he was at. I held out my phone for Luci to read. "Dev is here, out back behind the theater. They're going to be freaked. They don't know anything about magic."

Luci winked at me. "I'll go so fast they won't have time to fight me."

"Thank you," I whispered.

He disappeared, and I rushed over to pull Sammie into my arms. "Oh, baby, I'm so sorry. Are you okay? Did any vines grow around you?"

He shook his head. "No, I just fell asleep really fast."

"More than likely, he won't have many powers manifest until he hits puberty," Phira said, walking closer. Her gaze was frozen on Sammie. "Hello," she whispered. "I am so honored to meet you."

He blinked at her sleepily. "I'm Sammie."

Was that a tear in Phira's eye? I couldn't be sure. She looked down and if it had been there at all, it was gone now.

A minute later, Luci appeared with Dev and Jess staggering beside him. Both were barefoot, and Dev had his shoes in his hands. "What?" Dev gasped. Jessica just looked around, mostly at the Fae, with wide eyes and a gaping jaw.

"What?" Dev repeated when he spotted the Fae.

"Guys," I whispered. "There's a lot to tell you. It's going to be overwhelming. But you are safe. You have to remember that. You're completely safe here. Nobody and nothing will hurt you here. I promise."

They both slowly moved their gazes to me.

"Okay," Jessica said. "Okay."

That seemed to be all I'd be getting out of them. It was better than nothing and I'd take it. I hadn't expected them to call me at all.

"You know Ava?" I asked. They'd met her over Christmas at the party.

They both nodded.

"Okay, sit down. She's going to put her hands on your backs. It'll help you feel better, and in good time I'll explain how. Okay?"

They sat next to each other. Ava lowered herself behind them.

"Okay," both kids said in unison.

CHAPTER FIVE

How was I supposed to explain all this to my grown kids? Grown kids that really didn't want anything to do with me, thanks to their jerk father.

"Okay," I said carefully. Back to that word again. I sat across from them and took their hands. "Feeling a little bit better?"

They both nodded. "Yes," Devan said. "Why?"

I nodded toward my best friend. "Ava here is a witch."

They both jerked away, turning to look at her in horror.

"No, don't, she's helping you!" I held out my hands. "Don't freak out, now. Hear me out."

They settled back but looked more tense. "I'm not off to a very good start," I said with a sigh. "There are powers in this world that most people don't know anything about. Witches, shifters, vampires."

"Shifters?" Jessica asked weakly.

Ava interjected, "Like werewolves in movies, but more like shapeshifting. They're not evil entities out to turn all humans. And they can be any kind of animal."

Jess sucked in a deep breath and eyed Ava over her shoulder. "Okay."

And that was the word of the day. I guess it could've been worse.

"There are Fae and angels. Demons, too." I considered other creatures. "Ghouls, ghosts..."

"Mom," Devan gasped. "Seriously?"

I nodded and touched both of their legs. "Seriously. It's a big, wide world out there."

"What does any of this have to do with us?" Devan asked. "And the vines?"

"You had vines too?" Jess looked at her brother. "How?"

"I was in the bathroom at the movies." He slapped his hand on his face. "I left Carolyn there. And it was our first date. She's going to think I'm a jerk!"

"Text her," I said. "Right now. You've not really been gone all that long. Tell her you got sick, puking."

He grimaced. "I don't want to tell a girl that."

"Better than telling her vines started coming out of your ass," Jess said.

"Jess!" I furrowed my brow at her. "Language."

But that didn't get the reaction I expected. "First of all," she said, sitting up straight and cocking her head at me. "I'm a grown woman. I'm nineteen years old—" Ava snorted. It was hard for me not to, as well. Nineteen felt like grown at the time, but it was definitely still a baby. Jess shot Ava a glare. "I'm an adult. So I'll cuss if I like. Second of all, even if I wasn't over eighteen, who are you to try to parent me, now?"

She tried to puff up with bravado, but the tears in her eyes betrayed her.

"Oh, honey," I whispered. "I'm so sorry."

Devan finished his text and slipped his phone back in his pocket, then scooted over to put his arm around his sister.

"You're the one who left," Dev said. "We were just kids, and you left us."

I shook my head, at a loss. "We got divorced, honey. I didn't have a choice."

"You did," Jess hissed. "You left us."

They'd been nine and eleven when Carter had filed for divorce. So young. "I was a different person, then, yes. I wasn't the best mother that I could've been. But I never left you. Your father kicked me out. He wouldn't let me see you, and then during the divorce proceedings, you said you'd rather live with him. I figured I deserved that, since I hadn't been as loving or caring as I could've been when you were younger."

I'd been too hung up on being a mom... going to play dates dressed to the nines, doing all the classes and joining the gym to work out with other mothers. My kids had been another accessory to add to my purse. And I'd left them with the nanny all the time. Back then, I didn't know how to be a mom. Because my adopted parents had done the same thing with me.

"But I never left. I was right here in town." I'd stayed with my parents and contacted my children every chance I got. They'd rebuffed me more than once. Carter wouldn't let me see them. Because he'd kicked me out I didn't have money to fight him in court. It didn't matter what I did, he would always win because money talked.

"Then you met *him*," Devan said, glaring at Sam. "And had the kid, and it was like we stopped existing."

I gaped at them. An ache like I'd been hit in the gut rose up. I'd never wanted them to feel that way. "But you didn't. I tried, so hard, to get you to come over, to spend your weekends with me. I could've insisted, since that was the custody arrangement, but I wanted to respect your wishes."

"Well, Dad told us what a hardass he was," Devan said, not looking at Sam. "We didn't want to spend any more time around him than we had to."

"Uh, sorry to break it to you, guys," Ava said. "But your dad is a complete dick. Sam is the furthest thing from a hardass there is."

Jessica swung around and glared at Ava. "Our dad is *not* a dick."

"No, he's your father, and I believe he loves you," I said, drawing the attention away from Ava. She was feeling defensive of me, and I appreciated that, but this had to be done carefully. "Back to the matter at hand. You know I was adopted, right?"

They both nodded mutely.

"I found my birth parents recently. *Very recently*. They are Phira," I nodded toward the Fae, who walked closer and sat beside me. "And Luci, who you met." Luci plopped down on my other side. "The thing is, Phira is a Faerie, and Luci is...well, I'm not totally sure what he is."

Luci held out his hand to Devan, who took it and shook limply. "I'm what some people call a god," he said. "Others would call me a demon. I've been around for a very, very long time."

"What's Luci short for?" Jessica asked.

"Lucifer," he said brightly. "But I've had other names. Loki, Crounus, Hades, I was once even Cthulu, among others. It depends on the mythology."

Jessica and Devan stared at him in shock. "Lucifer? Like, *the* Lucifer? King of Hell Lucifer?" Jess whispered. "*Lucifer* is my biological grandfather?"

"I'm not as bad as they make me out to be," he said with his hands up. "A bit mischievous, maybe."

"When I was born, witches put a spell on me to hide my powers," I said, bringing the conversation back to explaining their newfound powers. "And now that spell has been removed, which unlocked my powers. We didn't think about the fact that when my powers erupted, it would unlock yours as well."

"That's why?" Jessica whispered. "Because you have powers now we have to have them, too? We're going to be total freaks?"

"Hey," I exclaimed. "We aren't freaks. This is kind of cool, really. I mean sure, it's going to be difficult to navigate having new grandparents, and it doesn't mean in any way my adoptive parents are any less your grands. We have a lot to work out, but it doesn't make you a freak." I heaved a deep breath.

"There's a good chance your powers will be a lot less than your mother's," Luci said. "My brother and I have powers which are a lot weaker than our father's."

"Your brother?" I asked, looking at him askance. I didn't know much of anything about him.

He sneered. "Thor. We don't really get along. He's a bit of a buzzkill."

Thor. Right. Of course. Uncle Thor. Why not?

"I think, while everyone figures this out, maybe you should stay with me," Ava said, bringing the conversation around. "You can stay here."

But Winston let out an audible groan that made Jess and Devan stare at the house wide-eyed. "Maybe not," I muttered.

"Stay with me," Luci exclaimed. "I have plenty of room and my house doesn't hate Olivia."

How had he known that?

Ava rolled her eyes. "Winston doesn't hate Olivia. Now that we know who she is, it makes sense. Olivia was born in this house, so maybe Winston knew all along."

"And likes to mess with me because?" I eyed Winston and a light in the attic window flashed on then off. Weird house.

Ava shrugged. "Being magical, he could sense the magic in you even though it was locked down. He's always been protective over my family."

I guess. I still didn't think he liked me.

Sam shook his head. "The kids will stay at our place. We have bedrooms for them."

But Devan shook his head and shot Sam a dirty look. "I'd rather not live under your roof."

I fisted my hands at my side and saw vines sprouting out of the ground nearby. Carter had made sure the kids would hate Sam to keep them from me.

We had a lot to work through, including what in the world their father had said to make them hate Sam.

"Why don't you *all* stay with me?" Luci offered. "The whole family, Phira included." He nodded at my Fae aunts and uncles. "You guys are welcome as well."

They didn't react at all. Luci looked at me again. "You'd be in a safe place to learn your powers, and if you mess up my house, I could just fix it."

I shrugged and looked at Sam. It might be a good idea.

He nodded once, telling me he'd go along with it.

"I guess so," I said.

"Yay!" Ava exclaimed. "Neighbors!"

Luci looked affronted. "You already had a neighbor."

"Oh, yeah." Ava shrugged, then she grinned at me. "Yay, *good* neighbors!"

I laughed and silently thanked her for breaking some of the tension. Clapping my hands together, I said, "Let's go inside and see about fixing Ava's living room."

Winston creaked like he was agreeing with my statement.

Jess stood beside me. "Is it safe in that house?"

I nodded. "He won't hurt you or anyone Ava likes because then Ava would be mad at him and Winston doesn't like it when she's mad."

Ava didn't anger easily. She seemed to take things as they happened. She freaked out on the occasion, but her life had been one chaotic mishap after another lately.

"After we get the vines cleaned out we can plan a

Halloween in June party for Ava's birthday next week." I turned and pointed at Sam. "And everyone will dress up."

Sammie perked up at that and clapped. "I want to be a skeleton like Larry."

"Um, Skeleton?" Devan stared at me like he wanted to run the other way.

Before I could answer, Luci stepped between him and Jess and threw his arms over their shoulders. "Larry isn't a skeleton anymore. Ava animated him to how he looked when he died."

I didn't think that really helped to ease their minds, but the kids shared a look and let Luci walk them inside the house.

I followed after and cringed at the mess that extended from the living room to the kitchen, through the opened office door, and hallway. "This is nuts."

Jess nodded. "So much worse than what I did."

Daven whistled. "Yeah, me too."

Phira floated up beside me. Yes, floated because there wasn't a better way to explain how she moved. "You can make them go away with your magic. Just focus on what you want to do."

Easy peasy. I wasn't banking on that, but I'd give it a try.

Before I focused on making the vines go away, I heard a muffled meow. Then Lucy-fur, Ava's ghoulish white cat, said, "Ava, you better get over here and get us out of this crap!"

Ava smirked and glanced at me. "Where are you?"

Snooze meowed again, and we followed the sound, finding them tangled up in vines about halfway up the wall next to the fireplace. Snooze was being held upside down with one vine around his chubby belly with another one wrapped around his tail. Lucy-fur was a few feet away and was more tangled up than Snooze. She must have put up a fight.

I glanced toward the kitchen, noting that Larry, Zoey, and Alfred watched us from the doorway. The vines weren't as dense there. Larry pointed to the cats. "I told them not to go in there."

Luci, aka my...er Satan, stepped close to the white kitty. When he reached out to help her she squeaked and said, "Stay back devil man."

Ava pushed Luci to the side and tried to untangle the mad as heck white cat, but the vines weren't moving.

"Move back, and I'll give it a try." I wasn't even sure how the darn vine had appeared in the first place so making them disappear was going to be interesting.

Taking a deep breath, I focused on what I wanted, like Phira had said. I wanted the vines gone so that was what I clung to. After a few minutes nothing happened. "I'm focusing."

Phira held out her hand to me. "Take my hand and feel how I use my magic to make them obey."

As soon as our hands touched, her magic tingled and wrapped around me like it was hugging me. Then it shifted to flow into the vines directly in front of us. The ones around Lucy-fur loosened enough that she slid out of them and landed on her feet on the floor. The white cat hauled tail out of the living room and up the stairs. I didn't think I'd ever seen her move so fast.

"Okay, I can try now." I understood what she'd done so I copied it.

I searched for magic inside me, and once I found it, I pushed it up to my palms then out to vines. They started moving and disappearing into the cracks of the wood floors. Ava caught Snooze as he dropped. But the fat cat didn't want to be held. He was mad and nipped at Ava to make her drop him. Of course he landed on his feet and ran up the stairs faster than Lucy had, surprising with his bulk.

When all the vines were gone, Winston sighed. At least that was what it felt like.

Happy with what I'd accomplished, I turned to the crowd. My husband, kids, new Fae family and my chosen family. That was what Ava and her magical menagerie were—my chosen family. "Because we only have a week and I need something normal to distract myself with, let's plan a costume party!"

CHAPTER SIX

ONE WEEK LATER

"Come in," Ava said with a big smile, swinging the door wide. It was her birthday, and we'd decided to throw a costume party. Halloween in June! With our crazy lives and all the magic involved in them, a Halloween themed party was more fitting.

Winston was hopping with guests, which most likely had him upset. He wasn't big on new people inside him, but that was too bad. Ava had a lot of friends.

"Happy birthday," I cried, pulling my bestie into a hug. "Sam is on his way." Sammie walked over with his brother and sister, bypassing Ava completely. In the time we'd been staying with Luci, they'd really gotten close. I was glad about that. "He's on duty." Sam, not Sammie.

Drew stepped forward and put his arm around Ava's shoulders. "Thanks to him, I'm here, so we'll forgive him for being late."

I couldn't stop my smile if I wanted to. Ava leaned into Drew pretty much the same way I did with Sam when he was near me. It was great to see her in love. Even if she didn't know she was in love.

I took my gift to the pile on the table against the far wall. Zoey stood by it, organizing everything to look pretty. "Hey, Zo," I said, smiling as Larry appeared from the direction of the kitchen with another gift. "How's life?"

"Great," she said, but barely looked at me. She only had eyes for the fully-fleshed and handsome Larry. His brown hair was getting long enough that the ends curled, but he wouldn't let Ava cut it. He said he went long enough with no hair, he was going to let it grow for a while. Zoey said she loved long hair and I was betting that was the real reason he wasn't cutting.

Ah, to be young and in love.

Those two made a great couple. Both had been given new shots at life... sort of at life. Unlife? Whatever, they had a new chance and were, at least for the moment, choosing to spend it together. I walked further into the living room to smile at a small group of witches from Ava's coven. I only knew Melody, who sort of operated as Ava's right hand woman.

"Hi," I said softly. "I'm going to need to talk to you soon. I'm not exactly a witch, but as it turns out, I do have some powers."

Melody brightened and peeled away from her circle of friends. "I'd love to talk to you about it."

"Maybe I'll come to the next coven meeting?" I asked.

She squeezed my arm. "I'd love that."

Devan, Jessica, and Sammie walked in. "Excuse me," I said and waved eagerly at my kids. We'd been at Luci's about a week. Things were still tense around Sam. Whatever my ex-husband had told them about my new husband, they'd taken it to heart.

However, they adored Luci. I wasn't sure how I felt about that. I did know that he wouldn't hurt them. And think of the devil—literally—he walked through the door behind them. He'd been working day and night with Dev and Jess to help them discover their powers and what they could do with them. Me as well, of course. There were no spells or sorcery with Fae and whatever magic Luci had handed down to us. It was all about intent and visualizing the outcome.

And that took a ton of practice, though memorizing spells would've been way worse.

Before I reached my kids, the shifter couple, the parents of the boy who Ava rescued in the fighting ring, stepped in front of me. Dana grinned. "How are you Olivia?"

I hugged her and shook her husband's hand. "I'm good. How are you?"

"Good." Dana patted my hand and then moved on to speak with another shifter couple that had come. I thought they were also parents of another kid that was in the fighting ring. The same one Zoey died in.

Glancing to where my kids were moments ago, I frowned when they weren't there. I scanned the party goers, waving at ones that met my gaze. My Fae uncles and aunts were gathered in one corner of the living room and I wondered if they were being snobs or just not comfortable with being around so many other magical beings. I really didn't care either way. If they were to accept me into their family, then they'd have to put up with my friends.

Eodh stood, said something to his siblings, then disappeared down the hall. I ignored him and moved toward the kitchen to see what Alfred was cooking up. About half way there Eodh appeared in front of me. "The lavatory in the hallway is occupied."

I almost snorted at his choice of words. "There is another bathroom upstairs. Second door on the left."

He gave a short nod and rushed up the stairs. I shook my head and smiled. He must really have to go.

"Where are my kids?"

My insides turned to frost at the sound of that voice. Oh, no. Not today. I knew that voice. It was the loud, demanding, entitled, completely assholish voice of my ex-husband, Carter. I rushed toward the door to intercept him away from Ava. "What are you doing here?" I hissed.

He glared down at me and suddenly I wished Sam was here already. Not that I wanted him to fight my battles for me. But I felt my worth with Sam. Every time I looked at Carter I felt tiny. Insignificant. Lesser.

Why hadn't I seen that when I first met Carter? The only good I got out of that marriage was Jess and Devan.

"I got a phone call from *my* daughter that she wasn't coming home. I get back into town to find that *my* son is also gone! What have you done to *my* children?"

His children? I'll have him know that it was me who spent hours in labor with each of them.

He stopped then, and looked around. So I tried to get his focus on me. Carter was human and as far as I knew didn't know about magic. I was betting he wouldn't take the news very well. He hated things he didn't understand.

"How did you know to come here?" I hissed and tried to push him out the door.

But he didn't answer. "What the hell is going on here?"

"Carter," Drew said and crowded past me. "It's time for you to leave."

But Carter had seen something. His focus was on whatever was going on behind me. I turned to see what.

Jessica was frozen in the doorway with Zoey beside her... and Zoey had ears. She sometimes didn't have full control over her shifting and around the house didn't try to. Her tiger wasn't a threat to any of us. Most of the time Zoey had her tigers ears out or her tail swinging behind her. I loved it.

But Zoey with tiger ears and Jessica beside her wasn't the

worst part. Jess was levitating. She was obviously showing Zoey, who she'd started to become friends with over the last week, how she'd mastered levitating herself.

And off to the right, Devan stepped forward holding a drink. The straw in the drink was stirring itself. My kids had grown comfortable using their magic in everyday things, while being careful not to let humans see. But there weren't supposed to be any humans that didn't know about magic at the party.

Until Carter showed up.

I swung back around to face Carter. "Don't freak out," I said. He wasn't listening to me. I could see his ears turning red with anger. "Carter!"

He stared at me in revulsion and sneered. "Freaks," he whispered, then raised his voice. "You're all freaks!"

Then he left, sprinting down the driveway to the road where his truck was parked.

Devan and Jessica shuffled forward to watch him go. "He hates us," Jessica said in a small voice.

"He didn't even give us a chance to explain," Dev whispered.

I put my arms around both my kids, drawing them into me. "Don't worry, and don't take it to heart. We'll get him to come around, okay?"

After pressing a kiss to Devan's head then one to Jessica's, I squeezed them closer. "It'll work itself out. I promise one way or another it will. I may have disappointed you before but I promise I won't again. We'll sort this out." I sighed. "As happy as I am to have you in my life again, we'll make sure you don't lose your father in the process."

And we would fix this. Somehow.

A KILLER MIDLIFE

A WITCHING AFTER FORTY NOVEL

ABOUT A KILLER MIDLIFE

Necromancer-witch hybrid Ava Harper has accomplished many things in the year since moving back home to Shipton Harbor. She's checking things off a bucket list she never knew she had.

Met—and started dating—a hot cop.
Caught a murderer. More than once.
Sent a couple of lunatics to Hades with the help of her devilish neighbor.
Visited Paris.
Saved a bunch of shifter kids.
Animated her cat's girlfriend.
Sold her old house and found closure.
Discovered her aunt's ghost.
Saved her mother's ghost from a dark evil blob.

The list goes on and seems to be never ending. Now Ava is faced with a new entity to deal with. Faeries! Who knew? They've dropped a bombshell on Ava and her best friend

Olivia. While they come to terms with all the insanity their lives have thrown their way, Ava gets more news from her mother.

Mommy dearest learned some interesting and relevant information while in the Inbetween. She has news about Ava's father that will change the course of Ava's life and take her down another new, exciting path.

Will this new thread in Ava's life prove to be more dangerous than she could've dreamed of? Maybe. But it's more likely that the truth about her father will be killer.

1
LUCY-FUR
—THE CAT, NOT THE DEVIL—

What in the ever-loving, hairball-causing Underworld had I signed up for? Better yet, what did that no-good Maine Coone Snoozer sign me up for? My new ghoulish life was entirely that big furball's fault. I mean I'm grateful, really, I am. And I like Snooze and Ava, most of the time, but I don't go around telling people that. I have a reputation to maintain.

And I'll deny everything.

Excuse me. I have an itch I just need to...Oh for whiskers' sake...Ah, that's better. Sorry you had to see me licking my back leg. How embarrassing.

If you haven't noticed by now, Ava's life is a little crazy... not to mention, she is a major chaos magnet. There's always something insane going on around her, and yet nobody ever seems to notice! How is that possible? The things that happen around this house and Ava have to be documented. And since nobody else is jumping up to do it, Well that makes me the right cat for the job.

First, I watched Zoey use that new social media thing, Tik Tak or Toe? Something like that, so I broke into her account—

ridiculously easy, as she never actually logs out—to see what it was all about.

That was when the idea hit me. Everything aligned in my mind, and I got so excited I was actually nice to Snoozer. Ugh.

I could do videos and talk about Ava's chaotic and unpredictable life. This could be a goldmine. It's not every day humans see a talking cat. Well, there was that silly lawyer man, but he doesn't count. He wasn't even a real talking cat, and look how much attention he got. So I'm almost guaranteed to get a plethora of followers.

Like that word? Plethora? It was on Ava's WOTD calendar.

Anymeow, about the talking cat thing... Yeah, it surprised me too when I woke up as a ghoul. We don't know why or how it's possible. I should've just been a cat, like Snoozer. Continuing my cat life, sunshine naps, eating, chasing string, all that good stuff. But talking's not all. I can read, too. Well, not like *actual* reading, I just understand the words on the paper. Ugh, it's hard to describe. Just come along with me. I'll catch you up.

I jumped up on Zoey's bed, my favorite in the house, by the way. Probably because of her shifter smell. It's alluring.

I padded over to where she had left her tablet and touched the screen with my nose. It flared to life, and I entered the code. Easy peasy. Zoey's tablet and phone were the only devices in the house that didn't have the face recognition turned on. She said it was pointless as it didn't work when her face was in half shift. Convenient for me.

Like me, Zoey was a ghoul. Unlike me, she was also a tiger shifter who unfortunately didn't have full control of her shifting. Most of the time around the house, her tiger ears twitched on top of her head, or her facial features looked more feline than human. Other times, her tail was out. I liked to chase it. Ahh, that was a lot of fun.

Once I had the Toe Top app open, I bunched the blanket

under the tablet, so it sat at an angle. When I got it just right, without flipping the tablet over, which wasn't so easy, I nudged the three-minute timer and hit the record button.

I backed into place, smiled at the tablet's camera, and started my story. "This week's update is about the newest thing with Olivia. Yes, boring human Olivia. She found out her mother is a Fae princess, and her father is Luci. Yes, that Luci, not me. I spell my name with a Y." I licked my front paw and smoothed a piece of fur away.

"So, that makes Olivia a demonic Faery princess. Sounds like a Halloween costume gone wrong, doesn't it? Anyway, Ava wrote it in some short story called Odd Mother or something stupid like that. It's at that big online e-book store if you want to read the full story. But I'm here to give you a spoilerific recap in case you missed it. To be clear. Lots of spoilers coming."

Sucking in a deep breath, I waved and let my audience know I'd continue in part two. These videos didn't last long enough.

Now for the hard part. I had to get all the hashtags on there. It took a while because my toe beans weren't situated to be able to do it—no opposable thumbs, you know—and my nose often missed. But eventually, I had them in. #catsoftiktok, #cats #catlover #shiptonghoul—to tie my stuff to the stuff Alfred had been doing on Insta—and a few more that were currently trending.

Then I started over again with part two. "In my last update, I told you about the black blob from the Inbetween actually being a Fae princess. Well, Ava and the coven tried every spell and counter-curse they could think of and couldn't figure out how to cure the Fae and turn her from an angry blob into a pretty lady. Then, one random day, Ava and Olivia went out to the blob and when they came back, they brought back the Fae all normal and nice. Turns out Olivia's blood was the key! Who could've guessed? Olivia's powers unlocked and the house sprouted vines and flowers, which Snoozer and I got trapped in." I gave the camera a flat, aggravated look. "I was not amused."

"What happened next was chaos from the noise. I was trapped in the vines, so I don't know all the details. Lucifer showed up and I guess they had a family meeting or something. The next thing I knew, Olivia's older children showed up. Turns out when Olivia's powers unlocked, so did theirs. Olivia and her family moved in with the Devil and the Fae princess to learn their powers. Then at Ava's birthday party, Olivia's ex-husband showed up and boy was he pis—"

"Lucy-Fur, What are you doing?" Ava's sharp tone scared the kittens out of me. I jumped and whirled around to face her. "Geez, Ava, you look like death." Her green eyes were dull and tired-looking, and her hair was greasier than I'd ever seen it. And that was saying something, considering she went into her office and didn't emerge for hours and hours, or days and days sometimes. She looked rough after a big writing jag like that.

To my horror, she reached down and snatched up the tablet, turning the video feed off.

I darted forward, but it was too late. "Hey! I need to save that!"

With her lips pressed together, she stared at me for a long while. I gazed back, not understanding what she was trying to do. Intimidate me? Ha! I think not. That wasn't possible. I was un-intimidate-able.

She looked down at the tablet and started swiping her finger across the screen. I couldn't see what she was doing, but I knew it wasn't good. Her voice came out all low and growly. Phlegm, maybe? "How many of these videos have you done?" No, it was anger.

I laid down and licked my paw, unconcerned with her fury. "A few. I have followers—" Over a hundred thousand, thank you very much. "—and they love me."

"Unbelievable. And it sounded like you were telling people about Olivia without changing names or anything. Everyone pretty much still thinks she's human! What were you thinking?" Ava lifted her head and paused as if she was going to sneeze. When she didn't, she called out, "Zoey!"

I paused in my bath and studied Ava. She'd been sick for the past couple of weeks, but today she really didn't look so hot.

A few seconds later, the young tigress appeared at the door of her bedroom. Her tail wasn't twitching around behind her, but her ears were out on top of her head. "Yes?"

Ava handed her the tablet. "Change your passcode. Did you know that Lucy was making Tik Tok videos?"

Zoey giggled and one of her tiger ears disappeared from the top of her head. "Yeah, of course. She has a bigger following than me. Besides, they think it's me using a filter that makes me look like a cat."

Ava looked supremely irritated and opened her mouth to say something but sneezed, then coughed. Zoey frowned and reached out to her. "You should see someone for that cold."

Ava waved her off, and I lost interest in the whole situation. It was no longer about me, therefore it wasn't important. "I'm going to go find out where Snooze wandered off to and disrupt his nap."

2
AVA

That cat was going to be the death of me. Or at least the death of my nerves. Shaking my head at her poofy tail as Lucy-Fur slinked out of the room, I turned my attention back to Zoey, who wasn't totally escaping my ire. She should've known better. "I'm concerned that hunters would want to come and investigate the talking cat. Drew says he has it covered, but you and Lucy need to be careful what you share on the Internet." I mean, really.

Zoey frowned and nodded, looking contrite. "Oh, I didn't think about that. I'll let Lucy know I need to review the posts before she submits them." Well, that was something, at least.

"Thank you." I wrapped my arms around my middle and shivered. I'm definitely sick if I'm cold. Being in the throes of perimenopause made me perpetually hot and sweaty. Plus, I'd always been hot-natured, anyway. Plus-plus, it was the middle of July! Winston's central heating and air—which he'd been surprisingly uncomplicated about having installed when I was a teenager—worked well, but it was older. We probably needed to replace it. Sometimes the house got hotspots, and Zoey's bedroom was one of them. If there's anywhere in the house I should be toasty warm in the middle of the summer, it was here.

Yep. It was definitely bedtime. I was just about to tell Zoey I was going to go lay down when I sensed my mother and aunt close by. "Mom and Winnie are here."

I rushed...well as much as I could feeling like roadkill, out of Zoey's room and down the stairs. Geez, I had to hold onto the banister on the way down. What the heck? I reached the first floor just as the front door opened with a creak. I stopped and breathed as deep as I could, ignoring the crud in my lungs in the process.

Mom and Winnie walked in, closing the door behind them. They looked like I felt. Mom's green eyes, the same shade as mine, a sort of bright sea green, looked filmy. Gross. And Winnie's hair was thin like a bunch had fallen out. Both of them had a pallor to their skin that made them look more like the ghouls they were.

Could ghouls get sick? Or was this them reacting to my cold? I hadn't been sick since I became caretaker of all these undead people and creatures around here. We had no idea what sort of problems me getting sick could cause. "Are you two all right?" I asked in a wheezing voice.

Mom looked at me and frowned, her filmy green eyes flashing worry. "Ava, honey, are you not well?"

"I asked first," I replied, then sighed as she drifted to me and placed a hand on my forehead, then my cheeks. Forever my mother, no matter that I was old enough to be a grandmother. Oh, geez, let the universe keep that from happening for a few more years, yet. Wallie was barely into college.

"You're not running a fever, but your energy is low." She tutted and put her arm around my shoulder.

I could have told her that before she touched me. But I'd missed my mom, so I wasn't complaining. She could mother me all she wanted. Especially now that I wasn't feeling great. She and Winnie had been gone for a week or so, looking for appropriate human bodies to one day transfer them out of their ghoulish bodies into. We'd begun looking farther from home so that once they took the bodies, we could hopefully keep them hidden from their real families. The spell would only work if they found someone whose soul had already left its person, but the body remained intact. Coma patients, mostly.

But we didn't want to cause any families any unnecessary pain by having to see their loved ones return, then leave again. It was a delicate issue. And definitely morally iffy.

Winnie stepped up beside her and repeated Mom's assessment of my wellbeing—forehead and cheek check. Of course, she did. She'd mothered me for longer than Mom had, really. Since I was eleven. "How long have you been ill?"

I shrugged and shuffled into the kitchen. Alfred stood in front of the stove stirring a pot of chicken noodle soup. Apparently, he'd either liked doing all the house-keepey stuff when he shared his body with Winnie, or he'd always been that way because I couldn't keep him out of the kitchen. I'd told him several times that with how many of us lived here, we could all share in the cooking and chores, but he insisted.

He reached a dried up, pasty grayish hand into the cabinet and pulled out a bowl, then filled it with the soup before walking it over to the table. "Sit and eat." His squeaky voice brought a small smile to my lips. Somehow, he looked like he'd be bigger, burlier if we ever got around to fleshing him out a bit. Things had been too crazy to get around to it yet. Now that everything had calmed down, I was sick and didn't at all feel like doing it.

I smiled weakly at him and sank into a chair at the table. If I felt better, I would have taken the bowl from him and gone to get a glass of tea, but as it was, I let him set it down in front of me. "Thank you."

Mom and Winnie took the seats on either side of me, both of them still looking worried and mother-hen-like. I inhaled the savory aroma of the soup and my stomach growled. It smelled so good. "Is this Winnie's recipe?" She made the best chicken noodle ever.

"It is," Alfred said with a grin. He looked proud as a peacock, which made no sense because his facial features didn't change. "I hope it is as good as she would have made it." He gave Winnie a head nod.

I scooped up a spoonful and blew in it to cool it off before putting it in my mouth. Oh, he'd hit the nail on the head. Winnie might get her feelers in a twist, but it was every bit as good as when she made it. "This is perfect," I said with a moan. The only thing that would've made it better was eating it in bed.

After my second bite, I sighed. It might've been better than hers, but I wasn't going to say that out loud. Then again, I could've just been so hungry and feeling so bad that leather would've tasted good. Either way, it made me feel a teensy bit better for the moment.

Footsteps pounded down the stairs, alerting me to Owen heading in my direction. At least I assumed he was coming in here. For all I knew, he could have been heading out, far away from me since I was sick. A few seconds ticked by before he filled the archway of the kitchen.

Owen turned his nearly-black eyes toward me with concern but some of the worry washed away when he spotted my soup. "It's good to see you're eating." He had a strong Severus Snape vibe, which had made us super leery of him at first, but now he was like the big brother I never had. What would I do without Owen?

"I've been eating. Just not as much. Don't have the energy to," I mumbled, then took another bite as Owen sat across from me at the table.

He studied Mom and Winnie and pressed his lips in a thin line while tapping his fingers on the table, assessing the situation. Assessing me. I held my tongue and let him analyze me while I enjoyed my soup. No doubt he was coming to the same conclusions I already had. My power wasn't limitless. Being ill was taking a toll on those who depended on me for… well, for life.

After a while, he sat back and tapped his fingers on the table. "I have a theory."

"Do tell, Dr. Owen," Mom said. She laced her fingers lightly through my hair. If she kept that up, I'd go right to sleep in my soup.

The corner of his lips lifted slightly. "Since you fell ill, Zoey and Larry have been having…issues." He shot me a quick look, but I nodded.

That was the understatement of the year. Larry's flesh was literally falling off and Zoey had been struggling with staying completely human more than usual.

"This cold or whatever this is makes it hard to function," I murmured. "I'm not keeping them up as I should."

"I think it's more than that." He sucked in a deep breath as if to give some big speech but paused when someone knocked on the door.

I was so not getting up to answer that. It was Olivia and Sam. They were due here about now. I was about to ask Winston to just open the door—despite his dislike of Olivia—when Zoey bounded down the stairs and answered it. "Hi! Ava is in the kitchen. Bye." She went out the open door once Sam and Olivia came into the entry. I gave them a feeble wave down the hallway from the kitchen. The table was situated to be able to see the front door from here.

It amazed me how my ghouls seemed to always know where I was. Then again, they were bound to me. But I couldn't sense their whereabouts at all times. It wasn't a two-way street. "Where is she going?"

Owen pointed behind me, in the general direction of the living room, and outside the house, toward our closest and most infuriating neighbor's house. "Luci's. She and Jess have become best friends."

Ah. Yeah. I should have known, but my brain wasn't firing on all cells at the moment. I took one more bite of soup and pushed the bowl toward the middle of the table. "Back to our conversation. What do you think it is?"

Olivia stopped next to my chair and placed a hand on my shoulder. Her magic seeped into me, and I sighed. She'd gotten her powers a few weeks ago, after we'd discovered that her mother was the mysterious blob-turned-Fae, Phira. And the big bombshell had been Luci. He was Olivia's biological father, and he was also Loki. And a whole bunch of other mythological bad guys over the years.

Olivia's magic was tied to the earth since the Fae were earth-creatures, and I was half-earth witch. Relief rippled through me and for a brief moment, I almost felt normal. "You're getting worse, not better," she chided.

I rolled my eyes at her, then looked at Sam. "Thanks. Where's Sammie?"

"At Luci's with his brother and sister." Olivia sat between Mom and Owen and smiled, even though I sensed a tinge of sadness. She was trying to rebuild a relationship with her two older children from her first marriage. Unfortunately, Jess and Devan didn't like Sam much, thanks to the venom that Olivia's ex-husband had spewed, and that made Olivia sad. It wasn't something she could control or fix right away, so it threw her off balance a little. Not to mention her newfound powers and birth parents turning her whole life into a complete uproar.

It was a good thing Jess and Devan loved little Sammie. And they'd learn to love Sam. Nobody knew Sam and disliked him. He was too good of a guy. And he'd been a stellar influence on Olivia. She wasn't the same person she used to be.

Mom looked up at Olivia then to Sam and Owen. "Why haven't you called us? How can you let her be sick for so long?"

Sam bowed his head. My mom was like a second mother to him or had been for our childhood. "We didn't see it at first."

Olivia added, "It all happened so slowly, like boiling a frog."

"What?" Everyone around the table said at the same time.

Olivia rolled her eyes. "You've never heard that old saying?"

We all shook our heads slowly at our eccentric friend. She always had a phrase or obscure advice. She was great in a trivia contest, though.

She sighed, exasperated at us. "If you want to boil a frog without it jumping out of the hot water, you put it in lukewarm water, then raise the temperature very slowly. The frog won't realize it's being cooked until it's too late."

"Gross," I muttered. "Why would you want to boil a frog alive? That's terrible." I didn't even eat lobster for that reason, and that was saying a lot considering I grew up in Maine.

She threw up her hands. "It's not literal. I've never actually boiled anything alive." Olivia shook her head at all of us. "You guys are hopeless, I swear. The point is that she wasn't that sick. It got worse slowly until now we're realizing she's very sick. Let's get you to a doctor, sweetie," she suggested.

But I shook my head. "No, it's just a cold. Sometimes they linger."

Just then Drew entered the house and came straight over to me. He didn't even knock or say hello. He picked me up and sat in my chair, placing me in his lap.

Oh criminy, how could I feel so bad, but his actions were so dang hot? If I wasn't about to pass out, I would've been turned on.

I snuggled into him, loving the feel of his warmth and his power, both physical and metaphysical. He was a born hunter and had a little magic of his own, although it was different from witch magic. I wasn't sure how exactly, but it was. That didn't stop it from being comforting, like a blanket of magic around me.

Drew rubbed circles on my back and said, "I talked to my sister, and she says it sounds like Ava has too many undead tied to her energy."

Owen clapped his hand. "Ha. That's what I was trying to get to earlier."

I lifted my head, alarms going off like crazy inside me. "You talked to your sister about me?"

Drew's sister, Lily, was an active hunter. As in, currently going after my ilk. Witches and vampires and shifters, oh, my! I didn't know what criteria hunters had about going after paranormal creatures. It was something we hadn't discussed as of yet.

Drew massaged the nape of my neck. "She isn't blinded like most hunters are. She has friends who are paranormal and will only go after actual rogues. There are a lot of hunters who do that now. Kind of like breaking old Guild protocols and making their own rules."

That was interesting news. "So, she thinks I'm being drained by my ghouls?"

"It makes sense," Owen said. He looked at Drew. "I assume she has access to the Hunters' library?"

"The what, now?" I asked.

"The hunters have a massive library," Drew explained. "It's digital now, but for a long time, it was kept mobile. It has facts and information about all the supernatural creatures and their powers."

Olivia perched onto Sam's lap, who sat next to Owen at the

table. I really needed a bigger table. This one couldn't expand as Winston could. "What are we going to do?"

"That seems simple enough. We need to figure out how to transfer some or all of them from her," Winnie said. "She has seven. That was what we were doing before we started looking like the undead." She gestured toward her hair. "Trying to find a way to get Beth and me off of Ava's power load, and into our own bodies."

Owen nodded. "But even in a living body, wouldn't you still need a necromancer's power to stay animated?"

"We're hoping not," Mom replied.

"I could take maybe two if it came down to it," Owen said. "We'd need to find another necromancer to take two more."

I wasn't sure I wanted a necromancer I didn't know to take two of my ghouls. They were a part of me. They were mine to care for. "I don't know," I said uncertainly. "That sounds like losing a lot of control."

"You've never been controlling," Winnie said. "Or possessive. Why now?"

I opened my mouth but couldn't answer. "I don't know, but somehow... you guys, you're all mine. What if someone else doesn't take as good care of you?"

Drew wrapped his arms around me, and I snuggled into him again. He looked at Owen. "Until we figure something else out, can you or the coven do a binding spell? You can bind me to Ava. That should be enough energy to balance it out for a little while at least."

Owen frowned and met my gaze. I started shaking my head as Owen said, "Binding yourself to a witch is for life. And since Ava isn't just a witch, there would be no breaking that bond. Ever. If she dies, so do you. And vice-versa."

"I'll do it," Drew said without another second's thought. Just like that. Drew was willing to bond with me to give me a boost? For life?

I wasn't so sure I was ready for that. Not to mention, if he died, so would I. It was a two-way street. This meant some major consideration. "What are our other options?" I asked. "What happens if I don't transfer some of the ghouls to someone else?" I didn't want Drew to bind with me for life. What if he regretted it later on? What if we got tired of each other or something crazy happened? There were too many questions.

Owen glanced away, out the window toward the cliff and the ocean. "If you continue like you are, you could die."

Well. Didn't that put a pallor on such a fantastic day.

3
AVA

"What do you mean, I could die?" I had another sixty-plus years before I had to worry about dying. Then again, I was a witch-necromancer hybrid and supposedly the most powerful one alive. So, it was possible I could live even longer. I wasn't meant to die in my mid-forties because of taking on too many ghouls.

Not according to Owen, apparently. He kept harping on about me finding a way to relieve myself of some of my ghouls. "You have seven ghouls drawing from your energy. Seven, Ava. Two is a strain on a normal necro." Owen glanced around the table, making me do the same. Everyone sat staring at me with worried gazes. Oh, good grief. Was this really that bad? Why all of a sudden was it a problem? It hadn't been for months and months. What had changed?

But still, I did the math on my fingers and Owen was right. I had seven undead tied to me. Snoozerton, Lucy. Alfred, Winnie, Mom. Larry and Zoey. And I'd been fine up until my birthday party. Well, maybe I'd felt a little off since going in and out of the Inbetween. But that couldn't be it, because Drew had also crossed over to the ghostly plane twice and he was fine. It had to be something else.

Speaking of Drew, I twisted around and glared into his eyes.

He lifted one brow in question.

"And what is with this binding your life force to mine?" I asked. It was such an enormous step. We hadn't even talked about it before and wham-bam, he was just ready to do it.

He brushed a lock of my hair behind my ear, setting my skin tingling everywhere his fingers brushed me. "If it will help keep you alive, I'll do it in a second." He used his alpha sheriff tone that sent a jolt of desire through me... which was quickly washed away with fatigue and aches.

Before meeting the sexy sheriff, I'd never known that I'd like an alpha, take-charge type of man. Drew was so much more than that, though. He was compassionate, powerful, and owned a piece of my heart. The latter wasn't something I'd let him know yet. I'd barely admitted it to myself. Things had progressed far too quickly thus far and showed no signs of slowing down. Certainly not with this on the table.

I poked him in the chest. "If it doesn't work, you will die with me." I couldn't come to grips with that part.

Holding my stare, he took my hand and pressed our palms together. Then a surge of warm magic flowed into me. The aches faded, the fatigue lifted, although just for a moment. I had momentary relief, and it was a little piece of heaven.

Sharing energy through touch was something witches could do, especially when they were a couple or bound to one another. Drew had told me once that he'd dated a witch before, and she had died at the hands of hunters. It was one of the main reasons he'd stopped hunting, and I couldn't blame him. He loved her, I knew that, but he'd never given me details on their relationship. And I hadn't asked because I'd sensed how painful the subject was with him. If he'd been anywhere as close to her as I had been with Clay, it had been intensely painful. It was no wonder he'd given up hunting.

Still, though, I hadn't expected him to push his magic into me in front of a room full of people. It was such an intimate thing, and I appreciated him so much.

He kissed the tip of my nose. "My hunter bloodline is one of the purest and one of the oldest."

Meaning his power was as strong as a high witch. At least as strong as mine, though he didn't use his in as obvious a way as I did. Before I could reply, he added, "By bonding, my power can help take the burden of ghouls. At least until we come up with another solution."

"Bonding with another magical being is not temporary," I reminded him. "And both of us still have a long life to live."

Our audience watched on in rapt attention as Drew chuckled and cupped the back of my head. He wasn't backing down from this, and I wasn't sure I wanted him to...but I also wasn't sure I didn't either. I cared for Drew—was pretty much in love with him or more. And since saying goodbye to Clay and getting his blessing to move on with Drew—not that I'd needed permission from my dead husband, exactly—one thing had become clear to me. Drew and I were destined to be together.

The Fates were running this show, and I hoped like hell they knew what they were doing. Something big was coming down the pipeline, and we'd be the ones leading our army to the battle. I wasn't sure what that was just yet. Or what we'd be fighting. Or why, how...maybe it was nothing and I was so tired I was making things up.

"I didn't say I wanted it to be temporary." He leaned closer until his lips caressed my ear. "The way I feel about you...I haven't felt like this in such a long time. I'm not sure I ever felt quite like this. It's right."

I let out an affectionate sigh and framed his face in my hands while studying him for a long moment or two. "But you won't be able to change your mind."

His nostrils flared. "This is the last time I'll say it. I don't plan to."

I frowned as my heart raced in anticipation. I hadn't even known Drew for a full year. Was I really jumping in with both feet like this? "We're doing this?" I whispered. A smile pulled the corners of my mouth up. I couldn't stop the excitement filling me. We were doing this.

He smiled and nodded. "We're doing this." The finality in his tone left me no real room for argument. The happiness in my heart told me I didn't want to argue.

Well, that settled that. I turned back to the table and realized that everyone had gone. Our audience had disappeared. "Where are they?"

Alfred stood at the stove, and when I looked at him, he pointed up. Drew said, "The ritual room." Which really meant the attic.

"Of course." They knew I'd agree before I even knew about it. I stood and held out my hand to Drew. "Let's do this." The thought of walking all the way up there made me a little nauseated, but if it helped me in the long run, so be it. I'd make the trek.

Why were stairs so difficult?

Drew took my hand and pulled me to follow him. The ritual room was a spiritually clean space used for high magic and, hence the name, rituals.

I also often used it as a quiet place to think and read when I needed to get away from the chaos that had become my life and the house. It was also our attic and a storage area. Nobody said we couldn't multitask. Multipurpose. Whatever, we needed the room. Even the ever-expanding Winston wasn't infallible with all these people under one roof.

The scent of frankincense and rosemary drifted in the air as we climbed the stairs. Owen had already started cleansing the space. We walked slowly along the upstairs hallway to the door at the end that hid the attic stairs. More stairs. Freaking seriously, again, why were stairs so hard?

I stopped in the doorway, panting, and Drew put his arm around me. "Come on. Let's hurry so you'll feel better."

Smiling at him, I shuffled forward into the circle of candles. "How does this work?" I asked. "I've never bonded with anyone." I chuckled. Over forty years old and still doing something new.

Owen stepped forward and smiled warmly. "It's pretty simple. I'll do the spell and Olivia will supply some power."

She bounced on her heels. "I wanted to do the spell, but I was vetoed." After shooting Owen a dark glance, she resumed her excited stance. "At least this way I'm still involved."

Owen grimaced and looked contrite. "It's not that I don't want you to do it. You're just so new and this needs to be right."

"I'm afraid I agree, dear," Aunt Winnie said. "You're just too green."

It was a battle for Olivia not to roll her eyes. She couldn't stop her nostrils flaring, though. "I know, I know."

"So, we just stand here?" I asked.

Owen held out a long piece of silky material. "We bind your hands. The silk serves as a guide for the magic, to twine your powers together."

Drew stepped around me, then turned to face me. As I looked up into his eyes, warmth filled me, and my aches and pains subsided a bit in the face of love. I smiled, butterflies really going crazy. I still couldn't believe I was doing this! It was really rather amazing.

"Ready?" he asked.

"Here," Mom said. She handed me a circlet that tinkled as I took it. It was gold and had small bells hanging off of little stars. The delicate circle was exquisite and looked expensive.

"What's this?" I asked.

After shrugging one shoulder, she laughed lightly. "It's probably superstition. But it's a crown of sorts, and the tinkling bells are supposed to confuse evil spirits so they can't invade the bonding. It's traditional for a witch wedding."

I gulped. "We aren't getting married, exactly," I whispered.

"No," Drew said. He leaned close to my ear. "This isn't how I wanted to ask you, but we can get married if you'd like to. I know I would love to."

I couldn't stop my eyes from widening. Had Drew just proposed to me... like this?

"We'll talk about it later," I whispered. I wanted to scream that I'd marry him in a heartbeat, of course!

But also, if he wanted to marry me, he could ask me properly. "Right now, it is about our bonding," I said. "This is for us. If we get married, it'll be a production."

This was just to save me, too. If we got married, it would be an eternal declaration of our intentions to stay together forever. More than just a quick fix to make me well again. Though, I didn't really believe that was Drew's only motive here.

"Ava?" Mom asked. "Are you going to wear it?"

I nodded, placing the circlet on my head. "Sure. We don't need any evil spirits here today."

"Join hands," Owen said.

Drew's big hands enveloped mine. The warmth was a balm to my poor freezing fingers. I wanted to wrap myself up in Drew and sleep for a good week.

Mom laced the silk material, which I now recognized as a tie, around our hands, binding them together pretty effectively. "Is this Luci's?" I asked.

Mom nodded. "Yes, Olivia brought it."

I grinned at my best friend. "Aw, your Daddy's tie."

Her blonde hair shined as she tossed it over her shoulder, even in the somewhat dim candlelight of the attic. "Hush and focus on your man."

That wasn't a problem. I grinned up at Drew while Owen and Olivia stepped forward and touched the tie with a finger each.

Power began to course through me. Owen's, I recognized, but Olivia's was still new and intriguing. It didn't feel like anything I'd experienced before. Her unique heritage gave her a pretty cool bit of magic. Half Fae, half angel-demon-god thing.

We still had no idea exactly what the heck Luci was. Demon, god, the devil? All of the above?

"Today we bind Ava and Drew. With destiny in our intent and love in our hearts. May they hold one another up in the darkness, a light to guide the way."

Olivia's power snatched hold of mine, like a hook on the back of my neck. I had to keep myself from staggering forward. By the look on Drew's face, Owen's power had just done the same to him. I breathed out a sigh as Drew's power lit up the scarf, quickly followed by mine. His magic looked like blue electricity, racing toward my green. My aura was earthy green, but the magic had it all lit up like Christmas lights.

I gasped when they hit one another, but to my credit, so did Drew. His energy and power filled me, chasing away the horrible feeling I'd been carrying around. I stood up straighter and stared in amazement as Drew's body glowed green. I looked down to see myself bright blue, putting off enough light to brighten the entire attic.

"This is amazing," I whispered.

Drew's entire self, his whole being hugged me, comforting

me and accepting me as I was, who I was. I'd never felt more empowered to simply be me.

The light began to dim, and the intensity waned, leaving energy behind. Not as much as I'd had when I wasn't sick, but enough to make me grin from ear to ear.

Once the flow of magic from the ritual settled around Drew and me, all I could do was laugh. My energy was completely renewed. I could actually feel Drew inside me.

Hey! Not like that. A dirty mind is a terrible thing to waste.

His power filled me, mingling with my own. I could also feel his emotions, pure excitement at the moment. Also, a lot of love. Perhaps more than I had, which I wasn't sure how I felt about that, but I hated feeling any sort of way about his emotions because then he would be able to sense me having a feel about his feels!

This was confusing.

I looked around at my friends and family standing outside the circle. Mom and Winnie looked ten times better than they had before the binding. Lucy-Fur and Snoozer chose that moment to enter the attic. Both looked better, too. And Lucy wasn't complaining, which was great. And rare.

Larry and Zoey had gone over to Luci's house to hang out with Olivia's older kids, Jess and Devan. I'd check on them in a bit. If they'd been showing any bad signs, by the power pounding in my veins, they were fine now.

Olivia grinned. "It worked!" She looked at us with slightly unfocused eyes. "I can see your auras. They've merged."

Like a bonded pair. I still wasn't sure how I felt about it. Oh, shoot. I had to stop feeling the feels. He'd know.

Drew took my hand and butterflies took flight in my belly. He tugged me close to wrap an arm around my waist. "I'm taking the boat out Friday since I have the day off. Want to come with me?"

Oh. Alone time with Sheriff Drew. Heck yeah, I wanted to go. "Sounds fun."

"Good." He kissed me quickly on the lips. "I hate to leave now. After our bond, I really don't want to leave you. But I have to go to work." He pressed another kiss to my temple. "I'll see you later." Then he left and I admired his backside until he disappeared out of the ritual room.

4
OLIVIA

"You need to focus, dear." Phira was endlessly patient, but I wasn't feeling it today.

"I am focused." Well, sort of. No, I wasn't. Let me be honest with myself and with you. I had too much on my mind. Ava wasn't well and I hated that none of us knew why. There was no discernable reason for her illness, none whatsoever. I wasn't buying the ghouls draining her bit. There was something else going on, but I couldn't put my finger on it. Even though she felt much better after the binding ritual with Drew, it was only temporary. We didn't fix anything, we only patched it.

The boost of energy was temporary, not the binding. That woman was now a bound female. It was more permanent than marriage. I hadn't had the chance to ask her how she felt about it. The bonding or marriage, cause I was pretty sure I heard him say something about getting married, which... I really hoped so, cause Ava was not all about wedding planning, but I would love to.

She'd seemed okay with it. On that thought, she hadn't put

up much of an argument with Drew about it. It was almost like Ava knew something the rest of us didn't.

How was that possible? I couldn't stop obsessing over how easily Ava accepted this whole thing.

"Breena."

I opened my eyes and glared at Phira, still not comfortable with calling her mother or mom. Not yet.

And that name. Breena. That was the name she and Luci had picked out for me before I was even born. Before Phira was sentenced to live the rest of her days in the Inbetween, which had made her go dark and turn into an angry black blob.

She had refused to go into the ghostly realm until after I was born. Ava's mom and Aunt Winnie had been the ones to put me up for adoption before they locked Phira in the Inbetween. At least I'd been adopted locally. And I'd had pretty good parents. Not the best. But by far not the worst either.

I put one hand on one hip and cocked my head at Phira. "My name is Olivia. It has been for forty-two years now. I'm used to it. I'm happy with it."

Phira drifted to me. Literally, she floated through the air, but yet I saw her feet on the floor as she walked. How did she do that? She took my hands and smiled at me despite the crabby tone I'd used. "And for forty-two years, I've only known you as Breena. In my heart and my imagination. You were and are my Breena."

I sagged in defeat. She was right. As a mother who had her kids taken away, I knew how hard it was to live without them. At least in my case, I was able to call and talk to them and see them. They just hadn't always wanted to see or talk to me, thanks to their jerk of a father. Not that I was blameless. I made my share of mistakes.

But Phira hadn't been able to see me or talk to me. She'd spent a few minutes with me after I was born and then they sent her to prison.

I really needed to be more sensitive to her feelings. However, the whole having magic thing was new to me, and I wasn't that used to caring about other people's emotions.

Not in a bad way, anyway. My adoptive parents raised me to believe that emotions made me weak. I had to always be in control and on top of things, absolutely all the time.

When I'd started dating Sam, I learned that was not the case. Sam was passionate, protective, funny, and full of life. He helped me see life through a different perspective. I'd learned how to express how much I cared about my family and figured out where I'd gone wrong with Jess and Devan.

It was better late than never, but I sure wished I'd known all this many years ago, before I nearly irrevocably ruined my relationship with my daughter and elder son.

The sound of laughter echoed from down the hall of the second floor of Luci's house. My father the devil had converted one of his weird collections rooms into a game room for Jess and Devan. Luci liked to collect things. All sorts of things, from lampshades to shoelaces. Not ordinary ones, of course. He had the first lampshade, and the shoelaces Elvis had on when he died. Stuff like that.

More laughter drifted down the hall. Larry and Zoey were up there, which was nothing new. They were here nearly all the time.

That made me smile. Ava had worried that Larry and Zoey wouldn't have a chance at a normal life. Well, normal for a couple of ghouls. At least with Jess and Devan, the two undead had a sense of normality while hanging out with Satan himself. And Jess and Devan didn't have to worry about hiding their newly developed magic from our neighbors.

"Breena...Olivia." Phira's calm, soft voice drew me out of my thoughts.

I met her stare and sighed. "I don't know how to focus." There, I said it. I didn't know how to do anything. Magic was intensely difficult for me. Ava had taken to it like a fish returned to water, but I felt like a bird trying to swim.

Fee, as Luci called her, studied me for a moment, cocked her head and brushed her white-blonde hair, so close to my own, out of her face, then took my hand and led me out the back door of the mansion. Once outside, she pointed to my feet. "Take off your shoes and follow me."

She didn't have to tell me twice. My Fae magic was connected to nature, thrived off it, and the feel of grass or dirt under my bare feet was as soothing as sinking into a hot tub on a cold winter night. But I needed to learn how to connect with my magic without the aid of the earth touching my feet. It'd been a small miracle I'd been able to do it when I helped Ava and Drew bond.

Phira stopped a few yards from the house and sat in the grass, facing the ocean. Ava's house blocked the waning sun to the left, and the sound of waves crashing against rocks below the small cliff teased my senses. I already felt more relaxed just by being outside.

I sat beside her and mimicked her pose, which was folding my legs like a pretzel that I was sure I'd need help getting out of later and my hands rested on my knees with my palms up.

"The more you connect with your magic, the easier it will be." She sucked in a deep breath and closed her eyes. I followed suit.

"Find your power," Phira whispered.

I did, rather easily, now that I was relaxed and the sounds and feels of nature helped me focus. It was right there, a river flowing and ready for me to pull the cool magic from the stream. I giggled as it danced around me, though I kept my eyes closed, watching the beautiful energy with my mind's eye.

"This is how you learn," she said in a voice so smooth it rode in on the tide and danced with my magic. "Spend time with your power, with your magic, and soon you'll find yourself unable to be separated from it."

I had to spend more time just like this. Connected. Grounded. It was the best feeling in the world. How had I been separated from this for my entire life?

I just prayed nothing ever happened to separate me again.

5
AVA

A terrible, awful, shrill sound blared through the room. With a big jump, I nearly fell out of bed and without trying, I conjured an energy ball. What the heck was that noise? Turning in a circle, I tried to figure out what it could've been, but nothing was really out of the ordinary. The house was quiet.

Movement on my bed brought me back from panicsville, population one, and I waved the magical ball away. Drew sat up and rolled to reach his phone on the bedside table. That gave me a perfect view of the curve of his back and down further. The man was all kinds of yummy. And he was all mine. Forever. In the permanent kind of sense. This was both exhilarating and incredibly scary.

Our new bond allowed for us to feel each other's emotions. Like right this moment, his ego was getting a healthy boost by sensing my desire as I ogled him. What a rat fink. Like he needed to be any more confident. He already knew how hot he was.

He rolled to his back and stared at me. "Are you okay?" A grin spread across his face as he stretched.

I shrugged, trying to play off my embarrassment for wanting to kill his phone. But I hadn't known what the noise was. I never used alarm clocks. My body knew when to sleep and when to wake. For the most part, whenever I could, I went with the natural flow of things. If I wasn't tired, I wouldn't sleep. When I did sleep, I slept as long as I needed. I was pretty lucky that I could. I didn't have to worry about a job outside the home, thanks to my books. How would I find time to be a necromancer and help lead the coven if I had to do a nine-to-five?

Yawning, I stretched too, hoping I'd be able to climb back into the warm bed and snuggle up. "Why did you set an alarm?" I glanced out the window noting it was barely light out. "It's still dark." Not a fit time to be awake.

He chuckled and got out of bed. My eyes roamed over his body on their own accord. I couldn't have stopped them if I'd wanted to, and I really didn't want to.

One perk of having Drew stay the night was he slept gloriously, beautifully stark naked. I felt a little overdressed with my sleep shirt that barely covered my rump. Tugging at it, I backed up to give him room and me a better view.

He stopped inches from me, and I turned my body to face him. The corners of his lips lifted as he spoke. "It's sunrise, and I want to get the boat out of the marina before it gets busy."

Smiling uncertainly, I nodded. I guessed he had a good point. It was summer in Maine, after all, and a tourist town at that. "Just as long as you don't expect me to wake this early every day." That would be enough to make me rethink this forever bond thing. Not that I could get out of it, but... a sleep-deprived woman would find a way.

"I wouldn't dream of it." He bowed his head, but the grin didn't slip.

Hmph. "Good. Just so we're clear." At least I didn't have to cancel this whole shindig.

He chuckled again, and man I loved the deep rumbling timbre. Leaning against his chest, I kissed him, letting it linger a bit as his arms wrapped around my back, pulling our bodies closer together. "I'm going to shower. Want to join me?"

"You bet," I said in a near purr.

It was about an hour later before we made it to the marina. And it was busy. I fully understood why he wanted to get up at the butt crack of dawn. However, I was not sorry for why we were late.

The boat was much bigger than I'd imagined. "This is yours?" I asked.

He puffed up a bit. Aw, how cute. He was proud of his boat. "Yep. All mine. I don't get to take her out nearly as often as I'd like, but I still manage once a month or so." I learned something new about this amazing man every day. He held one hand out so I could step on board. "She's thirty-five feet. Any bigger would be hard for one man to handle alone," he explained as I got my sea legs.

It'd been a long time since I'd been boating. "Sam and I used to go out with a group of friends during the summers growing up," I said, walking around the cockpit.

Drew squeezed my hand, then pulled me to the steering wheel. "Sam was the one who gave me the idea of inviting you. He said you used to love it. So, I figured, since the boat was sitting around not being used nearly often enough, we could escape for a day."

I leaned into him and kissed his lips before sitting in the seat behind him. "This is a perfect getaway." With a sigh, I sat back and watched him move around, preparing to go. "What are you doing?" I asked.

"Running the blower."

I nodded with my eyebrows up. Of course. I knew that,

from my time with Sam when we were much, much younger, but Drew seemed happy to explain.

"It makes sure there aren't any fumes built up."

I looked interested, but really, I was just checking out his muscles under the white shirt he'd thrown on. We drove the boat out for a while, Drew steering us toward the wide open ocean. When we got out to a quiet spot, he dropped the anchor and then sat beside me on the bench seat toward the back. Errr, the stern. Drew cupped the side of my head and kissed me.

Passion danced across my skin and tingled my insides. With a soft moan, I scooted closer and deepened the kiss. Drew wrapped his arms around me and slid one hand up my shirt. The feel of his warm hands made me sigh. Our magic mingled through the bond we now shared. This whole fooling around thing was extra special when I could feel his responses and he mine.

I didn't have to ask if he had regrets because I knew the answer. He didn't. One big perk I hadn't anticipated. A magical bond was the best kind of relationship security.

Drew skimmed his palm over my sensitive flesh as he pushed my t-shirt up and over my head, breaking the kiss in the process. He untied the top of my bathing suit, then pushed me to lay back on the cushioned bench, hidden by the upper part of the stern. Drew bent his head and captured one nipple into his mouth, drawing a hiss of pleasure from me.

My downstairs flared with heat and anticipation. This was just about to get really good.

An energy surge went off nearby, and at first, I thought it was us, but then Drew jerked to sit up, taking me with him, so that I straddled his lap as he tugged on my bathing suit, covering my breasts up.

"Dang it. I'm going to kill Sam!" Olivia yelled.

I turned my head toward Olivia's voice. Then I glanced

around, making sure we were still near the harbor. Actually, we'd traveled further out than I thought before stopping. Then again, I'd been a little distracted until one of my BFF's decided to pop in. Literally. "How did you get here and why are you here?" I asked, ignoring Drew's extremely hard lap underneath me. His fingers brushed against my back as he tied my swimsuit back up.

Olivia stood in the middle of the cockpit with her hands on her hips. Her blonde hair was up in a messy bun, and it looked like she hadn't even left her bed yet this morning. "Sam and I were arguing in bed. He brought up the fact that since I'm Lucifer's daughter I should be able to teleport. So, I tried it, intending on going from Luci's house to ours."

I snorted. Liv was learning her new powers and with her levels of patience, she was doing her best to fast track each lesson. Unfortunately for self-control, magic didn't work that way. "And you ended up here?"

Drew picked my shirt up and handed it to me. I slipped it on while Olivia explained as she waved her hands around, exasperated. "I was totally focused and visualizing our house. Then Sammie came into the room, said your name, and bam, here I am."

"Why did Sammie mention me?" Drew patted my thigh, silently letting me know I didn't have to stay on his lap anymore.

Olivia sat down in the seat across from us. "He's worried about you. I think he was asking if I talked to you today. Of course, I'm more empathic now thanks to the Fae magic, so I felt his concern and must have redirected my intended destination at the last minute."

"And here you are." I grimaced and cocked my head. She was not getting the point, not at all.

She nodded and sighed. "Here I am."

I continued staring at her with a raised brow. Well, with

both brows raised because I couldn't do the one-brow-lift. Olivia hadn't noticed what she teleported in on, yet.

She met my stare, looked down at my disheveled shirt, then looked at Drew, and then, finally, her eyes widened. "Oh, God! I totally ruined smexy time."

Drew chuckled and buried his face into my hair, which I was pretty sure was a mass of brown wavy tangles. That was probably where the term witchy hair came from. Really good lovin'.

I redirected my glare toward Olivia. "Can't you teleport back home?"

"Yes. I think." She closed her eyes, bouncing on her heels, and then...nothing happened. After a few minutes, she opened her eyes and pouted. "I can't."

"Try again," I snarled.

She had the good sense to blush. "I'm sorry," she whispered, then closed her eyes again.

Nothing.

"Come on," Drew said, tugging on his swim trunks and jumping to his feet. "We'll take you home."

Olivia and I sat back and chatted about how her learning was going—not well—while Drew maneuvered us back into the harbor.

We walked back to the car and Drew slipped his hand into mine as he started the car. Olivia sighed from the backseat.

When I turned to look and see what she was sighing about, she grinned big at me. "You guys are so cute."

I snorted and rolled my eyes, but my surge of happiness at her words met Drew's in my heart through the bond.

After dropping Olivia off, when we got back to my place, Drew put his truck in park and turned to face me. "I'm sorry the day was ruined."

I nodded toward the house. "It's not even half over yet. Want to come in?"

He sighed deeply. "Yes, I do. But I shouldn't. If I come in there, we'll go nap, and then we won't make it out of the bedroom. We'll be up all night. And I've got an early shift."

I pouted my lips. "Okay, but we're redoing this date as soon as possible."

Pressing his lips to mine, Drew then whispered against my cheek. "You got it. On my next night off."

I finally dragged myself out of the car and waved as he backed away.

Dang it. I really wanted him to come in. I was going to get the girl version of blue balls at this rate. Our time in the shower this morning hadn't been enough.

Maybe it was time to talk about Drew moving in. What was one more person in a house like this?

"Hello?" I called as I shut the door behind me. "Anybody home?" In a house so full of people, there should've been at least one or two of them around.

Sure enough, Alfred and Winnie walked out of the kitchen. "Hello dear, did you speak to Owen?" Winnie asked.

We went into the living room and sat down. "No, why?" No more bad news, please.

"He got a call from his father. His mother had a heart attack this morning. He had to rush out of here. Luci gave him a quick hop over to his parents' place in Connecticut," Mom said. "We were just about to set up a blessing you could do for his mom."

"Oh, what a lovely idea." I grabbed the candles and followed them up to the ritual room. Anything for my dear friend Owen.

6
AVA

Darn it! Urgh. I should have known the energy boost I got from Drew wouldn't last. It should have. It should've lasted forever, in theory. Yet, here I was feeling like total pooh. And not the chubby yellow bear with the red shirt. Crap on a crap cracker.

With crap sauce.

When I'd been feeling great the other day, and hoping it would last, I'd ignored the little voice in the back of my mind that had said it wouldn't, I'd agreed to pick up a few shifts at the bookstore for Clint. He wanted to take the morning off to help his sister with something; normally Owen would've covered him, but with him being out of town for a family emergency, I'd have to do it. I'd been taking fewer and fewer shifts of late, as my responsibilities as the high witch of the coven and author increased. I'd only been half paying attention when talking to Clint about it, though. At the time I'd just wanted to get out of the house after being cooped up and sick.

Yesterday was amazing on the boat with Drew. Even with Olivia, we had a blast. It had been far too short, and I'd wished for a happier ending, but at least it was a bit of Vitamin D and outdoors time.

Today, I was drained. Had I done too much while being sick? Or while feeling better? At least I only had another hour to sludge through here at the bookstore and it'd been a slow day.

Going back to dusting with magic, I moved the dust around to the beat of nineties pop on my phone in my bra pocket, but then I nearly jumped out of my skin when it rang. Pulling it out of my shirt, I frowned at Zoey's name. "Hi, Zo."

"Not even close."

Um... "Lucy?" How the heck did that cat learn to use the phone? She was getting up to no good, that much was sure. I was going to have to put some sort of video tracker on her.

"Whatever you've done to make your magic go away again, you need to fix it," she said in a haughty, irritated tone. Sounds of a struggle cut off her words. Maybe it was just rustlings of sheets of something, but my sick brain was making up its own version of the situation.

I had no idea what she was talking about, but we needed to get to the bottom of it. "Lucy?"

"Ava, it's Zoey. I'm sorry. I didn't know she had my phone."

In the background Lucy yelled something nonsensical at the top of her voice and it sounded like Snooze was yowling. "What is going on there?"

Zoey sighed. "Well, Lucy's fur is falling out in clumps. She is not happy about it. Snooze thinks she's going to die so he's being all dramatic." It sounded like Zoey pulled the phone away and whispered to someone. "It's just a lot of drama and chaos here right now."

Oh, no. I started feeling bad again and my ghouls immediately took a turn for the worse. "I'll call Clint to see if he can come in early. If not, then it'll be an hour before I can get there." I sighed and admitted what I didn't want to say out loud. "I'm not feeling so great either." This had to be something more than a cold. Something was draining my powers and it wasn't a dang cold. It wasn't something normal or human or some viral thing of the week. I was starting to really get worried.

Just then, thank goodness, the bell over top of the door jangled. I looked up to see Clint entering. He stopped, took one look at me, and drew his brows together. "You don't look too good."

"I feel worse than I look," I replied to his comment, then I said to Zoey, "Clint is here. I'm on my way."

I hung up the phone and Clint waved me out the door, mumbling about spreading sick germs all over the store as he covered his face with his shirt. "Go," he mumbled from behind his collar.

"I'm going, I'm going." I hesitated at the front door. "You might want to find someone for any other shifts you had me down for. I'm sorry to flake out, but I'm really worried about what's ailing me."

He backed up a bit and pulled the lower part of his face out of his shirt. "Go. I'll figure it out. Just get better, that's more important than covering a couple of shifts."

I waved at him with an appreciative smile and left.

Fifteen minute later I pulled into my driveway. Pretty much as fast as I could, considering I felt like death, I rushed inside the house only to stop a few feet in. Clumps of white hair were everywhere. "Lucy?" Geez this looked bad.

"Finally. What took you so long?" The haughty white cat stood at the base of the stairs. I followed her into the living room. "You need to fix me. At this rate I'll be bald in no time." She meowed piteously. "I'm not one of those hairless cats that looks like a ball sack! Fix me. Now."

Snooze entered the living room, yowling. He stopped in front of me and let out a meow so loud I was sure he'd wake

Wade up—my dead husband's uncle who'd been turned into a vampire several months ago when I went to Philly to sell my house. Thankfully, I was a powerful enough necromancer to convince them to release Wade into my custody, which broke pretty much all their rules.

Wade now lived with me. Winston had expanded himself to make the basement into an apartment for Wade so he would be protected from the sun during the day. It was nice having him here. He was a father figure, uncle figure, and all around friend.

"Snooze, will you shut up!" Lucy ran up the stairs, grumbling about why black widows killed their mates.

Lowering myself onto the sofa, I rested my head against a throw pillow and sighed. There wasn't anything I could do for Lucy at the moment. I didn't even know what to do about myself, much less anyone else. Turning to Zoey, I studied her profile. I didn't know if she realized it, but she wasn't looking too great either. Nowhere near as bad as Lucy-Fur looked, but not good either.

Something was definitely up. How would I even go about figuring it out when I just wanted to sleep?

Just then Larry entered through the back door and stopped at the archway of the kitchen. "Oh, no," I whispered. The poor skeleghoul had exposed bone in several places and flesh hanging off in others. The parts of him which still had skin were discolored, blotchy.

Really freaking gross. I got up to go make some tea and find my cell, but a wave of dizziness hit me, and I stumbled a little. I moved to the stairs and gripped the railing. "I'm going to have to lie down." Like now. More like five minutes ago.

I didn't wait for a response. Maybe a nap would help clear my head so I could figure out what in the Hades was going on.

7
AVA

When I woke from my nap, it was already dark outside. Drew lay beside me, sound asleep. I rolled to face him and brushed a few strands of hair from his forehead. His eyes opened, and he smiled but it didn't reach his eyes.

He was worried about me. And he looked exhausted. "I felt it when you woke up this morning and were off. And as the day wore on it got worse and worse." He sighed. "And now I feel awful, too. This isn't a normal cold." He frowned and cuddled up to me.

I sighed and melted into him. "I'm beginning to think so. I don't think it's my ghouls doing this either." I conjured my phone because I didn't have any energy to move and figure out where it was. Plus, Drew was warm and smelled so good. I wasn't moving. "You binding yourself to me isn't helping. Now you've got whatever it is." We had to figure this out, but I didn't know how, especially when I didn't at all feel like figuring it out.

Drew kissed my forehead as I dialed Olivia, putting her on

speaker because it took too much effort to hold the phone to my ear.

"Are you okay?" Liv's voice held concern for my well being. Someone must've told her I came home then immediately went to bed.

I sighed. "No. Drew and I are both sick now. I'm really thinking it's not a cold. But I'm not totally sold on the theory that the ghouls are draining me this much." I was just plain tired. And achy.

Olivia tutted and the phone rustled. "Call Melody and see what she thinks. I'll be right over. I need to let the kids know where I'll be." Olivia hung up without saying goodbye. No doubt hurrying.

I met Drew's gaze and shrugged. "I guess she's over at Luci's."

"Makes sense. Sam is on duty tonight and Olivia has been trying to split her time between Sam and Jess and Devan. Little Sammie is happy to go wherever." Drew sat up and looked at me over his shoulder. "Might as well go downstairs."

Moaning and miserable, I pushed myself up while punching the screen over Melody's name. This time I held the cell phone up to my ear.

"Hi, Ava!" Melody chirped.

Oh, geez. Too loud. "Hi, Mel." My voice came out all croaky. "Is there any chance you could come over?" I gave her a short summary of how I'd been feeling. "I'll tell you more when you get here. Could we test for a magical cause? Is that even possible?"

"Sometimes. Some spells aren't detectable, but I've never heard of any that would give you the flu." She paused, then added, "I'll be right over."

"Thanks." I hung up and trudged over to my dresser, then remembered I was already dressed. I'd collapsed into bed without stripping. Wow, my whole sense of time was off, which didn't happen often.

Drew and I headed slowly downstairs and as soon as our feet touched down on the first floor, the front door opened. Olivia let herself in, which was fine with me. She was here often enough. She stopped and studied us. "You two look like crap."

"Thanks," Drew and I said at the same time. His tone had just as much sarcasm as mine. I chuckled, enjoying this synchronicity, though I was too tired to really appreciate it fully.

I moved to the living room, where I dropped down on the sofa. When Drew sat beside me, I snuggled close to him. Being in his strong arms made me feel much better emotionally. Unfortunately, it did nothing for the aches, pains, and tiredness.

When Olivia didn't join us, I stretched my neck to see her. She was waiting by the door with it open. A moment later Melody entered with a smile until she saw Drew and me. How had she gotten here so quickly?

"Oh, you two look...bad. Sorry. I know it's not what you want to hear." She rushed over and touched my forehead, then Drew's. Shaking her head, she sat on the coffee table. "I'm not picking up on any magic. What makes you think you've been spelled? Or that this is magical at all?"

I shrugged. "Just throwing things out there. Owen seems to think it's the seven ghouls I have tied to me." I watched her eyes go round.

"Seven?"

I waved my hand, not remembering if I'd told her about Mom and Winnie yet. "I don't think that's it, but what else could it be? It doesn't seem to be any normal human virus or bacteria."

"Have you been to the actual doctor?" Melody asked.

I gaped at her for just a moment. "Well, no. I haven't."

She shrugged. "Maybe having them run your white blood cell count would help. If it's elevated, then you're just sick with something nasty."

I looked up at Drew. "But he's sick too."

Melody snorted. "It makes sense. You two are wrapped around each other. He'd be the most likely to catch it." She held up one hand. "I have a friend at the hospital's lab. He's a member of the coven, but you've only met him once when they swore you in. He's not a very active member. I bet I could get him to run some bloodwork."

She conjured a couple of those vials nurses and phlebotomists used when they took blood.

I took them from her, then focused on moving blood out of my veins and into the vials. "You don't think they'll see something magical, do you?" I asked.

Melody chortled. "No. Magic doesn't work that way."

I handed them to her, and she pulled out her phone. After sending a few texts back and forth as I laid my head back on Drew's shoulder, the vials disappeared with a twist of Melody's hand. "There," she said. "If anything looks off, he'll let us know in about a half-hour."

My consciousness drifted as we waited on the results. Olivia and Melody chatted in the high back chairs, but I didn't follow their conversation. I just drifted.

"Ava," Melody said a few minutes later. "He messaged me." She waved her phone at me as I struggled to stay awake and focus. "He says all your bloodwork is in normal ranges. It's not, well, most likely not, anything you're fighting off is a sickness."

"So, it is magical," Drew said behind me, his chest rumbling under my ear.

Sound from the hallway drew our attention to Wade as he exited the basement door and walked into the living room. I watched Melody because she hadn't met my undead uncle yet.

In my hazy state, I wasn't sure if she had any clue about vampires or not.

I sensed Mom, Winnie, and Alfred hovering close by, worried, though I couldn't see them.

Settling back against Drew, I let the concern go. I didn't have to be worried about Melody. She was my second in command when it came to the coven. We'd put each other through a series of trust tests when I first became the high witch. Plus, the blood oath everyone pledged to me kept them from doing harm to me or anyone else in the coven. So, anything she saw at my house stayed at my house. It was a house rule.

She walked toward Wade with a smile on her face but then turned back to me when I spoke.

"I'd like to research more on necromancers," I croaked. "Yes, I know I should have done that a year ago, but I need to know all I can right now." I sat up and put a little space between Drew and me. I'd end up falling asleep again if I stayed snuggled up to him. He was just so comfy. And warm. And perfect.

He chuckled, no doubt sensing my emotions.

I opened my mouth to speak but paused when I heard the familiar clicking of bones against the hardwood floors. Oh, no. Before he entered the room, I already knew from the sound that Larry had defleshed again. Larry descended the stairs and sure enough, he was a skeleton again. Like all his flesh has fallen off. "Oh, Larry," I moaned. "I'm sorry." A sob stuck in my throat, but I was too tired to finish it.

Melody followed my gaze to him. "Oh goodness. This is serious. But I think you're right. If they were draining you, they wouldn't be falling apart like they are." She shook her head sadly. "I don't think it's because of the ghouls."

Zoey bounced in from the kitchen. She must've come in from the back door or through the conservatory. Whatever this was hadn't skipped over the poor tiger-shifter-ghoul. She looked like she'd been in a grave for a couple of years. "There has to be something we could do," she said, looking down at her mottled skin.

Just then the doorbell rang. Larry, closest, moved to the door. "I'll get it," he said cheerily.

Olivia and I yelled, "NO!" at the same time. It took everything out of me just to yell. I couldn't have stopped him, magically or physically, if someone had offered me a million dollars.

It didn't matter. He was already opening the door. He'd done it without thinking. The poor mailman stared at Larry with wide eyes. After a few seconds, he blinked a few times, shrugged, then handed Larry a package. Larry took it like it was a normal day and he was not a skeleton and said, "Thank you." Then he shut the door and carried the package into the kitchen to Alfred. That ghoul was always buying something off the internet.

Olivia ran to the window, and I ignored my achy body long enough to get up and do a fast walk behind her. The mailman walked down the walkway, got into his mail truck, and drove away. Just like that. He didn't even run or hurry.

Liv met my gaze. "Do you think he's freaked out?"

Melody squeezed between us and squinted out the window. "Nah. George is my mailman, too. He sees all kinds of crap. This is just another day for him."

If seeing a walking-talking-sentient skeleton was just another day for him, I'd hate to see what else he'd experienced during his daily duties.

8
OLIVIA

My poor bestie! Taking her arm, I led her back to the sofa and helped her settle down beside Drew. Her skin was a little too warm, but as I looked down in concern, she shivered. I snatched a blanket out of the basket in the corner and covered her and Drew up as best I could. I wanted nothing more than to wrap Ava in a magical hug so I could feed her my power.

But that was what Drew did by binding himself to her. And his power was significant, according to Ava. And how long did that last? A few days. I had no idea how significant my power would be, since none of us really knew what I was capable of. No matter how hard I tried, I hadn't mastered my magic, nor had I found its depths.

Ava sighed, and sadness twisted in my heart for my friends while at the same time, anxiety threw a party in my brain. We had to get to the bottom of this and fast.

Phira materialized beside me. "I felt your concern." Well, look at that. The amazing appearing Fae princess.

One more thing to get used to. Apparently, we shared a

mother-daughter bond even though we were pretty much strangers to each other. "Ava's even worse than before." I sighed and looked across the room. My poor friend hadn't even noticed Phira appear.

Phira stared at Ava and Drew for a moment with her head cocked and silvery blonde hair cascading down her shoulders. Before she had a chance to say anything, Ava stood, shaky and breathing hard, and announced, "I'm going to get my laptop so we can tap into the Hunters' library."

"Ava, hon, let me get it," I said, darting forward. But she never made it to her office, and I wasn't fast enough. She passed out before she reached the hallway. It wasn't even like one of those old movies where the woman sort of swooned. She went down like a pile of bricks. Dropped. Whammo. I gasped and ran to her, praying to reach but Wade had beat me there. Dang vampire speed was no joke. He got there just in time to keep her head from cracking down on the ground.

Just as Wade picked Ava up, cradling her like a father would his own daughter, a loud thump sounded behind us. I whirled around to see Drew face down on the floor. Oops. We'd been paying so much attention to Ava we'd totally missed Drew struggling behind us. Poor guy.

A whoosh of air blew by me, sending the ends of my hair flying in all directions. I looked around trying to figure out what in the world had caused that gust of wind. Oh. Wade was gone with Ava. Seconds later he appeared at the top of the stairs and came down at a slightly more human speed.

When Wade picked Drew up and carried him up to Ava's room, I started to follow, but something stopped me. I sucked in a deep breath and turned slowly toward the kitchen, where Alfred stood staring down at two piles of ashes. "Oh, no." My heart sank.

Those were Ava's mom's and aunt's ashes. I didn't even want to know what happened to the cats. Nor did I have time for Lucy-Fur's drama at the moment. They couldn't be looking good, not at all. "Alfred?" I whispered.

He waved his arms ineffectually. "I'm okay...for now." Then he pointed to the ashes on the floor. "I'll get them put back into their urns, somehow. Go check on Ava."

The poor guy. He was pretty attached to Winnie. "Thanks," I said and rushed up the stairs with Phira and Melody right behind me.

My chest tightened as I entered Ava's room. The two of them slept on their backs, looking so incredibly still. Damn it. I wished Sam was there. I really needed one of his hugs.

Suddenly, I got the sensation of being watched, that there was something else in the room with us. In this house, there was no telling.

When I turned, I found Beth and Winnie drifting inside from the hallway. Not in their bodies, no such luck. They were ghosts, see-through versions of their former selves. "Holy Faeryland, I can see you two." I gaped at them, shocked. This was my first haunting. If I wasn't so worried about Ava, I would've been excited.

Winnie grinned, although it wasn't as cheerful or wicked as she might have intended. "Your powers are unlocked, of course, you can." Well, that did make sense. I was half-Fae, half...whatever Luci was.

Beth floated toward Ava and Drew, looking worried. Poor woman. She'd finally gotten out of the Inbetween and now she had this to worry about. We'd all been through a bunch of crap lately. We needed a nice calm vacation or something. A moment to rest and just breathe. But that didn't seem like it would be happening anytime soon.

I tugged on Melody's arm and pulled her close, nodding toward the ghosts. "Can you see them?"

Melody shook her head. "Not unless they want me to. I don't have death magic."

"Well, I don't either," I squawked, staring at her with wide eyes.

Phira nodded at me. "You do. Your father is Loki."

Ah, yeah. Him. Loki. AKA Lucifer, who liked to be called Luci. According to him, the list of Underworld and mischievous gods he'd been called over his lifetime was pretty long. And recently we added father to that list. Not that I was calling him anything but Luci. Not Loki or Eris or Lugh or any of the others.

Beth the ghost sucked in a shuddering breath with her hand hovering over Ava's forehead. "It's time to contact Ava's father." She announced, like it had always been the plan to do so.

For the record, it wasn't. It had never even been mentioned. At least no one had thought to tell me about that part of the plan. "As in his ghost?" I asked with my eyebrows straight up. Ava's dad had died when she was just five. That was long ago done and over with. He was at peace.

Beth wrung her hands in front of her as she floated closer to the bed, staring down at Ava. "No, not exactly. John is alive. I think."

I gaped at her until she shrugged sheepishly. Winnie turned her head to stare at her sister, too. Phira and Melody didn't seem nearly as invested or interested as I did, but they probably didn't know the whole story of Ava's father's tragic demise.

Beth glanced from me to Winnie, who grimaced, then back to me. She was giving me whiplash. "I don't know how, or why, but there were whispers in the Inbetween that the vampires have him."

Wade jerked his head at that news. "What do you mean vampires? Have they turned him?"

Beth threw up her hands, backpedaling a bit. "No. Vampires can't turn necromancers. In fact, they usually fear them because vampires are undead, and necromancers can control them just like a ghoul or any other undead being."

She paused, and all I could do was stare at her. Did Ava know all of this? Surely, she did, considering she had Wade in her house. Then Beth said, "Winnie and I have been trying to quietly get info on him without getting anyone's hopes up." So, Winnie knew. Beth continued, "Plus, we didn't want the vampire elders to know that we were searching for him."

Wade crossed his arms. "We don't want the elders coming here. As far as they know, I don't exist. I was turned without their permission. That's a big no-no and grounds for them to make me dead-dead." He was more ruffled than I'd ever seen him. He was usually a pretty unflappable guy. Right at the moment he looked...well... flapped.

Wow. His words registered to me a few ticks too late. "They would kill you because you were turned?" That seemed like a pretty extreme stance. I didn't know vampires from Adam, but that was barbaric.

Wade motioned to the door. "Let's take this conversation downstairs."

Nodding, I moved to the door, but I was reluctant to leave Ava. She looked so vulnerable lying there beside Drew. I wasn't used to seeing my best friend defenseless and I didn't like it. Not one bit.

Once everyone was out of the room, I waved at her prone form and pulled the door closed with a sad sigh. Whatever plan we came up with, we had to make sure that Wade's existence remains off the vampires' radar.

9
OLIVIA

With a sigh bordering on exhaustion, I sat back and tried not to sound too overwhelmed. " So, how is it possible that the vampire elders don't know about you?" I studied Wade, who stood a few feet from the dining table sipping blood from a coffee cup that said, "What's up, witches." One of Ava's favorites.

I needed a mug with a catchy phrase like that, but I wasn't exactly a witch. What in the world was I? A goddess?

Oh. Oh, I really liked the thought of that. I bet there were heaps of mugs with fun goddess sayings on them.

"Jaxon Parsons, the King of the US vampires, never told them." He cocked his head like he was listening to something only he could hear. I wasn't sure how I felt about vampires. Wade was the only one I've ever come in contact with.

"Wait. Who is Jaxon?" Did he say king? Royalty was just popping up all over the place all of a sudden. Next, we were going to find out Sam was Queen Elizabeth's long-lost grandson or something.

Wade walked over to the fridge and got out another bag of

blood. "He's the United States' Master Vampire. That's like a king or something. Honorary title, I think. His job is to keep us vamps in line and enforce the elder council's rules." Wade took a drink of his blood that I was pretending was just coffee.

Ew, he poured it in the mug cold. Oh no, wait. He grimaced and stuck the mug in the microwave. That had to be better. Warm blood. Blech. Maybe that wasn't better.

He continued as it warmed. "Jax turned me over to Ava as her responsibility but told the council he took care of me himself. Or, I'm not sure he even told the council about me, actually. I don't know. Honestly, I think he has his own drama going on at the moment and didn't want to deal with me and the council. Plus, Ava flat out told him I was coming home with her." He smiled as he looked down at his drink. "She's pretty forceful when she gets her mind set."

I chuckled at that, totally seeing Ava telling a master vamp how it was going to go down. If I hadn't been such a rich, snobby brat in high school, Ava and I would've been besties then, too. If I'd seen how awesome she was. Only the beginning of my young-life regrets.

Footsteps on the stairs made me lean sideways in the chair to see who was there. Had Ava or Drew woken up? I sincerely hoped so. As far as I knew, everyone who lived here was either here or out of town.

Luci strolled down the stairs with a look on his face that told me he was deep in thought. When in the world had he gotten here or gone upstairs? I hadn't heard the doorbell. And normally, Winston would've protested the sudden appearance of the devil. He must've been as thrown off by Ava's condition as the rest of us were.

When he entered the kitchen, I avoided looking at him. "When did you get here?"

Seeming to come out of his thoughtful stupor, my father drew my gaze and smiled, advancing straight toward me. I held in my groan, and fervently hoped he wasn't planning on hugging me.

Thankfully, he didn't, but he did sit in the seat next to me, a little too close. "I just heard about Ava and Drew and popped in to check on things."

Check on things? I stared at him for a moment and wondered if me being his daughter gave me a free pass to hit him or push him out of his chair. He could be so annoying. Did he think he was a physician or something? "And what is your assessment, Doctor Satan?" I arched one eyebrow at him.

He pursed his lips and looked troubled again. "Ava is under a deep enchantment. I can't place its origins, but it's familiar somehow. Yet, it isn't like any magic I've run across recently." He threw an arm over the back of my chair, which made him lean more into me. I scooted to the right just a little.

Luci didn't much like that I was struggling with the fact that he was my father. I couldn't help it, though, and the more he pushed, the harder it was to relax with him. Every time we were in the same room together, he tried to shower me with attention and conversation. I wasn't ready to get to know him. I literally just got comfortable with him being Satan. No. Not really comfortable with it. I'd... accepted it? Maybe.

I gave myself two gold stars for not jumping to my feet and running to the other side of the kitchen. My skin crawled with anxiety having him so close, and a little voice in the back of my mind screamed, "Father! Father! Father!"

Steering the conversation back to Ava's dad, I looked at Beth and sucked in the deepest of breaths before asking, "Do you know where John is or how we can contact him?"

She shook her head. "Only that the vampires have him."

Melody gave Luci a sidelong glance, then returned her attention to Beth. "Do you have anything that belonged to him? I could do a locator spell."

It took me a few to realize that everyone else could see Beth and Winnie, which meant that they had gone solid enough for everyone to see them. It was slightly difficult for them to do and maintain for very long, which was why ghosts rarely did it.

Beth turned to Winnie. "Where did you put his ring?"

Winnie sighed and gave Beth a sympathetic look. "It's all with your stuff. I think Ava has your jewelry box in her room." That was all Winnie had to say, apparently, because Beth disappeared.

A few seconds later she reappeared and handed Melody a gold wedding band. "That was his." Ghosts could pick up things, objects? I was learning stuff all the time, every day.

Melody took it and closed her hand around it, then chanted something similar to what Ava did when she did a locator spell. Usually a small floating orb appeared, but with Melody, nothing happened.

Frowning, Melody tried one more time. And still nothing. She tutted. "I need a world map."

Luci snapped his fingers and a world map appeared on the table, lickety split and easy as pie. Melody laughed. "That'll work." Some things about having magic really were convenient. I wondered if I could conjure something like that. I hadn't really tried yet.

She placed the ring in the center of the map... sort of the center. In the ocean between the US and Europe. The chanting once again went over my head. My magic wasn't much for words like witches. Mine was more about intent.

The ring began to slide on the map, very slowly, toward Europe. "Whoa," I whispered and peered down at it.

Unfortunately, the ring stopped in a spot that encompassed Germany, Austria, Italy, and France.

We needed a bigger map. "Um, Luci?" I raised my eyebrows at him. "We need to zoom in."

"Oh," he said with a chuckle. He didn't even look at the map, but it grew. And grew. Until it was the largest map I'd ever seen in my life, the sides all drooping off of the table. The ring now looked tiny, smack in the middle of France and Italy.

With a sigh and a grin at Luci, Melody focused again, repeating the Latin words. It didn't take a minute for the ring to shift a bit to the right, somewhere in Italy.

Luci smiled with the slightest tint of danger or evil in it. Spooky. "I know where he is."

I stood and faced him. "Then take us there."

"Oh, no." Luci held up his hands and slid out of his seat. "Not happening. He chuckled. "I'll go get him and be right back."

I shook my head. "No. I'm going too. I don't trust you to do this without causing a big ruckus or going way off the path."

He had the audacity to look offended. "What in the world have I ever done to make you think I'd go off course?"

I gaped at him, then looked at Phira, who looked secretly amused. Back to Luci, I crossed my arms. "I'm not even touching that." He opened his mouth, but I threw up one finger like when I had to put on my Mom face with Sammie. "No. We're going and that's that."

Luci turned toward Phira. "Can you help me with this?"

Her little secret smile deepened. "You're on your own. She's headstrong. Like you."

With slumped, defeated shoulders, Luci turned back toward me. "Only one of you."

I nodded. "Me."

With one last big sigh and flared nostrils, Luci nodded and held out his hand. "We have to try to stay quiet. I'd like to get through this without the vampires even realizing what we're doing."

"Fine," I said sharply. "Let's go."

10
OLIVIA

My whispered voice echoed around the large entryway. "Wow."

It was all that came to mind when describing the place...er, palace? which Luci was sure housed John. The stone entrance of the underground vampire palace seemed to melt into the walls of a subway. The architecture of the door and what I could see of the building was neo-classical with gothic flair. Black veins of onyx etched through the dark grey stone like tree roots seeking nutrition. Wow was a pretty appropriate description.

The vampire palace, where the elder councils lived or conducted their business, I wasn't sure which, was actually underneath the Royal Palace of Milan. The Palazzo Reale. Milan.

As I whispered the Italian name for the palace to myself, Luci spoke it out loud in a perfect Italian accent. I cut a glare at him as we walked up the stairs. Trickster god. That new title he revealed recently was starting to make a lot of sense. He was a tricky sort of fella.

The more I was around him, and that had been a lot in the last few weeks, the more I saw a little less evil devil in him, a little more fun loving guy. My kids loved him like he was the best grandpa in the universe, but it was hard for me to forget that we'd summoned him while trying to find Santa. He was the literal devil. We weren't supposed to trust him or like him, right?

If I stopped to think about the things he'd done to help us over the year or so we'd known Luci, I'd have been much more likely to be willing to get to know him. And that opened me up to a whole new level of emotions I wasn't prepared to explore. Better to keep him at arms' length.

For now.

He stopped suddenly and faced me. I stilled, listening, then raised my brows in question. We weren't supposed to be here and the fact that we were about to walk through the front door made me antsy. One part of my brain was preparing my body for someone to jump out and attack us. Because that had been mine and Ava's life for the past ten or so months. One emergency to another.

Luci snapped his fingers and a layer of magic settled over us. "That's better. Now no one will see or hear us."

As cool as that was, I still worried about being caught. I was too old to go to jail in a foreign country. Or to be held prisoner by vampires. "Why aren't we teleporting straight inside?" I asked. This whole thing was like kicking a hornet's nest. I didn't like it, but I'd do anything to help Ava and Drew. If that meant breaking a prisoner out of a vampire jail—a prisoner who was supposed to have been dead many, many years ago—well then, so be it.

He shrugged one shoulder. "Can't. Tried."

I rolled my eyes. "Thanks for the in-depth explanation."

Luci held out one hand. "Ready, Livvy?"

I snapped my gaze to my father, biting my tongue to stop

myself from being snarky with evil trickster dad, and nodded. "After you." I wasn't in the mood, not to mention too old to hold hands with my *daddy*.

Amusement lit up his eyes before he turned and opened the door. The sound echoed through the huge entrance way. Great. Like an alarm for the vampires. Hello! We're here!

Luci waved for me to follow him down a hallway to our right. I tiptoed down the marbled corridor, on tenterhooks that a vampire would appear out of thin air and attack, like some wrinkle-faced monster from Buffy.

We walked straight for a little way then wound to the left before stopping short. Doors to various rooms sat closed on either side, giving me a creepy dungeon vibe mixed with a five-star resort. Like an upscale destination hotel for horror fans. A low hum of magic in the air made my own magic dance in anticipation. "There's magic here."

He glanced over at me. "Some of the vampire elders dabble in it and have been known to keep witches on their payroll." Luci's tone was low. It said he didn't like their magical involvement at all.

"I don't care what they do as long as they stay away from me and mine." I opened the first door I came to and peeked my head. "What the..."

Luci pushed the door wide open and entered the room. "This is weird. I thought I had an unusual collection."

The room was full of Beanie Babies. They'd been extremely popular in the nineties, with everyone dying to collect this or that little stuffed animal.

Luci's jaw dropped. "Is that...?" He darted forward and peered down at a little fish thing. "I can't believe it."

"What?" I hissed. Looking up and down the hall, I sighed and pulled the door closed behind me. "I think we should be moving on, don't you?"

"Yes, yes," he said without moving. "I'm coming."

Yet, come, he did not. "Luci," I whispered. "Let's go." Darting deeper into the room which was absolutely chock full of the little animals, I looked down at what had his rapt attention. "What is it?"

"They have a 1996 Bubbles the fish," he said in a reverent voice. It was a little yellow and black stuffed fish. Completely unremarkable.

"Okay."

Luci looked at me like I'd offended him. "It has the errors in the tushy tag." He pointed to the little white tag under the fish's tail fin. "It's worth over a hundred thousand dollars."

With a sigh and a certainty I was right, I pulled out my phone and pulled up the eBay app. "Bubbles, 1996, tag error." When the results came up, I sorted by sold items and shoved my phone in Luci's face. "There's one that sold yesterday for $12.95. Now, can we go?"

As he read the results on my screen, his excited expression fell so quickly I almost felt bad for popping his bubble. He turned more stoic and headed for the door.

On a whim, as I followed, I re-sorted the results, found another with the same tag error, and hit Buy It Now for 19.95.

Hey, don't @ me. I wasn't ready to become his bestie, but I had a heart, okay?

The next room was full of various toys. Luci didn't go in, but he cocked his head. "I think they're all from fast food places."

Whoever collected these items was a child at heart.

At least, I thought that until we opened the first door across the hall. "Whoa," I said, staring into a room full of... "Are those sex toys?" I whispered.

The large bedroom was decorated in reds and blacks, and on every available surface were... toys.

Nothing like the toys of the previous rooms. Dildos, vibrators... oh, my. And a pocket p—

"That's enough of that!" Luci exclaimed, reaching around me to slam the door shut as I stood in shock.

Of all the objects in all the world, we had to walk into that little den of iniquity. Not the way I wanted to bond with my father.

"Excuse me," I whispered. "Does this palace have a bathroom I could vomit in?"

There were a few more random rooms before we found the one John was being kept in, including one with nothing but life-sized cardboard cutouts of pop-culture vampires. The Count Chocula was my favorite but Luci liked the Brad Pitt as Louis de Pointe du Lac.

We moved on, leery of the time we were wasting.

"This is it." I knew it was the right room because even through the closed door, I could feel his necromancer powers. They were muted, but definitely there. I knew that if they hadn't been so dampened, I could've found him much faster. He felt a lot like Ava, but... more sinister. Her dark necromancer magic was twined with her earth witch magic, giving her a unique feel. This was like meeting only half of my best friend.

Luci nodded. "Very good. You are adjusting well to your magic."

I had to admit that hearing his praise made me happy, but I didn't show it. "Should we knock?"

He shrugged and did just that. There wasn't an answer, so Luci opened the large door. Once we entered, I realized it wasn't a room, nothing like the others in this hallway. It was more like an apartment. We walked into a living-dining-kitchen combo, but it was quite large. It could easily accommodate a dozen people for a party. The decor was tasteful and simple. Nothing like the other rooms we'd seen, or the hallway, all dripping in opulence. This was more like something a home and garden TV show would decorate.

"Oh," Luci said. "Let me reveal us." He blinked a few times. "There."

All righty, then. We were, apparently, visible again.

John walked out of a door that I assumed was the bathroom and froze when he saw us. Oop. We really were visible. I smiled and waved. "Hello. Don't be alarmed. We're friends of Ava's."

He narrowed his eyes on us but before he could throw us out of his prison apartment, I rushed forward, stopping a foot from him. He pulled up his hands as if to unleash some sort of magic, but a warning came from behind me.

"I wouldn't."

I didn't turn to see what threatening thing Luci was doing. Instead, I rushed to explain, nearly tripping over my words. "Ava needs your help. She's been ill and at first everyone thought it was the fact she had seven ghouls tied to her but now I think it's more than that. Luci said she is enchanted but we don't know how to break it. Then Beth--"

"Wait. Stop!" He held up a hand, and I clamped my lips together. I hadn't meant to divulge quite that much information.

Luci took my elbow and pulled me back so he could step protectively in front of me.

John looked at Luci in the same dismissive, annoyed way Ava did a lot of times. I snorted and poked Luci in the back. "He really is Ava's dad. They get that same expression."

Luci glanced at me over his shoulder and rolled his eyes before facing John again. "Your daughter needs your help."

Just then Beth's ghost appeared behind Ava's dad. Oh, good. She made it. "John." Her voice, quiet and commanding, caused him to freeze. A look of quiet disbelief passed over his face.

Ha! I'd seen Ava make that look too.

Ava's dad slowly turned his head and stared at his wife.

They were still husband and wife even though Beth was dead, right? It wasn't like either of them had ever remarried.

"Beth?" He took a step, then another, before pulling Ava's mom into his arms. His magic made her solid and I had to sigh. It was beautiful. After a moment, he pulled back but didn't let go of her. "Is Ava ill? Why are you here?" The way John looked down at Beth. Ahhh. It made me want to rush home and hug my Sam.

"I'm scared for her," Beth whispered. "She's in some kind of magical coma. We've come to break you out of here."

Luci asked, "Are we ready? We should go now." He tapped his wrist as if checking a watch.

We all nodded, looking around expectantly, and waited for him to do his wiz-bang thing and pop us out of here. Nothing happened. I couldn't teleport home myself, and wouldn't dare try, because I hadn't mastered going from my house to Luci's yet. Never mind home from Milan. Luci growled. "The apartment is spelled. I can't teleport out." He looked about as mad as I'd ever seen him. "Explains why we had to start at the front door."

"Then we go out into the hallway." I moved to the door. Simple solution. I opened it and walked out, then Luci and Beth followed. But when John tried to come out with us, he bounced off some invisible wall. Literally. It was like the barrier punched him and he flew backwards.

Beth rushed back into the apartment to check on him. "John!"

I glanced at Luci, and he said, "I'll be right back." Then he disappeared, leaving me virtually alone in Milan, in the world's vampire headquarters. Fan-freaking-tastic.

"So, that answers the question of if the hallway is spelled," I muttered.

Neither one of Ava's parents said anything and when I

glanced into the room at them, I felt like I should leave. They were wrapped into each other's arms again.

Unfortunately for my comfort levels, I couldn't wait out in the hall. I slipped into the room, closing then turning to face the door, waiting impatiently for Luci to return.

Thankfully, the door opened about thirty seconds later. Luci walked in with a woman about my age, judging from the slight wrinkles around her brown eyes. "Hello," she said brightly, but then she didn't wait for responses. She walked around the apartment with her hands in the air and eyes closed. Somehow, even without looking, she never ran into any furniture or anything.

"That's Kendra," Luci explained in a quiet voice. "A witch friend of mine from Philadelphia."

I realized who she was, then. Ava had asked Luci to go help the woman, Hailey, who bought Ava's old house in Philly a month or two ago. Kendra was Hailey's best friend. And, obviously, a witch.

After a few minutes, she sighed, opened her eyes, and put her hands on her hips. "I think I can break the spell, but it'll be for seconds only."

"How?" Luci asked. "Can I help?"

Kendra shook her head. "No, it's a matter of stabbing through this ward. It's very strong. But it'll be like a blip. It'll push my magic back out pretty quickly."

"Let's not waste any time." I opened the door and peeked out into the hallway. "The coast is clear."

Everyone except Kendra and John walked out with me. "Ready?" Kendra asked.

John nodded. "Sure, yeah."

"Okay. When I nod my head, you run as fast as you can for the hall." She sucked in a deep breath, spread her legs into a sort of defensive pose, and held up her hands. Then, she straightened, shook her hands and rolled her neck, and went back into the pose. "Here goes."

Kendra grimaced, in an expression much like I'd imagine she'd make for a particularly difficult bowel movement. Gross. Then, she nodded once.

John took off, running into the hall so quickly he nearly ran right into me. At the last second, he stopped himself from bowling me right over.

Kendra came out a split second later, beaming.

"Here we go," Luci said brightly. The next second we appeared on Ava's front porch. Lucy looked around, clapped his hands together, and smiled. "Right then, I'm taking Kendra home. Back in a bit."

"Inside?" I asked, suddenly exhausted and praying John would be able to do something.

Beth took John's hand, and as I followed them in, I sent a quick group text to the family, letting Sam and the kids know I was back safe and sound. I also added that we brought John back.

We entered the house to find Phira talking to my uncle, Eodh. It looked as if he'd just arrived.

"Hello," I said, uncertainly. Eodh gave me the heebie-jeebies.

"I came as soon as I heard," he said. "I need to scan Ava and Drew."

In for a penny, I guessed. He could check them out, too. Maybe he'd have a bright idea the rest of us hadn't.

I couldn't keep the sigh out of my voice as I replied. "Okay, yeah. Thanks."

11
AVA

I stared down at my and Drew's bodies and wondered if all ghosts felt as confused as I did at that moment. I wasn't at all sure we were dead. Our bodies didn't look dead. I was pale, but not dead-body pale. And believe you me, I knew what dead-body pale looked like.

Yet, here we were, in a ghostly form with our bodies lying beside one another on my bed.

"This is weird," Drew said softly. His voice sounded fine, normal. As strange as this all felt, I'd half expected him to sound like he was miles away.

"Yep." I faced him and pressed my pointer finger against his chest. Relief flooded me when I could actually touch him. At least we had that much.

As if he was testing the same theory, he framed my face in his hands, then blew out a relieved breath. He laughed nervously and pressed his forehead to mine.

I was right there with him. This was unchartered territory. The last time we'd been in the Inbetween, we'd been here physically. This was different.

Voices drifted into the room from downstairs, so I shrugged at my body and walked out of my bedroom. Walked. I was a ghost type thing, but my feet firmly hit the floor as they had when I had... a body.

Drew followed me down the stairs and to the living room where I'd heard Olivia's voice coming from. "What do you mean, scan the bodies?" she asked.

The head Fae with a huge ego, who was also Phira's older brother and Olivia's uncle, stood with his nose in the air. Eodh. He'd been around all spring and half the summer when we were trying to break Phira out of her black, bubbly shell. In the end it had been all Olivia, but at least he'd tried. "To help you figure out what type of magical sleep she is in," he said.

He'd tried, all right, but there was just something about this guy. He didn't sit right with me, but I couldn't put my finger on exactly why.

"Luci already checked." Olivia crossed her arms and glared at her uncle. She didn't trust him either. Or perhaps she was just being overprotective of me and Drew. I was betting on a little of both. Maybe leaning toward overprotectiveness. Olivia was a total mama bear.

"And what did he find?" Eodh asked with a slight sneer to his upper lip. What a snob.

"Not much," Olivia mumbled. Oh, yeah, she really didn't want to admit that. She was pretty much keeping Luci at arms' length, but she'd rather keep Eodh at like...another realm's length.

I waved for Drew to follow me further into the room. That was when I saw him. I stopped short and stared.

It couldn't be. My heart raced as tears blurred my vision. "This isn't possible." Panic rose in my throat. "Did we go to sleep and wake up in an alternate universe?"

Drew put his hand on my lower back. "What is it?" He was

trying to sound supportive and soothing, but there was a definite undercurrent of panic in his voice.

I pointed to the dark-haired man standing almost hip to hip with my mother, who was back in her ghost form. Winnie hovered nearby, also a ghost. "That man is my father. My very alive-looking father."

Drew's jaw dropped and he looked back and forth between Dad and me.

As I spoke, I realized that no one could see us. "Winnie?" I questioned in a louder voice. "Mom?"

If we were in the Inbetween, which was where spirits went before they moved on, my father, mom, and Winnie should have been able to see us. But they didn't. To test my theory, I moved to stand in front of them and waved my hand inches from their faces. "They can't see us."

How the heck were we supposed to make contact with anyone? "Hello!" I shouted at the top of my voice.

Drew put his hand on my back. "We're not on the same plane as them. I don't know why we can see them, and they can't see us, but here we are."

This must be how ghosts felt most of the time. Frustrated.

And where the heck was Luci? There was no telling what he could see or not with his powers.

I turned to search the faces of my family and friends for any sign that they knew we were standing right in front of them. When my gaze landed on Eodh, he looked me directly in the eyes for a brief moment before focusing back on Olivia. "I need to be alone with the bodies."

"Hey!" I yelled. Lunging forward, I tried to grab his arm, but my hand went straight through him. "Damn it!" I didn't curse very often, but he was lucky I hadn't said something far stronger.

"Why?" Olivia's tone was sharp and mistrusting.

That was my girl! Don't let that creepy Fae in my room.

But then again, I was absolutely sure he could see me and Drew. Maybe getting him alone wasn't such a bad idea.

My magic still swirled around inside me, so I could use it. Hopefully. Moving closer to Olivia, I reached out and touched her forehead—why could I touch her and not him?—and pushed a small amount of power into her. "Let him do what he wants."

Drew drifted closer. "What are you doing?" he whispered.

I shrugged. "Trying a little persuasion spell."

I wasn't at all sure it would work, but I was getting desperate. A second later, Olivia shivered as if having a chill run up her spine. Then she rubbed her arms and frowned. Pointing at Eodh, she said, "If you harm one hair on either of their bodies, I'll bury you in vines." She looked and sounded fierce enough to pull it off.

"You tell him, Liv!" I hollered. I only wished she could hear me.

Eodh's mouth thinned at my outburst. Yep, he could definitely see and hear me. What a turd. What was his plan?

When Eodh moved to the stairs I went with him, right on his heels. Olivia followed, but her uncle turned and eyed her until she stopped and crossed her arms again, nostrils flaring. "Be quick," she said through gritted teeth.

Once inside my bedroom with the door shut, I asked, "What are you up to?" Narrowing my eyes, I crossed my arms and tapped one foot as he appraised me and Drew.

"I'm doing what I must to secure my place on the throne." Eodh moved the night-stand on my side of the bed and squatted down. A moment later, he pulled out a small bag and stuffed it into his pocket. Then he pulled another one just like it from a different pocket.

"Hex bags!" I couldn't believe this. How had I, of all people, with all my strength, not sensed the magic of a hex? "You hexed us?" I could barely believe it.

Drew stepped forward and shoved his hands toward Eodh, but the tall Fae smiled as Drew's hands went right through him. Drew gritted his teeth and tried again.

Eodh smirked. "Yes. I hexed you. During your silly little birthday party." He pointed to Drew and added, "He was dumb enough to bond with you, so he is hexed by association."

"Why? What do I have to do with you claiming the throne?" Of all people in my world who might affect his ability to become Fae King, I would've thought Olivia. Not me.

He placed the second hex bag behind my headboard and pushed the end table back into place. I was amazed how he was able to move the piece of furniture without a sound. The man was strong. "You are what they call collateral damage. I had an offer I couldn't refuse."

Drew balled his fists. "What kind of offer?" Oh, man. I didn't think I'd ever seen him this angry.

Eodh sighed and rolled his eyes. "Does no harm to tell you at this point, I suppose. My father was a ruthless leader. He believed in the purity of our people. The bloodlines are stronger when they are unadulterated. I believed in his cause and supported him. Then my uncle gathered his own followers and overthrew the king, taking his place."

studied his nails as if bored, then looked me in the eyes. Fire blazed in his depth as he smiled wickedly. "I was approached by a couple of powerful vampires. They wanted to form an alliance and with them in my back pocket, I will rule Faery and finish what my father started."

Vampires. My thoughts instantly went to Wade. I would kill them all if they touched my uncle. My non-existent blood boiled in my non-existent veins. "And what do the vamps want out of this alliance?"

Eodh grinned. "You."

Cold dread seeped inside me, cooling the rage. The United States master vampire, Jax, had told me the short version of the history between vampires and necromancers. Basically, vampires feared necromancers because we could control them. And the little capture of a rogue vamp while I was in Philly selling my house had put me on their radar.

"So, you thought you would...what?" I asked. "Kill me?"

"Weaken you." He shook his head like it was so obvious. "So, the vampires could do what they wish with you." He dusted his hands together, looked around and smiled. "Right." Eodh walked out of the room like he was done with the conversation.

Oh, I was so not done.

He turned when he reached the hallway and spoke in a hushed tone. "Don't bother to try to contact anyone. They can't see or hear you. It's all a part of the hex."

I stood there fuming over what he'd said. The smarty pants Fae jerkface thought he had it all figured out. I'd figure out a way to stop him. And the vampires to boot. This was not how we were going down.

I whirled around to face Drew. His brows were drawn, and lips pursed. But I hadn't really needed to see his face to know he was as mad as I was. "We need to find Lucy," I growled.

Drew raised his eyebrows. "How are you going to find the devil?" he asked. "Yell for him?"

"No, the cat. Lucy-Fur." I sighed and closed my eyes to focus on the white cat and my bond with her. The animation. I sensed her and Snoozer in the attic right above where we were standing. I grabbed Drew's hand and pushed off of the floor. Oh, ha! It worked. We floated to the ceiling. I laughed when we drifted right through the ceiling then floor of the attic. It was the strangest sensation. Like a tickle on my spine. "That was easier than I thought." We clomped down onto the attic floorboards.

"And weird," Drew muttered with a shiver.

Definitely.

I spotted the cats a few feet away. Snoozer was curled around Lucy and as I inched closer, I saw why. Poor thing was furless. She looked like a chubby sphinx. But for Pete's sake don't tell her that. Lucy-Fur could have a fowl mouth when provoked. And I couldn't imagine a vainer kitty.

"Lucy." She didn't move, but I sensed that she could hear me. One of her ears twitched slightly, just at the tip. "I know you can hear me. I need you to go downstairs and tell the others that Drew and I are under a spell. There is a hex bag behind my bed that is keeping us asleep."

Lucy lifted her head and snarled at me. "I am not going down there naked!" She took a shaky breath before laying her head back down and snuggling into Snoozer more. Snooze looked from me to Drew and meowed.

Well, he was no help.

12
OLIVIA

How long was he going to take? Geez.

I paced the living room, waiting for Eodh to come back down. I hated that he insisted on going up to her room alone. However, I could've sworn I'd heard Ava's voice telling me to let him go. Crazy, I know. That was it. I was going insane. My powers had worn me out and I was officially a lunatic.

The front door opened, and Sam walked in. We've all been doing that lately, coming and going without announcing ourselves. Ava didn't seem to mind. Winston didn't seem to mind either, which was another oddity. Could the house be worried about Ava too? Or maybe he liked me more now that I had powers. He'd always liked Sam.

I rushed into Sam's arms and sighed as his warmth enveloped me like a soothing balm. He kissed the top of my head. "Ava is tough. We'll figure it out," he whispered.

"Sam?"

At the sound of John's voice, we turned together. Sam frowned and studied him for a moment. I introduced him. "This is Ava's dad, John. John, this is Sam."

Sam nodded as he disentangled himself then held out his hand to the other man. "It's been a really long time." He cocked his head at the older man. "How are you not dead?"

Sam knew Luci and I had gone to Milan to get John, he just didn't know all the details yet.

John shook Sam's hand. "Long story and I'd like to wait until Ava is awake, so I only tell it once." He grimace-smiled at Sam. "I hope you understand."

"Fair enough." Sam pulled me into his side. "Where are the kids?"

I smiled up at my favorite person on the planet. "Still at Luci's. I told them I was here if they wanted to come over, but I think it's best if they stay there while we come up with a plan." Gods, I hoped we could come up with a plan. "Besides, Phira is over there with them."

I had to admit that she was great with the kids and had a special way of teaching them about magic without it being an actual lesson. It was especially helpful with Sammie.

Eodh drew our attention by walking down the stairs, nearly halfway down before we noticed him. His footfalls made no noise, even though he was a big guy. His features were void of all emotions, so it was hard for me to read him. Phira had been teaching me how to shield my emotions because Fae and other magical creatures could easily read them. Possibly steal secrets. Oh, how I wanted to steal Eodh's secrets.

"So," I said, facing him. Maybe we'd get lucky, and he knew how to help. It would go a long way toward me not thinking him a total creeper if he saved Ava.

No such luck. He shook his head. "I don't recognize the magic. I tried to imbibe them with some extra strength. Fortunately, it took hold and will help them stay alive until we can figure out what to do. I'll go discuss with the Fae healers to see what can be done."

Then he dematerialized. I was highly disappointed when

he didn't leave a trail of glitter or something. Maybe a small firework.

Shaking myself out of thoughts of Fae and glitter, I focused on everyone in the room. Beth and John seemed like they'd rather be on a second honeymoon, and I was right there with them. Well, not with them but I would've liked to go on my own little love vacation with my man.

Winnie paced in the far corner of the living room which was interesting to watch, because her feet didn't touch the floor.

Alfred drifted in from the kitchen carrying a tray with fruit, cheeses, small sandwiches, and tea. The ghoul liked to feed people when he was stressed. And when he wasn't. Pretty much all the time.

Larry and Zoey had gone to their rooms, away from unexpected guests and to avoid another mailman episode.

I'd caught Melody sneaking into Ava's office not long after I got back with John. Ava kept most of her spellbooks in her office now because it was easier to go in there than up to the attic whenever we needed to research.

Wade had come up while Eodh was upstairs. He walked out of the kitchen with one of his special mugs and sighed dejectedly before sitting in a wing-backed chair by the fireplace.

It was far too hot for a fire, but Wade sipped his blood and stared at the blackened bricks as if flames flickered merrily there instead of cold ash. After a minute, he stood with a sigh. "I'll be in my basement combing the internet for any mention of this if anyone needs me."

We nodded as he walked out, then sat in silence, everyone trying to come up with some answer.

Several times, one of us opened our mouths as if to suggest something, only to slump back down. I rubbed the bridge of my nose, a headache trying its best to form.

John broke the silence that seemed to stretch on because

none of us knew how to fix Ava and Drew. "Have you tried using the power source under the house?"

Beth, Winnie, and I looked at him blankly. What the heck was he talking about?

John furrowed his brow and looked at us like we were all totally nuts. "The chasm under the house is a never-ending magical source. Are you really telling me you haven't been tapping into it all these years? How is Ava able to have seven ghouls tied to her if not by channeling it?" John looked pointedly at Winnie like she should've known better.

Winnie glared back at him. "I didn't realize it was anything significant. I knew Winston was pulling from that power, of course, but I thought it was just a bit of extra juice to aid in spells and rituals." She shrugged. "Before I died, I hadn't even used it for years."

Beth nodded. "Me neither. It wasn't really something we ever needed."

John shook his head. "No, it's something that can be tapped into. Deeply. Didn't Yaya tell you this?" He looked totally shocked.

When no one spoke again, he continued to explain. "We might be able to use it to wake up Ava and Drew. It's a fair bit of power."

Winston began to shake and make creaking, groaning sounds. It was like the old house was agreeing with John's theory. Banging sounds came from the kitchen and dust rained down from the quiet fireplace.

"Well, I think Winston is saying we should try," I said dryly.

13
AVA

After being snubbed by the newly hairless white cat, and spending way too much time begging her to reconsider, Drew and I sat at the bottom of the stairs and listened to our friends plot out how they were going to save us. Lucy had decided she would rather turn to ash than come downstairs naked. So, here we sat.

The only way they could break the spell was to get rid of the hex bag jerk wad had placed behind my bed. By get rid of, I meant burn it outside so the fumes didn't get trapped in the house. That thing was a nasty piece of work. It didn't belong inside Winston whatsoever.

After the dirty Fae left, my dad—whom I still couldn't believe was alive!—started talking about a chasm under the house and how it was some kind of magical power source. Apparently, it was what kept Winston animated. I thought the house had just absorbed the magic from the hundreds of years witches had lived in it. I'd never dreamed that it had its own power source.

How had I not known this? Besides the obvious answer.

Just because I didn't practice witchcraft most of my adult life and didn't open up my necro powers again until almost a year ago, didn't mean that my aunt and Yaya had to keep me in the dark about what was underneath the house I grew up in.

"Oh, my gosh," I breathed. "Winston!" I jumped to my feet. "Winston! Can you hear me?"

A low groaning sound replied. Something coming from deep under the house. "Winston, is there anything you can do to tell them we're here?"

The kitchen cabinets slammed, and the front door rattled. Dust and soot rained down from the fireplace.

"Well, I think Winston is saying we should try," Olivia said.

"No," I moaned. "She thinks he's agreeing that they should check out the power source. They have no idea he's trying to tell them we're here." I stood. "I can't sit here any longer. Let's go check out the magic source under the house."

"I was about to suggest that," Drew said and followed me into the kitchen and through the wall to the backyard.

The house didn't have a visible crawl space. It had a secret tunnel that Sam and I had discovered when we were kids playing hide and seek. I was betting that was where the chasm was, but I didn't remember ever seeing it before. Surely, I would have sensed its magic.

Well, didn't that just spike my curiosity more to find the thing?

We walked—more like we drifted, which was just plain weird—around to the back of the house and stopped at the basement's exterior double doors. Enough light shined from the outside floodlights to illuminate the door. "Why didn't we go into the basement from inside the house?" Drew asked.

I stopped and stared at him. Why hadn't we? We could have just gone through the floor. "I'm not used to being a ghost. Besides, this way we bypass Wade's living space."

"Why? He couldn't see us, anyway," Drew muttered. "And the cats were no help. We're on our own."

"That's cats for you. They don't care. They never care about anything." But the idea to see if Wade could see us was a good idea. Eodh had said the spell kept us concealed from everyone. Was Wade included? One way to find out.

I floated through the basement doors and headed to Wade's bedroom. I'd only been down here a few times since Wade moved in. He'd gotten all of the stuff that we'd brought from his place in Philly and made the little apartment Winston had created for him a real home. It was neat and tidy. I smiled looking at pictures of Clay, Wallie, and me.

Drew was right behind me, so when I stopped suddenly, he slammed into me and gripped my hips. Flutters of desire raced through me at his touch, but I pushed it away because we were in my uncle's room. Wade might as well have been my uncle. Close enough.

Standing at the foot of Wade's bed, I said his name in a normal tone. He sat at a small desk, typing away on a laptop. "Wade," I said louder. Nothing. Not even a toe twitch. So, I called out his name even louder, though I knew from my upstairs experiences that it wouldn't do any good. Nada. I drifted to stand beside him and touched his arm. At least that was what I wanted to do. My hand went right through him. "Dang it." Straightening, I turned and poked Drew in the arm. He poked me back and I made a kissy face at him. "No sense in trying anymore. Come on, let's check out this magic source."

We exited Wade's underground apartment and headed to the other side of the basement, directly under the conservatory. There was a bookshelf embedded in the wall that opened like a door to a hidden passage that led to the caves along the coast. I pointed it out to Drew, and described how I would have opened it, had I been in my body. I looked at Drew, who widened his eyes. "Cool."

It was kind of neat to impress him like this. We walked straight through the bookshelf. "Yeah. Sam and I used to explore the tunnels down here all the time. But there's a door that we could never get open. I figured it was something Yaya spelled to stay locked, so we left it alone." I formed a small orb of light to float ahead of us as we walked. It wasn't as bright as one Melody would've been able to create, but I was learning. And she was a good teacher.

It helped that being the High Witch gave me an extra boost on abilities I didn't know I had. It was like something new popped up every day. "Do you find it weird that my magic works in the afterlife?"

"We're not dead, so I just thought that the hex only worked on our living forms. I don't know, I'm guessing." Drew took my hand. "We'll figure this out."

I moved a little closer to him, enjoying his warmth. Why did he feel warm like this? Why did I feel cold? This was so weird. "It depends on the type of hex and the chant that created it. We don't know his full intent besides handing me off to the vampires."

That still burned my rear end that the creepy Fae would do such a thing. To me, of all people! I wanted nothing to do with his plans of world domination. The jerk.

Walking along the path, I tried to sort out my emotions. If we didn't get this spell broken before the vampires turned up, which could be any moment, there was no telling what would happen. Would my father be strong enough to command them? Or would they overpower him, too?

We came to the door that Sam and I could never get open as kids and stopped. A pulse of magic vibrated through the door. Odd that I'd never felt it as a kid. Probably by the time I was old enough to have sensed it, I'd already begun repressing my magic.

Pressing my hand to the wood, I tested the magic to see if it would let us in. My hand went through the wood without zapping me with protective power, so I tightened my hold on Drew's hand and walked through the door, feeling a little nervous, which was silly.

The light orb zipped past us, illuminating the small room. More like a small cave, really. They must've done some fancy magic to get a door to fit like it did in the stone. The orb hovered in the center of the room, up high, chasing away the shadows of the corners.

In the center of the room, a small stone table held what looked like a tiny nugget of white and blue magic. As I glided closer, I realized it was a gemstone, a clear quartz. But it wasn't any bigger than my thumb. "That doesn't look very impressive."

"Look." Drew said, pointing at the floor.

A glowing thread of magic laid at our feet and into the far wall. It connected to the gemstone. "Oh, interesting," I whispered and followed the thread through the wall to find another tunnel I would never have known was there. When the orb caught up and illuminated the space, I raised my eyebrows at Drew. "There's no way into this tunnel." The end was closed off, a smooth stone wall, like someone had dug up to the house but stopped just short of that little room with the orb-magic-thing.

He looked around and nodded. "It looks like we have a unique opportunity to explore here."

"True. Who knows how long it's been since anyone has seen this?"

He grinned. "Let's go."

We set off down the tunnel that I hoped wasn't as long as it looked to be, following the thread of magic, thin but unbroken. We walked and walked. Okay. It was going to take a while. On the bright side, this gave me a chance to get to know my boyfriend better. Wait, he was my fiancé now, wasn't he? Kind of. I did like the sound of that. I asked him something I'd been wondering about, but we hadn't really had time to sit down and talk about it. "Do the hunters have an origin story?"

He gave me a quizzical look. "An origin story?"

"Yeah, like what stories were passed down to you about the first hunter or how hunters came to be."

He nodded. "Sure, of course. Though, I'm not sure how much of the story is true. It has changed slightly each time I've heard it. The story goes that a human man fell in love with a witch but didn't know she was a witch until their son was born. The child was magical, and the man demanded to know why, thinking his wife had an affair. When she told him she was a witch and proved it to him, he was so angry that she'd lied to him, he killed her. That was the first of many kills for him, because his heart turned dark. He raised his son to hate witches and to hunt them in order to purify the earth of evil."

"Wow. Talk about overreacting." I rolled my eyes. "Also, a human killing a witch? I call bogus."

He snorted. "It's possible. But like I said, it has changed over time."

"What do you think really happened?" I asked as we kept walking. The caves winded slightly, but for the most part the path was fairly straight. It was difficult to have a sense of direction under here, but from the direction we'd come from, we had to be going toward the caves at the beach.

He was quiet for a few seconds. "My grandfather told me a different tale that is a little more plausible. He said the man was spelled with a love potion. The witch used him to have a child and when she tried to leave with the baby, the man pleaded for her to stay. She broke the love spell and told him she didn't love him. They fought and he stabbed her with a dagger. She cursed him to forever crave the hunt of magic. Or something like that."

That was interesting and sounded a bit better, at least. "I bet it's a mix of the two stories."

"Yeah, maybe. Who knows?" He squeezed my hand.

The tunnel darkened and I peered at a room a few yards ahead. The orb had gone inside, lighting up the space, not leaving much in the tunnel. That was where the magical thread went also. "That's got to be it," I said. "Looks like we're here."

Drew and I picked up our pace. When we entered the room, which was a large cave, I gasped. "It's huge." I gazed into the large room with awe. How had I never felt this?

"And powerful." Drew looked at me and shivered. He'd told me once that his skin crawled when he was near a lot of magic. Yet, when he was with me, it didn't bother him. I took that as another sign from the Fates that we were meant to be.

"Yeah, it is putting out a lot of magic." Just outside the cave, I hadn't felt it. "It must be spelled so that it can't be sensed outside this room."

"Or it naturally does it itself?" he suggested.

"Maybe."

The thin thread of magic that had run down the hallway ended in the middle of the large room. At that point, the floor split and glowed with a bluish light. "It's a gigantic quartz crystal," I whispered as I moved closer and peered down into the rock. "There's no telling how far down it goes."

"You could power a city on this thing," Drew said.

I laughed and looked at him with delight. "This might be just what we need.

The only problem was there was no other entrance to this room. "We'll have to figure out how to get someone with an actual body in here," I mused.

Drew nodded. "And figure out how to use that power to break the hex."

I sighed, trying not to feel defeated. "Easy peasy."

Not.

14
OLIVIA

After heading downstairs and through the basement and taking a look at the unimpressive little glowing stone in the caves behind the basement, we traipsed back up to Ava's room.

By we, I meant everyone from the living room with the addition of Larry, Zoey, Wade and Alfred. It was easier than carrying Ava and Drew's bodies downstairs, especially if using the power under the house didn't work. We could've had Wade carry them, in theory. Oh, well. We were all crammed into Ava's large bedroom, which seemed tiny with this many people in it.

I looked at all the people in the room and watched their auras darken with sadness and worry. Zoey and Larry huddled into the far corner and kept their eyes on Ava. Larry was back to being a skeleton and Zoey looked...dead. Yet, they stood with their arms locked around each other. How sweet that they'd found one another. I loved that for them. Though, the thought of hugging a skeleton...or a dead and sort of rotting shifter.

Blech. I shivered and pulled my eyes away from the young couple.

Movement to my right caught my attention, and I glanced at John. He inched his way to the bed and stared sadly down at his daughter. Lifting a hand, he brushed a strand of hair from Ava's face and let his finger linger for a bit. "She's beautiful," he whispered.

Beth put her hands on his arms from behind and rested her cheek on John's shoulder. "She really is. Inside and out."

And she was naturally beautiful. Even when we were kids, she had this beauty that surrounded her and projected out. Ava could look like a hobo and still be pretty. I'd always had to work for it with designer clothes, my hair never out of place, and gods forbid I wouldn't have been seen in public without makeup. I'd hated Ava because of my own insecurities. I'd been jealous of her.

John's regret and guilt for leaving her when she was so young washed over me, thanks to my newly unlocked empathic abilities. I didn't even try to block the emotions. They met my own regret that I'd been such a bitch to Ava in school.

Would I ever move past the guilt of who I used to be? Of the person I'd been growing away from, learning to be better than? I really hoped so.

Melody was the first to break the silence, and I was grateful for it. I hadn't the first clue what to do now. This magical world was still new to me.

"If no one objects," she said. "I'll go first to try to pull power from the source and use it to wake them."

John nodded eagerly as if saying that she was welcome to try.

"Please," I said. "I feel like I'm flying blind."

Beth gave me a sympathetic smile. "I'm sorry, dear."

I stamped back the part of me that wanted to tell her she should be sorry. If she, Yaya, and Winnie hadn't put the spell on me, I would've had my magic all along. Maybe I wouldn't have been such a terrible person for so long.

But that wasn't fair either. They were doing what they thought was best for me. And if I hadn't been human for most of my adult life, I wouldn't have had my children or fallen in love with Sam, probably. Things happened the way they did for a reason.

Melody closed her eyes and lifted her hands slightly while we waited. Nothing happened. I looked around, surprised to not even feel a surge of power from her attempt. Stepping closer, I put my hand on her shoulder and then I could feel it. She was wrestling with some power, but it really didn't feel like all that much. Maybe combined with hers it would be a lot. Witch power worked differently from mine, so it was hard for me to say.

With a grunt, she released the thread of energy. "I feel the power, but something is blocking my attempt to direct it into Ava and Drew." Melody frowned down at their sleeping forms.

Phira stood on the other side of the bed from me, and I met her stare. She'd left Sammie with Jess and Devan and come to help. "Is there anything you can think of?" I asked.

She shook her head sadly. "I'm sorry, my darling. I can't sense what power is making them sleep like this."

Without warning, Luci materialized next to her. He looked around the room with raised eyebrows and asked, "What's going on?"

I swore there was a hint of worry in his tone as I settled back against Sam. Did he care about Ava after all? He seemed like he did, but why was it so hard for me to trust him? I had to work on it. I wanted a cohesive family unit, including my birth parents. "We're trying to pull from a magical source under the house," I said.

Luci nodded. "I would have suggested that earlier, but I

figured there was a reason why nobody had ever mentioned it." He tutted and looked down at Ava with his lips pursed.

Staring at him, I tried to figure out if I could zap him with power without hurting anyone else in the room. Probably not. "You knew about the power source?"

"Yes, of course. It's hard for me not to feel that." He watched me closely for a moment. "Judging from your expression, you did not."

I crossed my arms. "No. I didn't. None of us did until John told us." I took a breath to calm my emotions because my magic responded to how I felt. The last thing we needed was my emotions going haywire and causing an earthquake or something.

Phira took Luci's hand. "We could try together." That was sweet. They were together often and always seemed to touch one another.

Luci nodded and turned to face Phira, taking both of her hands. They pressed their foreheads together and everyone in the room fell quiet. This time I felt their power rise and the addition of another source of energy. And again, after a few minutes and repeated attempts on their part, nothing happened.

"There is definitely something blocking our efforts," Luci said with an edge to his tone. "When Fee and I get the stream of power close to Ava, it snaps back to the source." Oh, big bad Dad didn't like that he couldn't achieve something.

I was starting to see where I got a particular trait from.

John picked up Ava's hand and said, "I'll try and add in some of my own magic."

Hope filled me. As Ava's father, his magic could give the right amount of boost to break through whatever was blocking them. This had to work.

I sucked in a deep breath and leaned back into Sam, letting

his strong presence comfort me. Magically, he was absolutely no help whatsoever. Emotionally, he was my rock.

After a few moments, John said a low curse and let go of Ava's hand. "It's not working." He sounded as frustrated as Luci had.

Then, the floor under our feet rumbled. I spread my stance out to keep from falling as Winston let out a few creaks and groans. "What's happening?" Sam whispered in my ear.

"No idea, but—" Magic flowed over the surface of the floor and walls. I gasped as a stream of power headed straight to Ava. It glided like a sheet of light up the side of the bed, but when it got close to her skin, it bounced back. Damn it!

"Aww, how sweet. Winston is trying to help," Melody said.

"Because he loves Ava," Larry said. I looked back to see him embracing Zoey still.

Still creepy.

Zoey added, "We all do."

I nodded. We were all one big unusual and dysfunctional family. I was glad I was there to enjoy the ride with them all. Not that we were having very much fun at the moment. "John, why can't you just heal Ava?" I asked.

He looked at me like I was a little bit crazy. Maybe I was. "I can't heal her. Necromancers don't have that ability." John looked from me to Beth.

Ava's mom smiled. "Ava has been able to use her necromancer power to heal." She shrugged. "Or maybe it's a separate ability altogether."

John looked back down at Ava and smiled. "She carries the power of her ancestors. That ability hasn't been seen in hundreds of years. Maybe longer."

Just then, Luci moved closer to the bed and did what looked like a scan. That was the only way I could describe it. He hovered his hand over Ava's chest with his eyes closed. When he opened them, he frowned. "She is weakening."

My heart leaped into my throat, and I clung to Sam. We couldn't lose Ava. This was unthinkable.

Beth made a choked sob sound as she said, "It's time we called Wallie home." Oh, no. Poor Wallie. How would he handle losing his mother?

Winnie nodded. "As well as Owen."

Maybe once everyone was here, we could do some sort of spell that combined our powers. We couldn't give up now.

15
AVA

When Drew and I returned to the house, it was quiet. Like creepy quiet. "Where did everyone go?" We emerged up the stairs into the hallway after cutting through Wade's apartment, rather than going around the house.

"It is odd to see the house this empty," Drew whispered. "There was just a roomful of people here."

Sure was. "Where'd everyone go?"

A knocking sound echoed above us, making me look up like someone was walking on the ceiling and wanting my attention. Not likely in a normal situation, but the house, aka Winston, was magical. "I think Winston is telling us that everyone is upstairs."

Drew rocked back on his heels. "Only one way to find out."

We took the stairs to my bedroom, hurrying up, and it wasn't until we reached my bedroom door that I remembered we were in spirit form and could have floated through the ceiling and floor of my bedroom. But whatever. I was tired and wanted to be alive again.

I entered the room first and stopped short at the sight of

every one of my friends and family, except the kids and Carrie, inside my room. They were really squeezed in there, too. "What the heck are they all doing in here?"

Larry was a full-blown skeleton again, and oh, my goodness. Poor Zoey. She looked positively awful.

Drew shrugged, and at the same time, Luci turned as if he'd heard me speak. But that was impossible. Nobody could hear me.

But then, miracle of miracles, he stared right at me. His jaw dropped and his eyes widened much larger than normal. In the next second, he rushed around the bed to stand in front of me. "Where have you been? You aren't dead, so how are you in this form?" He reached out and grabbed my shoulders. "How are you here and there?" he asked, looking from me to the bed at my body.

He was able to touch me, so he obviously didn't realize we were just spirits.

Olivia turned and stared at Luci like he had lost his mind. It was the same look I gave him all the time. Liv asked, "Uh, Luce? Who are you talking to?"

He furrowed his brow. "Ava and Drew. They are in spirit form." Oh, so he realized we weren't in bodies. Luci waved a hand in our direction, but Olivia and Mom were looking in the wrong direction.

Enough was enough. "Luci, there is a hex bag behind my bed. Eodh put it there. He is trying to make me weak so the vampires can come to collect me." I went on telling him what the crazy Fae had told me about the vampires and forming an alliance to take over Faery.

Anger colored the devil's face, and he fisted his hands at his side as he seethed. "I knew he was rotten. He always turned his nose up at Fee and me before she was taken."

Everyone stared at Luci with rapt attention while Phira glided closer to him. I wondered if she could see me. If so, she hadn't let on that she could. She focused on Luci with concern etched in her features. "Who, dear?"

Luci took her hand and pulled her close. "Your eldest brother. He is responsible for the enchantment."

As soon as Luci let go of Fee's hand, he hurried to the head of the bed and moved the nightstand out of the way. He moved it just as easily as Eodh had. He was stronger than he looked.

Luci dropped down on the floor to look behind the headboard. "Bugger," he muttered. When he stood, he had the hex bags in his hand. "This is why he wanted to be alone with the bodies for. He hexed them in order to turn Ava over to the vampires."

Everyone in the room gasped at the same time. Luci cupped his hands around the bag and tightened his grip around it. "Outside," I squawked. "Don't release that energy in here."

"Oh," Luci said. "Good point."

"What's a good point?" Olivia asked. "What is she saying?"

Luci ignored her and walked toward the bedroom window.

"Luci," Olivia said warningly. "Please answer me."

He was focused on the bag, though. With one hand, he waved his fingers and the window opened.

"Dad!" Olivia yelled.

Luci froze and turned to face her with the biggest expression of hope and happiness on his face. "Sweet girl. Ava wants me to do this outside so as not to release the energy within the house."

Olivia nodded once. "Fine, then."

He stuck his hands out the window, and within seconds they were engulfed in flames. He destroyed the bag and its negative magic with it.

As soon as the spell was broken, my spirit snapped back to my body. I sat up with a gasp then before I could speak, everything started to spin. Olivia and Sam were at my side instantly while Mom and Winnie floated over my bed. I sat for a moment and let my body acclimate to my spirit again as Drew moaned and sat up.

"That's not fun," he muttered.

As my vision settled and the nausea passed, I looked back at Mom and Winnie. The two of them were ghosts. "Where are your ashes?" I asked.

"I put them back in their urns," Alfred squeaked. I swung to look at him hovering worriedly in the corner of the room opposite from the one Larry and Zoey stood in.

"Can you go get them for me?" I smiled at him. Might as well get everyone back to normal. I was already starting to feel my magic strengthen.

Drew let out a soft groan and I looked down at him. I squeezed his hand and pushed a tiny bit of magic into him to give him a little boost to help him reorient himself. Poor guy.

When I looked back up, I met the stare of my father. My heart thumped wildly, and I wanted to fly into his arms. But I also wanted to ask a million questions. The first one being why he left me. Why had I thought he was dead? Had he faked his own death?

But first we needed to deal with Eodh and the vampires. "So, Eodh made a deal with a couple of powerful vampires, and no he didn't tell me who they were." I rolled my eyes. "And we were so shocked by it all. We didn't think to ask."

Drew sat up and leaned into me. "We may be able to use the chasm to help fight them. I can call Lily to come help." He was still a little woozy from the spell. I could feel it through our new bond.

Olivia launched herself at me and wrapped me in a hug. "Hey, frand."

"Hey," I whispered. Squeezing her tight, I thanked my lucky stars for this wonderful woman now in my life. Too bad we hadn't been able to make things work and become friends when we were younger. "Thank you for leading the charge for saving me."

She sniffled and backed away. "Of course. Nothing you wouldn't have done for me."

Luci perked up at the mention of the chasm, and I remembered nobody knew about the chasm. Luci glanced around the room and asked, "What chasm? Are you talking about the ley line under the house?"

Ley line? I shook my head. "No, it's a power source. The one under the house is a small stone that glows. But it leads to a gigantic chasm filled with quartz and power. The power! The magic coming off of that thing is amazing. But we noticed it because of a thread of magic that went along the tunnels of the caves. Drew and I followed it and found this stone that was ten times bigger and more powerful."

"A hundred times bigger," Drew said under his breath.

I nodded. "Probably. It is self-contained, somehow, so it can't be sensed outside of the cave. And there's no way to get to it. We only were able to because we didn't have bodies."

"There is," Luci said. "I can sense it even now. I just assumed you all could too. There's a cave near the beach that leads to the paths under the house."

We all stared at him in shock. "You need to learn to share," I said.

Alfred returned with Mom and Winnie's urns. I stood and took them from him while motioning for everyone to give me space. Melody, Olivia, Sam, and Phira moved to stand in the hallway in front of the door so they could still hear and see what was going on. There just wasn't room in here for everyone.

I took the urns and one at a time dumped them on the floor, then said the chant while pushing magic into their ashes. Quickly, their bodies formed around their ghostly forms. Olivia ran into the bathroom and came out with a couple of towels to cover their nakedness.

As they got to their feet, I turned to Luci. "I never knew ley lines had power sources. That was the biggest quartz I've ever seen."

Luci nodded. "Oh, yes. There are many of these sources placed in crossroads of sorts under the earth and they feed the lines. Witches of old used to use the lines to travel from place to place. A witch's way of teleporting."

Melody and I exchanged a glance. That would have been helpful to know on a number of occasions. Mom and Winnie, once they'd dusted themselves off and wrapped the towels around to cover them, pulled me into a group hug and started kissing my cheeks.

"Sweet girl," Mom said. "I was so worried."

My stomach growled and we all chuckled. "I guess my belly wasn't a fan of my extended sleep."

Olivia and Melody ran out of the room and returned a few minutes later with tea and some snacks. Alfred, who I hadn't seen leave, came in several minutes after that with a bowl of soup and handed me two spoons—one for me, the other for Drew.

I waved my fingers at Zoey and Larry, sending a stream of magic their way. Larry's flesh grew back while Zoey changed from zombie-like to human with tiger ears. They both laughed in delight and patted themselves. Zoey snatched up one of the towels Mom and Winnie hadn't used and covered Larry. They all left to change clothes.

When I headed to the door with my soup, my dad stepped in front of me. Tears blurred my vision as I looked at him. "Dad."

He pulled me into his arms. Drew slipped the soup from my hands as warmth and love surrounded me, and I sank into my father. I never imagined I'd be able to feel his arms around me again. Or smell his cedar and rosemary scent. "How is this possible?" I whispered.

He framed my face and studied me for a little while before saying, "I'll explain to everyone as soon as you rest up." His smile was enough to make me feel like I'd slept for days.

Which, I had. "Rest up? Drew and I have been doing just that for the last day or so." I didn't even know how long we'd been out.

Dad kissed my forehead and turned me to the bed. "And you had all your power drained by a hex. That will mean you need to rest."

I looked around at everyone else, and at Mom, Winnie, and Larry. They'd just returned from putting on clothes. They all nodded, agreeing with Dad. Fine. I wasn't going to argue. At least I got to cuddle up with Drew while we recharged.

"Everyone out," Olivia commanded. "Let the lovebirds rest." She winked at me. "We'll be researching the vampire situation. Nobody will bother you."

I smiled gratefully and took the soup bowl from Drew. "Thanks," I whispered.

Once everyone was gone, I sighed and looked over at my partner in crime. "Well, then. Let's get around to resting."

16
AVA

After a good long cuddle—that led to other, sexier things—and an even longer nap, I woke up just as the sun rose. "Gross, morning," I muttered. I hoped my body didn't want to make this a habit. Rising with the birds was, well, for the birds. But going back to sleep wasn't an option because I was wide awake. I felt like I could've run a marathon and then come back and cleaned the whole house.

Drew was still softly snoring beside me, so I decided to let him sleep and slid out from under the covers. After a long shower, I got dressed and skipped down the stairs feeling more refreshed, balanced, and energetic than I had for a long while. Especially not since that jerky Fae hexed me. But I felt even better than I had before all this happened.

Oh, of course. Now that I didn't have the hex bag draining me, I was feeling the effects of the bond with Drew.

Heck! This was fantastic!

I followed the scent of coffee and something savory toward the kitchen. I stopped short in the archway and stared at my dad as he moved around the kitchen. He seemed to be the only one up. Or at least the only one downstairs. Not even Alfred was shuffling around yet.

Dad's hands wrapped around a coffee mug as he looked out the window. "Are you going to have a seat or stare at me all morning?" He turned and smiled at me, and I wanted to cry. My emotions went absolutely haywire looking at him.

Playing it cool, I moved to the counter to fix myself a cup of coffee, which I hadn't done often since Alfred moved in. "Where is Alfred?"

Dad said, "Laundry, I think he said." I should've known he'd be up. When had he ever slept longer than me?

Wait...come to think of it... Did Alfred sleep? Yes. Surely, he did. Or I'd know if he didn't. Right?

I'd been about to say that I hoped he didn't wake Wade, but as a new vampire, he'd sleep through a tornado. Instead, I said, "So, you're alive." Way to slip into it gently.

It might've been a lame thing to say, but I didn't know what else to talk about. I had so many questions. Once my coffee was doctored just right, I moved to sit at the table across from him. "You are alive, right? Not undead."

With my luck, he was some new sort of ghoul-slash-vampire or something.

He chuckled and shook his head. "I'm alive." He grabbed my hand and held onto it tight. "I was captured by the vampire elders and held prisoner."

I gaped at him. "But how? How did vampires take down a necromancer?"

He smiled sadly. "Using Fae. We have no real power over the fair folk." He squeezed my hand and looked off out the big windows. "They made it look like a car wreck. I have no idea how they convinced anyone that body was me, or what else they did. They knocked me out and I woke up in the same place your friends saved me from."

"Dad," I said, shocked to my core. "That was thirty-eight years ago."

He nodded sadly. "All that time, I had no way to contact you. When the elders taunted me with your mother's death, I tried and tried to find a way to get word to the afterworld to try to contact you. But I don't think it worked. They had my room warded against magic." He let go of my hand, and as soon as he did, I wanted to reach out and grab him and hold on for dear life.

"Mom said she heard rumors that you were alive." So, his spell must have worked to some degree. "But she didn't tell us at first."

He nodded. "She explained. She didn't believe them, and only told everyone about them as a last resort. She feels terrible now for not coming to find me as soon as you pulled her from the afterworld."

"The Inbetween," I murmured.

He raised his eyebrows. "That's right. I'd forgotten that's what the witches call it." After taking a long sip of his coffee, he smiled at me. "I'm told I have a grandson?"

I clasped my hands together. "Wallie. I can't wait for you two to meet. You're going to love him."

"I have no doubt about that." His face softened. "I haven't been formally introduced to your beau, but you have my condolences on the loss of your husband."

I pressed my lips together. "Clay was the love of my life. He's at peace, and now I've been blessed to find love again. I'm a lucky woman."

"Indeed, you are." Dad smiled. "In this family, it never hurts to ask. Are you sure your Clay is...uh..."

"Yes, he's definitely dead, and he's not in the Inbetween. He's moved on."

Dad nodded his head. "Good. Never hurts to check when you're a necromancer."

That was the truth.

I sensed Drew before he appeared in the kitchen entrance way. He was dressed in his uniform, ready for work. That wouldn't do. Frowning, I asked, "Can't you take the day off? I mean we almost died, surely that's a legit excuse to call out sick."

His lips lifted in a sensual smile, and he advanced to me. Magic flickered in his teal eyes. Our shared magic from the bond. "I could, but I thought Sam could use the day off since he's been covering for me."

He was so selfless. Bless him. "Oh, Sam will get over it," I teased while playing with the buttons on his shirt. Flashes of our tangled bodies entered my mind, waking up the desire I felt for him.

Dad cleared his throat, reminding me he was there. Oops. I introduced the two of them. Even though they knew who each other was, they hadn't officially met. "Dad, this is Drew, Sheriff of Shipton Harbor. Drew, this is my dad, John, who is back from the dead."

Drew chuckled and held out his hand. "People usually come back from the dead around Ava. It's a pleasure to meet you."

"I noticed," Dad teased with twinkling eyes.

I rolled my eyes and stood. Drew didn't move so when I rose to my feet, our bodies pressed together. "Do you want a coffee to go?" I asked, hoping to keep him here for another moment. Funny how quickly I'd gone from enjoying his company to not wanting to be parted at all.

Alfred entered the kitchen a moment later and waved at Drew and I to sit. "I'll fix him a cup, but he can't leave until he eats. You two sit. The hashbrown casserole is almost done."

The mention of food made my stomach growl.

Drew chuckled and sat in the chair beside mine. The temptation of a home-cooked breakfast was too much for him to refuse. "I won't make you twist my arm, Alfred," he said. "I know how good your cooking is."

Soon after, Mom and Winnie joined us at the table. I tried to watch my parents as they smooched and cuddled each other. They needed a honeymoon or something. I was going to suggest that when Dad spoke instead. "I want to transfer your mother's care over to me." He didn't take his eyes off of her as he spoke.

At first his statement confused me, though. Did Mom need care? Like a hospital or something? I thought she was pretty healthy for a ghoul. Oh. Duh. A ghoul...who needed a necromancer to care for her by giving her life. That was what he meant.

I grinned at them. "Okay, sure. I mean, she's not a drain on me. That was the hex Eodh the Stupid put on me. I don't need you to."

Mom patted my hand, then gave it a squeeze. "We know, dear. But, he's my husband."

I grinned at her. "Right-o." In other words, she would rather be bound to her husband than her daughter. That was okay with me, because if I had the same decision to make, I'd choose my husband. "I said it's okay. I'd rather be bound to my soul mate than anyone else."

The room got really quiet. Even Alfred stopped doing whatever he was doing at the counter behind me. Everyone was staring at me with creepy grins. It was Dad who said, "You already are. When is the wedding?"

I started choking on air, not expecting Dad to ask something so pointed and something that I hadn't had time to fully think about. Not that there was a lot to think about, since the deed had already been done. I stared at my parents, intending to tell them that we weren't going to have a wedding. I personally wanted to elope and not tell anyone until it was done. Like some celebrities did to avoid the paparazzi. Only in my case, it was to avoid the person of the week who wanted necromancers dead at the time of the wedding.

However, I couldn't tell them any of that. Both had missed my first wedding. I couldn't take that away from them. So, I shot Drew a glance and changed course. "We haven't set a date yet. The bond is still pretty new. Besides, the way my life has been for the past almost year, I'll have to hire security to make sure we all survive it."

Everyone laughed. It wasn't truly funny, but yet... it was. One of those, we're going to hell for laughing, sort of things.

"We'll survive it," Drew said, then kissed my temple. I sighed and leaned into him.

Dad stretched out his hand over the table. "Give me your hand."

I did and as soon as our palms touched, both of our dark necromancer powers curled around our hands. My instincts took over, and I knew what to do like I'd been practicing death magic all of my life. "I, Ava Harper, gift to you, John Lowe, my undead Mom, Beth. Do you promise to protect her and treat her like a queen for the rest of your existence?"

Those might not have been the correct words used in the traditional transition of a ghoul, but they felt right. And magic was a bit more about intent, especially necromancer magic.

Dad smirked. "I promise."

Something tugged inside me. A bit of power flowed down my arm and circled our combined hands, then disappeared. I didn't feel any more powerful than I had before... or any less. But still, I missed her being connected to me.

She looked radiantly blissful, making me happy for both of them. They were reunited and here with me. My childhood had been nearly ruined by their absence, but now we could make up for all that. I couldn't wait to get to know them.

Just as Alfred brought our breakfast over to the table, Olivia materialized a few feet from the table. We stared at her for a split second, amazed, as Phira and Luci popped in right after her. Olivia grinned and said, "I did it."

"Yay!" Then again, she'd been able to teleport to me the last time. It had been way the wrong moment, but hey. "It's easier for you to teleport to me?"

She let out a dramatic sigh and rolled her eyes. "Yes."

"Aw, that means you love me." I stood and went to her.

She pulled me into a hug. "I thought I lost you and Drew."

Tightening my grip on my best friend, I swayed us back and forth. "Never. You're stuck with us."

"I'm more than okay with that." Olivia gave me another squeeze before letting me go. "We need to go to Faery. Phira arranged a meeting with the king. Or is that an audience with the king?" She scrunched her face as if trying to figure out which is the right terminology to use.

Luci held up a hand. "I'll be sitting this one out. Ava, you, Olivia, and Phira will be the only ones to go." Nice to have a choice in the matter. Pfft. But I did want to deal with Eodh. And soon.

Drew shook his head and opened his mouth to protest, but Phira said, "She will be perfectly safe with me."

Sitting back in my seat at the table, I placed a hand on Drew's arm. "I'll be okay. We're linked and you will know the moment if I'm not okay."

"That isn't all that reassuring, considering I can't just pop into Faery and rescue you." He searched my face while working his jaw. Then he nodded and kissed me quickly on the lips. "I still don't like it."

I motioned for Olivia and Phira to sit. "Alfred made a hash brown casserole. Eat with us and tell me what one should wear to meet a king."

17
OLIVIA

Having magical parents came in pretty handy, especially since I didn't have full control over my own magic. Luci had conjured up two gowns for Ava and I that were similar to Phira's floor length A-line.

As soon as Ava had asked what we were going to wear, Luci just snapped his fingers and poof, the clothes we wore changed into dresses. Mine was teal, which I'd always thought went well with my blonde hair. The skirt flowed out to the floor, and had a beautiful princess scoop neckline and short, flowy sleeves. I felt like a Faery princess in it.

Ava's was gorgeous as well. Ruby red, her skirt was similar to mine, flowing with lots of a deep V neck. I squinted closer. The V was held together with a thin layer of nude mesh. Clever. Hanging off of the top of the sleeveless dress was a cape that made her look like royalty.

It was fitting. The Fae princess and the necromancer princess, going to meet the Fae King. A meeting of the supernatural aristocracy.

"Oh, these shoes are so comfortable." Ava said, lifting up the hem of her dress to admire the shoes. They were flats and the exact same color as her dress. They looked delicate like they'd fall apart the first time she took a step, but they wouldn't. Luci wouldn't have allowed it.

She was right, though. These slippers were incredibly comfortable. I'd never had anything that felt like it was made just for my feet before. Was Luci's godly magic at work? It had to be.

"Are we ready?" Phira moved to stand between Ava and me. When we nodded, Phira pulled a stone out of the pocket of her dress. I peered at it interestingly.

"It's a Luz opal," she said, showing me the smooth rock. "It looks like it has an entire galaxy inside." She curled her fingers around the smooth, oval stone and closed her eyes.

That was when my attention went back to the fact that Phira had pockets in her dress. I checked my dress and giggled when I found them. Ava poked me in the arm and I glanced at her. She mouthed, "Pockets!"

"I know," I mouthed back. Luci got some major brownie points for thinking of pockets in the dress.

A whisper of magic flared in front of us and when I focused on it, my jaw fell open. "That's cool."

I'd seen a portal before when we'd gone to Faery to meet with Carrie's grandfather, the king of the Sprite Fae. But this, Phira's portal, was different. The magic was larger, and the space that opened up looked like the galaxy inside the stone. Maybe it was just a visual representation, but I felt like we were going to walk among the stars.

"This is cool," Ava breathed. She pressed a kiss to Drew's cheek, then we took Phira's hands and stepped through.

As soon as we were fully on the other side of the portal, the Fae magic reached out to me, teasing my own power. Everything was so colorful. The trees had different colored leaves and flowers. The green was a mix of bright and dark greens. All the colors were more vivid, opaquer than anything on Earth.

My soul sang being here. I wanted to dance barefoot through the fallen leaves and climb all the trees. Swim in the river and fall asleep under the stars.

I peered upward. The clouds. They were so close to us here! Like this place was closer to the heavens or something.

Phira pointed straight ahead. "There is the palace."

And what a palace it was. It was more beautiful than any fairytale castle that I'd ever seen. "This is amazing." The spires and turrets reached up toward the sky, made of some sort of metal that both contrasted and complemented the nature around it. Was it silver? Surely the Fae didn't have whole buildings made out of silver.

Too bad I didn't have time to explore. I wondered if I could bring Sam with me and the kids. Oh, this was going to be our next family vacation spot for sure. This place was better than any possible resort we could've stayed at. I opened my mouth to ask Phira if that was okay, but she spoke, answering my unasked question.

"You can come back whenever you want and as many times you want. And, yes, Sam is welcome too. After all, as your husband, he is family." Phira waved us to follow her down the cobblestone road, which was a mix of grey, blue, and deep purple rocks.

Ava leaned close. "This place is so cool."

"You too are welcome here, Ava," Phira said. "As long as you have me or Olivia to accompany you."

With a big grin, Ava grabbed my hand. "Honeymoon!"

I chuckled and squeezed her fingers. "Leave it up to your matron of honor. I'll plan it."

But I looked at her, worried I'd overstepped my bounds.

"Oh, sorry. I didn't mean to make it sound like I was inviting myself to be in your wedding party."

She put her arm around my shoulder. "Don't be silly. There isn't anyone else in the world I'd rather have by my side."

When we reached the palace, two guards wearing uniforms of greens and browns stood outside the large double doors. I squinted at their clothes. If I wasn't mistaken, this was some sort of Fae camouflage. If they stepped into the forest, they'd blend right in. Yet at the same time, the threads were absolutely gorgeous.

They recognized Phira and bowed to her. When they noticed me, their eyes went round as if they knew I was her daughter. They bowed to me and then Ava.

Wow. "They bowed," I hissed once we passed them. "Holy crap!"

"I know!" Ava replied. Phira just chuckled.

We walked through the doors and into a large open foyer. A set of stairs split in the middle at the far wall and went left and right, leading to galleries on either side of the enormous foyer. Hallways led off of each of them.

The decor inside the palace was much like the outside, and now I could confirm the walls were made of silver. Intricate drawings of regal men and women adorned the walls, floor to ceiling and enormous.

Phira led us to the right and down a hallway lined in carpet that...

"Is the carpet made of moss?" Ava asked.

"Indeed," Phira replied. "Many things in this palace are living, carefully cultivated to thrive and support us.

We walked into a throne room where, again, we were met with two more guards. They bowed as they opened the throne room doors.

The throne room was more barren than I would've

expected, the focal point being the enormous throne on a dais in the middle of the room. In here, the walls were gold, not silver, and light from high windows streamed in.

King Mitah sat on his throne with two of Phira's sisters on smaller thrones on either side of him. I couldn't remember their names right off. Anxiety spiked as reality set in about what we were here for. We were ratting out their eldest brother, my uncle, for trying to kill Ava. This wasn't going to be easy.

King Mitah rose to his feet the moment he saw Phira, which made me stop in the middle of the room. I watched as he advanced to Phira and pulled her into a tight hug. When he pulled back, he framed her face with his hands. "Phira, my dear niece. It is good to see you looking so well."

She put her hands over his and smiled up at him. "It is good to be alive and well. Thank you for seeing us today." Phira's face was full of love for her uncle, and I wondered if she loved him more than her crazy father. I wouldn't ask that because it would be incredibly rude, but I wouldn't have blamed her if she did. At least, I wouldn't ask Phira. I'd wait to ask Luci later. I felt more comfortable asking him rude questions. Huh. That was something. If I felt comfortable going to him with any questions, that was an improvement over how I'd felt just a few weeks ago.

She turned to Ava and me and took our hands. "This is my beautiful daughter, Olivia, and her friend Ava."

King Mitah bowed slightly at the neck and kissed each of our hands. "Welcome to my home." Then he motioned for us to sit at a large rectangular banquet table that had not been there just seconds ago. "What brings you here today? I understand this is not a social visit."

Phira sat beside him and frowned. "It is not. I wish it was. But we have some upsetting news about my brother, Eodh."

"He tried to kill Ava," I blurted out then slapped my hand

over my mouth. Geez. I should've let my mother handle this part and kept my dang mouth shut. But I was so darn mad at Eodh. I wanted to punch him right in the junk.

Ava sat in the seat across from them and pulled on my arm until I dropped in the chair next to hers.

The king bunched his eyebrows together and studied me and Ava for a long while. "That is a serious accusation." His grave tone didn't tell me how he was going to go with this. Believe us or not?

Ava spoke next. "It's not one I take lightly. I don't think his goal was to kill me. At least not himself anyway. He wanted to weaken me so when the vampires showed up at my door, they could kill me, or take me prisoner."

"Eodh made a deal with the vampires," I added. "He plans to unite the Fae with them and take the throne from you."

There was a long stretch of silence as Mitah considered what we told him. Then he placed his hand on the table between him and Ava. "Your mental shields are strong, necromancer. Please take my hand."

Huh. Nice to have strong mental shields. As I understood the Fae so far, each was born with different abilities. My guess was that Mitah was able to read thoughts through touch. Either that or he could tell if she was lying.

When Ava placed her hand on his, palm against palm, she sat incredibly still. A few moments later, Mitah let go of her hand and curled his into fists. "This is a betrayal to the throne and all of Faery."

Oh, okay, then. I knew which side his bread was buttered on now. Even though Mitah seemed calm on the outside, his magic was anything but. It whipped around him, ready to strike Eodh down. That might be just what he would do. Though, I hoped not. I didn't want to see an execution today. I wasn't in the mood for gruesome.

Mitah snapped his fingers and Eodh appeared a few feet

from us. His eyes turned into big saucers as he stared at us, and when his gaze landed on Ava, his mouth opened slightly. Eodh fully opened his mouth to speak, but no sound came out. Mitah stood and moved towards the traitor. "Eodh Keyric Keana Zyltris, you stand accused of treason. Your trial begins now."

18
AVA

I really didn't know what to expect from a Fae trial, but I was happy that the king was taking us seriously and doing something about it. After all, it wasn't only me who Eodh planned to double-cross. No, he was out to destroy his own family, his king, and the whole Fae race.

Once Mitah announced there would be a trial, his guards sprang into action. One of them took hold of Eodh and pushed him into a chair that had appeared out of nowhere in the center of the room. Two other guards stood, one on either side of Eodh.

A door in the far right corner of the room opened and Phira's siblings entered, all taking their seats at a table to the left of the throne. How Mitah had gotten them all together was a mystery, though it probably wasn't much difficulty for a man who had been able to snap Eodh into existence right in front of us without so much as a flutter of his eyelash.

The brother, Aeden, looked madder than a cat stuck in a plastic bag while the sisters didn't look surprised by Eodh's betrayal. There was one sister, though, Evie, I thought her name was, who appeared to be nervous. That was interesting. The other two, Scorpia and Octavia, were cool as cucumbers.

King Mitah walked to an altar against the far right wall and pulled out a wooden box with beautiful carvings on it. He opened it and pulled out an amber gemstone. The Fae were big on their rocks. This one looked like a garnet of some sort. Not that I was a stone expert, but we did use them often in witchcraft.

Phira leaned forward at the table and whispered, "That enchants the room so no one in here can lie."

That was a neat little trinket. I'd have to see about getting one for the house. Winston would love that. Luci would probably use it to torment the town.

The king sat on his throne and stared at Eodh—who was now on his knees—for a long while before speaking. "Eodh, It has been brought to my attention that you plan on overthrowing me and claiming the throne for yourself."

Whispers came from Phira's sisters. Ah, so they didn't yet know why they'd been summoned.

Eodh sneered. "It was a brilliant plan until they ruined everything," Eodh said and pointed right at us, Phira included. After the words left his mouth, he jerked his attention back to Mitah. It was apparent that Eodh hadn't meant to confess so early on in the trial. That stone was pretty good.

Too bad so sad, buddy. But that was the purpose of a truth spell.

This one was powerful, cause he couldn't stop talking as he gazed up at his uncle. "With the vampires at my side, I'd have enough power to kill you and all who are loyal to your weak ways of ruling. Our race needs to be purified from all its imperfections and tainted bloodlines." Eodh snarled, then chucked wickedly.

Hey! He was talking about my best friend's tainted blood. It wasn't really tainted. Olivia had the potential of being extremely powerful one day. More so than Eodh could ever dream of and that was with her tainted bloodline. I glared at him as he lifted his nose in the air as if he were better than the rest of us.

Well, I hoped Mitah sent him to his own special kind of Hell. Maybe Luci could help with that. He was the devil after all.

And on the heels of that thought, Mitah swiped a hand through the air, cutting all sound coming out of Eodh's mouth. I let out a snort, then pressed my lips together so no more noise came out of me. The rotten, meanie Fae still continued to talk. It was funny to watch his lips move like a fish without any sound coming out.

Eodh's face turned pink, then red, then purple as his mouth moved faster and faster. He really wanted to confess all of his sins. Instead, he was comical in his frustration.

King Mitah ignored Eodh's elaborate way of communicating with everyone in the room. "Eodh, I sentence you to 100 years in your own prison world."

Mitah clapped his hands and Eodh vanished.

The king returned to the table. "His mind will make a prison for him worse than anything I could think up." He smiled wanly. "Will you be staying for dinner?"

Olivia looked at me and I shrugged. "You stay; I have to get back. I'm not sure when the vampires will be showing up but I want to be there to see their faces when I tell them that their plans failed."

The dark power from my necromancer half flared to life inside at that comment, ready to show the undead the error of their ways. Remind them of why they were so afraid of me in the first place.

Mitah nodded as if understanding, then he added, "The vampires will come for you at sunset."

I gaped at him. Sunset? Tonight? "How can you be sure?"

He winked. "It is what I pulled from Eodh's memories of the agreement he made."

I nodded. "Can I ask one question, assuming the truth stone thingy is still working?"

Mitah inclined his head. "Of course."

I looked over at Phira's brothers and sisters. "Were any of you involved in this plot?"

Mitah's brow furrowed as he realized he'd overlooked the possibility that Eodh had worked alone. He turned in his seat with his spine ramrod straight. "Well?"

One by one, Eodh's brother and all of his sisters either shook their heads or murmured their innocence.

I sighed in relief. "Thank you," I said. "Sorry to have to ask, but I needed to be sure."

The brother winked. "We understand, necromancer. Go in peace."

On that note, Olivia and Phira decided to come back home with me, and I was grateful because I would likely need the support. So, we said our goodbyes—I bowed to Mitah, and he bowed to me, then the brothers and all the sisters bowed, so I had to bow back to them. Then all the other people in the room, who had come in while we were otherwise occupied, bowed, and I wasn't sure who any of them were, so to be safe I bowed back. By the time Phira walked us outside the palace to open the portal home, my back was hurting from all the bending over.

We stepped out of the portal into the middle of my living room and to my pleasant surprise, Wallie and Michelle were walking in the front door.

"Hey," I cried. "You're home!"

When my sweet son saw me, he flew at me, gathering me into a tight hug. He was taller than me, so my nose squished against his shoulder. "Wallie, I can't breathe," I squeaked.

He let me go and took a step back while studying me

closely. Then he turned to Olivia. "I can't believe you didn't call me sooner. If my mom is sick, I need to know the instant she becomes ill. Not three days later."

Olivia looked chagrined, but I patted him on the shoulder. "It started way before three days ago. But it's all handled now, and you need to focus on school. I'm okay now. Promise."

"I was at a witch's retreat, Mom. It hardly qualifies as school. It's July." He kept hugging me until I pulled back.

"Really, I'm fine now. And a witch's retreat is good learning."

He didn't look convinced, but it was a good thing I had the perfect distraction. Taking his hand, I pulled him into my office where I thought my father was. But the office was empty. "Come on, there's someone I want you to meet." We checked upstairs, and I looked out on the front porch, but Dad was nowhere to be found.

By the time we returned to the living room, Dad was there. "Ah," I said. "Here he is."

When Dad turned toward me, both he and Wallie froze and stared at each other. The thing about my dad was that he didn't look much older than he had when he died. I knew from my training with Owen that necromancers aged slower because of their ability to reanimate the dead.

I don't think he had explained it quite like that, but that was how I'd understood it. Then again, Dad could have aged slower over the last thirty something years because he was being held by the vampires in some magical room. Who knew?

I squeezed my son's shoulders and beamed at my father. "Wallie, meet your grandfather, John Howe. Dad, meet your grandson, Wallie." I smiled at the confusion on my son's face as he stared at Dad.

"How?" he choked out.

"The vampires have had him imprisoned all this time," I said.

Mom stepped forward. "I'd heard the rumors but dismissed them. Winnie and I had been trying to figure out if they could be true, but then when your mom got sick, I decided we had to intensify the search and told everyone. Luci helped us go get him out."

The two men, one younger, one older, stepped toward one another and clasped hands, shaking until Dad pulled Wallie into a hug. "I can't tell you how happy this makes me," Dad said in a choked-up voice. "More than I could ever express."

Larry and Zoey walked out of the kitchen, looking a lot better with Alfred on their heels. Wallie and Dad sat on the sofa murmuring. I smiled and let them have a moment to get to know one another as Winnie came through the front door with Owen.

Sam and Drew were working, so I'd have to fill them in later when they got back here. "Okay," I said. "Long story short, King Mitah sent Eodh to a prison world. And he told me Eodh knew the vampires would be coming at sunset." I peered out the window. "What time is it?"

"Two," Olivia said.

"We need to prepare," I muttered.

"But he didn't say when the vampires would come, only at sunset?" Dad asked.

That was true. "We'll have to take turns watching out for them."

The floor under my feet started to vibrate, telling me that Winston was on security detail. "And Winston is on the case."

"Come on, Wallie," Larry said. "I'll fill you in on what all you've missed."

Zoey looped her arm through Michelle's. "We'll go too."

"We should go fill Luci in," Phira said. "He's at home?"

Alfred nodded. "That's what he said."

Phira smiled at Olivia. "Come with me?"

Olivia patted me on the back. "See you soon."

"Come, Owen," Mom said. "Winnie and I will get you up to speed.

As my friend and mentor walked by, he pressed a kiss to my cheek. "You look good."

I squeezed his arm. Owen was my family, as much as any of the rest of them. We were all connected now.

Soon it was just me and Alfred left in the living room. "Melody left?" I asked.

Alfred nodded. "Yes, you might want to see if she can come back this evening."

That was a really good idea. I headed upstairs to change, rest and text my friend. Between me, Owen, Dad, and Wallie, it seemed unlikely we'd need the coven, but it didn't hurt to be prepared.

19
AVA

THREE NIGHTS LATER IN THE WITCHING HOURS...

The whole house shook, waking me from a dead sleep. Seriously, I hadn't slept this well in months. Why couldn't they just let me sleep? I moaned and squinted into the dark bedroom.

Once the fog of my sleepy brain lifted. I realized that Winston was trying to wake us up. Something was coming. The vampires who hadn't arrived when we'd expected them.

Scratch that. Someone was coming. Several undead someones.

"The vampires are coming! The vampires are coming!" Lucy-Fur's voice echoed from the hall. By the sounds of it, she was also running up and down the hallway. Her little footfalls could barely be heard over the moans and groans of Winston sounding the alarm.

"Your potential ghouls should come with warning labels before you animate them. Lucy's label would have said, 'able to talk in complete sentences and can cuss like a sailor,'" Drew said as he got out of our bed.

Yes, our bed. He was officially moving in as soon as we took care of the vamps and moved his stuff from his house to mine.

"Potential ghouls?" I tossed him his pants and shirt and rushed to the closet where I blindly grabbed a pair of jeans and a t-shirt. No need for a fancy dress when I was just going to be taking down some vamps.

He dressed in two seconds flat, which was impressive. I was still tugging my jeans over my hips. Ugh. I'd grabbed the snug pair. Dang skinny jean fad. I was ready for the baggy boot cut to come back. Or wide leg. Oh, yeah, I'd loved wide leg.

"Yeah, as in the dead, as a whole, when you're around." He grinned at me as he tightened his belt.

I pulled my shirt on and once my head was through the hole, I rolled my eyes at him, knowing he was teasing me. I was ready to fire off a tease or two right back at him when Winston started rattling and slamming doors. That was our cue to get our booties downstairs and outside to deal with the vamps. "Come on," I cried. "I think he means business."

When I opened my bedroom door, Lucy-Fur stood in front of it, looking annoyed. "Did you not hear me? The vampires are here! What are you, deaf?"

Not bothering with arguing with the grumpy white-again cat, who I should've left naked in punishment, I raced down the hallway. It wasn't until I reached the bottom floor that I realized I didn't have shoes on. Whatever. I didn't have time to go get any, so I'd fight barefoot. At least it was warm outside.

Oh, but wait, I wouldn't have to actually fight because I was at my full strength. In fact, I felt stronger than I evaer had, thanks to my new bond with Drew. My boo. Heh.

"Close all the windows!" Dad yelled from the kitchen. "Winston, do it yourself if you can!"

The house moaned and the sound of several windows slamming shut all at once made me grimace. Why had they been open to begin with? We were too sure of ourselves.

Wallie blew past me from the hallway, heading to the living

room. "On it. Do we have salt?"

Wha—? I turned to Wallie and furrowed my brow. "Salt? To keep vamps out? That doesn't work on them. Neither does garlic."

He shrugged. "I don't know! They do it on TV."

I chuckled at the thought of those cute Supernatural boys helping us take down these vampires. It was a nice thought, but they were too close to my son's age for me to ever be attracted to them.

Well...maybe that older one.

The house shook again, then let out a loud groan. "The vampires are trying to come in," Wallie said. "I thought they couldn't enter a home without being invited."

Dad walked out of the kitchen, shaking his head. "That's only the case with human-owned homes."

"Oh, great." I glared at the front door as Wade entered the house from the basement, slamming it behind him. "Where were you?" I asked.

"The ocean to feed. Shark blood is pretty tasty." Wade grinned, then pointed to the front door. "They're getting pretty desperate."

"The sharks?" Dad asked.

Larry and Zoey appeared at the top of the stairs. Larry laughed and said, "That brings a whole new meaning to shark week." Then he laughed uproariously at his joke while jogging down the stairs.

Wade turned to grab the handle of the door while looking at me over his shoulder. "The vampires are getting desperate."

Right. "Then let's go meet our guests." I grinned and called my dark magic to the surface, then nodded for Wade to open the door. "And then you get below stairs," I whispered. He sighed and obliged, opening the door then moving with his special vamp speed back toward the basement stairs.

Walking serenely, I exited the house with my entourage

behind me. My dad on my right, Drew on my left, and Owen and Wallie were behind us. I raised my hand and said, "Stop."

The small group of vampires, six of them, halted, frozen in place thanks to the power a necromancer had over a vampire. "You may move, but don't come any closer to me." I didn't recognize a single one of them.

A few of the vamps in the back relaxed and retreated a few steps. Chickens. However, the one in the front, a scary-looking mofo with a scar across his cheek, snarled at me. I raised my brows at him. He did not want to mess with me. It was the middle of the night, and I was not in the mood for crazy.

"Here's how this is going to go. You will leave here and never come back to bother me or mine. Understood?" I waited and watched each one nod their head. All except for Roadrash in front of me. He looked like he had a death wish.

As soon as that thought formed in my mind, the jerk charged forward faster than I could track. He plowed into me like a linebacker sacking the quarterback. My back hit the ground, knocking the wind out of me. It also royally pissed me off. Anger bubbled inside me, meeting up with confusion about how the heck the crazy scarred vamp had been able to break my compulsion over him. Without a second thought, I slammed my hands into his chest and pushed all my power into him. It happened so fast that Drew hadn't even had time to move, and he had crazy Hunter reaction times.

Roadrash yelped and flew off me like he'd been zapped by a million volts of electricity.

By the time I sat up, the vampire was nothing but a pile of ash. Drew appeared at my side in an instant and helped me up. Dad picked something up off the ground and handed it to me. My lips curled as I saw a hex bag.

"Seriously? What is it with you people and hex bags?" I snatched it from Dad's hand and squeezed it, still a little mad about the whole thing. I should be sleeping right now!

That was when I noticed the sparks of electricity circling my hand. Drew stepped in front of me to hide my newfound magical ability from the rest of the vampires. We didn't need those jerks knowing about this. Holy crow. I'd shot lightning at that vampire from my hands. I took a breath and calmed myself. Relief flooded me when the electrical magic vanished.

Straightening my spine, I opened my hand to reveal that the hex bag was now ash as well. I snarled at all the vampires in my yard. "Anyone else want to play with the necromancer?"

They all shook their heads and started backing up. Ha. I hadn't thought so. "You will go back home and tell your elder council, whoever the heck they are, that I know their secrets, and I will be coming for them. Oh, and Eodh has been dealt with and will be out of the picture for the next hundred or so years."

They turned and took off, disappearing into the woods.

Winston groaned, this time sounding like he was relieved. It was done.

"Spoken like a queen," Dad said and kissed my forehead before ducking into the house.

I glanced at Drew and crinkled my nose. "Good gods, I hope not. The last thing I need is to become the vampire queen."

Drew chuckled and wrapped an arm around my waist as we moved into the house. "More like the undead queen."

Blah. That was even worse. What kind of crown would I have? A crown of bones? Ew.

Would my life ever get back to normal? But what was normal? Boring was what it was.

Once we were all in the living room, I asked, " So, where'd I get the power of electricity from?"

Everyone laughed, and Owen shrugged. "At this point, I'm not surprised by anything coming out of you."

20
AVA

A WEEK LATER AND—GASP—NO DRAMA

The fire stretched up towards the sky, the flames dancing to the beat of its own music. I watched it carefully to make sure it didn't come alive and start attacking everyone around it or something else totally insane. The bonfire on the beach was amazing, but my worry was caused by the fact that Luci had been the one to create the fire. Hell fire at that. I had good reason to be skeptical.

Drew came up behind me and wrapped his arms around my shoulders. With a sigh, I leaned back against him, sucking up his warmth. There was a slight chill in the air as the sun set on this early August night. The temperature in Maine had already started to drop a few degrees, indicating that fall was close. I couldn't wait until the leaves started to change.

"We should have a fall wedding," Drew whispered in my ear.

My heart jumped in my throat and whirled in his arms to face him. "That's only a month and a half away."

"And?"

"That's not enough time to plan a wedding." All the things that needed to be done started swirling around in my mind. Cake. Dress. Food. Decorations. Guest list. And the list went on and on and on. I was getting stressed out just thinking about all the stuff that needed to be done.

Olivia walked over to us. "That's plenty of time. I'll get started on making lists and making calls. We can get the coven to help. Oh, this is going to be fun!"

Then she ran off to talk to Sam, who was sitting with my parents. Crap. I eyed Drew, now grinning like an idiot. He was my idiot, and I loved him. I stood on my toes and kissed his lips, letting mine linger against his for a little bit before I said, "Looks like we'll be getting married at the end of September."

"Ava," Dad called out from the entrance of the cave where Phira had been kept when she was an evil blob. That same cave also led into the caverns under my house and the huge chasm, aka power source for the ley lines. Which meant there was another hidden entrance to that tunnel Drew and I had found.

"Well, here we go." I took Drew by the hand and tugged him behind me. We stopped at the mouth of the cave, and I stared into the darkness inside. "Are we all going in?"

Dad shook his head. "Just you and I. We'll go in and carefully take seven pieces of the stone and bring them out here to connect each of the ghouls to the power in the stone."

That sounded simple enough. But if I'd learned anything, it was that nothing in Shipton Harbor was ever easy. At least not since I returned home. "Alrighty, let's do this."

Together we entered the cave and followed the tunnel to where the big room of stone just waited, almost aching for me to harvest from it.

"How did we never know this was here?" Dad whispered.

I shrugged. "I didn't even sense the trickle of power that leads up the house, which gives Winston his juice until I was right on top of it."

"If you hadn't been cursed and put in that weird spirit form," Dad said, "we might never have found this amazing source of power. Something about it protects itself from being felt or found."

I nodded. He was right. "Now we just have to figure out how to best use it."

"Starting with letting it power your ghouls." He squeezed my shoulder."

"Any idea how?" I asked.

"Well, I'm a full necromancer. My magic won't allow me to do this. Your mother did it for me once, not here, when we found a small cache of quartz in the mountains on vacation in Tennessee. She used her Earth magic to charge them for me."

Well. That meant it was up to me. "Okay."

I walked as close as I could to the chasm, then sat down. "Hello," I said quietly. I had no idea what made me want to speak to the quartz, but here we were. "I could use your help. I need a few pieces of you. Seven. So that I can take the weight of six ghouls off of me and one from my dad. Would you mind if I did that?"

Nobody and nothing answered me, of course. It wasn't like Winston. But still, it felt right to ask permission.

Drawing on the power of my mother, my Yaya, and my Aunt Winnie, I focused on the quartz and wrapped a little bit of magic around a small piece that looked like it would make a nice necklace. Slowly, I squeezed it until the rock broke off of the main part. It continued to glow as it floated over to me.

I wrapped my hand around the rock and sighed. "Thank you," I whispered.

Five more times I did that, drawing out small stones that would make good jewelry.

On the last stone, a rather large one that would make a lovely brooch for Winnie, the ground rumbled. And then it positively shook. "Uh," I said uncertainly, jumping to my feet. "Should we get out of here?"

Dad looked pretty freaked out himself. "I don't—"

He was cut off by a horrible tearing and ripping sound. The center of the stone, the chasm, opened up and something came pelting at my head. Instinctively, I held out one hand, and what landed in my palm couldn't have shocked me more if it had been a giant dildo like Olivia found at the vampire's palace.

Oh, yeah. She'd told me about that. My only regret was that I hadn't been there with her to tease her about finding such a room in front of her dad!

In my palm, long and proud, was a gigantic sword.

"What in the ever-loving hell?" Dad whispered.

The ground shook again, and the horrible sound filled the cave. The crack in the chasm closed and everything went back to deadly quiet.

"What is it?" I asked.

Dad shook his head and studied it. "It looks incredibly old." He squinted at it. "Yet it's in such good shape. I need to see it in the light."

With my gaze still on the chasm, I backed uncertainly out of the cavern, then finally turned and led the way to the beach where everyone waited.

When we exited the cave, one of Phira's sisters was standing outside, talking with Phira and Olivia. "Hey," I whispered to Dad. I didn't want to say it out loud, but I didn't want anyone to see that sword. Not yet.

He tapped his nose, understanding and taking the weapon from me. He disappeared into the cave for a second before returning to exit with me.

I pocketed the stones from the chasm and made my way over to them. Olivia turned to me and said, "You remember my aunt? Well one of them. Scorpia. She comes bearing gifts."

"Really?" I was intrigued. Why would the Fae bring a gift?

Scorpia handed me a small box.

"The king is grateful for bringing Eodh's treason to his attention. We had our suspicions that our eldest brother was more like our father than we wanted to admit." A sadness washed over Scorpia, but it was gone almost as fast as the emotion appeared. "But, we didn't have enough proof to confront him until you came."

I accepted her gift and took her hand. "He was your brother and for that, I'm sorry for your loss."

A ghost of a smile formed and Scorpia stood a little taller. "Eodh is an idiot, and he deserves his own personal hell. My uncle also wanted me to offer you an alliance. If there is anything you need, simply call us."

Wow, that was huge and very much appreciated. "Thank you. I accept and offer the same. After all, you are my best friend's family."

Scorpia seemed pleased with my acceptance and offer. She and Phira walked off arm in arm and chatted for a bit longer. As they walked away, Scorpia turned back. "Oh, Ava, that will only work for your magic. Just prod a bit of your essence into it and it'll work just like ours at the palace."

I nodded uncertainly. "Thank you."

Olivia faced me and stared pointedly at the box. "What is it?"

I shrugged and excitedly pulled on the end of the bow. When I opened the box, I grinned. "Oh, excellent."

Holding out the stone, we peered into it, at the beautiful amber stone. "A truth stone," I whispered.

Olivia's eyes lit up. "Awesome. What to get someone who has anything." We dissolved into giggles.

After we spent a few minutes oohing over the stone, I pulled Mom, Dad, and Winnie close. Dad and I told them about the sword. "As soon as the tall and leggy contingent has gone, we'll get it out," Dad said. "Might have to come back for it."

Phira and Scorpia were almost back in earshot.

"Someone change the subject," I whispered.

"Do you know when Luci's birthday is?" Olivia asked.

"No. I'm not sure he actually has one. Was he birthed or created? I've come to the conclusion that he is a god of sorts." And as much as I'd tried to get rid of the devil, I was growing to actually like him and all his quirks. But don't tell him that. His ego is already too big.

Studying Olivia, I could tell she was starting to accept the fact that her parents were her parents. That was a good thing. She needed to be able to trust them to teach her how to use and control her magic. "Why do you ask?"

She shrugged. "I might have gotten him a gift. I just don't know when to give it to him."

A smile tugged at my lips. I took her hand and gave a gentle squeeze. "You'll know the right time."

Dad smiled and asked, "Are you ready?"

"Yep. Let's do this."

Dad faced me and I handed my gift from the Fae to Olivia, then called all the ghouls to gather around Dad and me. Once all seven of them were positioned in a circle around us, Dad and I took out the stones we got from the chasm. I'd tucked the ones I had carried in my pocket to keep Scorpia from seeing them because I hadn't known why she was there at first. Eodh had given me trust issues. But like the coven, I would learn to trust the Fae.

Dad and I faced each other while holding our stones in our palms. I wondered if the transforming of the ghouls' animated lifeline would be the same as when I transferred Mom's to Dad.

"Hand each of them a stone." Dad moved to Mom, then Winnie and Alfred, placing a stone in each of their hands.

I moved to Zoey and Larry, then looked around for Snooze and Lucy-fur. They weren't there. "I'll have to do the cats later."

Just then the two felines made their way down the path from the small cliff that led to the house. When they took their place in the circle, I said, "Nice of you two to join us."

Lucy huffed. "Make this quick. I need a nap and a bath."

Of course. I bowed my head at the little cat. Now there was our Queen.

Instead of handing the cats their stones, I held onto them. I would need to put them in a collar so they could keep their power source close to them at all times. "Everyone hold your hands out with the stone in your palms."

I hoped this worked. When Dad took over as Mom's necromancer, he did the pulling of the magic from me to him. It seemed too easy. Then again Dad had been in tune with his powers a lot longer than I had. The stones from the power source couldn't pull the magic from me, so I had to push it into the crystals.

Closing my eyes, I held my hands out in front of me with Snoozes and Lucy's pieces of quartz and focused on the lines of power that connected me to each of my ghouls. I sensed Dad doing the same with Mom. I started to ask why he was bothering since they were bonded now, but I knew the answer. He didn't want Mom to die because he did. Plus, this would give each of them their own sense of independence.

Once I had all their tethered lines gathered inside me, I pushed those threads out and directed them to each ghoul and their crystals. Magic flowed around us, weaving in and out like it was searching for something.

Worry seeped into my bones as I feared it wasn't working. Then Drew's hand pressed into the small of my back. My focus realigned with the purpose.

I could do this.

And with that confidence, the threads of magic snapped to each of the quartz pieces, giving my ghouls their own portable magical source that kept them animated. Now they controlled when they would die and didn't depend on me to stay alive for them.

Not that I planned on dying anytime soon. But with all the things that had been thrown at us over the last eleven months, something was bound to get lucky.

Once the power transfer was complete, Luci, the devil, appeared and walked over to me. He took the cats' crystals from me. I frowned. "What are you doing?"

He winked at me but didn't say anything as he transformed the crystals into the most beautiful collars for each of the cats. The stones were polished until they shined. Lucy's collar was a beautiful deep pink and Snoozer's a rich brown. He put them on Snooze and Lucy-Fur. They both arched their backs when Luci snapped their new fancy collars on them.

I expected the white she-cat to complain about the collar, but she actually loved it.

"Thank you, Luci," I said warmly.

He beamed at me, and I rolled my eyes, adding, "Don't get too excited. I haven't decided if I like you or not."

Luci laughed. "But you are warming up to me."

Then he walked off. I leaned back into Drew and smiled when he said, "You're going soft."

"Oh hush," I teased.

Just then Jess jumped to her feet. She, Devan, Wallie, Michelle, Larry, and Zoey sat a few feet from the bonfire. "Mom!"

Olivia whirled around like she was about to battle a monster for threatening her daughter. "What's wrong?"

"It's Dad," Jess said, handing her phone to Olivia. "He's missing."

Don't miss Ava and Olivia's next adventure in A Grave Midlife!

DEDICATION

Dedicated to Claire and Amanda. Our early morning heroes.

WITCHING AFTER FORTY SERIES

Witching After Forty follows the misadventures of Ava Harper – a forty-something necromancer with a light witchy side that you wouldn't expect from someone who can raise the dead. Join Ava as she learns how to start over after losing the love of her life, in this new paranormal women's fiction series with a touch of cozy mystery, magic, and a whole lot of mayhem.

A Ghoulish Midlife
Cookies for Satan (Christmas novella)
I'm With Cupid (Valentine novella)
A Cursed Midlife
Birthday Blunder (Olivia Novella)
A Girlfriend For Mr. Snoozerton (Novella)
A Haunting Midlife
An Animated Midlife
Feary Odd-Mother (Novella)
A Killer Midlife
A Grave Midlife

A Powerful Midlife (coming soon)
A Wedded Midlife (coming soon)
More to come

READ AN EXCERPT FROM BITTEN IN THE MIDLIFE

Bitten in the Midlife is the first in a new spin off series featuring Hailey Whitfield, whom you met in this book. The new series is titled, Fanged After Forty and we hope you love Hailey and her friends as much as Ava's.

Get your copy of Bitten in the Midlife Here

Here is the first chapter of Bitten in the Midlife.

Chapter 1

The day had finally come, and I could hardly contain my excitement.

I never knew starting over at the not-so-ripe age of forty would be so freeing. It was like a huge weight lifted off my whole body. And I was *free*!

I didn't have to look at my ex-fiancé's face anymore. Nor

did I have to watch him openly flirt with all the other nurses. I didn't have to watch him move on happily with the tramp he cheated on me with.

Jerk.

He was a lot more than a jerk, but I was *not* thinking about him anymore. Plus, karma always got back at people who deserved her wrath. And I was starting my new life in a new city, in my new-to-me house.

The best part of this move was that my best friend since we were in diapers was my neighbor.

We were celebrating this glorious day together with champagne on my front porch, ogling the movers as they unloaded the truck and carried all of my things into the house.

It was a great way to celebrate on a Monday.

See? All Mondays weren't bad.

Another thing that made this move better for my sanity was that I was closer to my two older brothers. One I adored and loved, Luke. The other was the eldest of the five of us, and... the poor guy wasn't everyone's favorite. We all loved him, but we wouldn't walk out in front of a bus to save him. Oliver was just...Oliver. He was a hard person to figure out. Oh, calm down. We'd save him. We might just shove him out of the way extra hard.

Pushing away thoughts of family and ex-jerkface, I went back to supervising the movers. It was a tough job, but someone had to do it.

"What about that one?" Kendra asked.

I hid my smile behind the crystal flute she had brought with her.

My bestie had taken the day off to celebrate with me. She was a lawyer and had just won a big case, so that gave us double the reasons to celebrate.

Good times!

I watched mister tall, dark, and delicious with rippling abs, a luscious tush I could've bounced a quarter off of and one of those cute little man buns carry a large box toward us.

He was young enough to call me mama but still legal. Maybe being a cougar wasn't such a bad idea. Just as long as he left before the sun was up. I had no plans to wake up beside another man, ever.

Did you hear me? *Ever*.

It would give my eldest brother Oliver something else to turn his nose up at and lecture me about why it wasn't a good idea to date a man young enough to be my son.

At least Luke would support a fling with the hot moving man. On second thought, Luke supported orgies and any manner of sexual escapades. That was a little too many hands, arms, legs, and bodies for me.

No, thank you. Although... maybe... Nope.

As the cutie with the man bun walked past, he batted a pair of lashes that looked like someone had dipped them chocolate, and I glanced down at his pants, totally by accident.

No, really. I didn't mean to.

But oh, my. His pants fit like they'd been painted on. Molded to every move of his body, but also like they were begging to be torn off. It'd been a while since I'd had a back to rake my fingers down.

Kendra, my bestie for as long as I could remember, cocked a dark brow, then shrugged. "I have socks older than he is."

I snorted, then giggled. It was probably the champagne, but who cared. "I didn't say I wanted to marry him."

God forbid. One bite of that sour apple was enough for me, and even if spitting out that second bite wasn't my choice, I was over the whole idea. Kendra had it right. Her love 'em and leave 'em lifestyle was my inspiration from now on. New start, new motto.

Broken hearts were a young woman's game, and I wasn't young enough to be willing to risk another. No way, buddy.

"Since when is a little bump and grind enough for you?" Skeptical was Kendra's middle name, while a smile flirted with her lips. The skeptical part sure helped in her budding law career as her last name was Justice, after all. Literally.

Kendra didn't trust easily, which was why she'd stayed single after her divorce almost fifteen years ago.

I shrugged and watched a mover lean against a dolly full of boxes while he rode the truck gate to the ground. Shirtless, muscular, and blond were apparently my new turn-on. Who knew I had a type? "Being left at the altar was eye-opening and threw my entire life in a new direction," I mumbled.

And this direction's sheen of sweat, when combined with the champagne, put thoughts into my head. Fun thoughts. Sexy thoughts. Thoughts a newly single woman with no prospects had no business having. Or maybe every business having them.

The best part was I didn't have to wake up next to anyone or answer to anyone. Ever. Again.

"Have you found a job yet?" It figured Kendra would change the subject to something more serious. What a way to snap me back to reality.

She was such a buzzkill sometimes.

"No, but I put in applications and sent out resumes to hospitals within fifty miles and every doctor's office in the greater Chestnut Hill-Philadelphia area. I also found an agency that offers private nursing. I'm thinking of checking it out." At this point, I had to take what I could get. My life savings had gone into the sanity-saving move.

Kendra nodded. Her approval wasn't essential, but the validation was nice. "Have you met the neighbors yet?"

She knew I'd come to tour the house and talk to the previous owner about a week ago. Kendra had been on some witch's retreat.

Pointing to the house on the other side of mine, she said, "Sara lives there with her 2.5 kids and a husband that is never home. She's nice but on the snobbish side. She is one hundred percent human, like you. But don't tell her anything you don't want the whole neighborhood to know."

Kendra had connections with the neighborhood I didn't yet. There were two reasons for those connections. One, she was a witch. Two, she'd lived in this neighborhood for the past fifteen years. She'd moved right after her divorce to start a new life with her kids. Of course, now she had a great relationship with her ex. They made better friends than lovers, as it had turned out.

It had been the same years ago for me and my ex-husband, Howard Jefferies. Our divorce had been messy and painful, mostly because I hadn't wanted to admit we'd fallen out of love with each other. I was bitter for a long time before we'd finally become friends.

"No. I've been here a couple of times, but always during the day when people are working, I suppose." I hadn't met a single soul besides the previous owner, Ava Harper, who was also a witch, and her extended family that had been with her.

Kendra hid her smile with another drink. "The neighbors across the street are," she leaned closer to me and lowered her voice, "*weird.*"

"Yeah?" I glanced at the house across the street. "How so?"

It was a large three-story, modern brick home with a balcony that wrapped around the top floor. I wondered if the top floor was one large room or a separate apartment or living space.

Black shutters accented the windows, which appeared to be blacked out. The front door was crimson with black gothic-looking embellishments. There was a front porch on the ground level that was half the length of the front of the house. The lawn was perfectly manicured with lush green grass and expertly trimmed bushes.

"You know, weird." Kendra cocked an eyebrow. "*My* kind of weird."

Maybe she'd had too much to drink, or I had because I wasn't following whatever it was she hinted at. Then it hit me. Oh! *Her* kind of weird. "You mean like...." I lowered my voice to a whisper as I looked around to make sure there wasn't anyone in earshot. "Witches?"

She shook her head, and I grinned. A guessing game. Awesome. I so sucked at those.

I kept my voice low enough so only the two of us could hear. "You said there's more than witches out there. Is it one of the others?"

This time, she tapped the left side of her nose and smiled. Kendra so loved her dramatics.

"Werewolves?"

"No."

"Werepanthers?"

"Nope."

"Bears?" I paused for another negative reply then ran through a list. "Dragons? Lions? Cats of any kind?"

"No, no, and no." She kept her brow cocked and her smirk in place. She loved torturing me with these crazy guess games.

"Llama, dog, sock puppet?"

She burst out laughing at the latter, drawing glances from the movers. We laughed together like old times. God, I'd missed her so much. Being around Kendra was soothing after everything I'd been through.

"If we were playing the hot-cold game, I would say you were getting hot, but you're very cold." That helped so much. Not. Cryptic hints were her thing. "Brr." She ran her hands over her arms and faked a shiver. Then cackled like the witch she was.

"Zombie? Something in the abominable category?" Now I was reaching into the tundra. While Philly was cold in the winter, anything of the snow critter variety wouldn't stand a chance in a Pennsylvania summer.

"Warmer with zombie, a little too cold with the snowman."

My tone dropped to reflect my almost boredom. "Ghoul? Ghost? Alien?" She was losing me.

"Oh, come on!" She stood to her full height and leaned against the rail on the porch to stare at me. "You're dancing right around it." She let her tongue slip over her canine.

Oh, snap! No way.

"Vampire?" I whispered that one, too, because somewhere I'd read vamps could hear every pin drop in a five-mile radius. Then again, that article was on the internet, and you couldn't trust anything on the web. At least I didn't.

I stared at the house again after her wink, indicating that I guessed right. Finally. Now, the gothic embellishments and blacked-out windows made a little more sense. However, the home looked normal at the same time.

"Wow." Were they friendly vampires?

"Yeah." She nodded with her lips pursed.

We both shifted to look at the truck, then as one of my boxes went crashing to the ground and the sound of breaking glass tinkled through the air.

I groaned inwardly and hoped it wasn't something valuable in that box. The movers would be getting a bill for it if it was.

Later, after the hotties had left and the sun began to set, Kendra started unpacking the kitchen while I worked in the living room. Thank goodness they'd put the boxes in the rooms they belonged in, thanks to my OCD in labeling each one.

I was knee-deep in opened boxes and bubble wrap when the doorbell rang. "I'll get it," I called to Kendra in the kitchen.

Not waiting for her to answer, I swung the door open and froze.

The most exquisite man I'd ever seen stood in the doorway.

Hellooooo handsome.

This guy was...tall. Well, taller than my five-one height, but then, most people were. He towered over me with a lean, more athletic than muscular form. His deep amber eyes reminded me of a sunset while his pale skin said he didn't spend much time in the sun. Light hair, something in the blond to strawberry variety, brushed the tops of shoulders. Shiny, clean, and begging for my fingers to run through the strands.

Smiling as if he could read my mind, Strawberry Man handed me a basket strongly scented by blueberry muffins. The smell made my mouth water. Or was that him? Maybe he was Blueberry Man. Oh, geez. I hadn't even said a word yet. Had I?

"These are for you." He nodded toward the basket, looking a little uncomfortable.

Oh, yes, they were. His large hand brushed mine as I grabbed it, and I sucked in a short, quick breath. At some point, I'd become awkward. And ridiculous.

And I remembered I hadn't brushed my hair all day since the movers arrived. Damn.

The porch was smaller with him standing on it, somehow it had shrunk, and I couldn't draw in a breath around him. Dramatic, yes, but so true. Or maybe he was too hot, and all the oxygen had evaporated in his presence. Either way, I found it hard to breathe and think.

"Th-th-thank you." I was like a nervous teenager who'd just met her very first pretty boy. I chuckled, hiccupped, and would've fallen out the door if not for the frame I'd somehow managed to catch my shirt on.

He nodded and tilted his head, smiling. Damn if my knees didn't go weak. "No problem. If you need anything at all, I'm Jax, and I live right over there." He pointed to the house across the street. And the back view of his head made my heart pitter-patter and my belly rumble as much as the front.

"You're the...." I didn't know if he, if they, were loud and proud with their creatures of the night status, and I didn't want to take the chance of outing Kendra for telling me. Unfortunately, I thought of it a second *after* I started speaking. "Neighbor."

His grin hit me like sunshine poking through the clouds on a rainy day. Ironic, since vampire meant allergic to the sun in a deathly kind of way.

"Yeah."

I didn't know if I should invite him in. What if there was a Mrs. Vampire? The last thing I needed was to become a jealous vampire wife's main course.

Like the queen of the dorks, I held up the basket, gave it a sniff, then hiccupped again. "Thanks for the goodies."

As I spoke, I wished again I'd taken a moment to brush my hair or put on a clean shirt before I answered the door. Vampire or not, this guy deserved a neighbor who combed her hair.

SNEAK PEEK INTO A NEW SERIES COMING SOON

A bunny bit me on the finger and everything went sideways after that.

That's just the beginning of my insane life. The Fascinators, the local ladies' club, suddenly are incredibly interested in having me join their next Bunco night, which is a thinly veiled excuse to drink and gossip.

I've been dying to get into that group for years; why now? I'm over forty, my daughter is grown, and all I do is temp work. What's so special about me?

After I shift into a dragon, things become clearer. They're not a Bunco group. The Fascinators are a pack of shifters. Yes, shifters. Like werewolves, except in this case it's weresquirrels and a wereskunk, among others.

And my daughter? She wants to move home, suddenly and

suspiciously. As excited as I am to have her home, why? She loves being on her own. It's got something to do with a rough pack of predators, shifters who want to watch the world burn. I hope she's not mixed up with the wrong crowd.

There's also a mysterious mountain man hanging around out of the blue. Where was he before the strange bunny bite? Nowhere near me, that's for sure.

Life is anything but boring. At this point, I'm just hoping that I'll survive it all with my tail—literally—intact.

Preorder your copy today

MORE PARANORMAL WOMEN'S FICTION BY LIA DAVIS & L.A. BORUFF

Witching After Forty https://laboruff.com/books/witching-after-forty/

A Ghoulish Midlife

Cookies For Satan (A Christmas Story)

I'm With Cupid (A Valentine's Day Story)

A Cursed Midlife

Birthday Blunder

A Girlfriend For Mr. Snoozleton (A Girlfriend Story)

A Haunting Midlife

An Animated Midlife

A Killer Midlife

Faery Oddmother

A Grave Midlife

Shifting Into Midlife https://laboruff.com/books/shifting-into-midlife/

Pack Bunco Night

Prime Time of Life https://laboruff.com/books/primetime-of-life/

Borrowed Time

Stolen Time

Just in Time

Hidden Time

Nick of Time

Magical Midlife in Mystic Hollow https://laboruff.com/books/mystic-hollow/

Karma's Spell

Karma's Shift

Karma's Spirit

Karma's Sense

Karma's Stake

An Unseen Midlife https://amzn.to/3cF3W54

Bloom in Blood

Dance in Night

Bask in Magic

Surrender in Dreams

Midlife Mage https://amzn.to/30MFNH3

Unveiled

Unfettered

An Immortal Midlife https://amzn.to/3cC6BMP

Fatal Forty

Fighting Forty

Finishing Forty

ABOUT LIA DAVIS

Lia Davis is the USA Today bestselling author of more than forty books, including her fan favorite Shifter of Ashwood Falls Series.

A lifelong fan of magic, mystery, romance and adventure, Lia's novels feature compassionate alpha heroes and strong leading ladies, plenty of heat, and happily-ever-afters.

Lia makes her home in Northeast Florida where she battles hurricanes and humidity like one of her heroines.

When she's not writing, she loves to spend time with her family, travel, read, enjoy nature, and spoil her kitties.

She also loves to hear from her readers. Send her a note at lia@authorliadavis.com!

Follow Lia on Social Media

Website: http://www.authorliadavis.com/
Newsletter: http://www.subscribepage.com/authorliadavis.newsletter
Facebook author fan page: https://www.facebook.com/novelsbylia/
Facebook Fan Club: https://www.facebook.com/groups/LiaDavisFanClub/
Twitter: https://twitter.com/novelsbylia

Instagram: https://www.instagram.com/authorliadavis/
BookBub: https://www.bookbub.com/authors/lia-davis
Pinterest: http://www.pinterest.com/liadavis35/
Goodreads: http://www.goodreads.com/author/show/5829989.Lia_Davis

ABOUT L.A. BORUFF

L.A. (Lainie) Boruff lives in East Tennessee with her husband, three children, and an ever growing number of cats. She loves reading, watching TV, and procrastinating by browsing Facebook. L.A.'s passions include vampires, food, and listening to heavy metal music. She once won a Harry Potter trivia contest based on the books and lost one based on the movies. She has two bands on her bucket list that she still hasn't seen: AC/DC and Alice Cooper. Feel free to send tickets.

L.A.'s Facebook Group: https://www.facebook.com/groups/LABoruffCrew/
Follow L.A. on Bookbub if you like to know about new releases but don't like to be spammed: https://www.bookbub.com/profile/l-a-boruff

Made in the USA
Coppell, TX
07 October 2024